THE DUBIOUS WIT
OF KARL SHO

What the hell. So I'm an enabler. That's why I go to AA but not to Alateen. Got an opinion about that? ▮▮▮▮▮▮ you.

I thought how normal kids were spending their Friday nights after a game. Probably having pizza, or road drinking, or making out. Whereas I was standing on Mug Me Street in Toledo, Ohio, with a baseball bat and a purse.

I like a guy that will do too much for a friend, and try to hide it from them. Makes me feel like I'm just another fool instead of the biggest one in the world.

It never occurred to Harris and Tierden that I had figured out their favorite trick. But then it also never occurred to them that no one liked them. Or that they were a pair of ▮▮▮▮▮▮s. They just weren't real occurrable kind of guys.

I was a little tired of Philbin's but then I was a little tired of a lot of places—such as my house, Lightsburg, Ohio, the United States, and Earth.

OTHER BOOKS YOU MAY ENJOY

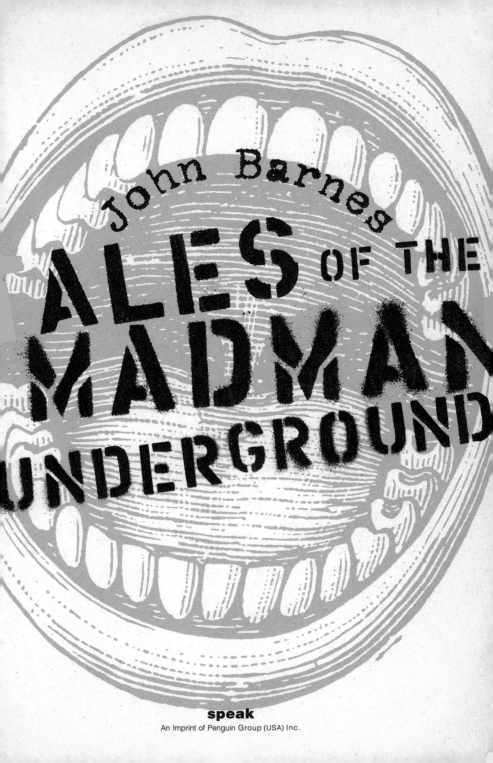

John Barnes

TALES OF THE MADMAN UNDERGROUND

speak

An Imprint of Penguin Group (USA) Inc.

SPEAK

Published by the Penguin Group

Penguin Group (USA) Inc., 345 Hudson Street, New York, New York 10014, U.S.A.

Penguin Group (Canada), 90 Eglinton Avenue East, Suite 700,
Toronto, Ontario, Canada M4P 2Y3 (a division of Pearson Penguin Canada Inc.)

Penguin Books Ltd, 80 Strand, London WC2R 0RL, England

Penguin Ireland, 25 St Stephen's Green, Dublin 2, Ireland (a division of Penguin Books Ltd)

Penguin Group (Australia), 250 Camberwell Road, Camberwell, Victoria 3124, Australia
(a division of Pearson Australia Group Pty Ltd)

Penguin Books India Pvt Ltd, 11 Community Centre,
Panchsheel Park, New Delhi - 110 017, India

Penguin Group (NZ), 67 Apollo Drive, Rosedale, North Shore 0632, New Zealand
(a division of Pearson New Zealand Ltd)

Penguin Books (South Africa) (Pty) Ltd, 24 Sturdee Avenue,
Rosebank, Johannesburg 2196, South Africa

Registered Offices: Penguin Books Ltd, 80 Strand, London WC2R 0RL, England

First published in the United States of America by Viking,
a member of Penguin Group (USA) Inc., 2009
Published by Speak, an imprint of Penguin Group (USA) Inc., 2011

1 3 5 7 9 10 8 6 4 2

LIBRARY OF CONGRESS CATALOGING-IN-PUBLICATION DATA IS AVAILABLE

Speak ISBN 978-0-14-241702-7

Printed in the United States of America
Set in Century Schoolbook
Book design by Jim Hoover

*This book is dedicated, with deep gratitude,
to two loyal friends who insisted, for years,
that I ought to write it,
and then that I could write it,
until finally I did write it:
Ashley Grayson and Jes Tate.*

. . . and he was so grateful, and said I was the best friend old Jim had ever had in the world, and the *only* one he's got now; and then I happened to look around and see that paper.

It was a close place. I took it up, and held it in my hand. I was a-trembling, because I'd got to decide, forever, between two things, and I knowed it. I studied a minute, sort of holding my breath, and then says to myself:

"All right, then, I'll go to hell"—and tore it up.

It was awful thoughts, and awful words, but they was said. And I let them stay said; and never thought no more about reforming. I shoved the whole thing out of my head, and said I would take up wickedness again, which was in my line, being brung up to it, and the other warn't.

—Mark Twain, *The Adventures of Huckleberry Finn*

"God, you don't want to stay with me," he said to the girl. "Someday you'll be in difficulty and need my help and I'd do to you exactly what I did to Leo; I'd let you sink without moving my right arm."

"But your own life was at—"

"It always is," he pointed out. "When you do anything. That's the name of the comedy we're stuck in."

—Philip K. Dick, *The Three Stigmata of Palmer Eldritch*

Contents

PART ONE

(Wednesday, September 5, 1973)

The Year of Being Normal

I HAD DEVELOPED this theory all summer: if I could be perfectly, ideally, totally *normal* for the first day of my senior year, which was today, then I could do it for the first week, which was only Wednesday through Friday. And if I could be normal for that first short week, I could do it for the next long week. After that I'd just have to repeat the have-a-normal-week process seven more times. I'd worked that out on a calendar.

Far as I could remember, nobody ever got their ticket after about Halloween, unless they spazattacked in class.

My alarm went off at 7:15, and my eyes opened on the sun smearing across the yellowing roughcoat of my ceiling. *Get up and be normal. Just for today.*

It was kind of like an idea that I'd gotten from my dad back when he was alive—"one day at a time." Just this past summer I'd found out it wasn't his idea, he got it from AA. Anyway, good idea or not, it was my theory, which was about to become my plan, and I was going to stick to it. *Like a coat of paint*—for Dad, everything that stuck, stuck to everything *like a coat of paint.*

Thinking about Dad was a bad way to start the plan, because it could make me blow acting normal all to hell, and nobody would understand, since he'd been dead for almost four years—four years exactly on October 17. Which I had noted would fall on Week Six of Operation Be Fucking Normal.

Don't think about that. I shoved that whole thought away like I shoved away the two hungry cats that jumped up onto the dining room table and headed for my bowl of raisin bran. Since I could tell Mom was still passed out solid, I didn't worry about looking like I was being all gentle and caring with those nasty hairy fuckers; I just pushed them off the table.

No matter what you heard, they don't always land on their four feet. Starlight did and stalked away with most of his dignity, but Prettyangel flopped on her back, and came up snarling.

"You're supposed to be graceful, asshole," I said, but the cat was already gone, charging into the living room. There was considerable yowling and screaming; with cats everywhere and all perpetually hungry and pissed off, any cat that moved fast was gonna get jumped.

I finished my cereal, dumped the milk down the sink to keep it away from the cats, and rinsed the bowl. They always fought over any food that was left out, even if it was just something to lick, and made an even bigger mess than Mom's kitchen was naturally.

I spritzed my pits, splashed my hair, combed it out, and checked myself in the hallway mirror. T-shirt: red and gray, not white like a farm boy. Jeans: faded, moderate flare, Levi's, not dirty and written on like a stoner, not chinos like a nerd, not polyester or big flared groovy-boy cords like a Christian jock. Tennis shoes: low-tops, scuffed but not too scuffed. Look groomed without looking like I had groomed. Normal normal normal.

I combed the hair out again, riffled it with my fingers. Straight, fine, mudcolored—it clung blandly to my skull like chocolate pudding running down a bowling ball.

Probably I was worrying way too much. Nobody normal was always trying to figure out the rules.

I shut the door to my room good and tight; I had my time planned kind of tight for that evening and didn't want unexpected cat messes in my room. Sometimes when I came in late I didn't have time to do cat turd patrol in the whole house, and just had to catch it the next morning, but I drew the line at cat shit in my room.

Especially 'cause one of those evil furry bastards

liked to shit on my bed, and even Hairball, the big orange one that was kind of mine, would pee on my throw rugs if he could. I had the only room in the house where you didn't need an ax to cut through the cat stench, and I was gonna keep it that way. The doorknob held when I tugged. Okay, if Mom didn't open the door and forget to close it, I was catproof for the day.

I picked up the old coal shovel I had for the purpose and ran through; I'd gotten so good I could do this in less than five minutes, like the world champion Easter egg hunter except of course it was for cat turds. More piles than I could count, as always—I was never completely sure how many *cats* we had at any given second—because no matter how many litter pans I set out, the big cats always guarded them and the little cats ended up crapping in the corners.

Most of the cat pile was wormy; I didn't look too close because I hated to see. Mom didn't believe in fascist things like veterinarians, vaccinations, or spaying. When SkyMusic had gotten clawed up by a raccoon and been in godawful pain from his infected wounds, I'd broken down—I had sworn I'd never spend a dime on those cats but he was suffering so bad—and taken him to the vet myself, and Mom had screamed at me all that night about it, and taken SkyMusic's painkillers for herself, and flushed his antibiotics down the toilet because all he needed were herbs and love. He went into a coma or something and died a couple days later; I remember crying the whole time I was burying SkyMusic (I gave him the spot by the lilac bush near where he used to hang out). Usually burying cats was just a job, something I did a couple times a month, but I could still get sad and pissed off and near tears when I thought about SkyMusic.

I was gripping that shovel so hard you'd think I'd bend it in half, and I made myself relax before I spilled any. I opened the back door and slung the shovelful under the trellis. People always wondered why our morning glories were so impressive.

At least there weren't any dead cats this morning, and it didn't look like anybody had lost a fight with a raccoon, skunk, or owl. I hadn't seen BeautySong in a while, though, so maybe she'd run out of luck.

Ocean, Starlight, LoveJoy, and Tundra all padded past me, off to kill birds and raid garbage cans in the neighborhood, as I closed and locked the back door. I'd lost two minutes to getting into a rage about cats. Fuck. Normal guys did *not* do that.

One last check in the mirror. It was still me, Karl Shoemaker, Prospective Normal Guy. Normal normal normal. One like him on every street corner. Think normal thoughts, stop being a chickenshit, get moving.

Check on Mom, like always; you never knew what might be breaking and shaking, because she broke things and shook things the way cats have kittens. So I quietly opened the door to her room, slipped inside, and looked around. Trouble, definitely—Neil was there.

Shit. *Real* trouble. Whenever Mom went out at night she dressed like she'd gone to a costume party as a gypsy—big clunky black boots, baggy skirt in about twenty colors that looked like an old quilt, lots of fake gold and silver chains and loops, baggy shirt, bright head scarf. But this morning the junk jewelry lying on the nightstand and the clothes thrown around the room were new, and in the ashtray beside all the Kent butts, there were a couple roach clips with a not-smoked-down joint in each one.

Fuck.

This close to her paycheck, she could only have gotten the money one way.

I slipped back out, down the hall, glanced around, opened the closet door, lifted the carpet, flipped up the little take-out piece I'd made in the floor there, and sure fucking enough. The big Ragú jar there was empty except for a note that said "Tue. Sept. 4 1973. I.O.U. $226.00. Put it on my tab, Beth Shoemaker."

I had a familiar numb, sick feeling as I pocketed the IOU. I'd paste it in my account book later. She'd just wiped out what I'd made last week selling radio ads, or what I'd made gardening in a month, or three McDonald's paychecks. Figure it any way you liked, there were some days of my life I had worked for nothing, and sure as shit I was never getting them back, because Mom's IOU wasn't worth wiping your butt with.

"I had to do that, sweetie," she said, behind me. I turned around. Her jaw was set forward; she was pouting. In the early morning light her skin was pale and ashy, showing every fine wrinkle. She really needed to learn to wash her face before going to bed. The heavy electric-blue eye makeup looked like some kind of a disease, and her lips, crusted with pink lipstick, looked kind of sick and dead. She was wearing a Lightsburg Wildcats T-shirt, probably Neil's, since it hit her about midthigh. "I really needed some freedom last night." She looked away, her face disappearing behind her loose hanging hair. "I'll pay you back when I get my real estate license, it'll all come out of the first sale to pay you."

Her thick, long, dyed-yellow hair was wet on one side where she'd drooled into it. "You slobbered on your hair again, Mom."

She touched it, yelled, "Ucky ucky!" and ran into the bathroom to splash water into it and brush it out. Good. That would give me my minute to get out the door.

She was still yelling "Ucky ucky ucky!" in the bathroom as I grabbed up my books. She got that from back when she used to be a substitute teacher; she liked really little kids and kind of naturally got down on their level. I guess doing that "ucky ucky" thing every time she got spit all over her hair was cute, maybe the first few times she did that, back when I was in eighth grade, right after she started to grow it out and dye it. Most of the guys who came through seemed to think it was cute, anyway.

Dashing for the door, I plowed right into Neil, who was naked. His shoulder-length brown hair smelled like a fire in a rope factory, his rumpled beard brushed over his mound of chest hair, and he was kind of waddling toward the bathroom, looking like Primitive Man in the diorama at the Toledo museum; slumped like an ape, big jaw hanging half open, peering around like he was afraid someone would hit him but hoped someone would feed him.

He reached out and rubbed my head with his hand, which was probably as much cleaning as that hand would get today. "Hey, little dude. You oughta stick around. Your mommy got some money. Betcha she takes us to breakfast."

He'd thought that was fucking hilarious for years, pretending like he didn't know where she got it. Sometimes he'd helped her look for my stashes.

"I gotta get to school, Neil." I slapped his hand up off my head.

"School's bullshit," he said as I opened the door, and "Hey, what's with the little dude?" as I closed it behind me.

I was almost as tall as he was, and in better shape from work (something he wouldn't know much about), but I was sure as *shit* not as heavy.

Off my schedule. Shit, right in the first twenty minutes. Now I'd have to hurry, no slack in my timing.

It was a nice, bright summer day, no trace of fall yet. I had to catch the early bus, and make it look like an accident, so I could just accidentally miss seeing Paul Knauss.

Paul and me had been best friends since we shared a playpen—our dads had been best friends for like five years before we were born. We were like two pieces of the same guy; I got the muscles and the common sense, he got the talent and the face. I told Paul that once, and like right then, not even a second for a breath, he said, "How do you know we're not two parts of the same ugly, puny, untalented dork?"

See, he could always crack me up. And we'd been through more shit together than an old plumber's snake. So I wasn't mad at him or anything—I just needed to duck him for a few weeks, and get people to stop saying KarlandPaul like it was one word, and disconnect myself from his weirdness, since being *un*weird was critical for Operation Be Fucking Normal.

Paul and me had always been on the same bus since the first day of kindergarten, so to make ducking him look like an accident was going to be tricky. Usually we'd be at the stop just *after* the early bus, on purpose, to goof some till the on-time bus came. Today I needed it to look like I accidentally took the early bus.

I glanced down at my watch—I had been walking slower than I meant to. Three blocks to cover, *now*. I ran down the street, sunlight flashing in and out of my eyes as I passed through the deep morning shadows of the big old trees. The early bus was at my stop, the last kid just getting on, so I started a serious kick, finishing in a blaze along its bright yellow side and jumping up onto the black rubber steps, landing tiptoe and rocked forward.

So much for looking like I caught it by accident.

Jolene Weber, the driver, was one of the ladies that got drunk with my mom. She grinned at me. "Made it, kiddo," she said. "Two more steps and you'd've been hanging from the back windows on the way to school."

"Yeah, well." That's what you said, in Lightsburg, when you were supposed to say something and couldn't think of anything.

She swung the steel handle that thumped the door closed and hollered, "Everybody hang on, I'm peelin' out."

In the aisle, the guy in front of me turned partway around.

It was Paul. I was surprised to see him but I figured, oh, well, hitches in the plan were bound to happen, I couldn't very well dodge him clear till Halloween, and come to admit it, I didn't really want to. I'd have to sit with him.

But Paul stared at me like I'd just gotten off a flying

saucer, and sat in the first open seat, next to one of those invisible sophomore girls that fill up the halls in school.

Plenty of double seats open, just a couple steps further back. I went and sat in the nearest open double, two rows behind Paul, watching the back of his head.

Paul and me'd been friends since before we could talk. We'd been in the Madman Underground ever since we'd gotten our first tickets in the first week of fourth grade.

I guess up until just a few years before Paul and me went into it, there wasn't much mental health care in schools, which explained everything about the older generation, if you asked me, which is probably why nobody asked me.

When I asked Dad why I had to go to a shrink, back in fourth grade, he told me Mr. Knauss, Paul's dad, had worked really hard to get school psychologists into the budget, which was good enough for me right there. Then he leaned forward and looked me right in the eye and added, "Karl, we are finally advanced enough to admit some kids need help, and provide it for them." (Which told me I was one of those kids.)

But like Paul's dad always added, this was still Ohio, the Cheap Bastard State, so they got the cheapest shrinks they could get—either fresh out of grad school or just up from a first job at a prison. First thing shrinks did when they got into the Lightsburg schools was start mailing out résumés to bigger school systems or real clinics, and they'd get hired away from Lightsburg pretty fast. Our therapy group went through like three to seven of them a year.

The school system didn't exactly know what to do with the shrinks, either. Teachers had a list of who got out of class to go to group therapy, and you got sent off to it on the same period and day every other week, the same way the kids who talked funny went to speech.

Now here's what was plain old wall-to-wall stupid: the *teachers*—*not* a shrink, *not* the kids, *nobody* who knew jack shit—the *teachers* decided who went to group therapy. Or sometimes the guidance counselors, which was not any better, since all our guidance counselors were coaches who were too stupid to teach. Which meant you got your ticket either because they knew your life was full of real bad shit, like Paul, or because the teacher caught you doing something weird, like me. And once you were in, they put a note in your file that said you were in therapy, and all your teachers saw that file.

They might as well have tattooed CRAZY on your forehead. The next year every teacher would be watching you for the first weird thing you did—and has there ever been a kid who never does anything an adult considers weird?

First thing you did, bing-o, back into therapy. They kept our same therapy groups together year after year, so almost always the newest person in the room was the shrink. Get one ticket once and it was good for free tickets every year afterwards.

Teachers have *no* sense of perspective. The first time I got a ticket it was in fourth grade, because Mrs. Daggett was reading a story and I got a crying jag like I did sometimes.

Stories *nailed* me. I was one of those kids that has to know how a movie comes out before I could see it. I couldn't handle suspense, not even a little. And if I *did* know how it came out, and it wasn't happy, that was even worse.

Mrs. Daggett was reading us "The Steadfast Tin Soldier," the part right before the end when the paper doll blows into the fire. I started to cry because I knew we were coming up on the part where they would find the tin heart in the ashes, and just knowing that was coming was too much for me.

When that happened at home, Mom or Dad would just go out to the kitchen, fix themselves a drink, and wait till I'd stop. Then if they remembered, they'd come back and finish the story. No big deal. But Mrs. Daggett didn't know me, and she was one of those pushy people that just have to try and help, so she put her arm around me.

That got me crying so hard I couldn't breathe, let alone explain. So I was making these weird hiccup noises and my face got all purple. Daggett called in the school nurse.

That was that, I got my ticket. The next week I was excused from class and started going with Paul to group therapy.

Paul had been going since the start of school that year. He got *his* ticket because everybody in Lightsburg knew about what had happened over the summer. His mom was going to take a picture of the kids just before going to church, so she had Paul and his big brother Dennis and little sister Kimmie lined up in front of the house. She had one of those old kind of cameras where you look down into it instead of through it, and you walk back and forth to get things right in the picture.

So she was down at the foot of the front yard, in the grass between the sidewalk and the street, trying to get it perfect, and she stepped one more step back without looking, and her high heel slipped over the curb and she fell over backwards in front of a speeding car.

The driver was some high school girl. Her family only lived in town that one year. People said they just weren't Lightsburg people; I guess it was a shame that Mrs. Knauss didn't get killed by a real local.

The tire went right over her neck, and she died that second. For years people in town said she didn't have time to suffer. I think everyone always has time to suffer.

So I got my first ticket because I did something crazy, and Paul's first ticket was because something awful happened so he was supposed to be crazy. Same story with all the other Madmen—once we got our first ones, from then on we got them because we'd had them before. We were gonna be in the Madman Underground till death or graduation.

But it couldn't be absofuckinglutely impossible to not get the ticket, because now and then a kid was only there for a year and then left the group.

I was going to try being normal, starting today. Who knew what might follow? A social life. People off my case. A non-Madman girlfriend. The road was wide open, so I was pedal-to-the-metal-and-let-her-roar flooring it towards being more normal than anybody.

Still, I wondered what Paul's problem was. Okay, so I wanted to avoid him. That didn't mean *I* wanted to be avoided.

The bus pulled up at another crowded stop and a bunch of kids piled in. Some rabbity-nervous freshman girl, carrying a big heavy pack for some reason, stood next to my seat. "I'm harmless," I said to her.

"Excuse me?"

"I'm harmless," I said. "That looks heavy. Sit down."

She blushed but she sat.

I kept staring at the back of Paul's head. Of all the group, Paul was the one I most needed to avoid hanging out with, because he was the heart and soul of the Madman Underground, the one who had named it.

For some reason, back when we were all in eighth grade, Paul had gotten hung up on reading *The Catcher in the Rye* and *On the Road* and he'd just kept reading them over and over all year, first one then the other, about one week per book. They sounded real boring, so I never read either. From what Paul said, they had three things in common: One, they were both classics, ten or twenty years old. Two, they were about young guys that didn't give a shit what people thought. Three, both books used "madman" as a compliment.

So Paul started calling the therapy group the "Madman Underground," and everyone else picked it up. The name stuck like a coat of paint, at least inside the group.

And supposedly nobody outside the group knew there *was* a group. Of course we all knew that wasn't true. High school was like the little clear plastic tunnels that Paul's hamsters lived in: you could run a long way but never get out, and always, everyone could see you.

So I was going to change tunnels. This year, no ticket for me. No Madman Underground. Normal normal normal.

Fuck. I wondered what Paul's trip was.

The bus bottomed its shocks on the turn into Oakbrook, the closest thing that Lightsburg had to a suburb: a tangle of winding streets just outside the city limits, with houses that started looking fake the day they were put up, lawns that had no sidewalks or fences, station wagons or pony cars parked out on the street, and wide driveways full of the toys you saw on TV.

Oakbrook houses had "rec rooms" and "dens" and "foyers" and all kinds of pretentious shit like that, but what they were was plywood and Z-Brick boxes with plastic "ironwork" and pot-metal "brass" and hollow chipboard columns on the front. The last couple years, I'd made some money sticking all that frouf back on with Liquid Nails.

Everybody out there talked about their houses like they were always for sale, calling them "homes" and saying they lived in "a three-bedroom New England saltbox home" instead of "a big white house with siding and a sloped flat roof."

But no matter how much molded plastic and pot metal you stuck on those cheap-bastard houses, the cheap-bastard just came bleeding through. They were on septic tanks so the yards stank all summer, especially after the low spots flooded. Because they only had county street maintenance, they had potholes the size of townships. And the kids from there were always in town anyway, paying a quarter to use the library, the pool, and the skating rink, because Dad and Mr. Knauss had fought to put in nonresident fees (and been called cheap bastards themselves for that).

Back when Dad was mayor, they'd tried to annex that land and the developers had put up a big fight and the city had lost. Later, while Oakbrook was being built, Paul's father, on City Council, had tried to annex them and make them pay property taxes. Nobody else on the council wanted to do anything that would actually make the Oakbrookers pay their fair share, but sticking their kids up for candy money was pretty popular.

"Lightsburg politics in a nutshell," Dad used to say. "A perfect balance between spiteful and ineffective." That was one of a million things I missed, and Paul missed, too—we could still crack each other up talking about the way our dads would get rolling on the subject when the families'd do cookouts together. "Maybe they should just incorporate and get their own school district," Dad would say. "Put in some used singlewides for the town hall and school if they can get them cheap enough." And Mr. Knauss would add, "They could be our cross-town rivals. Come on out Friday night and see the Lightsburg Wildcats versus the Oakbrook Fighting Cheap Bastards."

The school bus bucked and slammed along through Cheap Bastard Acres, picking up more people, and Jolene hollered and made everyone find a seat.

At school, I was one of the last people off because I'd sat so far towards the back, and I wanted to give Paul a head start.

Jolene gave my arm a squeeze. I don't know why all of Mom's friends were always touching me, but I didn't mind much when it was Jolene. "Have a great year, kiddo."

"Thanks, but I have other plans."

How the Most Expensive Pizza of My Life
Resulted in Delayed Gratzification

MY FIRST CLASS was college-track senior lit, taught by Coach Gratz. It bit the big hairy bag. I'd had Gratz before, twice, and that was like about four times too many.

How I happened to be taking this class from Gratz kind of happened in two stages. The first stage, last spring, was God's punishment for my taking my mother out for her birthday.

I *knew* it was dangerous to get all dumb and sentimental. And yet all the same, right when I was about to sign up for my senior year classes, I tried to really celebrate Mom's birthday, instead of just giving her the money to get drunk, high, and laid, like I had the year before. This time, I told her, she was going to be just slightly spoiled, and I was going to take her to Pietro's, the semidecent pizza place in town. It had red-checked tablecloths, if you didn't mind that they were fake plastic-coated canvas, and slightly better than decent pizza, if you were flexible about what you called decent.

"Are you sure you can afford this?" Mom asked, as soon as we'd already ordered.

"It's your birthday, Mom, and I don't spend money I can't afford." I wasn't sure whether she was trying to be my loyal protective concerned mother, which would be nice for her to at least try for a change, or if she was setting me up for one of her sermons about "ucky ucky money," so I played it neutral. "You know I have a bunch of jobs and I'm a miser, Mom. It's just that last night I was visited by these three ghosts, the Ghost of Mom's Birthday Past, the Ghost of Mom's Birthday Present, and the Ghost of Mom's Birthday Yet to Come, and they all showed me the true meaning of Mom's Birthday, so I ran out into the street in my nightgown and started giving money to urchins and stuff. That's why I ordered us the El Supremo Dreamo Extra Large. It's twice the size of Tiny Tim. Of course *we're* gonna both be twice *our* size by the time we finish—"

She was giggling pretty good by then, so even if she had been setting me up for a sermon, I'd managed to step out of *that* bear trap pretty neat and clean. "So what's new at work?" I asked. She could always crack me up by saying mean shit about her coworkers.

She took a moment to light one of her Kents, take a deep drag, and pose with it; Mom used her cigs to wave around at least as much as she smoked them, so she probably only got like half the cancer she paid for. "Dull as *shit* all day, Tiger." She always kind of emphasized the swear words when she was talking to me, I guess to remind me I had a cool mom that would say *fuck* and *shit* in front of me. "So I did one whole chapter of my real estate course, and filled out the answer sheet, and mailed that in. If the school is even still in business, now I've done eight chapters, with seventeen to go. So there's some progress in my personal world, anyway."

She'd started that correspondence course three years ago. Every couple-few months she'd do another chapter, mail it in, and get a grade back a couple weeks later, always an A because the assignments were retarded-chimp easy, and open-book besides. Supposedly once she finished the correspondence course she'd be all set to take the exam for her real estate license, but she could have just walked in and taken the exam; the course wasn't like a requirement or anything. I'd speed-read the whole book in one long weekend last year, but then I'd been real disappointed when it turned out that in Ohio you had to be eighteen to sell real estate (I figured it couldn't be any harder than selling radio ads, and it paid a lot better).

Come to admit it, I knew good and well that Mom was

taking the course so slow not because she wanted to get her license but because she wanted to avoid it. I had no idea why she'd want to stay a secretary/receptionist, but that was what she wanted.

Meanwhile, though, she could sure tell a story. She took another drag, then posed again, one arm across her chest to shove her boobs up, the other holding her cigarette vertical, head cocked to the side, the basic clever-and-flirty she did all the time when she was pretending to listen to Neil and the other losers.

She talked quite a bit of dirt about Mary, the part-time office help, who was a couple years older than me and screwing two of the married sales agents, which was why she never actually did anything "except her nails and hair," Mom said, "which she does at her desk for hours. And whatever she does to her nipples to get them to stick through her blouse like that all the time," Mom said. "That doesn't happen naturally till you've had like ten babies. Oh, and she does talk to her girlfriends on the phone, but since we have to keep the line open she only does that maybe half the working time in the day. I just think of her as not really an employee, more like a benefit, we supply the sales guys with hot and cold running slut."

Then she got going on all the weird gross stuff they found out at the Merton house when old Pearl Merton finally died. There were all these cat skeletons, boiled and cleaned like for a science fair project, with tags on them naming which cat they'd been (I almost asked Mom if she'd like me to start doing that for her cats instead of maintaining the cat cemetery in the backyard, but it was her birthday so I was being nice). Old Pearl also had a stack of Bibles all the way up to the ceiling at the northeast and southwest corners of every room, and three waist-high pyramids of carefully washed beer bottles in her attic. It didn't seem to me like it meant much more than that old Pearl was crazy.

After that, Mom got into how she thought her friend Judy might lend her some money to write and publish a book about the connection between Nixon and flying saucers.

I knew that wasn't going to happen. I mean Judy wasn't going to give her the loan—Judy was lucky to keep the doors of her little head shop/record store, Officer McDoodle's, open.

Come to admit it, I figured Nixon would leave on a flying saucer well before Judy would loan Mom money or Mom would get her real estate license.

So she rambled back and forth between her jokes about Mary the Slutlette, which I wished she hadn't been quite so loud about because like everyfuckingbody in town went to Pietro's, and Pearl Merton's whole closet full of unopened tins of Christmas cookies, and how Daniel Ellsberg used to work for national security and must have had the secret codes for contacting the good saucer people ("elves"), and Nixon and his bunch must have been trying to steal the codes to give them to the bad saucer people ("grays").

I don't know what got into me to ask her, "So why would Ellsberg leave the codes in his psychiatrist's office? Instead of in a safety-deposit box or something, I mean."

"Because a psychiatrist is like a priest or a lawyer, baby, they can't divulge your secrets. And he'd *never* put it into a safety-deposit box at a *bank*—they're all *in it*."

"In what, Mom? I'm falling behind here."

"Yes, you are, sweetie." She leaned forward, holding her cigarette down low so that smoke went up past her face. I think she was trying to look extra mysterious. The candlelight caught her face on the underside, which made her makeup look like she was telling stories at a Halloween bonfire. "I'll show you. Show me a dollar bill. Actually we just need the back of a dollar bill."

"The front comes with it," I said, fumbling in my wallet.

"Oh, you." She giggled, so she was still cool—good. "Has anyone ever told you that you're very literal, Tiger?"

"You, just now."

"Hah hah. Now look here at the back. What does this say and what is that?" Her fingers rested on two spots.

"This says 'Federal Reserve Note,' and that is an eye in a triangle floating over a pyramid, Mom," I said.

"You went all through this a couple times last winter, so I looked it up. The Federal Reserve is the bank that all the other banks use to clear checks, and the eye over the pyramid is supposed to be the eye of God, or a Masonic symbol because a lot of the Founding Fathers were into Freemason stuff, and nobody really knows whether the Masons on the committee that created the seal put it on there, or if people just liked the idea of God watching over us all. Personally I like the idea of God watching over my money." Not a real subtle hint.

She dragged my dollar bill toward her with the two fingers she'd been pointing with, daring me to point out that it was mine, and I felt like it, but I also decided it was her goddam birthday and she wasn't getting this easy an excuse to spoil it.

With the dollar bill safely in her purse, she glared at me, puffing out smoke fiercely. I could tell she was having an idea, which was always scary.

Just then Lyle, the waiter, showed up with our pizza. Mom sat back and turned her radiant-happy love-you-sweetie smile on him. Lyle had been a senior when I'd been a freshman; he was a shy, gawky guy with shoulder-length gray-blond hair, and always seemed pretty startled that anyone noticed he was there. Mom cranked the wattage, asking him how he was, remembering things about him, and getting him all stammery.

Once she had him flustered, she said, "Well, I guess

we have to let you get back to work. Oh, and Lyle, please get us a bottle of your house red wine, and two glasses."

"Um, I'll need to see some I.D. for him. Um."

That was what she'd been waiting for; she opened up her could-cut-glass stand-up-for-your-rights-voice to half-scream. "No you sure as hell *don't* need to see any I.D. for him. I'm his *mother*! I say it's fine for him to have wine, and who the hell's business is it besides mine?"

Everybody stared at us.

"Those are the rules," Lyle said, hitting Mom's overdrive button with a hammer.

"The *rules!* The *rules* are why soldiers are killing babies in Vietnam! The *rules* are why we don't have a woman president! Why don't you think a little more about freedom and a little less about the *rules*?"

I was hungry. I wanted to eat some of that pizza, which I'd be paying for whether she calmed down and we ate, or we got thrown out, or she sailed it into the kitchen like a Frisbee, and with Mom any of those might happen.

I needed to say something, but the truth—that I didn't *want* any wine, I just wanted to eat—would *really* get Mom up on her hind legs, mad at me for not standing up for my freedom.

Then I thought of the winning strategy. "Mom, I want you to have a good birthday." I kept my voice very soft.

She got that crazy scared look in her eye, and she leaned across the table and hissed at me. "Karl, controlling

people's access to altered consciousness is the first thing
the oppressors do."

"Lyle, just for today, so my mom can have a nice birthday, you go right ahead and oppress me. Bring a bottle of
wine and *one* glass. And watch me like a hawk to make
sure I don't alter my consciousness. But I warn you right
now, buddy, when the Revolution comes, I'm putting you
up against the wall *personally*."

Lyle laughed, thank God, and looked relieved, so Mom
decided to laugh, too, and just like that it was cool again.
Everyone at the other tables saw the show was over; I
got the root beer I actually wanted; Mom got a bottle of
wine all for herself; and Lyle got a safe escape and a big
boost in the tip. Mom and I settled in to eat, and as the
wine hit her, she got all silly and girly and funny. Damn
if it didn't look like the best Mom's birthday I'd seen since
about sixth grade, before Dad got sick.

She was eating more than usual, and drinking to keep
up, and she got funnier and funnier, rambling on about
her girlfriends, the "super super ladies." To be a "super
super lady" you had to be a middle-aged lady that wished
she was a twenty-year-old hippie, with extra points if you
were divorced, did witchcraft or astrology or other weird
shit, and smoked pot. Whenever that crowd acquired a
new member, and Mom would tell me about her, she'd
finish up by saying "She's a super super lady."

Lots of times she'd say that after talking nasty about

one of them, too; *"so she's blowing the mailman and she sold her kids for medical experiments and she's eating Dex like it's Milk Duds. She doesn't take shit from anybody. She's a super super lady."* Like that.

As she went on, I realized that she thought I was also going to give her night-out money like I had last year, in addition to the dinner and the wine.

That was pretty fucking pushy, come to admit it, but this is what I had money for, to keep Mom happy so bad shit wouldn't happen. She was going to have a happy birthday if it fucking killed both of us and the whole town of Lightsburg. Actually, killing the whole town of Lightsburg might make it a happy birthday for both of us, but since *that* was out, I was ready; I'd brought along an emergency wad. "So," I said, "about how much is it going to cost for you and the super super ladies to go terrorize the town?"

Mom brushed her hooker-blonde hair back, wrapped one arm across her chest, held her cigarette upright, and looked at me across a sip of her glass of wine. "Me *and* the super super ladies? So, Tiger, are you implying that your old mother is *not* a super super lady?"

"You're in your own category, Mom. A *super* super super lady. One full super ahead of the rest."

"And you're a big phony super suck up."

"Why do you think I'm such a good salesman? All right, you're a half-super super super lady. Only half a super above the rest. But that's my final offer, and if you don't like it I'm getting a new Mom, which I *hate* to do for a steady customer like you but—"

She was laughing real hard again. "Oh, Tiger, when you flatter your old mother like that, I ask myself, 'Beth, how long is it before there's a whole squad of pregnant cheerleaders on the front porch?'" This would usually have been her cue to try to piss me off by loudly asking me if I'd fucked Bonny, the girl I took to the prom. But apparently I'd mellowed her so much that she just topped up her glass and reached for more pizza.

So I had another piece of pizza myself—I had an infinite capacity—and right as I was figuring I could probably hand her two twenties and a ten, the price of a good tear through the bars back then, and make her birthday perfect for both of us, she pulled out a real mood-killer. "So what are you signing up for, for your senior year? Gary O'Grary in the office was bitching about Larry signing up for a lot of puff courses."

I tried to deflect her. "What can you expect from a whole family that rhymes?" That was our standing joke, since Larry's grandfather was Harry, his mother was Mary, and his sister was Terri. We had no idea why they hadn't gone on to have two more kids, Barry and Sherry, but maybe they were trying to leave room for future generations.

She laughed but she said, "All right, Karl, I'm drunk

but I'm smarter than that, sweetie, and I know this is the week you sign up. Now what are you planning to take next year?"

I shrugged. Maybe she wasn't really interested. "Gov, gym, Mod Lit, probably French, and then either Wildlife Ecology or wood shop."

Mom was looking way too focused. "Correct me if I'm wrong. None of that is college prep track."

"French is," I said, "third-year languages all are. And I only need a semester of science, the government class, and six units overall to graduate, so I'm taking more than I need to—"

"Unh-hunh." Mom could always just drop the drunk when she wanted to, maybe not enough to drive, but more than enough to talk. "Let me tell you what worries me here. You're not lazy, Tiger, and sweetie, your mother may be an old bimbo and a fake hippie and a drunk—I know what people say—but I do know you, and know how you think. So when you *don't* take college prep, it means you are *not* planning on going to college."

Like a moron—maybe I used up all my strategy earlier or something—I sat there and nodded, instead of making something up quick.

"You couldn't be dumb enough to be thinking of staying here in Lightsburg," she said, not making it a question. "You *know* this whole stupid little armpit of a town is dying, the jobs are going, the people are going, all that's going to be left is ucky ucky old turds that don't want anything to change ever and hate everyone's freedom, this town will look like the Ohio State Rest Home for the Elderly Stupid in another twenty years. You need to get *out*, Karl, I'd be getting out if I had a way and something to do. So if you're not going to college, what *are* you doing?"

The whole time she'd been jabbering I'd been shoving pizza into my face. I figured I was about to lose my shot at it if I didn't get it inside me soon, and it was good and I'd paid for it. So when she suddenly asked that question, I had a great big mouthful, and the perfect excuse of having to chew and swallow, to give me time to think. Unfortunately, even when I'd finished, I still had no idea what to say.

I guess the Brain Fairy had visited but forgotten to leave a quarter. I just blurted, "I'm planning to go into the army."

Dad had done that when he was eighteen—joined the army to leave Lightsburg—like he said, they were definitely hiring in 1942. He was no hero type or anything, he jumped for every clerking job he could find, said he'd personally fought the Japs all the way back to Tokyo with his adding machine and four tablets of graph paper, and like that. It would crack me up.

"Oh, for the love of God," she said. She looked at me like I'd blown my nose on her shirt. "At least give yourself a chance, Karl, it's the least you can do. All right, we're poor and things aren't going very well, but it's not like we live in the projects and you're going to be hanging out on street corners."

I shrugged. "It'll get me out of Lightsburg, and after a few years they'll pay for my college. And Vietnam's over, Mom—"

"Oh, fuck, fuck, you stupid fuck, you don't mean you believe the shit they put in the newspapers? They're still over there burning villages and spraying chemicals, it's just secret since Kissinger came back and lied about having a peace treaty so McGovern would lose the election. That's part of what Watergate is supposed to cover up for. Get real. They'll put you under some big black sergeant and he'll beat the shit out of you all the time."

"I don't believe any of that," I said. "It won't be all that bad."

She gulped her glass of wine and poured another. "Christ, I can't believe I have to argue with you about this at all. Sometimes you're so much like your father I could just slit your throat, you know?" She heaved a sigh. "Karl, my father and both my parents went to college. Even *Doug* managed to make it through night college after we got married, though it wasn't easy . . . I mean, his *grades* . . . and all right, so I only did one semester, and I didn't like it, but I *tried*, and I found out I *could* have done it, that's how I know I have the brains to do my projects now . . . it's just—you know?—important?" Her sharp focus of a minute ago was fading.

"And I know maybe you're thinking about Doug . . . aw, shit, Karl, I didn't get along with your dad and all but I did love him and I miss him, too . . . shit. What I was going to say is he was the *mayor* here, they elected him *three times*, and Shoemaker Avenue is named after his great-grandpa, and the whole fuckin' ceme-trare—cemetarary—cemetery, cemetery, cemetery, your old mom isn't as peep as some thinkle drunk, Tiger!" She flashed her *God I'm cute* little-girl smile at me. "The ceme-te-ry is full of his people and my people and *we all go to college.*"

"And then to the cemetery."

"Getting cute will *not* get you off the hook this time. Why would you want to go into the ucky ucky army, anyway, sweetie? Right now the college campuses are just . . . they're places of peace and love, Karl, I wish I was your age and going to college . . . can't you feel all that harmony and peace settling in? I know you don't like my astrology stuff but it's the age, Karl, it really is the age of Aquarius, and you want to put on a uniform and go be all Piscean . . . I mean, don't you even want to smoke a little grass and get laid while you're young?"

From what I'd heard from guys I knew that were in the army, that wasn't going to be a problem.

"Karl, all I'm saying—I don't want to be all fascist

and controlling with you, Tiger Sweetie—is give yourself the courses so that even if you do go into that ucky ucky army, at least you can go to college after."

Well, she kept getting louder. Finally, so I could get her quiet, give her a nice birthday—and okay, eat the rest of the pizza in relative peace—I had said, yeah, I'd take the college prep classes my senior year. Hell, I'd even take the SAT, it was just one more test. After all, I reminded myself, soon as I turned eighteen, on June 29 after I graduated, I'd be pounding down the door at the recruitment office, and get on that bus to freedom.

But to get a shot at the last of that pizza, I had promised I'd take the college prep classes, trig and senior lit and honors gov.

At the time I agreed to it, it hadn't seemed so bad. I was okay at math, and I knew I could get through trig. Honors gov was the class everyone called "Agreeing With Harry," because a third of your grade was participation, and Harry Weaver did these humongous long riffs about how Castro was going to invade, the Supreme Court had made praying illegal, and Martin Luther King was a Communist. He also insisted that we call the Civil War the War Between the States, because he was from some hillbilly state and couldn't get over being forced to wear shoes and share drinking fountains. As long as you nodded, and woofed all that back to him on the work sheets and tests, Harry gave you your A.

But the best deal of all had been taking senior lit from Mrs. Kliburn. In fact five of us Madmen had signed up for that first period college-track lit class. Our therapist last spring had been a young-looking eager guy named Vic Marston, who thought stress made people crazy and the thing you had to do was avoid it and get rid of it and never let stress into your life, which it seemed to me would be okay if you were a cow, but I think old Vic wanted everyone to mellow out and coast, I guess like he did when he would get high with students at parties sometimes.

Vic had set up a list of all the "low-stress" and "high-stress" teachers, gone to the principal, and insisted us Madmen only take classes from low-stress teachers. And Mrs. Kliburn had been Low-Stress Teacher Number One, because she was into this thing called "full-success learning" where supposedly her objective was to always have a hundred percent of the class score a hundred percent on every assignment. Paul's dad said he didn't know what it did for the students, but it was great for football and basketball, and that was good for bond issues.

So I didn't think I was giving up all that much by agreeing to do college prep. It was like giving Mom her going out money—more than I expected but not impossible.

Anyway, it didn't really matter right away. Mom got into getting drunk and overeating, and by the time we got home, it was a little late for her to call Jolene, who still lived with her husband, or Judy, who had to open up her record shop in the morning, so Mom decided to delay going off to Mister Peepers to pick up sales guys and lawn maintenance workers for another night. By then she was all sloppy and sentimental and hugging me and calling me Tiger Sweetie, and messing up my hair, and I more or less dumped her onto her bed, facedown so as not to choke on her puke.

By the time I got her tucked in, and my McDorksuit on, the clock said 9:48, and I had to practically run all the way, a good mile and a half, to be on time for my job cleaning out McDonald's. I punched the clock at 9:57—three minutes to spare. That queered my mood bad. I liked being a guy who was always way early.

So I was whizzing around, burning off energy scrubbing counters and wiping down tables and all that, and since none of my friends had shown up to watch me clean, I pulled out the bottle of Rosie O'Grady that I kept in my school bag.

I was thinking about what Mom had said. Even though she was weird about it, I *did* need to get out of that little dying town.

Something or other made me think for just a sec, maybe, too, about Dad having gone through AA.

I looked at that bottle of cheap fake wine and saw things real clear, the way you see them just before you start to drink to get drunk: I would drink away my money and time and energy, and be a fucked-up failure all through my twenties, probably hanging around the high school looking for loser chicks I could fuck. Then I'd dry out and get Jesus when I got old.

It wouldn't take long. Thirty is old in drunk years— this was Mom's thirty-ninth birthday and she was definitely an old, old drunk.

I realized after I got Jesus, I'd marry "that good woman who put me right with the Lord, got me away from the bottle, and taught me what life is really all about." Which was to say, some church girl that resembles a pile of loose fat upholstered with pale goopy skin, and whose whole life is chocolate cake and visiting her sister.

Then we'd have kids—two or three whiny little failures who never succeeded at anything, or maybe a smart one who went off to college and never came home and despised his old man as much as his old man despised himself.

All of a sudden, with that vision of my future, I just said to myself, *fuck it*. If I kept drinking I'd never leave Lightsburg. If I stopped right now I could not only skip Jesus, I could skip the church girl. It was like, right there, with that cool smooth bottle clenched in my fist, the screw cap still in my other hand, I could smell cheap scent not quite masking fat-girl sweat, and hear her warbly voice singing country music and gospel hymns beside me in our broken-down fourth-hand pickup.

I screwed the cap back on the bottle and went out to the Dumpster. I thought about having one last drink.

Decided that would mean there'd never be a last one. Threw it hard against the back of the Dumpster. Great little smash.

I went inside and cried because Dad was dead, and I wanted, so bad, to tell him about it. At the same time, I was so grateful that I felt like thanking Jesus for not existing.

Next day I went to my first meeting. By the end of school two weeks later, my life was noticeably better, so I stuck to AA like a coat of paint.

It wasn't all happy. Bonny dumped me because she wanted a guy who would drink with her. Paul still drank but never around me, and hung out with me night after night, talking and goofing and just being there with me at McDonald's, making me pour Sprite and Coke down myself till I washed the poison out. Mom decided that since I was broken up with Bonny and constantly with Paul, I'd turned queer, and screamed at me till I admitted I'd just stopped drinking, which offended her even more. Every time we ate together she'd be trying to get me to take a drink.

Still, by the end of June, I was busier than ever but getting more sleep, and a lot of times Paul and me would be up till three or four in the morning talking about life and stuff; I remembered more of the day-to-day stuff. The blur was sharpening, and I was getting to like things better with hard edges.

I kept right on going to AA, and got a sponsor, Dick Larren, the cook at Philbin's where I was hopping the counter for the summer.

By July, Mom stopped hassling me about being a fag, and then about being an "ucky ucky Puritan," and went back to hassling me about going to college. Since I'd already agreed to do college prep, and application deadlines were a long way away, it just wasn't that big a deal.

Then less than a week before school started, Kliburn's husband suddenly got a job in Boise. The class was going to be taught by Gratz. I about shat my shorts.

Gratz was an asshole Vietnam vet. I know they didn't *all* bayonet babies and set villages on fire and shit, despite what Mom said. I bet most of them just followed orders, and were just real glad to be back, and their friends got killed and stuff, so we should respect them or feel sorry for them or something nice like that. I shouldn't be all down on every whacked-out flag-waving hates-everybody psycho that came back from Vietnam.

Just the *bad* whacked-out flag-waving hates-everybody psychos, the ones that machine-gunned old farmers and bombed grade schools and got the clap from twelve-year-old hookers and didn't have any sensitivity to the culture and all.

Gratz carried Vietnam like this twenty-ton chip on

his shoulder, and we all had to admire his chip. He wanted everyone to hear how sincere he was every time he said "God bless America," and notice how often he stood up and told everyone exactly what the facts were. When he lost it in class, which was often, he would slice some poor kids to the bone, humiliating them until they half-drowned in tears and snot. Then Gratz would get all apologetic and I-care-so-much-about-you.

I think that's why us Madmen loathed him. Switching back and forth between this-is-the-way-the-world-is, my-way-or-the-highway tough, and remorseful big-wuvvy-teddy-bear sweet, was what a lot of us saw at home—the behavior of a father that beats his kids or fucks them.

Rude hollering asshole teachers always get way too much respect from adults, so lots of people in Lightsburg were Gratz fans. When I hopped Philbin's lunch counter, every old fart with too much mouth and not enough brains blabbed about how Gratz was a great wrestling coach, and how much he cared, and what a great teacher Gratz was, and it was so good for the kids to be taught by a real man, a guy who had been a Green Beret and still got choked up at the national anthem and always sang real loud in church and knew there was one right way and would keep the kids on it. The old gomer would take a big drag on one of those nasty unfiltered cigarettes, and like, arf up half a lung, and thump the counter and glare at me. "He keeps those kids in line and he really cares about them."

Unh fucking hunh.

Literature, in the Gratz universe, was good for us because it would make us manly. (Especially the girls.) Every single book or story you read in one of his classes, every line of poetry, every paragraph of every essay, you were supposed to get all these lessons about being manly men. I guess all the great authors really just wanted to write pep talks for the Fellowship of Christian Athletes.

I tried to get out of it. I told Mom, "Hey, I'm trying to avoid a screaming hollering Vietnam vet fascist asshole."

It didn't work. Instead, Mom had looked up from her almanacs and flying saucer books and all that, and set down her glass of white wine, and thought seriously, or at least looked serious, and said, "Well, I know you don't like him. I don't like him either. But he really does make kids learn things, and he was one of your father's very best friends, even went into that awful AA program with him, and I think you should probably take that class, Karl, I'm sorry you don't want to, but I think you should."

For just a second she sounded just like the Mom I remembered from before Dad died. I don't know why, but that really got to me, and I didn't ask again while there was time to switch classes.

So, anyway, that's how my deal with having to take Gratz happened, that's who Gratz was, that's how Mom's birthday pizza turned into some of the most expensive pizza I ever ate, so here I was. Like the army except with an extra-abusive sergeant, no pay, no free stuff, and no promotions.

Gratz for breakfast, and no alcohol. My senior year was shaping up fucking great.

3

*Eight Madmen, the Biggest Asshole
in Ohio, and One Very Normal Guy*

BECAUSE I HAD caught the early bus, I got
into Gratz's classroom so early that only Cheryl Taliaferro was there.

Cheryl had a lot of thick brown hair permed into ring-
lets, and perfect makeup—her stepmom took her over to
Cleveland to see a professional cosmetologist every few
months. She had on a tight tan jacket, a loose blousy top,
and nice tight pants that rode low, and the soles and heels
of her shoes probably added three pounds to each foot and
three inches to her height.

Cheryl was the queen of the socials—all the cute
perky girls with big smiles that knew everybody. She
was the secretary or the vice president for every club
and committee, always at every party, and never missed

a game. She was always tits-up go-team super-positive gosh-I-love-it-here-and-everything-is-so-wonderful and all-my-friends-are-my-specialest-funnest-buddies. All the regular teachers and counselors adored her, and all the cool intelligent teachers hated her guts.

But even though she was Queen of the Socials, Cheryl was even more the Queen of the Madman Underground.

I squatted down beside her. "Hey, haven't seen you at McDonald's in a while." She usually came to hang out and talk while I cleaned, once in a week or so.

She made a face. "Grandpa stayed the summer."

"Were you and Sammy okay?" Her sister Sammy was a freshman this year.

"Basically, but I had to make excuses and stay in, like, after nine P.M. and till he'd pass out about one in the morning, so that I was stuck in the house. I guess I could bring Sammy by McDonald's—she's in a therapy group now, we could start another generation of Madmen."

"Any time, you know."

"Yeah, I know. Anyway, it's not so bad now. Grandpa's scared of me; I told him to his face that if he messes with Sammy again and I catch him, I'll tell the cops. But the threat only works while I'm right there. So instead he's been doing a lot of that same old creepy stuff in front of my parents. He told me in front of Daddy that my boobs are even bigger than my stepmom's were at the same age. Daddy sat there and nodded like a good doggy, like he always does, and Barb said, 'Oh, she's so beautiful,' just like he'd complimented both of us. I don't think I ate anything all August. At least my jeans fit great."

Cheryl and her sister got punished if they "disrespected" the old troll.

"Well, *that* all sucks the big one," I said.

"Yeah." She was looking down at her desk.

Stacy Hobbins came clattering in, and just started telling Cheryl about a phone call she'd gotten from a guy the night before. Cheryl acted all interested and stuff. Since I'd just become invisible, I sat down.

After Stacy the room filled up pretty fast with the usual group of brains and socials you found in college prep classes. The only one I didn't know was a pale, skinny girl with bad acne who came in, looked bewildered, and then took a seat behind me.

The next Madman in was Danny, in his FFA jacket. Paul always said that he probably slept in it and you couldn't prove he didn't have it on under his football uniform. He was a one-man two-clique wonder, leader of jocks and farm boys alike. Three-clique, really, the smart kids let him hang with them to show they could be tolerant.

Four, I guess, if you counted the Madman Underground.

Danny was a brainy all-American jock that most parents would trade their real kids for in a heartbeat. His old man hated him for being a success and threw it in his face all the time, or all the time he could spare from drinking and screwing up the farm. Danny always got his ticket in the first week because he'd get awful crying jags.

The next Madman to arrive was Darla Pilsudski, who was super-intense and super-smart and ultra-beyond-super-weird. She plucked her eyebrows into strange wickets and wore huge circular tortoiseshell glasses and bright blue eye shadow. Her daily uniform was a hot pink or electric blue leotard, sprayed-on jeans, and huge clunky heels. Darla fit into no cliques. She was a fox but she didn't hang out with either the socials or the hoods. She was a brain and super-serious about books and grades, but she dyed her hair hooker blonde, smoked, and cut school. She always had a couple of steady jobs and every employer loved her but she was always in trouble with the cops.

Darla read books nobody else read, had records from bands like two years before they were on the radio, and went out with art students from Plantagenet College who had little stripped-down motorcycles and big built-up attitudes.

She always carried Mister Babbitt, a stuffed rabbit she talked to out loud. Most people thought that was so weird that they never actually listened to what she said, so she got away with saying all this fucking hilarious shit right out in public.

She got her ticket for being weird and obnoxious but she really did have problems, like burning herself with cigarettes and cutting little bits of skin off with a razor blade. When she was in ninth grade, the cops came to her house and she had dragged her seven-year-old brother, Logan, into the bathroom and threatened to blind him with Drano. Gist County Child Welfare had put Logan in foster care and tried to get Darla locked up, but it was pretty clear her parents didn't really want Logan back anyway, and that was right when the group had Shirley Reloso for a therapist. Good old "Doctor Shirl" responded to any negative comment about any of the Madmen with "Prejudice city! There are no bad kids!"

Reloso had gone to the judge and sworn up and down that Darla wasn't a bad or evil person, she was a *good* person who did extremely brutal, violent, nasty things, and—who the fuck knows what or if grown-ups think?— they gave Darla supervised probation and left Logan in the foster home.

A week later Darla's parents left for six months in Hawaii. Most of the kids would tell you that her parents were never home because her dad was a Hells Angel, and they dealt drugs and were always on the road. Older people knew her dad had made a bunch of money as a stockbroker, then married a Prentiss, which used to be the big family around town, bigger even than the Shoemakers, and they'd been living off her trust fund.

Darla had told us that her parents were "pussy-nerd wimp-ass trustfunders who inherited a fuckload of money and spend it all in New York, L.A., Aspen, Acapulco, all those shitholes. They always come back complaining it was nothing like what they expected, but they always go again."

She usually had the house to herself, a big old place on the hill. Old people in town said that house had once been *the* place to be invited. Now it was *the* place for the kind of party that parents didn't want their kids at—or most kids' parents, I ought to say. I'd run into my mom at two of Darla's parties, but I think she was just there to score pot, or because Neil had crashed it.

Darla's big plan was to go somewhere east to school and never come back to Lightsburg at all, so she played serious-student real hard. Like always, today she sat in the center of the front row, opened a pad to take notes, and set four neatly sharpened pencils beside it to the left. (Paul and me had timed her once: class hours were fifty-four minutes, with six in between for getting to your next class, and sure enough, with Mr. Irish, this one obsessive science teacher we had who always started exactly on time, Darla changed pencils every thirteen minutes and thirty seconds, exactly one quarter of the class time.)

She stuck the suction cup on Mister Babbitt's ass onto the desk so he faced her. She plucked at his ears for a moment to make one stand up straight and the other droop at whatever exactly the right angle was.

Paul came in, and took a seat far away from me, over in the corner behind Danny. He didn't look at me at all.

I wondered if maybe he had a crush on that invisible sophomore girl he sat beside on the bus. Normally he got crushes on prom-queen all-American shampoo-commercial girls whose major conversational gambit was "What?" and whose huge boyfriends would beat the shit out of him.

He was my best friend but he wasn't perfect, you know? I was worried about him, and, come to admit it, pretty hurt.

Coach Gratz walked in on the balls of his feet, arms held away from his body like he expected someone to yell, "Ready, Wrestle!" He had gold-blond hair, piercing blue eyes with little crinkles in the deep tan around them, and a hard-edged cleft chin. He wore dorky stretch-knit shirts, the ones that go over your head like a T-shirt but have a few buttons and a collar, to show off his hard muscular body and keep Mrs. Gratz horny. He always wore the same bolo tie with a turquoise and silver slide, because the dress code for male teachers said a tie, but it didn't say what kind.

He slung a big stack of books onto the desk with a bang. I don't think anyone jumped as much as he'd've liked.

"Hi, since I've had everyone in this room for one class or another, sometime in the past, you all know I'm Coach Gratz, and I'm not Mrs. Kliburn. For those of you who took this class because you heard Mrs. Kliburn was easy, tough. For the rest of you, we're gonna learn some stuff. It won't all be easy, and it won't all be—"

"Excuse me, sir," the new girl behind me said. I looked around. She had very thick, messy, wavy blonde hair that sat on her head like a thatched roof. Her wire rim glasses perched on chipmunk cheeks smeared with acne, above a mouth full of braces. The white T-shirt she was wearing was too big on her; she looked like she'd missed her last three months of meals.

"I haven't been in one of your classes before," she said. "My name is Martinella Nielsen. Most people call me Marti."

Gratz frowned. "Well, *Marti*, that is *very* interesting. Normally in my class you speak only when there is a reason for you to speak."

"I'm sorry, sir. I didn't mean any disrespect."

That was about twice as polite as anything Gratz was expecting, and he kind of half-froze in shock.

The moment for tearing into Marti slipped right away. When he launched into the tirade for the second time, it just didn't have that old Gratzical energy.

Anyway, Gratz announced, "with great pleasure," that we were going to read *Huckleberry Finn* first, because it was "the greatest American novel." We knew that because Hemingway said so. Or something. Then he hollered about how our literature was just as good as anybody else's literature, so there, and if you didn't know *Huckleberry Finn* you "didn't really know what it was to be an American." Once he slipped back into his groove, I tuned out.

One thing about Gratz was kind of funny in a pathetic sort of way—you could tell that he really did like books and poetry by the way his eyes would light up, especially when he got off his lecture notes and just talked. The Budweiser company didn't want people to drink beer half as much as Gratz wanted us to like poetry. But the poor guy just couldn't shake his terrible fear that literature might be for fags.

He finally said, "Far enough for today," and made a pencil mark on his lecture notes so he'd know where to start the next day. "Paul, Cheryl, Karl (uh, Karl Shoemaker not Carl McGwinnick), Danny, Darla, and *Marti*, see me after class. It will just be a minute."

That was annoying. Us Madmen didn't associate with each other in public. We didn't need some dumbass football player or one of the jackoff smart kids to come up to us and make bibby-bibby noises with his finger and lip. Even though it was the seventies and like half the people you saw in movies were seeing a therapist, it was cool in the movies, but not in real life. Kind of like being black—every cheap bastard in Oakwood watched Flip Wilson, but you should have fucking heard them when they thought a black family was going to move in.

We surrounded Gratz's desk. Cheryl and Darla stood with arms wrapped around themselves, Paul looked at the floor, Danny leaned across Gratz's desk and hung his head, as if to hide his face. Marti stood behind me.

Gratz pulled a letter from his stack of paper and waved it like a summons. "It says here that Doctor Marston suggested that all of you should continue on in therapy this year, except for you, Marti, but your old school doctor recommended it.

"Now, I know a lot of you kids hate therapy, and I don't really like having six kids missing from class every other Monday. What I wanted to tell you all is that if you don't want to go this year, I'm on your side. If you need me to write a letter or something, well, I'll be happy to. Okay, that's all."

We turned and had to struggle out through a bunch of sophomores coming in for Gen Am Lit. When Paul and me had both had Gratz for that class, we had called it "Read Like a Man." Last year, that had become the nickname among all the kids a year younger than us; we were hoping "Read Like a Man" would stick this year, too, and eventually be what everyone called it. This is the sort of thing legends are made of, at least in places like Lightsburg.

Cheryl and I had Hertz's trig class next, over in the other wing, so we walked there together. "I can't believe he did that," Cheryl said. "Couldn't he have just said 'All the mental cases, please see me after class'?"

"Gratz," I agreed, "absofuckinglutely pure Gratz."

She made this growly, frustrated noise and shook out her thick mass of curly hair. It reminded me how pretty my friend was, and what a great body she had. Knowing how creeped out she'd be, I hated myself for noticing.

"So is Gratz the biggest asshole in Ohio or just in Lightsburg?" Danny asked, behind us.

We both laughed and Cheryl gave him five.

"I don't know if I'd want to do the research, checking out every other asshole in Ohio," I pointed out.

"Good point." With Danny walking just behind us, I was reminded how big he was, and how tiny Cheryl was; it made me feel safe to have him standing over me and it made me feel like her protector to be standing next to her, and just then I didn't give a shit that a normal guy wouldn't be with the Madmen. *Normal is still important, I'm still going to be normal, but normal isn't everything.* It was my new idea. I was going to stick to it like a fresh coat of paint; the old idea obviously was just the primer.

Mrs. Hertz wasn't really a pushover. No math teacher can be because they can see your bullshit too easy. But she was nice, and she hated to say "you're wrong," and best of all, she was as heavy a smoker as my mother, so between classes she was always charging down to the teachers' lounge to suck down those nasty skinny brown almost-cigars, and it usually made her a couple minutes late to class, so there was more socializing and less math in my life.

Which was good because Bonny was early to class, and I hadn't really seen her all summer except to wave to. It had been kind of a relief when she'd dumped me last spring, but I still wanted to be friends. When school was out, we didn't see much of each other because she worked as much as I did, maybe more.

Her parents had an import shop up in Toledo. They'd go on long trips to buy stuff for it, but the shop only made about enough to pay for those trips, plus to pay the help and keep the doors open, not much more. Now and then they'd get a jackpot, some guy would come in and buy up a lot of stuff, and then they'd give Bonny some serious money to keep the house going, maybe two or even three months' worth of money, but that only happened maybe once a year.

Meanwhile, Bonny had to have money for groceries, clothes for her younger sister and two brothers, the house payment, and all that. She said her parents never asked her where she got it, didn't even seem to be aware that most of the time when they were away they weren't sending any money.

The shop paid straight into her parents' account, which Bonny couldn't take money out of, so if they didn't send a check, like they usually didn't, whatever money the shop made might as well have been on the moon.

She wasn't going to nark on her parents, since that could mean the kids being taken away or even her

parents being busted and doing jail time. So Bonny
made the money, one way and another. And she was in
the Madman Underground because now and then she'd
throw a fit of temper or a crying jag in front of teachers. Bonny would never explain that the screaming and
throwing things wasn't "just for no reason" as teachers
would say about her, but because she was getting by on a
couple hours of sleep and worried sick about paying the
mortgage and hadn't heard from her folks in a month
while they knocked around the south of France. She had
at least a couple of those a month, so she got her ticket
every year like the rest of us.

Except me, of course, Mr. Normal. Remember, this
was my year to be normal. With friends, of course. In my
guise as the normal member of the Madmen.

Bonny was a cheerleader because she did anything
that would look good on those college apps—cheerleader,
choir solos, Service Club, plus all the science clubs, math
team, and chess team, but she wasn't much of a conform-
ist. Today she was looking sort of like Grace Slick or Ja-
nis Joplin after a three-year famine, in three layers of
skirts and a vest with a lot of gold piping over a blouse
that looked like the curtains from a funeral home, and
enough bracelets for any six regular girls, and her red
hair was spilling out of a purple scarf, like maybe she'd
been thrown off the belly dancing squad for overdoing it.

"So," I said, "still robbing thrift stores?"

She slapped my arm, not hard. "Ask me about my new job, Karl. Big hint, I can't dress like this there. I have to wear a uniform."

"Oh, my god, I'm being replaced. I knew Mayor Mc-Cheese was a treacherous bastard and he'd stab me in the back. Just watch out when you're alone with Ronald McDonald—he likes to squeeze the meat and pat the buns."

She snorted. "Actually it's even grosser than mopping the McPiss off the McFloor in the McCrapper. Not the clown—the monkey."

"Pongo's?"

"Yeppers. They had a girl quit and Darla got me in before they even advertised it. Steady hours and it won't conflict with choir or cheerleading. How's that for cool?"

"Cool," I agreed. "How many jobs you have right now?"

"Oh, cleaning out those offices downtown, handing out cigarette samples at the concerts in Toledo, the paper route, and this. So four. Where are we?"

"Still tied," I said. "I have cleaning McDonald's, selling ads for WUGH, helping Browning deliver couches, and my gardening and handyman racket. It's a good thing school is such a joke or we'd be so fucked."

Cheryl coughed.

Mrs. Hertz had come in behind me and heard that. Shit.

Danny and Bonny and Cheryl were all fighting down laughter, and so was Larry O'Grary, the weird sci-fi hippie freak kid that was hanging-out buds with me and Paul.

At least it was Hertz, so I wouldn't be getting a ticket for this. She was cool and smart enough to know that hating school wasn't crazy. Another reason to hope she didn't blow out a lung before graduation.

She started right in where geometry had left off, without even a *hi* or a *how was your summer*, and kept us busy. Okay with me, really—I got to spend like forty-five minutes being normal without having to think about being normal.

I know smart guys are supposed to hate gym class. I loved it and signed up for it every term. It beat the shit out of study hall, I can tell you that. I always seemed to have so much energy, and it felt good to burn it off and get to play with the other guys, it was usually a whole hour when nothing could bother me, and it came with a free hot shower that didn't smell like a litter pan. That was another reason I was looking forward to Army Basic; gym all day, not much homework, and no after-school job.

Danny and me suited up fast in those silly "uniforms" they had for gym—a pair of purple shorts with a built-in jock that would only give you any support if you were hung like King Kong, and a sog-baggy yellow T-shirt with a picture of a wildcat on the front. Opinion was divided as to whether the Lightsburg Wildcat looked puzzled, drunk, or constipated.

Coach Korviss was an okay guy. Even though he was the gym teacher, he was a lot less of a coach than Gratz. "All right," he said, "obviously we're all here to get a workout every day, so we're starting out today running, just to see what kind of shape you're all in."

By that time it was steaming Midwest summer outside, but it was so nice to just have a mindless hour that I didn't care. About halfway through the first lap, a familiar voice said, "So, you think you'll have some work for me this fall? And maybe for Tony?"

"Squid, you know you're always the first I bring in on a big job," I said, "and Tony's great too." I glanced left at Squid Cabrillo and slowed a little; he was pretty much the right side of the line for our football team, but asking him to run distance was like asking an elephant to tap-dance.

His squashy nose ran all over his always-serious trollface. You could cliff-dive from his single eyebrow, and his eyes were two olive pits set between his bulging cheeks. His big square jaw looked like he could take a bite out of a car bumper.

Next to Paul he might be my favorite Madman.

Squid didn't get his ticket because he acted weird—he

was a case of *something awful happened to him, we don't want to think about it, put him in counseling.*

When he was seven, his father had gone to the state pen at Mansfield for beating the living crap out of a nice old farmer, taking all the pay envelopes for the pickers, and going down to Columbus for a whiskey-and-whorehouse spree. His mother had taken a job as janitor at Saint Matthew's Lutheran here in town, to be close enough for visiting days, which Squid said she'd never missed while his old man was in. Also once a month, she had taken a homemade meal to the farmer and asked him to pray for the Cabrillo family.

The farmer said he forgave them and prayed for them and all, but it didn't look like it had worked. Papa Cabrillo had gotten out of jail, divorced his wife, and taken up with a fat Kentucky chick fifteen years younger than him who'd been writing to him while he was in prison. Then Squid's mom had killed herself when he was in eighth grade. Somehow old Cabrillo had gotten the house and moved in with his hot hillbilly honey. Laws and judges being stupid, they got custody of Squid and his younger brother Tony and sister Junie.

I'd seen the marks on Squid's back in the gym class showers; I'd helped him out with a place for him and his two younger sibs to sleep; there had been a couple sacks of groceries I'd gotten for them—maybe more than a couple, come to admit it. But tempting as it was, I'd never ratted out old Cabrillo, because Squid made all us Mad-men promise not to.

I guess maybe we could have. Officer Williams (one of those cops whose name just logically begins with "officer" the way some teachers are just always Mr. or Miss), the family-court cop here in town, seemed like a good enough guy. But none of us ever narked, because we knew it wouldn't help. I mean, what was I going to do, have them take my mom away, lose our house, lose everything? What would Cheryl do if they arrested her grandfather and her parents threw her and Samantha out of the house?

And could anyone expect Squid to send his dad back to prison? I mean, yeah. He sure as shit deserved it. But it was his dad.

The sky was like a hot metal bowl overhead, and our shirts were all soaked, but it felt good to be moving and using the muscles just because I wanted to and not because I had to. Squid plodded along beside me and I kept the pace comfortable for him; if Coach wanted me to run faster, he could tell me to.

Halfway round the next lap, I asked, "So, you do the usual this summer?"

"Yeah. Worked my ass off, got some stuff for the kids, got some savings. Mostly picking tomatoes and detassel-ing corn, my cousin got me some of that, plus I kept the bagging groceries job at Kroger. It sucked and I hardly saw Tony and Junie at all but now I won't *have* to do much more than some bagging to get through football season. But you know, more is always nice. So you think you'll have any gardening you need help with?"

"I always do. I've got to turn compost under and build some beds for spring, bunch of places."

"Hey, if you fellas have breath to talk, you ain't working hard enough," Coach Korviss said. "Pick it up, Esquibel. Karl, run with me a second."

Squid *ooph*ed on ahead, and I waited for the question Korviss always asked me just once. "Karl, I know you have endurance and speed. It's your senior year. Are you sure you don't want to come out for cross-country this fall, and maybe for track in the spring?"

"It would be fun, Coach, but I work all the time."

"I could talk to your mom."

"She's not the one making me work."

He ran beside me for like half a lap before he finally said, "Well, your life is your life. We'd love to have you. And I know you'd enjoy it. Give it a day or two and then get back to me next week if you change your mind, all right? Only time I'll ask this year, I don't want to pressure you. Now show me what you can do, will you? Put on some speed."

So I opened up and ran hard the rest of the time, and it was good and brainless and mind-clearing, even if my uniform did end up soaked so that I'd have to take it home to wash right away. That conversation with Korviss, I don't know why, gave me some incentive. I lapped a couple guys from his cross-country team, put some pressure on his miler, and finished with a two-lap kick of running like a flat-out crazy bastard just to see if I could keep it going that long.

I didn't bother thinking about how I felt about Coach asking me. I just didn't do extracurriculars. Stuff happened at my house, sometimes, and if it conflicted with the extracurricular, I'd have to let someone down.

Besides, Korviss didn't pay you to run.

He was right, though, it could've been fun, spending time every day just running. I kind of wished life was different, but it wasn't.

In the showers, Squid said, "Hey, you still got that night shift job at McDonald's, right?"

"Right." There was a fresh mark on his back, probably the buckle. "Anytime you need a place for you or the kids to sleep, door's always open."

"I just always like to know," Squid said.

4

How to Get Your Very Own Madman Nickname

THEY CALLED ME Psycho after I killed the rabbit in seventh grade, and that's actually the worst thing I ever did, but it was also how me and Squid got to be friends. If there was anything good about it, it was all Squid; I brought the disease, he brought the cure.

See, seventh grade was pretty bad.

The summer between sixth and seventh, as I was getting all psyched up for junior high, Dad had me out with him on a lot of jobs, kind of learning how to work, and paying me a little bit. So I was there to see it when Dad kept getting tired and he couldn't hire enough help to make up the difference, and paying so much more in wages instead of doing the work himself, so his contracting business was going all to shit. Then one soggy hot

August day he passed out on a roof, slid down, and fell into Mrs. Caron's yard.

I was scared, I can tell you that, but Mrs. Caron called an ambulance, and Mom met us at the emergency room. I could smell that she'd had some wine; the last year or so she'd been doing that when no one was home. But it was still a relief when she hugged me, and when we went in to see where Dad was sitting up, with an IV in his arm, and getting a stern lecture from the nurse about drinking enough water in hot weather.

But before they let him go, the doctor got interested in the way Dad was coughing, and did some tests, and they found lung cancer.

By November, he was puking a lot from all that stuff they did to him, and losing hair, and looked a million years old. He could still sit next to me on the couch down in the basement, and we'd sit and watch old movies together, usually two per night, but he'd fall asleep on my shoulder, not the other way round.

He couldn't come out to see me play seventh grade football; it was too far for him to walk, he'd lost his license from too many DUIs, and Mom wouldn't drive him, she said it was too much bother and besides I only got in for maybe one or two plays a game. Whenever I came home, I seemed to be interrupting a fight; a lot of it was because Dad had quit drinking but she was making up for him, and whenever he wanted her to drive him someplace, it would turn into a major battle.

Anyway, I guess it was okay that Dad didn't actually see me play. There really wasn't much to see. I was a scrawny fast guy—didn't really get my growth till a couple years later when I'd been doing heavy work for a while. Little fast runts like me were only useful for real long passes, and we didn't have a QB who could throw for shit. Coach sent me in exactly five times in three games, and Al never passed on any of those plays anyway.

Really, I never even knew if he *could* throw. But I did know for sure that Al could punch ribs like a son of a bitch.

He was a mean dumb bastard, only the quarterback because he got his growth early and he could run with a bunch of seventh graders hanging on to him like baby possums. I think he knew in the depths of his ape-brain that as soon as the other boys' bodies caught up he'd be nowhere, and it made him mean, or meaner anyway, while he still had the chance to beat on other kids.

So Al would beat the hell out of me. And all the time, Squid, his then-best buddy, would be standing right beside him, saying, "Come on, make him cry so we can go talk to the pussy." "The pussy" meaning Cheryl, who was Al's then-girlfriend.

Whenever I thought about Al's then-life, and his now-job at a tire store and the now-wife he'd had to marry last year, I'd get a smile that nobody wanted to see.

But even if it turned out all right later, back in seventh grade, there was nothing I could do to save my ribs.

I couldn't quit the team. It was a big deal to Dad. He saved the stories from the *Lightsburg Lighthouse*—they did a "preseason" about us, a story about each game, and a "postseason," where Coach Stuckey mentioned me in a list of about ten guys he was expecting more from next year. Dad put yellow Hi-Liter on my name; that and the honor roll were the only times I appeared in the paper while he was alive.

I'd come home from practice and go downstairs to sit on the couch with him, or he'd be doing some fix-up on the house and teach me how to do it, and he'd want to know what all I did in practice, and—well, I couldn't quit. And I couldn't really tell him, "Oh, Coach said I'm a fast runner, he always says that, and then Al beat on me in the locker room, here, look at the bruises up the side of my ribs."

Because for one thing my stupid old man would have said to fight back, and what was I gonna say, *well, I used to try, but he just knocks my hands out of the way and keeps on pounding?*

I knew Dad. He would tell me to keep trying. I mean I know it's good to keep trying and all, but sometimes, like when you just get pounded twice as hard for twice as long, you have to do what works instead of what's good.

I guess I could have told Coach Stuckey, but I didn't want to be a nark and a crybaby. I'd have to go away to the State Home for Terminal Pussies with a big *P* tattooed on my forehead. Besides, who the hell were they going to believe, the popular QB, or skinny little Shoemaker whose dad used to be mayor before being the town drunk? Al's dad, who was at every game cheering like a nut, or a spooky ghost like my dad, a dying bundle of sticks and scraggly hair?

I knew where I was on the ladder. And where Al was.

Anyway, so I'd walk home, sometimes crying all the way from the beating I'd gotten, and then wash my face and tell Dad how much I loved football and how well I was doing at practice. That was the fall of seventh grade.

I don't remember exactly what tipped me over. Maybe I just thought my ribs were fucking sore enough. So one Sunday Al was riding his brand-new ten-speed over to see Cheryl—he was always bragging on how he was feeling her up all the time—and I stepped out from behind a bush with a ball bat and spoked his bike, and he went over the handlebars, and as he stood up, I swung the bat real hard at him, and clipped his right elbow. (I couldn't do anything right. I *wanted* his ribs).

They said I chipped the bone, so he didn't play that fourth game. Neither did I, of course, because good old *Al* had *no* problem with narking on *me*.

Everyone kept saying I was lucky I didn't break his spine or rupture his kidneys (I always thought he was luckier) and was all sympathetic for him, and nobody ever did give a shit that Paul and me and Larry had spent months being bruised and afraid. Pain only matters when it happens to someone important.

Instead of hitting him a lot more like I planned to, when I saw him holding his arm and yelling like a baby, I ran away.

If I'd left it at whacking Al's elbow and destroying his bike wheel, I guess people would've understood eventually. Or if Al's mommy had called the cops as soon as he came home and tattled, instead of rushing off to the emergency room and waiting for X-rays and shit, I might have gotten busted before I did anything else. But nobody stopped me, especially not me, and what I did next, well, I fucking made *myself* sick.

That night, I went into Squid's backyard, pulled down the chicken wire enclosure, grabbed his pet rabbit, cut its throat with a box knife before it knew what was happening, then tore it up with garden shears—it didn't come apart as much or as easy as I planned, so I just kind of opened up a couple big rips in it. Then I left it in the yard for stray dogs and cats to tear up some more, and for him to find in the morning.

Squid cried in school for like a week and the social girls were all over him—they all thought it was so cute how he wuvved his bunny wunny, and him such a big strong football player too. I think I probably got him laid.

I got six days of in-school suspension for hitting Al

with the bat, which they could prove. And that was well worth it.

I didn't draw any penalty for the rabbit, because the cops said *could've been a dog did it*, but Williams watched me real hard because he found out Squid had been in on beating me up—Al told him. Like I said, Al was a fucking nark.

So later that week, Williams dropped by to talk to my parents while I was doing my bench time at school. When I got home that afternoon, Dad took me down in the basement and made me drop my pants and bend over the couch. Coughing and gasping for air, he took a metal yardstick and lashed the holy fuck out of my ass.

Then Mom came down screaming at him, and got between me and the yardstick. She yelled at Dad because he hadn't known what Al and Squid were doing to me, and they both started yelling about how I was turning out and whose fault I was. I pulled up my pants and went out and sat in the toolshed till Dad came and got me to tell me it was dinnertime, they'd ordered in a pizza, sausage and green peppers, my favorite.

That night, as Mom rubbed salve into the welts, she was crying and talking about going to the cops but she didn't; I guess I didn't want her to.

Come to admit it, I realized a while later that what I had done had really changed something. My parents were scared of me. So were the other kids for a while.

And the teachers and Officer Williams all watched me like I was gonna explode.

I guess maybe they thought, next thing, I might cut up a little kid or something, but the only person who asked me directly was this one therapist, a weird little East Coast guy named Bradshaw, months later.

It was a little chilly, windy and cold. Doctor Bradshaw took me out to shoot baskets one afternoon, got me out of school and all, and then when I was pretty well worn out, way after school closing time, he sat down with me on the bench by the basketball courts in the park, and we just talked.

Bradshaw was being so nice he got me crying, and I told him how I felt sick as fuck about that rabbit, sometimes I had bad dreams about how its jaw had worked against my hand, the way it rubbed its nose on my palm wanting to be petted, the second when I could feel the pulse in its soft throat, and then the ripping feeling in my hand and the warm blood squirting all over my arm. Come to admit it, it was the first time I'd cried in months, and it was pretty hard to stop once I got going.

When I was all cried out, Bradshaw took me to a sandwich shop for dinner, and bought me a big sub sandwich and pile of French fries, and I always wondered if he slipped a drug into it or something, because I got pretty sleepy. He took me back to my parents' house and told them, straight to their faces, that I was fucked up but not dangerous—he said it in psychology-talk but that was what he meant—and I think he told the cops and teachers that too, and after a while people forgot and I got some slack. And Paul stayed my friend through the whole thing, too, which helped.

The next month Bradshaw got a job at a university counseling service. He left his address with me and I wrote him like three letters to say I was okay, and he always wrote back to say it was good that I was okay. He sent me a sympathy card when Dad died the following fall, and we traded Christmas cards once, and then I guess there just wasn't much for either of us to talk about. I think I was probably the only Madman who remembered him.

But though killing the rabbit was the worst thing I ever did, that wasn't the worst part.

The next fall I didn't play football because Dad was sick all the time, dying, and I wanted to spend as much time as I could at the hospital. And that meant I didn't see Squid at all.

One thing I remembered, though, at Dad's funeral in October, it seemed like half the town was there, but nobody my age was except Paul, and his brother Dennis and sister Kimmie.

I really remembered how much it helped to have Paul there standing next to me. Maybe because Mom was being so weird and quiet, maybe because everyone was just

walking up to me and saying, "I'm sorry," and then walking away like they were afraid I might talk, maybe just
because it was a friend who was there for me. I don't remember Paul saying anything. After the graveside service he touched my shoulder and said he'd come by the
next day.

When he did, he just sat with me all day, not talking,
which for Paul was like not breathing.

I needed Paul real bad and he was there; I couldn't
imagine how bad it would have been not to have anybody.
And right there he set me an example, one I must have
decided to live up to, though I can't remember thinking
that in words.

If anybody ever needed a friend—a real one, I mean—
it was Squid. That guy never had any kind of luck but
shitty. On the April Fool's Day after my father died,
Squid's mom killed herself. Harris and Tierden, these
two real hateful guys that would have been our class
clowns if they'd been funny, were making jokes about it
the next day, when Squid wasn't in school, so I treated
them to my best Psycho expression and they went creep-
ing away. First time (but not the last) I saw the useful-
ness of being Psycho Shoemaker. Doing Squid that favor
got me thinking.

Squid's mom'd been depressed, everyone noticed that.
A lot later Squid said, in group therapy, that old Cabrillo
had been calling his mom up to tell her she was fat and

ugly and how he hated her, and how much he loved his new no-shoes teenage hillbilly honey.

So on April 1, 1970, Squid's mom was walking home along County Line Road from one of her cleaning jobs, out in Oakwood, and she looked right at an oncoming semi—the driver said she "looked right through him"— the *Lighthouse* went and *printed* that. I guess Squid and Tony and Junie weren't anybody, so it didn't matter how they felt about it, and it sold newspapers.

Semis really barrel along that road; he had no way to stop. He laid on the horn, and stood on the brake the whole way to her, and rolled the trailer trying to swerve, but she just walked straight toward the front grille till she hit and went under.

Everyone said Catholics weren't allowed to do that and she wasn't supposed to get a Catholic funeral, but Father Robert, at St. Ignatius, basically told everyone to stop being an asshole. Maybe Father Robert told the bishop she was crazy or blind or something, but he gave her a Catholic burial.

I had Paul's example. I had scared Harris and Tierden into not being shitheads. I felt like I was committed but hadn't yet done enough. So the afternoon of Squid's mom's funeral, I slipped out of the junior high, ran home, grabbed my jacket and a tie, and went over to St. Ignatius's Church. I didn't know when to stand or kneel or how to cross myself, I'd never been to anything Catholic before, but I watched the rest and figured it out.

There wasn't much of anybody there—just Squid; Tony, who was nine at the time; Junie, who was seven; Squid's great-aunt, who didn't speak any English; a lady from County Welfare; and Father Robert.

The two kids clung to Squid like he might evaporate. After the service, since I wasn't going to go out to the graveyard, I came up to Squid and touched his elbow and said, "I'm sorry."

He nodded, his face almost expressionless, and said, "Thank you."

I don't think that was what made us friends, though.

See, the next Monday was our second or third therapy meeting with Ramscik, one of the worst counselors we ever had, the one after Bradshaw, so I hated him extra bad already but he fucking deserved it, I can tell you that. It was Squid's first time in therapy, since he'd gotten his ticket for having his life stink.

Ramscik kept badgering Squid about letting his feelings out and shit, and Squid just sat there and looked at the floor and wiped his eyes, which I guess didn't count as letting his feelings out.

That went for I don't know how long and everybody else was staring at the wall or the ceiling. Then my voice said, "Leave him alone," real loud.

Ramscik stared at me.

I said, "Squid can talk when he wants to talk. And

he's not all alone. He's got his aunt, you heard him. And me and Paul're gonna go shoot baskets with Squid Saturday morning. Maybe he'll talk to us." I still don't know where that came from. It got Ramscik off Squid's case, though, and back into talking to us about staying away from drugs and peer pressure and sex.

After therapy, in the hall, Squid said, "I suck at shooting baskets," and Paul said, "Me too, and besides I have clarinet practice on Saturday mornings. What were you making up, Shoemaker?"

"Something to get that asshole off Squid's case," I said. "If you had a better idea you should've been faster."

"'Preciate it," Squid said. He touched my arm just for a second, and kind of half smiled. I smiled back for all I was worth. I couldn't stand to think how lonely the guy was feeling. Christ, if that wasn't a lesson—lose your rabbit and other kids swarm all over you, lose your mom and you're invisible—what a thing to know about your friends. I wanted to be a friend for him worse than I'd ever wanted anything.

Well, I guess I managed it. Squid followed us to lunch like a lost puppy. It was like a month before his jock friends started hanging out with him again. Meanwhile, since Squid and me were both lonely kids, and we knew what was wrong with each other, and didn't want to talk about it, before we even realized it was weird, we were friends.

Just before school got out, the judge decided that the house and the kids went to old Cabrillo, which meant Squid's dad was in there on his mom's bed with a girl just seven years older than Squid, and a lot of the nice way his mom had fixed the place up went all to hell. And my mom got serious about being a pretend hippie philosopher and a real drunk bimbo. Squid and I started running into each other at older-kid parties, where we got pretty good at stealing or begging booze. By the end of eighth grade, Squid and me were pretty regular drinking buddies, and all that summer, we'd get odd jobs together, then go to whatever party we could get into, and wind up in a vacant lot or behind a building, drinking till we passed out. We talked whenever it was necessary. Mostly it wasn't.

Okay, here's the worst part. I don't remember ever talking about it, but Squid knew about the rabbit. I could see that in his eyes. He never said a word, he just knew.

But Squid forgave me. Really forgave me, I mean, all the way to trusting me and accepting me as his friend, and I would swear I didn't have a more loyal friend from then on.

Which I'd never have done for him. I can be an okay guy but I wouldn't have it in me to be that good to someone who'd done something so awful to me.

So my revenge was a mixed bag. I kept Al from playing his last game as quarterback and deprived him of the peak of his life. But killing that poor rabbit—all I accomplished was to prove that Squid might have a mean streak, but he was still a much better guy than I was.

Me? I was a vicious crazy bastard who hurt helpless things when he thought he could get away with it.

So that's how I got to be called Psycho Shoemaker and why the name stuck. I earned it, I deserved it, and it was all my doing.

Normal *Guys Walk with* Pretty *Girls Who* Giggle

LARRY O'GRARY WAS just getting into line when I got to the cafeteria. He wore his blond hair halfway down his back; he was "about six feet tall and weighed about six pounds, or it might be the other way round," as he said, every time he got the chance.

That was one of many things he said to be weird. I mean, Larry really *was* weird, no question, but I guess not being innately weird like the Madmen, he felt he had to work at it.

You know how a girl who isn't naturally pretty will wear too much makeup and get way too careful about matching colors? Or the way a not-so-smart guy who wishes he was smart will always bring up some really hard book he read, or keeps repeating the only fact he knows about a subject? So you always keep noticing that she's not really pretty, or he's not really smart, and they can feel you noticing that, so they get all insecure and keep doing it more?

That was Larry and weird.

I think he was afraid someone would notice that he was just a guy with long hair who read a lot of sci-fi, knew all of Firesign Theatre by heart, and stole a lot of one-liners from *MAD* magazine.

Larry did lights for the school plays, took photos for the school paper, and was a moderately shitty reliever for our immoderately shitty baseball team.

I never saw him over a summer; he went to camp. Just this moment in lunch line he was telling me about some girl named Allison that he'd finally lost his virginity to. First thing every fall, he'd have to tell everyone that this year at camp, he'd lost his virginity. He never remembered that he'd said the same thing the year before. I thought about asking him if Allison'd gotten into any fights with Jen, who was the one from last year. But I didn't; I'm a cowardly shit.

Anyway, another ten years and he'd lose his virginity for real. Probably three weeks after I lost mine, come to admit it.

We got up to the head of the line and Larry tried to freak out the cafeteria lady by asking for sea creatures and boiled wheat, with spoiled milk. He looked kind of disappointed when she just plopped a serving onto the tray.

Since it was the first Wednesday of the school year, we had Wednesday meal number one, tuna noodle casserole, corn, and apple crumb cobbler. They hadn't changed the rotation since Mom stopped packing my lunch back around third grade. For thirty cents more I could've gotten hamburger-with-fries, but I always got the main meal, for variety, because between all my jobs and my hanging out I was already eating like five thousand hamburgers a week.

Larry and me headed for a vacant table on the main aisle. Paul would have lunch this period too. After a whole morning getting caught up with all the other Madmen, I'd come to see that, like it or not, they were the friends I had—and anyway avoiding my best friend wouldn't exactly be normal. So I had added another operation to Operation Be Fucking Normal.

Operation Restore Best Friend would go like this: Paul would sit with me, we'd have a normal conversation, and then on the way out he'd suddenly tell me why he was avoiding me. He liked to drop the big one on you just as you were saying bye—as an actor, he wanted the curtain line.

Paul came out of the serving line. Larry waved at him. Paul walked right by us and went to the picnic tables outside.

"Wonder what's wrong with that there laddie, 'e's a weird one 'e is, eh, eh, eh? A weirdie you know. Eh?" Larry was probably quoting some movie I hadn't seen, to judge by the fact that he was doing a really bad accent, bad enough I didn't know which he was trying to do. He did that a lot. I don't know if he was hoping people would recognize something he quoted, or afraid they would; knowing stuff nobody else knew was a big deal to Larry.

"Hunh," I said. "He seemed kind of fucked up earlier today too. But you know, sometimes Paul's just like that." I was lying—I'd never seen him act like this before—but I guess I just wanted to keep it sounding normal. Maybe I wanted Larry to agree I knew Paul real well.

I ate a couple bites of corn while Larry launched off into some rambling thing about what if all your friends were replaced by aliens, which I think was like his *MAD*-magazination of a Philip K. Dick book. I was watching my tray like it was naked television.

When he stopped to breathe, or I think maybe he asked me a question, I said, "Hey, I'm not hungry. You want to finish this for me?"

"You only ate, like, a few bites, man."

I shrugged. "If there's not enough of my germs, I could sneeze on it for you."

He laughed. "Good one, Karl. I wish I'd thought of it."

"You will if you're ever not hungry." I passed him my tray. "I have to grab something from the library."

"First Paul, then you. Is it my breath?"

I got up. "No, that's what keeps *girls* away." He snarfed, so I said, "Hey, I offered to sneeze on it for you, you don't have to do it yourself."

Like Paul always said, you don't waste a curtain line, so I went.

After not being hungry at lunch, I was starving all afternoon and couldn't concentrate in chem, or in Agreeing with Harry, or even in French.

Walking home—I usually did if the weather was good and I didn't have to get over to Browning's to deliver a couch—I mostly watched my shoes and didn't go very fast. I was going to buy dinner at Philbin's Drug Store rather than try and find anything clean and not-cat-chewed at home. The one problem I didn't have was poverty, and at Philbin's I could get a science fiction novel or a mystery or even just a comic book to enjoy with dinner.

"Hi," a girl said behind me. "I'm going to introduce myself to you because—"

I turned. "Your name is Marti," I said. "Coach Gratz made sure *everybody* would remember."

I could tell from how she flushed that that was a real stupid thing to say. For just a sec I felt like shit.

Then she made herself smile, revealing her braces. "This is the part where you tell me *your* name. That way you can say 'Hi, Marti' and I don't have to say 'Hello, geek.'"

I laughed. "My name is Karl Shoemaker. I'm sorry."

"Oh, that's all right, I was *hoping* for you to have a *good* name, but don't apologize, I'm sure your parents liked it."

I was so out of it I almost went on to explain that no, I meant I was sorry about having brought up the thing with Gratz, then finally got my head together enough, and realized what she'd said was funny. So after an interval just long enough for her to decide I was retarded, I said, "Uh, yeah. Um, I'm kinda thinking too much and I'm a little slow about everything. Uh." I was sounding fucking brilliant, I can tell you that. "So you're new this year. Where'd you come from?"

"Prison," she said. "Are you going this way for a while? I'd like to try to make friends."

"I'm going downtown," I said. "Walk along if you like."

She was bony, with about as womanly a figure as I had. Her belted-in jeans bunched and sagged around her ass. She was wearing grody old loafers without socks. Her frizzy blonde hair bunched around her head so that she looked like a tree drawn by Dr. Seuss.

"Most people, when I say I came from prison," Marti said, "either laugh like they're afraid I will think that they didn't get the joke, or they're so literal-minded that they ask 'really?' Most people don't stay dead silent, when I say that."

I wasn't going to tell her that I'd been trying to figure out exactly how small her boobs were. "I figured if I waited a little, you'd tell me."

"Karl, you're a great person," she said. "A really great person."

I had no idea what she was talking about. "So what prison were you in?"

"Prison with style. My dad kept putting me into genius schools to teach me discipline so I could live up to my potential. It didn't really work out."

"You didn't learn discipline?" I asked, feeling stupid.

"No, that's *all* I learned, was discipline. I had to— there was so much homework and it was so hard. After a few months, I'd start to cry all the time, and then he'd move me to another genius school." She sighed. "I didn't actually have any potential. Well, not, didn't have 'any,' any, but not like the kids that go to those schools do. The trouble is that Dad *is* a genius, a real one I mean, and he thinks since I'm his kid I should be a genius, and— I mean I'm smart enough and all that shit, but *not* a genius. Not the kind of daughter that Doctor Martin Nielsen should have, and Doctor Martin Nielsen gets what he wants, or he thinks so. Or at least he gets what he wants except when it's his daughter." She shook her head as if she wanted to slap herself and said, "Wow,

Marti. Brilliant. Confess your whole life. Scare the shit out of the guy you're trying to make friends with."

A normal guy would've found a way to ditch her right then, but I wasn't doing so good with being normal at the moment. "So you've never been to just regular school before?" I asked. "I'm guessing Lightsburg High has to look easier?"

She twisted her mouth sideways. "I'll probably get A's. Which Dad will use to prove that I really had all that potential he wanted me to live up to. But I am still *not* a genius. 'Kay?"

"Sure."

"Sorry, I guess I really overdid that, didn't I?"

"Yeah. Is that what all geniuses do?"

She swatted my arm, not hard. She knew it was a goof. She'd've had a great smile if she'd been showing teeth instead of miles of wires, but it only flashed for a half a sec before she started checking the sidewalk for land mines, open manholes, or rattlesnakes. "I think Dad finally decided that I'm not going to live up to my potential, or maybe Mother won an argument. She does sometimes."

We walked half another block before I thought of anything to say. "So you were in therapy before at your old place?"

"Every year since second grade. How about you, Karl?"

"Since fourth. I was a late bloomer."

She made a weird snorty-fizzy noise that I realized must be her laugh. "That's funny."

"That would be why you laughed."

Another fizzy noise followed by a snort and a gasp. "Karl, you crack me up."

Normal *guys walk with* pretty *girls who* giggle *at their jokes*, I thought.

She hesitated, then said, "Can I ask you a stupid question?"

"Sure."

"There's posters all over the hall for this First Day Dance thingy?"

"It's a come-on to lure freshman girls for the annual Massacre of Virgins."

"Okay, but—seriously—socially speaking, is it like, serious? I don't know this stuff because I've never been in regular school before and nobody tells me anything."

"The password is 'Dingleberry.'"

"Seriously, please?"

She looked kind of frantic, so I said, "Okay, seriously."

"Well, then." She drew a deep breath. "If I don't go— or if I do go—will I get social leprosy?"

"Depends on who you want it with. If you *do* go you get social leprosy with the drama types, the school paper, the Poetry Club, and both the serious intellectuals."

She grinned. "Both?"

"Spooky Darla and her hypothetical male counterpart. So if you want to be in with the people that make a big deal about being brainy and too cool for kid stuff, don't go. They'll all be at Pongo's Monkey Burger across town, the place with the monkey on the roof, smoking and trying to be too cool for each other. On the other hand, if you *don't* go to the First Day Dance, you get social leprosy with the socials, the jocks, the Glee Club fairies, the hoods'n'sluts, and all the clubs that begin with *F*."

"Clubs that begin with *F* . . . okay, let me try, I'm gonna get this place figured out if it kills me. The guys in the blue jackets—"

"Future Farmers of America. Guys who take ag classes and are going to inherit the farm. Hot shit around here, they have a couple guys in every clique, and they stick together, 'cause they know they'll be seeing each other every week for the next sixty years. If you go out with the right one you might could be Dairy Goat Queen at the next Gist County Fair. Wow, you can stick your tongue out a long way."

"Is there really a Dairy Goat Queen?"

"More real than Santa or Jesus—Stacy, in Gratz's class? She was DGQ just a month ago. Probably still has her tiara."

Marti shook her head. "I am not sure I will ever fully understand the strange ways of your tribe."

"Well, then we should definitely be friends, because I sure don't. Okay, three more *F* clubs."

"Hunh. Well, I saw a sign for an FCA get-acquainted picnic."

"Fellowship of Christian Athletes. Jock club that gets together to fake the churchy adults into thinking they're responsible young men with bright futures. The ones with long hair that's perfect, brown cord bell-bottoms, big sincere smiles, Good News Bibles in their back pockets. No girls, because there's no girls' varsity anything here."

"Imagine my disappointment."

"They sponsor a lot of coed events that are pretty dull and involve a lot of talking about the Lord before they sneak out back to drink Little Kings."

She grinned. "Karl, I feel like you just saved me a month of confusion. What are the other *F* clubs?"

"Future Homewreckers—FHA—the dumb girls that are majoring in clothes and makeup. French Club, because French is the social language."

She looked puzzled, then caught it. "You mean the language of the socials."

"Yeah, socials don't take Spanish because Mexicans speak it, or Latin or German because the teacher for those is a hard case. And the last *F* is the Freshman Council, which is all the freshmen that are going to be on student council and prom committee and all that shit."

"That's *five* clubs that begin with *F*," she pointed out. "You said there were *four*."

"You're the one who didn't want to go to genius school. See what we're like here?"

"How utterly splendiferous!" she said. "That means 'real good.'"

"I'd take vocabulary notes, but they don't let me have sharp objects. Anyway, as for whether you'll get social leprosy by going or not going—" I shrugged. "Depends on who you want leprosy with. I've had three First Day Dances to deal with. I went to one, I went to Pongo's another time, and last year my buddy Paul and me stayed home and got drunk in his basement and watched *The Three Stooges*."

"And this year?"

"I'm going, I think."

"So am I," she said, "based on your excellent advice. It'll be good to have someone I can say hi to by name," she said. Okay, her eyes were a weird shade of storm-blue, and about as nice as her smile. She was still a woofer, but not a 100 percent woofer. "Would you do me a *humongous* favor?"

"Sure."

"Ask me to dance at least twice tonight. In the first hour. Not when the floor is empty—when some people are already dancing. So I don't have to start *off* looking like a reject. 'Kay? Just, you know, friend for friend?"

"Sure." Actually this meant not having to worry about starting off shot down, *and*, since *she'd* asked, it wasn't a pathetic loser deal. At least not for me.

We were almost to the old redbrick downtown.

"This part of Lightsburg is kind of pretty," she said.

"As long as you don't notice all the boarded-up store-fronts."

"Does the Chamber of Commerce pay you to be this cheerful, or are you on happy drugs? Here's where I turn off. If I say it was nice talking to you, can you *not* say something sarcastic?"

I said, "Uh—I'm glad I met you." That didn't seem like enough, so I added, "Really," which, I realized a second too late, didn't help at all.

God, she had a great smile, if you could deal with all the metal. "Oh, I'll believe you. Tonight. We dance twice, and make it look like you want to! Bye." She turned away down Pierce Street, walking in that funny, stiff-legged strut that some girls get from being yelled at about moving their hips when they walk—Kimmie, Paul's little sister, walked that way—like she was trying to hold a corncob in her butt.

A Word from My Sponsor

PHILBIN'S WAS AN old dump: linoleum checkerboard floor, busted-up Naugahyde-topped stools shaped like conga drums, one of those butt-ugly steel counters. Lots of dull old chrome, and enamel in fridge-mold green and baby-shit pink. Outside, over the street, one of those old neon-tube signs (which didn't work any-more, thank god) said, PHILBIN'S DRUG STORE SUNDRIES SANDWICHES ICE CREAM.

I guess the place was mondo keen, maybe even groovy, in 1955, but nowadays they probably couldn't donate it to the Museum of Embarrassing.

Philbin's stayed open selling comic books and candy to younger kids, lunch and breakfast to the downtown workers, and lunch and medicine to the old people who'd been coming to this place since Philbin's granddad had opened it. I figured I'd come back from the army sometime and it would be boarded up like a lot of the other places in town.

They got *no* after-school crowd. Philbin and his daughter Angie both had asthma and wouldn't let kids smoke, so the hoods went to the poolroom up the street or the Catholic juv center instead. Heads went to Judy's stupid head shop, which was called (I wish I was kidding) Officer McDoodle's Shredded Wheat and Records Emporium. It had some tables and served herbal tea, and Judy let the fourteen-year-olds smoke. The jocks had practice, and the socials did cool extracurriculars like Show Choir and Key Club, so they hung out with the jocks at Pongo's Monkey Burger later in the evening.

Angie was sitting at the counter reading last week's *National Enquirer*, and Philbin was staring at an old black-and-white TV, watching the Indians lose as usual. "'Lo, Karl. Gettin' dinner here tonight?"

"Guess so. But first I'm going to get something to read, and do homework, and soak up some of that *fine* coffee."

I first started going to Philbin's after school in eighth grade—right after Christmas, we had some big blizzards and I got a bunch of snow-shoveling jobs. It was the first time I had some extra cash, and a good thing, too, because food was getting pretty irregular at home—Mom sometimes just fixed baloney sandwiches and Campbell's soup and went to bed, and other times took off to drink her paycheck. I could make mac and cheese or a sandwich, of course, if there was anything in the house, but often there wasn't.

Back then with only the snow money and the paper route money, I had to squeeze every nickel till the buffalo shat, so I got to drinking coffee with the afternoon special, because it was hot, only cost a dime, and refilled for free. But I'd been raised pure Ohio: the Zeroth Commandment was Thou Shalt Not Be Any Trouble to Anybody Ever. I didn't want them to make a new pot, even though the last customer had probably been about three hours before me, and what was in the pot was lukewarm, with a greasy sheen on the surface, and thick as motor oil.

Philbin poured the old stuff down the sink. "Ooops. Just spilled it. Have to make a new pot." It was our particular joke. Not exactly a knee slapper, but it always made me feel at home.

I found a few new paperbacks in the spinner racks. I could buy them all if I wanted. I still had a ton of money, even after Mom's most recent raid on my cash.

I touched her IOU in my pocket; not as much as I would have had. She was never going to pay me back. I had her IOUs for more than a year's mortgage.

The first one had been right after she cleaned out my

bank account—May 17, 1970, probably about two P.M., Mom took all $171.38 out of my savings account to buy wine, snacks, and pot, so she could "have some people over for a meeting to just share some feelings and talk about how everyone felt about Kent State and Cambodia and all." It was about six months after my dad died.

The second time she cleaned out my savings account was that fall, when I started ninth grade: $392.67 of garden work, paper route, sweeping out Philbin's, and some corn detasseling. Mom could take all the money in any bank account I opened because the law was, I couldn't get an account without her as a cosigner till I was eighteen. So in fall 1970, I started keeping money in hiding places, and I never told anyone I was doing that, not even Paul. It took her almost till Christmas to figure out what I was doing and get together with Neil to rob one of my jars, and by that time I had several stashes scattered. It had been a long hard run, but I was staying ahead of her.

The Madmen didn't know what I did with the money, but they sure knew I worked for it; Squid and Bon worked almost as much, after all. Every single shrink the group had ever had, since I was in ninth grade, said that the way I lived, always working and always making money, was a "defense."

They always said it like it was something wrong. *There is nothing wrong with having a defense if you're attacked*, I said, inside, where they couldn't get on my tits, trying to make me say, "Oh, now I understand everything and I am all better Mister Shrink Sir and now I will live just like you think I should."

Anyway, I could pretty much afford all the books, records, clothes, and meals out that I wanted, and still sock money away in my stashes. If I would've had a car I might've been able to do something about getting a bank account that Mom couldn't get into—drive up to Toledo, with some adult I wanted to trust to never nark me out to Mom or take the money themselves, and have them cosign—but that'd mean narking out my own mother.

And the car itself would've been another problem. I'd need to put deposits in a couple times a week, and she'd notice I was going somewhere that often. Not to mention insurance, which was fucking murderous; probably it was cheaper to just hide money.

So I was always spending it, too, because I got to keep things I bought, any money I spent was money Mom didn't, and she couldn't take a book or a record or a restaurant meal away from me and go spend it down at Mister Peepers.

Once, she'd sold a bunch of my records at Officer McDoodle's, but since I handled that ad account for WUGH, I kind of leveraged Judy hard, so she gave my records back to me. It was kind of a wash; she pushed Mom so hard to pay her back that Mom finally dug out one of my cans and gave that money to Judy. Mom still brought that up sometimes when she got mad, about how I had humiliated her, and "blackmailed" Judy, and how she didn't think she should have to pay on that one IOU.

"Hey Karl," Angie said. "One of those books really pissing you off?"

I was grinding my teeth and balling my fists tight enough for my nails to dig into the palms. "It's like a muscle thing," I said.

She came over and started rubbing my back. *Not* what I had in mind. Angie was okay for a twenty-three-year-old fat chick still living at home and working in the family business, I guess. But it reminded me of the way some guys are always offering back rubs to cute girls, and I didn't like it when Angie just started to, not even asking.

"It's okay," I said, trying to keep my hands from shaking because the fury was getting worse and I didn't want anyone to see. "Really it's okay. It goes away by itself in like a minute."

"Jesus," she said, continuing to rub, "your back is in *huge* knots. Maybe we should just *iron* you."

"Angie, don't fondle the customers," Philbin said. "Or at least fondle someone like Tom Browning, who will like it."

She let her hands slide down my sides and let go of me. "He's so old God calls him 'sir.'" She went back to her seat.

"Exactly. When Karl's that old, you can feel him up."

"I was *not* feeling—"

"Angie."

"Well, I wasn't." She went into the kitchen and started slamming stuff around, pretending to clean it. That was weird. But I was glad her father had stopped her. When I got those black rages, I was really afraid I might hurt someone.

"So how's the school year look so far, Karl?"

"Okay, I suppose." I made myself keep my voice real soft and offhand. "Harder than I wanted. Mom said I had to take the college prep track."

"How's Betty been?"

"She likes to be called Beth now."

"Right, sorry, Beth. I forget because I knew her for so long before."

If Philbin'd been like most of the old people in Lightsburg, he'd have had to point out that my parents met when she was hopping the counter and he came in for lunch for three months straight, but Philbin knew that I had heard that story all my life, and skipped straight to asking, "So, anyway, how's she been?"

"She's fine, you know, same old. Working in the real estate office, studying for her license, she's got her things with her friends."

He looked right into my eyes. Nice a guy as old Philbin usually was, he had some of that closed mind that

Lightsburg turned out like soybeans and corn. I knew what he wanted to ask. *Are you okay with the way she fucks around? Is she ever sober at night? Does she let Neil hit you? Should I call the cops about anything?* I knew he wanted me to nark on Mom.

I gave him a slack face, hoping I looked like I was thinking about hitting him, afraid I looked like I was about to cry, probably just looking like I was real dumb.

He left me alone while I looked through that rickety wire rack of paperbacks. I wasn't sure whether I wanted a good story, or something that it would impress Larry to say I was reading. I settled on a Philip Dick novel, *The Three Stigmata of Palmer Eldritch*, because it had a pretty cool cover and besides I always felt like Philip K. Dick, at least he had some idea about what the world was really like—full of hidden trapdoors with tanks of shit under them. People said it was because he took a shitload of drugs but I think he took the drugs because he knew what was going on, not vice versa. I couldn't always understand his books, but come to admit it, that was another way they were like real life.

Philbin's Drug Store was really dead that day. I read *The Three Stigmata of Palmer Eldritch* for twenty minutes and no one came through the door until Dick, who cooked there.

I don't mean Philip K. Dick cooked there. It was Dick Larren, a nice old guy, forty or so, my AA sponsor.

(Though holy *shit* it would've been cool if Philip K. Dick *had* been cooking there, I can tell you that. The Young Republicans, which was a group of middle-aged ladies—definitely *not* super super ladies—had coffee together there on Wednesday mornings, and I'd've *loved* to see what would happen after Philip K. Dick fixed them up with some extra special apple pie.)

Dick came over to say hi; that was okay, talking to your sponsor is a good thing to do. "Hey, are you feeling okay? Or is it a depressing book?"

"I'm a teenager. I *live* to read depressing stuff."

"Yeah, I remember that. Wait'll you hit your mid-twenties and find out smiling is okay again. But you're okay?"

"Hey, are you my sponsor or my mother?"

He blinked for a second, but then just smiled. "Well, sponsor is more than enough work for me. And I know what you eat like, so I'm glad I'm not buying the groceries. Anyway, you always know where I am if you need to talk. One day at a time, Karl."

"Betcha. Really, I'm just kind of tired, is all."

"Okay. Not a problem. Just making sure you're okay."

Really feeling better, I smiled. "Nothing worse than the usual."

From the first days I'd started coming here for meals, long before I'd started going to AA, Dick had been slipping me extra food. He lived alone, in a big apartment over a furniture store downtown; he had it fixed up nicer than a lot of people's houses—very clean, and actually decorated rather than just furnished. When AA met there, the coffee and the sandwiches would always be way better than average. It would have been fine with me if we met there every time, but Dick said it always took forever to get the stink of the cigarettes out of his drapes and rugs, and you can't ask people not to smoke at AA, you really can't.

When he wasn't working he dressed neat and fussy, so there were rumors he was a homo. I was pretty sure he wasn't.

After two more chapters, I had to admit to myself that I pretty much didn't get *Three Stigmata*, though it seemed very cool. I decided I'd finish it anyway. The Indians lost and Philbin and me talked some about that, just enough to establish that we were friends again. Philbin was about as nice a shop owner as you're going to find in a little Ohio town—nicer, actually, most of them are fat hollering self-satisfied flag-waving assholes for Jesus, not to mention their bad qualities. I hadn't meant to get so close to a quarrel with him; just sometimes, when people got nosy about Mom, I got pissy.

I pulled out my homework. The math was all review so I took about ten minutes to do that. Then I filled out Harry Weaver's standard twice-a-week worksheet; he had transcribed some sentences from the book onto a mimeograph page, leaving a blank, and your job was to replace the blank with the word. Every other blank, the word was *freedom*. Pretty silly that we had gov at all; if you were going to vote and stuff, you'd learn all this, and till you wanted to, why learn it? I mean nobody learns the rules to poker until it's time to play, do they?

Then I looked over the chem. So far that was all stuff I remembered from eighth-grade science. The French worksheet was all review from last year, too. Coach Gratz had said not to start reading *Huckleberry Finn* till he put the magic mojo on us, so I didn't look at it.

Now it was 4:30 P.M. Dick was thumping around in the back getting ready for the old couples that came in to eat dinner here. The water he splashed on the grill to test the temperature made a little *phit!-sput-sputter*. I grabbed a pad off the counter and scribbled "CB/dlux—cof—apl—choc S," wrote my stool number at the top, and clipped it to Dick's turntable.

I had hopped the counter here, off and on, usually whenever Angie took classes at the community college, ever since the summer after eighth grade, so Philbin had long ago told me to just grab a pad and scribble an order, and if I was in a hurry or they were busy, just ring it up on the register when I finished.

Like always, Dick way overloaded my plate. My cheeseburger came with about a triple load of fries, the slice of apple pie was like half a pie, and somehow or other not only was the shake all the way to the top of the glass, but the can was brim-full too, which seemed to defy both the Law of Conservation of Matter and the Law of the Five-Pound Bag.

I ate it all and read another few pages of *The Three Stigmata of Palmer Eldritch*. More and more confusing, but *still* very, very cool.

By now it was happy hour at Mister Peepers, a safe time for a fly-through of the house. I needed to change my shirt, get my McDorksuit together, and grab a shower before going out again. I was shoving homework and notebooks into my old Boy Scout pack when Philbin put a hand on my shoulder and said, "Ask me about a possible job."

"You got any possible customers?"

"Fair question, bub. You know that this weekend they're going to reopen the Ox? You must've noticed all the fixing up going on next door."

The Oxford Theater had closed when I was in sixth grade, after a long time when they just ran second-run movies and kiddy matinees. Lightsburg hadn't had a movie theater since.

"Unh hunh. And so?"

"So the new owners happen to eat lunch here a lot. It's a young married couple, Todd and Mary Urlenstein. They're English profs over at Plantagenet College. They have decided to bring culture to the benighted masses of Lightsburg."

"Aren't they going to show movies?"

"Oh, no. Not from what they tell me. They are going to show *films*. If anyone shows a movie in there, they will wash the screen afterwards. They are going to make it a *re-per-tor-y ci-ne-ma*."

"Foreign movies?"

"Foreign movies, and old movies that are supposed to be classics, and I kinda suspect, now and then, artsy dirty movies, which is what will make any actual money, if any actual money gets made. *If* they can square it with the churchies."

"Good luck on *that*. How long you figure they'll be open?"

"Well, I've done lots of talking with Todd. He comes in here for lunch and coffee while he frets over how they're fixing it up. I *know* they're undercapitalized. I'd guess that they probably have four months of mortgage payments for that place in the bank, but operating costs're gonna get'em before then. Movies cost money, you know, even old ones and foreign ones. On the other hand there isn't much to do in this town, and the nearest competing 'repertory cinema'—Christ I can't do that phony accent he puts on when he says that—is up in Toledo." He stared up at the ceiling a second; Philbin usually seemed to find the God of Business Analysis in an old spot of water damage just above the cash register. "Figure, hmm, they'll get some draw from Gist County, anyway—college kids from Vinville, at least the artsy ones and the students who need to suck up to their profs, and probably some people from Delos, Arthur, and Lincoln Bridge.

"Plus one good thing, Mary's picking the movies, and she's smart enough to start off with some popular oldies. Just a weekend double feature till about Christmas, and then add a Wednesday–Thursday show if that goes. Anyway, this Friday night they open with *Casablanca* and *The Maltese Falcon*, which are good movies but you can see them on TV a couple times a year if you hop around the channels a little and you don't mind big scenes getting interrupted with hemorrhoid commercials."

"Hunh. Friday is the football season opener and a home game," I pointed out. "They'll get all three Lightsburgers that wish they were artistic, plus their own students and friends from Vinville."

"'Fraid so. But, anyway, here's the thought I have. For the few months they'll be open, they will have a crowd getting out around ten thirty on weekend nights, when the only thing open in town is Pietro's, which is on the other side of town, and the Dairy Queen, where the grill closes at nine. Michelson, that owns that Pongo's Monkey Burger, has already told me he ain't gonna change his hours. Now, if people coming out of the theater smell some burgers grilling and maybe some fresh pie baking . . . you see?"

One reason why I liked talking to Philbin, he was

always looking for some way that the drugstore could make money and grow. That kind of stuff was way more interesting than school crap that you talked about with teachers, or "say, fella, how's your football team doin'?" that regular town people would try and make conversation with, and way-way-*way* more interesting than flying saucers and astrology and Nixon, like Mom and the super super ladies talked about.

It was kind of funny—and a shame, though, since I did really like to hear about business and making money and stuff—that in the whole town, the guy who talked about business best was a doomed loser.

Philbin thought real good about what might make money, or lose it, for anybody else's business, but he managed to never quite see that his own shop was stuck behind the eight ball. If it had been anyone else's he'd have laid it out, neat and clean as an isosceles triangle of pie on a plate with a sphere of ice cream beside it, but instead he was always trying to think of the magic formula to turn his dusty old dump of a drugstore into a gold mine. Somehow whenever he thought about his own place, he stopped seeing the FOR SALE signs and boarded-up stores around it, and failed to notice that he had empty seats at the height of his lunch rush.

But I wasn't going to point that out. I just said, "So you'd need someone on counter this Friday and Saturday?"

"Yeah, weekend nights for as long as the Oxford stays open. I'll cook, Mrs. P will bake. That will put us ahead on homemade desserts for Monday lunch when we always need a lot and usually have to switch to storeboughts, so it won't be a total loss even if no one comes in. But I'll need someone on the front, and Angie has taken up with a drug-crazed hippie biker—"

"Pop, he *just* has a *motorcycle!*"

"—and will want her weekend evenings free. Now—"

"He has a good job. At a bank."

"I'm sure he's just casing the joint. Karl, I'm not going to pretend it's all that promising. I don't know how long the job will last, and it would just be Friday and Saturday nights, waiter's minimum plus tips, and you know, like your dad used to say, Lightsburg is the Buckle on the Cheap Bastard Belt; I swear we have the chintziest tippers on the planet. But all that said, the Oxford *should* last till Thanksgiving even if it doesn't work out, and I'm guessing we'll get some decent trade some nights, so at least you'd make some extra gift money for Christmas or something, eh?"

"Well, yeah, I'd be *very* interested. Show up Friday at—"

"Say six P.M. Got to do the tax paperwork and all, maybe get you outfitted with a spiffy new apron or something."

"Will do." We shook on it.

Shoemaker's Kid

I ALWAYS LIKED that time of day, when people were shutting up their shops, putting the town to bed for the night, going home to do normal stuff with their normal families. I wondered if they got to enjoy being normal, to know just how terrific it was, or whether it was just invisible to them like air? Sometimes I got so pissed off at how easy the normal people had it that I just wanted to walk down the street shaking them and screaming into their squishy self-satisfied faces.

In those first few weeks of school, still really summer, it stayed hot till past six. The radiated heat from the red-brick walls could practically give you a sunburn, and the cloudless sky was more gray than blue, as if the heat had baked the color right out of it.

Mom and me and all those fucking cats lived on Mac-Ready Avenue, in what Dad had said was gonna be their starter place back before I was born. Turned out it was his finisher place, too.

MacReady was like every other street in that part of town. The houses, once all Norman Rockwell–y frames and shingles and clapboards, were now your basic Do It Yourself Duct Tape White Trash Shithole, with all kinds of new cheap crappy stuff stuck on—white aluminum siding, rusty iron wire fences on green steel posts, big glider davenports from Sears to replace the porch swing, sheet metal sheds out back with the doors never put on.

I'd been trying to keep our house up. Dad had left me a list, month by month and week by week, when to do all the stuff he'd shown me how to do. I couldn't always keep up with it, between Mom and the cats. I knew it would all fall to shit the minute I left for the army. Still, mostly, I kept it up. Nights when I couldn't sleep, I'd just turn on my desk lamp, point it at the wall, and read that list to myself till I knew where I was in the world again.

As I trotted up our front walk, a voice wheezed from next door. "Karl, your place don't look too bad." It was Wilson, this real old guy with no teeth who liked to watch me work while he sat out on his porch, smoked Camels, drank animal beer, and talked to anybody passing by.

I leaned over his fence and said, "Well, the window-sills want scraped and painted before winter, and I gotta start on storms this weekend."

He coughed real hard. When he'd finally forced all the ashes, tar, and goop out of his filthy old lungs, and sucked in what air he could, he wheezed, "Goddam doctors!" Then he set up his favorite joke. "You're good with your hands, bub, it's a shame you have such a hard time keeping up."

I played along—he was a nice old fart. "Well, it's hard to make myself fix stuff at home for free, when I can do the same thing for other people for money."

"Shoemaker's kids always go barefoot." Maybe he was just slapping his knee due to the coughing fit that laughing at his own joke had sent him into. I hoped so. He finished with a long *hraaak!* and leaned sideways to slobber over the side of his lawn chair. "Goddam doctors."

I bet they kept trying to tell him he needed to stop smoking, the mad fools.

I opened the door. Forest, Loveheart, and Sunnyjoy ran out. "Have fun, kitties, there's a lot of nice tires to go under just up the street," I said.

I scooped the mail up from the floor in front of the slot—just the electric bill, which I pigeonholed, and a BankAmericard thing that I buried in the trash so Mom wouldn't see it and apply.

I looked at the clock. Mom would be at Mister Peepers at least another hour and a half. I dialed Kathy's number, and she picked up on the first ring. "Just checking in and letting you know I'll be there tonight," I said.

"I saw you coming out of Dad's place. How is he?"

"Exactly the same as ever," I said. "He's adding an evening shift Fridays and Saturdays because some new people are reopening the Ox. And Angie has a new boy-friend, a banker that rides a motorcycle."

"Hey, tell her to give me a call and tell me all about it, 'kay?"

"Absolutely," I said.

"Have a quiet evening, Karl. You take care."

"You, too."

Funny the way people could be. From the day Kathy, Philbin's older daughter, had bought the franchise for the McDonald's out by the interstate, old Philbin had refused to speak to her. But he'd offered, before she did it, to mortgage the drugstore to give her a stake to launch her own downtown burger stand. He wasn't mad that she was competing with him—it was that it was McDonald's.

Everyone in town always told Philbin, to his face, that his hamburgers were better than McDonald's. They were, too, bigger and greasier and with buns from some bakery up in Toledo, and the onions and tomato were all locally grown in the summer, and Dick and Mrs. P didn't cook them into hockey pucks, and they were just better, all kinds of ways.

Just the same, the people who said they loved Philbin's hamburgers, whenever they chose to go out for a burger, took their kids to McDonald's, because that's where the kids wanted to go, and the French fries were better,

She was yelling, all pissed, and shoved me out the door, so I walked around town for hours and was just sitting on the steps of the roller rink when Officer Williams saw me and said I had to go home, it was past curfew.

He must've seen I was upset, because he insisted he'd take me himself. When I got home Mom had had all the windows open for a while, so I don't know if Williams could smell the pot (though I still could) and the minute I got in the place she was yelling at me about running away and having been worried sick, just like she was still being a real mom. Williams left quick and as soon as he was gone, Mom slapped me and told me not to ever bring pigs around the house again, then shoved me out the door and locked it.

That was the first time I got locked out. It was warm, so I just went around to the back alley behind First United Methodist and lay down on the back stoop, using my shoes for sort of a pillow because the concrete was pretty hard on my head. I didn't sleep much.

Next morning, I went back. Mom had left the house unlocked before going to work; in a little town like Lightsburg, people did that. I got my books, went to school, got through the day somehow, and went right home and to bed. Next morning when I got up everything was normal. Mom never said anything about it.

That made me think about getting a key. The hardware store was open till eight on Wednesdays, so the next Wednesday, while she was on the phone talking all soft and sexy to some guy, I slipped into her room to go into her purse and get her key.

But it must have been on the bottom of the purse, or maybe she had it in her pocket, so instead I found a fifth of gin, a few joints, and some loose rubbers.

That had freaked me out. Back then I barely even knew enough to recognize the stuff. I felt so bad I just went upstairs to lie down and read some dumb book for the rest of the night, and never tried again. So I guess it was really my fault, like a lot of things.

Nowadays I had several different ways to get back in, depending. Before the storm windows went up, it was always real easy because Mom didn't notice sash locks.

I grabbed the coal shovel and made my high-speed rounds through the house, getting a full shovelful of wormy cat crap in no time, and stepped out on the back porch to fling it behind the trellis. That's when I saw Sunflower; it looked like she'd had a serious argument with the old boar coon that lived down by Hawthorne Ditch and foraged into our garbage now and then. I thought, *I can't imagine what that old raccoon would be doing out in the daytime.* I reluctantly headed for the toolshed; I couldn't leave Sunflower out there for Mom to find.

As I came out with the shovel, I heard a goopy cough, and old Wilson wheezed at me, "Karl, I'm sorry, I meant to tell you about that. I think your mom's kitty got killed under my lilac bush last night, and then this afternoon that collie Trixie, that belongs to the Ramsay kid down the street, had drug it out and was messing with it, so I threw a rock at her and she ran off. But I think it was that old raccoon that got your mom's kitty—I think Trixie just found it."

"I'm sure it was the raccoon," I said. "Trixie's never done more than chased them and she wouldn't eat half the cat the way the raccoon did." I grabbed a garden spade and a posthole digger from the shed—the ground was soft from yesterday's rain, but not soft enough to dig with my coal shovel—and I walked over for a good look.

No question it was Sunflower—that cream-and-orange blotchy pattern was distinctive, even with the face torn up pretty bad. She must've gotten in a couple good bites, but that old boar coon was a twenty-five-pounder at least, and those teeth on coons are like butcher knives.

Definitely the raccoon. We had a couple cat-killing dogs in the neighborhood, but they usually didn't eat the victim, and especially they didn't tear into the belly and bite out everything from the back legs to the ribs and leave the poor cat like an empty rag. Not a dog, obviously not a car, and not a hunter either. The corn was still in the fields; too early in the fall for a quail or pheasant hunter to have shot her—they did that because free-roaming cats killed chicks and ate eggs. Besides, if she'd lost that much of her guts to birdshot, she'd never have made it back here.

I felt like Sherlock fucking Holmes; over three years of experience had taught me to recognize most of the ways that Mom's cats died. "Obviously, Watson," I muttered, "this is the work of Professor Moriarty, the Napoleon of Lightsburg varmints."

"Remarkable, Holmes," Wilson said. He'd hobbled right over behind me, and I about jumped out of my skin at his voice so close.

We contemplated the mauled remains of Sunflower together. There was a leg missing, and most of the tail too, but I wasn't going to go looking for them; probably the nephew that did Wilson's yard would rake them out from under the bush later on.

I flipped her over, gently, with the spade. Sunflower hadn't had much of a personality except that she was about half wild like all of Mom's cats; it was that splashes-of-yellow-orange coloring that was unusual. I couldn't think of a thing other than that I remembered about her.

There was plenty of room in Cat Arlington, as I thought of the back end of the backyard; when you bury them right next to each other you can fit a lot of cats into a small part of the yard. Muffin's headstone—a nice piece of ply that I'd worked up with the wood-burning set—was still in pretty good shape, at the far back corner; she'd died while still a kitten, back when we just had that one litter, by pulling a bookcase onto herself. Next to her, starting the first row, was Starpeace, who I'd only found after a couple dozen cars had flattened him. Sunflower would make the third grave in the fourth row of the not-yet-completed ten-by-ten grid. I figured we'd probably get to somewhere in the fifth row before I left for the army.

I made four neat cuts and lifted out the sod in a block. Old Wilson hawked one up and spat onto the grass. "God-dam doctors. Ever thought about putting the Lightsburg Coon Hunters' Club onto the job?"

"Mom makes me promise not to. I don't think she believes me when I tell her it's that big old raccoon. She always says he's natural, beautiful, and free and therefore he would never harm a natural, beautiful, free kitty." I shrugged; at least Wilson knew something about what Mom was like, because she occasionally leaned across the fence and harangued him about switching to organic tobacco, or asked him if he'd sensed any spiritual forces in the neighborhood, so I could tell him the kind of things she actually said without feeling like I was narking her out.

"Might could be." He wheezed, gasped, and started over. "I might put a word in an old friend's ear. I ain't been out on a coon hunt in a long time and couldn't now, but some of those guys would love to get one that big."

"'Preciate it if you did," I said, "just don't let Mom

know I had anything to do with it. God, look at that. I hope that coon slashed her throat *before* he started eating. That looks like it hurt."

I took my posthole digger and screwed it down into the heavy earth, pulling out a plug of about a foot and a half of dank clay. Sunflower went into the hole headfirst, in kind of a loose heap—not much of a ceremony, but I figured I had things to get to and *she* was past caring—and then I busted the plug into pieces on top of her, tamped it down, and slid the sod back into place.

When I went back to the shed to return the spade and posthole digger, I picked up one of my "headstones"—a big plug of Readi-Mix poured into a plastic milk jug bottom. I carried it out, turned it over onto the grave, and with a Sharpie marker, I wrote, SUNFLOWER SHOEMAKER, 9/5/1973, GOOD KITTY RIP on the plastic top. The neighbors' dogs would mostly be too lazy to try to dig in through the sod around that block of concrete.

Have to remember, sometime soon, to pour a few more headstones; I was running low again.

"For sure," Wilson said, "I'll remember to tell him next time we talk. Your mom's ain't the only pets'at get killed by him." He shuffled back toward his place, shaking with smothered coughs.

"Thanks, Mr. Wilson," I said.

I checked my watch; I'd cut myself plenty of time, and just needed to dust my pant legs, recomb my hair, and get moving; still plenty of time to walk to the high school for the First Day Dance. Dead cats, crazy mothers, all in a normal kid's day's work, right? Nothing to worry about but staying normal.

I walked back to the high school at a comfortable pace, with lots of time to spare. Lightsburg, with all its bricks and white columns on older expensive houses, could be kind of pretty in the golden early evening. Between the trees overhead there were already a couple bright stars, though the tops of the trees were still glowing with sunset. Cicadas were going at it like they had amps, drowning out people out on porches talking about sports and weather and Watergate, and even the screams of the little kids playing on the lawns. Everything felt warm and moist and crawling with life.

Good evening to be a kid.

Good evening to be some poet with a girl to write about.

Or, I thought, being me, *with all those bugs around, it would be a great evening to be an exterminator.* I could never help thinking about who made the money.

Around the high school grounds, lots of kids on foot crossed every which way, between and among new station wagons trying to snake through to drop off bunches of freshmen and sophomores; old beaters trying to get up enough room to go fast for a second or two; and a few late models, containing our few rich kids, cruising by slowly to make sure we knew they were there. I saw Cheryl go by in a '72 Barracuda, but she was with Bret, this rich FCA guy, so I didn't wave.

I went into the building but not into the gym, not yet. The band would still be setting up and the Spirit Club would still be getting their concession stand organized, and that would be all there would be. And until the sun was off the gym windows, it would be an oven in there.

So I wandered around the dim, cool hallways, past other people just wandering around, and stopped by the Alum Case. It was a fund-raiser; the school took bids from all the different alumni classes, and each month the display in the case went to the high bidder. This month it held several yearbooks open to different pages, some rusty trophies, two football helmets, and remnants of a science fair project from the Class of '61. Row after row of guys with different ziphead haircuts and girls with bubble hair, all smiling just like something good was going to happen to them.

"Are they all your cousins, or are you trying to memorize old sports records?" Marti asked, behind me.

"Just killing time. I do a lot of that."

She moved around to see what I had been looking at. "Class of 1961. Just twelve years ago. They all look so *normal*."

"That's pretty much what I was thinking. I can't tell who was a social, who was a dork, or anything."

"The big guys were probably jocks," she pointed out.

"Yeah, but after that, who can tell? The clothes and stuff were all different from now, and they kind of all look the same. I do know who some of them were"—I looked at the names on the roster—"him, him, not him but his kid brother, her kid delivers our paper, she got killed in a car wreck. Neil, there, went out with my mom for a while, till he found out how old she really was—he's not the smartest guy in the world, you know, guess he couldn't subtract or something—and he still comes by sometimes and sees her, or they come home from the bar together, but they don't, like, go out on dates or anything anymore. That greaser hood guy there, the only one with any sideburns? Now he teaches at Vinville High, and coaches debate and their chess team. Some people change, some people go away, most people don't do either. That's what my dad used to say."

"He doesn't anymore?"

"He's dead."

"Oh, I'm sorry—"

"Three years, eleven months, and twelve days ago. *I'm* over it. It's the *rest* of the people in town who aren't. Dad was kind of a big guy in town here, though—mayor when I was little—so people pay too much attention to me, you know what I mean?"

"Why, no." One eyebrow went up and her mouth kind of twisted, like she'd just eaten something and everyone was laughing and she was waiting for them to tell her what was in her mouth. "I have no idea what it's like to have people pay too much attention to you because of who your dad is."

"Sorry."

She touched my arm. "Hey, I didn't mean—"

"Naw, that's okay, I just kind of forgot that other people have troubles, too, and everyone has the biggest troubles in the world. Which is another thing my dad used to say. I don't think he said an original thing in his life. Probably why so many people voted for him." We both stared at those meaningless old yearbooks and trophies for like half a minute, or maybe half a century, something like that, before I glanced sideways at Marti. She looked like she really *was* trying to memorize the sports records. "Hey, *you're* pretty interested for somebody who just got here."

"Yeah, well. . . . After that, like, breakdown thingy I had last May, the doctor made Dad promise me I could stay a whole year in one place this time, some place where I could just have some fun and be a kid. I've never had a whole school year in one place."

"And this causes an old trophy case to hypnotize you?"

"You'll laugh at me."

"Only if you say something stupid."

"Gee, thanks. What a pal." She made that snorting noise. "I like your sense of humor, Karl. It probably keeps any poor girl from talking herself into having sex with you."

"And I thought it was the warts."

Neil's senior picture had hair as short as Dad's. Even then Neil had piggy little eyes and looked like he was mad that everyone thought they were better than he was, and they were all 100 percent correct.

Shit, in 1961, Mom had already been the mayor's wife for three years. How could Neil tell her he didn't know how old she was later on? What kind of stupid excuse was that?

"You're clenching your fists," Marti observed.

"Too much history," I said.

"Yeah." She sighed. "The reason everything about Lightsburg fascinates me is pathetic. Since I finally get to have a home town, just like a regular, ordinary, normal person, and people know all about their home towns, I want to know everything about Lightsburg, right now, because once I do it will *really* be my home town. Am I making sense?"

"I guess people only appreciate what they don't have— which is another stupid thing Dad used to say."

"You miss him a lot," she said, "and that doesn't sound so stupid."

"I don't think he ever said a smart thing in his life. I've lived here all my life and I can't wait to leave."

"I bet you're pissed because no matter what you do in the future, Lightsburg is always going to be your home town. Right?"

"I'll never forgive it for that." Our eyes met, seriously, for just a second. "Well, I'll see you inside, then."

"Remember, ask me to dance, twice, in the first hour."

"I hadn't forgotten."

"See ya."

We went in opposite directions, looping back through the corridors to the gym entrance. Was avoiding looking like we were with each other normal?

At the gym doors, the crowd filled the hallway, but no one was going in just yet; still too hot and too light. Paul was leaning up against a wall looking lonely and bored and all tucked into himself, the way he got when things got shitty but not *real* shitty at home. I thought I'd try to just walk up and say hi, real casual and light.

He saw me coming toward him and went out the door.

I didn't know what had knotted *his* shorts, but it was tiresome. The only positive side to it was that avoiding him, like I fucking *meant* to, was gonna be duck soup.

Pretending I hadn't been headed for Paul, I turned and walked the other way fast. Unfortunately, I wasn't looking where I was going, and my hard swerve took me straight up to Bobby Harris and Scott Tierden.

Other high schools had class clowns that were funny. Not poor old Lightsburg. We got Harris and Tierden.

Their idea of funny was to bring a whoopee cushion to a choir concert to fuck up Bonny's solo, or go into Philbin's, order a banana split, and turn it upside down on the counter with a two-cent tip under it for me. They didn't like Bon and me much because we worked a lot; they picked on Paul because everybody picked on Paul, for being a faggot. They didn't fuck with Danny, Darla, or Squid much, and they left Cheryl alone.

Picking on Madmen, or trying to, was one of those things they did, like playing rotten tricks on retarded kids, saying dirty shit to shy churchy girls, and sitting in the back to hassle anyone who was up front doing something.

There was no one behind them, so I couldn't pretend I'd been going to talk to anyone else. I turned to head back the way I'd come.

Bobby Harris—short pudgy redhead with blotchy freckles and a haircut that looked like a sloppy copy of Moe Howard—said, "So you making your rounds, shaking hands and saying hi, like your pathetic old man used to do? Gonna be like big hot shit in this shithole town someday? Everybody's always talking about how you're such a go-getter, you know. Full of pep. Hardworking boy. King of shithole Lightsburg."

I swear I hated Harris so bad right then that I felt like defending *Lightsburg*. So I just walked up to the pudgy little asshole, real slow, and kept walking till he shoved his wire-rim glasses back up his shiny snub nose, took a step backward, and did this little ha-ha laugh that meant he was nervous.

Tierden, who I guess you could call the brains of the pair if you kept in mind that it's all relative, was about my height and maybe half my weight, with awful acne and thin oily shoulder-length blond hair. Even in this heat he wore cowboy boots and a denim jacket on which he had sloppily lettered, in very dark worked-in ballpoint pen, WHO GIVES A SHIT?

He rode to Harris's rescue and asked, "You gonna go out with the titless genius?"

He meant Marti, obviously.

I took another step so Harris would back up another one, like Tierden wasn't even worth my attention. "I talked to her a couple of times, she's really nice, and I hope we're going to be friends."

"'I hope we're going to be friends,'" Tierden said, mincing it in a way that I was sure I hadn't. "Oh. Oh. We're almost a British person, aren't we? 'I hope we're going to be friends.'" His version of a British accent was half Monty Python, half Ringo, and all duh. "She's got no tits and a pizza face and 'I hope we're going to be friends.'"

"Well," I said, "you've got no brain, and a pizza face with extra sauce and cheese, and I hope you're going to swing at me because it'll give me an excuse."

"You are *so* pathetic, Shoemaker. *So* pathetic. You make me fucking sick. What you gonna do, try and make time with her? She don't even have nipples, man."

Something blonde moved in the corner of my eye. That was why they were doing this. Marti was a few feet away and they wanted her to overhear.

There were times when I liked being Psycho Shoemaker. I moved close enough to Scott Tierden to smell his nasty breath; his little rat's-eyes widened to near-human proportions, and his drowned-corpse skin got even paler, and he backed up against the wall.

"Fuck you." I let my face go all flat, stared right into his eyes, dropped one hand to crotch height, and stood close enough to give him the horsebite. "Marti and me are friends. Leave my friends alone, got that, Scottsy? Not every pair of friends has to have sex. Unlike a couple of queerboys I'm thinking of, Scotty-poo."

Tierden looked pretty pissed and I thought the horse might have to bite him, but then Gratz, behind me, said, "What's going on here?"

"He tried to kiss me, Coach," I said.

"Oh, fuck you, Shoemaker," Tierden said.

"Well, Tierden," Gratz said, "we don't allow language like that at school events, anyway, so you're out. Bye."

Tierden went slumping away with Harris trailing after him. At least they wouldn't be hanging around on the bleachers staring at girls' butts all night, like the dance was a strip show, which was what they usually did.

"You okay, Karl?"

"Yeah, Coach, I'm fine."

"Good."

And he walked away. Well, this wasn't too bad. I heard tires scream and Gratz charged out the door to get the plate number; peeling out in the parking lot was a big no-no. He came back in writing something down, so I figured he'd probably tagged Harris's old pile of shit Ford Galaxie.

Paul came back in and went by me like he didn't see me.

I let a few people get in line behind him before moving in behind two funny-looking freshman guys, who were talking nasty about other kids in their class—probably the Harris and Tierden of the Class of '77. Maybe that was an essential niche in the ecology, like lampreys or slime mold.

Inside the gym, it was still hot. They were playing records while the band was tuning up, and little circles of freshman and sophomore girls, who really wanted to dance and didn't care about whether or not they looked stupid, were twitching to "Brother Louie."

I small-talked my way around the gym until the band got going, and people started dancing. The dark really helps guys dance; a lot of girls are real graceful and pretty and stuff, but most guys just kinda stomp and shake our butts. But not too much so we won't look like homos. Most of us are at our best dancing in total darkness.

The bass player could play and the lead guitar almost could. Anyway it was a high school dance and nobody cared much that you couldn't tell one song from another.

I tagged Marti for a dance early on; she wasn't a great dancer—better than all the boys but only about half the girls. Then I kind of wandered around and danced with Bonny, for old times and another sure thing to get my confidence up.

After a while I saw Paul on the other side of the gym, so at least I hadn't completely ruined his evening. I talked with people I knew, got a couple of Cokes from the Spirit Club table, and wandered along the walls, meeting people and nerving up to ask pretty girls I didn't know to dance.

"Rounding up votes for later?" Gratz asked.

"I just have a lot of friends." Jeez, that was the second time some asshole had to bring that up tonight.

"That's what your dad would have said when he was in high school. Hey, Tierden didn't really try to kiss you, did he?"

I shrugged. "He was saying really cruel stuff about a friend of mine, so she'd overhear."

"Marti."

"Yeah."

"She looked like she was going to cry. That's why I

headed over. Then whatever you said—don't tell me what it was—she heard that and she smiled."

"The way they were trying to hurt her pissed me off, Coach. I'm glad you turned up 'cause it was pretty close to a fight."

"I could tell. Stay out of stuff like that, Karl, will you? I'm perfectly sure you were in the right, but I don't want to have to go through any more PTA meetings with Tierden's mother whining about how the school isn't fair."

"Yeah, sorry, Coach. I'll try to stay away from them. Just, you know, when they start hurting people for fun—"

He laughed. "Doug Shoemaker's kid, to the bone. Defending the helpless and shaking hands." He clapped my shoulder and walked away. I resisted the urge to wipe my shoulder.

About 8:15 I broke away from cracking stupid jokes with Larry and asked Marti to dance again.

We danced one song, then the band announced that they had to replace a broken string. "How can they tell?" Marti asked.

"Good question. Hey, thanks for dancing with me."

She smiled. "Thanks for standing up to those two creepy guys."

"You weren't supposed to hear that."

"They were making sure I heard them be assholes. It's okay that I accidentally also heard you being a gentleman, Karl. I promise I won't let any other guys find out that you are. For a small fee, of course."

It wasn't that funny, but I laughed. There wouldn't be much laughter in the world if people didn't like each other, because there sure as shit aren't that many good jokes.

She asked, "Maybe we could dance the first song after the band comes back?"

"Shit, Marti, sorry, but I can't. I should be going right now. I have to be at work before ten, and I have to get home, get into my uniform, and get out to McDonald's. I ought to be running right now but I'm having fun talking to you."

"I thought McDonald's was closed at night."

"I sweep out."

She slapped her forehead. "Duh, Marti." Something about that gesture was fucking great. "Look, I've got a car and no curfew. Why don't we dance when the band comes back, you hang around till nine-fifteen or nine-thirty, and then I'll give you a ride home, and from home to work? It's no problem, I'd rather not be at home till late anyway."

Marti was going to be a Madman, all right. I wondered what happened at home: did they hit her? Nobody sober after noon? Fights? A heap of coke on the coffee table? Bedroom visits from her mother's creepy boyfriend? Wall-to-wall crosses and nonstop prayers? All of those were certainly possible, based on the other Madmen.

I didn't ask. I'd know, soon enough. One problem with an underground, you always know too much about what's buried. "I'd really appreciate the ride, and getting to dance some more," I said.

Her bony shoulders dragged her T-shirt up and down like a sticky drape. "I really just want to talk to somebody for a while, preferably somebody that's going to be a friend." Marti pronounced *preferably* PREFFer-ubbly like all the educated grown-ups, instead of preeFUR-a-blee like the coaches, the kids, and the vice principal. "So this way I have a friend trapped in the car while I babble. And it's so cool to know that if I make any friends I get to keep them."

"Well, keeping them is a whole different kind of problem."

She looked puzzled. Luckily the band kicked off into an almost-recognizable version of "Satisfaction," too loud for us to talk over, so we danced again.

8

Tales of the Madman Underground

NOBODY LEAVES A dance half an hour before the end. At that point the people who had to leave early have already left and everyone else is staying. So Marti and I had the parking lot to ourselves as we walked to her car—her parents', so I guess they had money— a '71 LTD, cherry red, with a big old air intake on the hood and a stick. I didn't know shit about cars, so she quoted me a bunch of numbers and I nodded like I was impressed.

She drove it like a guy, laying a little rubber on her way out of the lot. "Half a demerit," I said, "if they catch you doing that in the school parking lot."

"Half a what?"

"Demerit. Like a bad point. If your average goes

above two demerits a week, you get a one-day suspension; if it goes above three, you get three days; four and up, a week. Of course there's lots of shit you get suspended for right off the bat, but all the chickenshit goes through the demerit system. And they erase demerits every nine weeks."

"What happens if you keep your average under two?" She floored it up Courthouse Street toward the downtown.

I didn't know shit about cars, like I said, but I liked the way the acceleration pushed me back into her passenger seat. I explained, "They don't do shit, not even talk to you. It's a great system. You only have to watch your ass if it's getting close to Friday and you've gotten caught a lot. Mrs. Brean, the secretary, figures up everyone's average on Friday afternoon. Takes her most of the afternoon with charts and graph paper and an adding machine and all. Mom says it's our tax dollars at work."

"So, like, at the end of nine weeks, I can have seventeen and a half demerits?"

"Right, that's the total everyone tries for. For anything you can do it's either half or one, so seventeen and a half is the closest you can get. Peeling out's a half, getting thrown out of class is a one, making out in school is a one, leaving your tray on the cafeteria table is a half, not standing for the school song at a pep rally is a half . . . if you're short on sleep, ask Mister Emerson, the vice principal, to explain it to you."

"Why doesn't Mrs. Brean just make up a cross table, once, that says if you have X demerits in the Yth week your average is Z? Then she could just draw a red diagonal with 'too many' below and 'okay' above, keep running totals, and be done in an hour."

"Because they'd make her do something else with the time she saved."

"Seems inefficient." She gunned it to beat her third yellow in a row. "After downtown, which way do I go?"

I directed her through the dark streets between white splashes of glaring streetlights, her headlights sweeping over front porches with columns and high steep steps up from the street, and broken-up crappy plastic toys, rusty bicycles, cars on blocks, vis-orange roll fencing, trash cans with stacked boxes of twenty-four empty Bud cans beside them; now and then a cat's or dog's eyes would flash out of the dark at us.

"My house is right here. I'd invite you in to meet my mom while I change, but, uh, at night things are sometimes . . ."

"I'll wait here." She killed the lights and engine and switched up the radio.

"See you in a sec." Seeing the lights that were on, I ran around the back of the house.

I opened the kitchen door, and the stale cat piss and fresh cigarette smoke slammed into my sinuses. Mom was at the kitchen table writing her big loopy scrawl in her notebook. She had four big books, paperweighted with cats, open in front of her: her big old leather-bound astrology guide, a 1958 nautical almanac, her big UFO book with crappy grainy photos of dark spots in the sky, and Nixon's *Six Crises.*

Of course it *would* explain a fuckload if Nixon was an alien, but even if he was, I didn't think Mom was going to be the one to prove it.

She looked up from her work, the yellow hair falling around her face, and took a drag from the cigarette that had burned down, unheeded, in her propped-up left hand while she scribbled. "Hi, Tiger. Home for the night?"

"Still have to work." I thought about not telling her and decided it was better to get it over with. "Uh, Mom, Sunflower got into a fight with that big old coon; she was dead in the yard when I came home from school."

"How could she be fighting a raccoon in the middle of the day? They only come out at night!" I couldn't tell if Mom was angry at me, the raccoon, or Sunflower.

"Wilson said Trixie was dragging her around in the yard. He thinks she got killed last night under his lilac bush. I'm sorry, Mom, I know you really loved her."

She was wiping her eyes, staring down at the table; sometimes she'd just put her head back and howl, sometimes she just shrugged, but for some reason, whenever the coon got one, especially when he chewed up a kitten, she'd be like this, quiet but so sad.

"Uh," I said, wanting out of there, "I have to get my

uniform and get to work and I have a ride waiting." I let the last few words trail over my shoulder as I charged up the stairs to my room. The door had held; no cat crap to clean up. So far so good.

I yanked off my pants and shirt, pulled the thin polyester trousers over my shoes, zipped up the smock of my McDonald's outfit. At least the army would mean a much cooler uniform.

When I turned around, Mom was standing at my door. Her makeup was still a little smeared from crying over Sunflower, but she had plastered on a big phony smile. She was making an effort; for some reason that always made me feel better. "So," she said, acting all bright and happy and all, "how was—"

"School looks pretty good this year. I got all my homework done and got dinner at Philbin's. I went to the dance, and danced several times, with girls. None of them had to slap me."

Mom giggled, and now it was real. I could nearly always get her to giggle. "Karl, I wanted to ask you, do you think maybe we could take my paycheck off direct deposit, and stop all those automatic payments?"

"You haven't bounced a check in six months since we put you on that plan, Mom, it looks like it's working."

"I bounced two checks at Mister Peepers last month and now they won't take my checks."

"That's because we get your bills paid first, Mom, the

things you *have* to pay. You haven't bounced a check anywhere that *counts*. Did you sign the checks I wrote out
for you?"

She held out a sheaf of unsealed envelopes—I'd
learned to always check that she had actually put a check
in there and not fucked it up somehow.

I took it. "I'll record these and drop them by the trustee's desk at the bank, tomorrow. And I'll figure what's in
your account for you for your weekend."

"It's just kind of hard to have a social life when you
and the trustee control all my money," she said. "And it's
embarrassing to tell my friends that a boy is running my
life. And that trustee fee is like a week's groceries every
month."

Or an ounce of pot, I thought, but I said, "I'm just
making sure you pay your bills. That's all the trustee
does, too. You know you didn't like it when they used to
garnish your wages. The judge said if we do *this*, you don't
have to do *that*. That's all. I don't like doing it either."

"Maybe if you didn't do it, if I could just have my check
the regular way, when I needed some freedom and some
space, I wouldn't have to take money from your jars. I
must owe you like a thousand dollars now."

*Actually, two thousand nine hundred thirty-seven.
And forty-one cents.* I shoved the thought away like a cat
away from my plate. "You did that before." *You just don't
make as much money as you want to spend.*

"I don't see why I even pay a mortgage on this old place anyway. It's too big for two people and the neighborhood is all falling down and we'll never get any money for it when it's time to sell it, and it just means you have to spend every Sunday working just to keep it up. So I don't see why I have to pay the mortgage."

"We'd have to pay someone somewhere anyway, Mom, just to have a roof to live under. Mortgage here is cheaper than rent anywhere else, and nobody'd let you have all those cats."

She blew a cloud of cigarette smoke into my room, and sighed. "I guess it's pretty weird that you're being all adult and I'm being the kid and wanting my freedom. You aren't going to let me just deposit my checks, are you?"

"Mom, I can't. The judge says."

"Yeah, the Man's really got us all down, doesn't he?" She sighed again. "Neil told me he's dumping me, again."

"He'll be back, he always is."

"Yeah." She dropped her cigarette butt on the carpet in front of my room and crushed it with her toe. "Fuck, first you comfort me 'cause my kitty got killed, and take care of burying it, and then you make sure the bills are paid, and oh god, now you're consoling me about losing a boy. And I do mean boy. We're *so* fucking backwards, you know that?" She looked like she might cry again, but then she reached out, put her hand on the back of my neck, and rubbed gently, like I remembered her doing when I was little. "Try to relax. Don't let it all get to you, Tiger. Your neck is one big ball of tense, you ought to see Judy about some herbal tea or some yoga lessons since you won't smoke up." Her hand on my neck felt good, even if I didn't like her cigarette smoke and we'd just been quarreling; it was something she still did just like when I was a little kid. "Don't be out too late cleaning up after corporate America. You have better things to do with your life than mopping out bathroom stalls. You are a special child of the universe, and the starlight falls on you. Never forget that. 'Cause if you do, Tiger, Mama gon' kick yer butt." Mom had read some book about how to talk positively to your kids, but she had too much of a sense of humor to be any good at what the book said. "Do you know a girl named Martinella? Martinella Nielsen?"

"Uh, yeah, new girl. She's in a couple of my classes."

"Well, I met her mother today when she came in to get some office supplies. Rose Lee Nielsen is just a super super lady. We got to talking about, you know, things, and she and I are going out for a little drink later this evening, and I'm going to explain the town to her, and we're both interested in each other's projects. So I might not be home when you get back from work. You take care of yourself, 'kay, Tiger?"

"I'm glad you found a new friend, Mom," I said. I gave her a peck on her soft, clean, dry cheek. My mom was still real pretty whenever she took care of herself; that was what everyone said.

"Um," she said, "when Neil dumped me—he called me an old bitch and he—"

I reached for my wallet. "Did he hit you or hurt you, or make any threats?"

"You're not going to the cops about any of my friends."

"He doesn't sound like that good a friend to me, but suit yourself. He took the money you had left, didn't he?"

She looked down at the floor. "Yeah. Yeah."

What the hell. So I'm an enabler. That's why I go to AA but not to Alateen. Got an opinion about that? Fuck you.

I handed her a twenty, which would get her drinks and some lunch the next day. "Now don't be out late and don't go past second base with boys you don't know."

She giggled again and hugged me. "Have a good time, oh Favored Heir of Ronald McDonald."

"Are my feet growing and is my hair orange?" I asked, walking backwards down the stairs. "Because I've always been afraid there was something you wouldn't tell me about that pair of striped socks you keep pinned to a dried rose in the back of your closet. Pull that door closed tight, please—thanks!" I waved bye-bye and nearly fell over that fat orange hairy slug of a cat. I bent to scritch his ears, said, "Guard, Hairball," and darted out the door.

Safely back out on the dark street, I plunged into Marti's car. "Hope I wasn't too long."

"Two songs and four commercials. I like the 'We came up the hard way,' one. From the way you came out of that house I feel like I'm driving a getaway car."

"Yeah, well." I fastened my seat belt. "Hey, Marti? I really appreciate this."

"You're welcome. And you're keeping me from getting home, which is more than returning the favor."

"If it makes any difference, your mom isn't going to be there. She's going out drinking with my mom."

"Shit," Marti said.

"Sorry I gave you the bad news."

"It's okay, really," she said, like any Madman said when it sucked right down to the root.

We turned the corner and went three blocks. In the flashes of blue-white light from the streetlights, between the dark under the trees, I could see she wasn't crying or anything but she seemed to be far away, inside herself. We pulled onto Rolach Street and headed toward the interstate exit where McDonald's was. After another block, she said, "Can I ask you something personal?"

"Six inches but I tell everyone eight."

She laughed, that weird fizzing noise, as we pulled into the McDonald's parking lot.

I said, "They don't mind if a friend hangs around and talks with me while I clean."

"That would be *cool!*"

"Watching a guy clean out McDonald's is cool?"

"First day of school and I'm out late talking with a friend. I feel so normal I could just shit."

"Well, do it before I clean the ladies'."

The night crew had left five regular cheeseburgers, a very soggy Big Mac, a heap of dried-out fries under the warming light, and two Quarter Pounders, plus an urn of hot coffee.

"They do that so I can eat what I want and throw the rest out. If you sit here, we can talk while I work. I just clean the customer area, counters, and bathrooms—Pancake Pete cleans the kitchen at four A.M."

"Don't they leave food for him?"

"Naw, he gets a huge breakfast after he finishes up. We all call him Pancake Pete—he gets a kick out of it—because sometimes he'll put away like six orders of pancakes and sausage. He's a retarded guy, real nice." I moved all that food to the table on one overloaded tray. "Usually I just grab food and gulps of coffee as I go by, and I'm not fussy about what I grab, so just help yourself and try and make sure your hand doesn't look like a cheeseburger."

"My hand's the one that contains actual meat. I'm not eating your supper, am I?"

"There's always tons more than I can eat—don't worry about it."

I shot around the room, getting tables, counters, and edges wiped down and making sure the sticky spots were gone, grabbing food as I went by, and we talked about everything while I mopped and scrubbed.

"You're practically done and it's only been half an hour," she said.

"The bathrooms and the food counters will go slower, but yeah, these places are designed to be cleaned really fast, and I went through and read the manual, mostly 'cause I got real bored and tired one night and forgot to bring a book and it was snowing like a crazy bastard outside, and I knew I was locked out, so I stayed here to have somewhere warm to sleep and I needed something to read. McDonald's has this whole system—like, I can finish in about an hour, but they pay me for two and a half, so I study or read till it's time to clock out. The time I spend studying here, and over dinner, is about all that keeps me afloat in school."

"I was talking with that girl Bonny and she said you're always working somewhere."

"Yeah, Bon's that way too. We kinda compete to see who can have the most jobs."

"How many jobs do you *have*?"

"Uh, five."

"Five?"

"That's a lot, I guess. One, this one. Two, moving couches for Mister Browning the upholster. Three, I take care of the heavy work in four old people's gardens plus do some handyman stuff for them and their friends. Four, I sell ads for WUGH, the country radio station here in town. Five, starting Friday night I'm going to hop the counter at Philbin's for the after-the-movie crowd, weekend nights. I guess that's all."

"'That's all'? Do you *sleep*?"

"Some, but they don't pay me for it."

"Are you saving for college?"

"Naw, I'm going into the army. But if I don't get right in, I want to make sure I can live for a while in a strange town. Because I don't want to come back here, at all, ever."

"I don't think I've ever met anybody that wanted to join the army before."

I shrugged. "Well, shit, I want out of Lightsburg. I'll always be the Shoemaker boy, here. And I'm not one of your peace-and-love never-comb-your-hair never-take-a-bath never-finish-a-sentence just be-be-be me-me-me free-free-free and love-me-'cause-I'm-so-mellow-groove-a-delic hippie freak types, anyway. A reliable paycheck with free bed and food, and a ticket out of town for good? And all they want me to do is char some babies? Well, all right then, a deal's a deal, line up the cradles, hand me the flamethrower, and fetch me the barbecue sauce."

Marti started laughing.

"God, that's a relief, I wondered how far I'd have to go

before you knew I was shitting you. Talk loud, I've got to clean the food prep counters now."

"Thought you didn't do the kitchen."

"Food prep counters get two cleanings, me and Pete both. Keeps the burgers from getting cooties, or it drives away the evil spirits so they can't possess the French fries, I forget which."

I went back into the kitchen and Marti moved a burger and her coffee to the service countertop, keeping napkins under everything so as not to make a mess where I'd already cleaned.

"Hey," I asked. "What was that super-personal question you were going to ask me, that I got away from with that dumb joke?"

"Maybe I shouldn't ask you. It might piss you off."

"I promise I won't get pissed off," I said, "or even if I do, I promise I will get over it and still be your friend."

She gave me that great smile. "Back at the dance, just before the band started up again, I said something about getting to keep the friends I had made, and you said something kind of strange about how that was a problem. And you just looked so—sad. I thought I hit a raw spot. So I was wondering if maybe you'd tell me what the matter is? I mean I know it isn't really any of my business, and you don't have to, like if it's too personal, but you really looked so sad, you know?"

I only thought for a second. Some people you just

know are cool, from the first second you meet them. "Well, you know how Gratz called a bunch of us together after class—the Monday first-period therapy group?"

"It's hard to forget."

"Well, we've all kind of been like family with each other for ages. You know Paul Knauss, the super-skinny guy with the light brown fro? You danced with him—"

"I just knew his name was Paul."

"Well, Paul started calling it the Madman Underground . . ." I filled Marti in on the basics. "It's not all that cool, really, just kind of a club for weird kids that know each other's sad stories. Anyway, Paul and me were playing together when we were too little to remember, our dads were friends forever, Paul's my best friend . . . you know." There was a sticky spot I had to rub extra hard. "I'm just—well, lately—well, just today, I don't know why, but he's definitely avoiding me."

"That's awful."

"Yeah. I don't have—"

Tires and brakes shrieked. Bobby Harris's ancient cream-colored Ford Galaxie roared through the big rutted puddle out front, slapping brown muddy water all over the big windows. It made a sound like having your head in a bucket that someone whipped with a big wet towel. Harris fishtailed hard left and accelerated out of the lot, back onto Rolach Street.

By the wall clock, 11:30 on the dot.

Over the fading roar of the ancient engine and scream

of bald tires, Marti said, "Shit, shit, shit," looking down at where she had dropped her coffee onto her pants and the freshly mopped floor.

"Are you all right? You didn't get burned?"

"No, the coffee was practically cold. Just startled and wet. Sorry about your floor. Would you mind if I rinsed my pants out in the women's room? I'll make sure it's spotless when I'm done."

"No problem. Sorry I didn't think to warn you that that was gonna happen."

"Thanks." She went into the women's room. I mopped up the spilled coffee, then rolled out the big trash receptacles and flipped them over into the Dumpster. If Harris and Tierden were going to make a second pass they did it within five minutes or so, so I allowed enough time before I got out my bucket, squeegee-stick, and hose, and cleaned the front windows. I hadn't had to redo the windows in months.

It never occurred to Harris and Tierden that I had figured out their favorite trick. But then it also never occurred to them that no one liked them. Or that they were a pair of assmunches. They just weren't real occurrable kind of guys.

As I was putting the bucket and the squeegee-stick away, Marti came out of the bathroom in wet pants, did a big mock salute, and said, "The bathroom is ready for inspection, sir."

I looked inside and it was perfect.

"Who was the asshole?" she asked. "You sounded like he does it every night."

"Assholes plural, or is that assholi? Harris and Tierden, those two creepy guys—"

"That call me the titless genius."

"Yeah, them. They have a nasty nickname for every girl in the school. They're petty and mean and hateful and if you listen to them for even one second, you're *really* not a genius."

She smiled again. It was so cool.

"What they are," I explained, "is pure raw fuck-me-up-the-butt small-town dumbass dickweed loser assholes. I don't like them, by the way. Anyway, they do that. That's why I wash the windows last. They think I don't know who does it; they're always hinting to see if they can get me to complain about having my nice clean window splashed and having to work extra time. Besides, they're so *proud* of figuring out how to splash a window—must've took 'em weeks. They pick on the Madman Underground when they can—we're like their little wet dream of being able to hurt people who are better than they are, and get away with it."

Marti made a face. "We had nasty guys who thought they were hot shit in genius school, but most of them were geniuses."

"Well, these guys sure aren't."

"So are they going to hassle me all year, like they started to today?"

"Probably. They have minds like steel traps, get hold of an idea and never let it go even if it's dead. But they won't dare to hassle you too much. Last year we kind of took care of that."

"Took care of that?"

"It's another Madman Underground story. Maybe our finest hour, which is pathetic if you think about it. Last year their favorite target was Cheryl Taliaferro, you know, the cute social with the curly brown hair and the big, um—"

"She definitely has a big um. If her um got any bigger it would rip her sweater apart." She saw my expression. "Sorry."

"Well—the thing she's in therapy for—you'll hear all about it but she should be the one to decide to tell you—anyway, it makes her pretty sensitive about her body, and comments, and shit.

"Anyway, so for like weeks they were always saying gross things about her big boobs, whenever there wasn't any teacher to hear.

"So there was this pep rally, where they had all the cheerleaders doing their cheerleader stuff. And Cheryl did this stunt where her legs were way apart in midair. So Harris yells 'Nice shot!' and Tierden shouts 'Tuna!' and Cheryl kind of stumbled coming out of it, and Tierden

said something about her boobs bouncing, and that's
when Mrs. Emerson, who's the cheerleading coach and
the French teacher and is married to the vice principal,
grabbed them both and marched them out of there, but of
course Cheryl was already humiliated and it wasn't going to make much difference that those guys were going
to serve some detention time, shit, they have reserved
parking slots on the bench in the office, you know?

"The next day they were making like it was a big joke
and like everyone should think they were heroes for, I
don't know, putting Cheryl in her place, or standing up
to the forces of busty cheerleaderism. Anyway, trust me,
none of it was funny."

"Oh, I trust you that none of it was funny."

"So we were lucky. That Monday the therapist, Vic
Marston, was a little late, and we got to have a conversation."

"Don't Be an Asshole," Explained in Easy-to-Understand Terms

FOR EACH THERAPY meeting, Marston always wrote up an agenda on a whiteboard. When I got there that Monday morning, everybody but Cheryl was already there, and Marston was off loading up his big coffee cup.

Number one on the whiteboard was CHERYL, BULLIES, BODY ISSUES.

Everyone was quiet—we often were. I mean, Monday morning, not a lot of small talk subjects, how would you launch a conversation?

So, how's the medication working out?

Hey, too bad your mom got arrested again.

Hey, aren't the new sheets on the Salvation Army bunks great?

Today, though, we were even quieter.

One thing I hated about Marston, he had *no* sense that sometimes you just *need* to skip a fucking subject. He was like always trying to be a movie shrink, get right to whatever the matter is, nail us to the wall, make us say the bad thing in our lives, like that would instantly make us all better and totally grateful and we'd write our life story for *Reader's Digest* and he'd be able to get a real job.

So he was on us all the time, telling me that my money was a defense, or Paul that he had to accept being gay, or riding Darla about drugs. For a guy who didn't believe in stress he sure liked to push and push and push, you know?

So: #1. CHERYL, BULLIES, BODY ISSUES.

He'd push her about how she didn't trust boys, how she didn't set boundaries, shit that had nothing to do with Harris and Tierden. Somehow it was all going to be her fault, because Marston liked to make girls feel weird about sex. Probably that was why he went to shrink school in the first place.

I don't know what anybody but me and Paul was thinking, but him and me were pretty much sitting there feeling sick and not knowing what to do.

Cheryl came in, and she was wearing her cream-colored silk blouse and her black cutaway jacket and slit skirt with big clunky shoes, which she called her "cheer-up suit" because she felt pretty in it and wore it to make herself feel better.

She took one look at that on the board and just *ran* right out the door, into Vic Marston, coming in. His coffee splashed all over her, ruining her favorite clothes.

She started yelling and crying, and he was trying to be all shrink with her out in the hallway where anyone could see.

The rest of us had to hear all of it because that room had just one exit.

Finally Marston said he'd give her a ride home so she could change and try to save her blouse, and came in and told us we could go back to class, or just sit and talk, as long as we *all* did one or the other. Then he left with Cheryl, who was keening like her puppy got run over.

As soon as he was gone, Darla pulled out Mr. Babbitt and said, "What's that, Mr. Babbitt? Why, you're right. It's a pity we don't have a gallon of vodka here, so we could all get drunkies as drunkies can be, and then go back to our classies and tell the teachers that good old Doctor Vic gave us the vodka. We could even say he told us to keep quiet while he went home to help Cheryl take her blouse off. Wouldn't that be just the mostest special-est funsies, Mr. Babbitt? Oh, you're right, you naughty bunny, it would!"

I couldn't have laughed any harder if we'd been taking turns writing "I want you to know I'm concerned about you," Marston's favorite phrase, on Marston's dick with a wood-burning pen.

After we got done gasping for air, Danny said, "Well, personally, I agree with the rabbit. I'd do it even though I don't drink, just to get rid of Marston. Fuck, yeah."

Darla covered the rabbit's ears. "Why, Mr. Babbitt, don't faint, Danny said *fuck.*"

"Danny does, when he's *really* pissed off," Squid observed.

"Yeah. *Fuck* yeah."

Two fucks out of Danny in less than a minute. Definitely a red-letter day.

Squid looked around at us. "You think anybody's gonna fucking do anything about it that will make Harris and Tierden stop hurting Cheryl?"

Paul said, very quietly, "Not unless we do it."

Squid nodded. "That's what I'm thinking."

Bonny was nodding, too. "Marston and Emerson and all them are either going to be all concerned about the de-*velop*-ment of those poor misguided boys, or they're going to want Cheryl to express her feelings. Either way Harris and Tierden get all the attention they want. There might be seminars and mandatory meetings and all that shit till doomsday, but those assholes won't feel a bit of fear or pain about this."

"Unless we make them," I said.

"Well," Darla said, "anybody doing anything tonight,

say eight? It's always dead on Mondays at Pongo's but I work till closing."

"Might have to park Junie in the corner with a coloring book," Squid said, "and it's kind of a long walk, but I can be there."

"I'll give you a ride," Danny said.

"Bring Tony, come early, and I'll buy all of you dinner," I said.

"Split it with you, Karl," Bonny said. "We want you there, Squid. This is important, and you're essential."

Squid slammed his fist into his palm. "Deal."

"Then Pongo's, tonight, eight P.M., where the elite meet to be indiscreet," Darla said. She got up and held up her silly rabbit. "Wave bye-bye to our friendsies, Mr. Babbitt, and think naughty bunny thoughts all day."

The teachers must have thought therapy was working great, because we were all back in our classes fifteen minutes into the period, and all of us were in a real good mood all day long.

Three days later Paul and me were shooting pool with Danny and Squid at New Life, which was supposed to be a "coffeehouse" but was actually just a storefront fixed up with a couple pool tables, foosball, Ping-Pong, and some board games. There were a few tables and a little soft drink counter. Some of the churches here in town fixed it up for us youths, I guess to keep us from stealing hub-caps and making zip guns. Anyway, it was somewhere you could be for free with some stuff to do. When us Madmen were in junior high, it was our refuge a lot of times.

Rev Dave, the Youth Minister there, was sort of all right, for a guy who probably just never really recovered from spending his high school years in church youth group. You just had to make sure you didn't give him a chance to go after your soul, because as a sales guy he was a slow warm-up but a hell-on-wheels closer.

The New Life didn't want you to hang out there and then go out to drink or toke up or have sex, so you had to sign in and out, and you had to let Rev Dave look at your pupils and smell your breath every time you came back in. I always wondered how he found out if you'd been having sex.

Anyway, a nice thing about New Life, you could get phone calls there, and make local calls. That was why two of the biggest dealers in the school hung out there. Rev Dave thought he had them about 95 percent converted, and had no idea why he couldn't close the deal.

Now, Harris and Tierden were what you might call predictable guys. Wednesday nights they'd hang out at Pongo's Monkey Burger till sometime after the DQ closed, daring each other to talk dirty to Darla (neither of them ever had the nerve). Then they'd go smoke dope in the Dairy Queen parking lot and crank up Iron Butterfly on the eight-track, till it was time to splash water on the window at McDonald's. It was a full, busy life, you know? Both of them being all that they could be.

So that Wednesday night, after Paul's play practice, me and Paul went to New Life together, and Danny and Squid happened to be there. We all decided to split a pool table because it was crowded. So there we all were, being good but troubled youths, basically good kids with just a few problems at home, shooting pool together. You could've taken pictures of us for the fund-raising brochure.

The phone rang, and Rebecca behind the counter— Rev Dave's daughter, in ninth grade, a Madman herself— announced it was for me, handed me the phone, and wound up the two-minute egg timer.

"Hello," I said, leaning against the wall and cradling the phone like I thought it might be a girlfriend.

"Hey," Darla said. "Two assholes just left me a fifteen-cent tip after tying up a table for three hours sharing an order of fries. Do you think anyone would like to beat the shit out of them?"

"I'll ask Rev Dave," I said, "but it would be better if you asked him yourself."

"Tell the Reverend I'll give him a blow job if he breaks Tierden's nose."

That bit was off script. I had a hell of a time not laughing like a crazy bastard. "I think he'll have some kind of answer but it would be better if you came down yourself."

"Yeah. Hey, tell Danny and Squid I want all the details."

"Everyone's coming to work with me, after," I said, "so you can catch up with us there if you want."

"Cool. Good luck. Say something about Rev Dave one more time."

"Like I said," I said, "I think it would be better if you talked to Rev Dave yourself."

The egg timer went off just as I handed the phone back to Rebecca.

Now, Rev Dave thought he was the last of the hot-ass arguers, and kept all these cartoon pamphlets in his office behind the counter, ready to go in case anyone wanted to argue. So when he heard me say "I'll ask Rev Dave," he was already gwomming his holy diapies for a chance to argue some Jesus into a youth, but coming out of his office acting all casual, like he just happened to be there.

I said I had this friend, Paul and me wanted her to come down to New Life with us, Danny and Squid had asked, too, stuff like that, making it real clear that this was a lost friend with big problems, a messed-up young sinner fit to make a youth minister salivate uncontrollably, who said she wasn't going to come in because God was bullshit. "See, Rev, every now and then she calls me because she thinks up some stupid question, like the one about God making a rock so big he can't lift it. It's just her excuse to not come in and give it a try."

"Oh, and what was your friend's question tonight?" Rev Dave asked, stroking his little beatnik beard like he was flexing before stepping into the ring.

"It's so stupid it's embarrassing."

"There are no stupid questions."

Only stupid people, I thought, but said, "Well, I think it's even dumber than the one about the rock. She asked why God lets there be all this pain, and suffering, and war and death and shi—um, *stuff*—in the world, since he could stop it, and if he has the power to stop it, doesn't that make him responsible for it?"

"Well," Rev Dave said, "that's not really a dumb question at all. That's a very *important* question." He settled his rimless glasses high on his nose.

Paul drifted over from the pool table, like he was interested, and pretty soon Rev Dave had warmed into the subject and there we were, him talking to Paul and me in his office, with the Rev pushing a lot of cartoon books across the table at us and earnestly explaining how this was called "The Problem of Pain" and it was very-very-*very* important to *Christians.* Darla's boyfriend at the time, who was majoring in religious studies, had really come up with a perfect one to get Rev Dave going. Paul and me started to wonder whether the Rev would ever stop. He had *three* pamphlets on the subject, so you could tell it was important. And we went over all of them in detail.

Squid and Danny said later that we had the hard part of the job and they had all the fun. With Rev Dave's back to the door, Rebecca gave Danny and Squid the high sign; they were out the door in zero flat, ran two blocks to the back of the Dairy Queen parking lot, sneaked up behind Bobby Harris's rolling rust pile, and used a little added touch that Squid thought of—they each turned on a flashlight and shined it in the window on their side, and Danny yelled, "Out of the car, long hair!" just like Kenny Loggins in that song.

So Harris and Tierden opened their doors, already pissing down their legs because they were pretty far into a bowl and thought they were busted. Squid got Tierden by his long dirty hair ("felt like washing my hands for a week afterward," he said). Danny grabbed Harris by the boy-boobs, right through his shirt, and lifted him off the ground.

They body-slammed those two assholes up against the car to take the breath out of them, and then just hit them till they were both crying and all curled up with their hands around their faces. Later that night, at McDonald's, Squid said Tierden's ribs thudded like a bass drum; Danny did a pretty good imitation of Bobby Harris keening "no-o-o-o" as his head got slapped back and forth.

Squid and Danny worked fast but they made sure they hit about every surface there was to hit on those assholes. Then they pantsed them both, pants and shoes

and underwear and all, dragged them over to the freez-
ing-cold ditch that runs by there, and pushed them in.
Squid said they were crying real hard and hanging on to
each other like a couple of homos.

Then Squid stood guard to keep them standing there
in that icy water up to their waists, and Danny took their
pants and stuff and sprinted up to a streetlight up on
Courthouse Street where lots of cars go by. He dropped
the pile there and then him and Squid took off, running
back to New Life. The way Squid put it, they had explained "don't be an asshole" in terms anyone could understand. Even Harris and Tierden.

"Wow," Marti said, "that was doing the *job*. So how many
demerits was that, sixty-two million?"

I swallowed some coffee let my big smile build the
effect. "Not even one."

"Those guys must've narked, though, they're such
losers—"

"Of course they narked. Now we're getting to the
beautiful part. See, Danny and Squid had only been gone
for like ten minutes, so they came back to the pay phone
just outside the door of New Life, called, and asked for
me. I pretended I was getting another call from my friend
who was all messed up and hung up on the problem of
pain, and Rev Dave started trying to get onto the phone
with 'her' over my shoulder.

"Meanwhile Paul dashed around, opened the side door, and he and Squid and Danny cruised back in. Then my 'friend on the phone' turned out to be mad at me and hung up, and the three guys acted like they wanted to get another game of pool going, and when I called my nonexistent friend back—Darla's house, just in case Rev Dave got nosy—she wouldn't answer."

"Nonexistent friends can be like that."

"You bet. I won't date imaginary people anymore. My friend Larry keeps losing his virginity to them and it never works out."

"Larry in math class? Okay, that's another story I have to hear—"

"Oh, you will. Have faith in Larry. Anyway, meanwhile, back at the story I *was* telling, I apologized to Rev Dave, and us four guys shot pool for another hour and went home. Next day in school, Harris and Tierden turned up looking like raccoons and walking like old men. So of course, being pussies—"

"Pick a better word."

"Uh, so, being wimps, they went to Emerson, the vice principal, and narked out Danny and Squid."

Danny and Squid, of course, said they had an alibi, so Emerson called me and Paul in.

He made this big show out of asking us before we saw Danny and Squid, and not telling us what all the questions were about. Of course me and Paul just said, yeah, yeah, yeah, we shot pool with Danny and Squid— or Daniel and Esquibel, trying to sound super-sincere for the adults—all night at New Life. And of course we hung out and rapped about that groovy Bible thing with Rev Dave.

I mean, it was *true* except for about ten minutes out of four hours. Do the math, that works out to ninety-four percent true, that's an A in truthfulness anywhere.

Emerson got the weirdest smile, and called New Life.

Rev Dave checked his check-in book and found that all four of us had had Pool Table A for an hour and a half before, and an hour after, Harris and Tierden said Danny and Squid beat them up. Rev Dave even added that he especially remembered us because we'd really rapped seriously about some heavy issues, and he thought he might have turned us on to the Book, and that we were really a bunch of far-out kids.

You really had to be there to see Emerson repeating, into the phone, in that flat vice principal voice, "Yes, Reverend, yes, I got that," and writing down "turned on to the Book" and "far-out kids" on his yellow legal pad. We could hear Rev Dave's voice through Emerson's head because of all the enthusiasm the Rev had.

Now here's the real good part—Emerson knew perfectly well we were bullshitting him. But remember

Mrs. Emerson was the cheerleading advisor, and she'd spent a lot of time taking care of Cheryl, who was one of her pets.

In fact Mrs. Emerson had given those assholes so many demerits for hassling Cheryl that Mrs. Brean stopped taking demerits from her about them—Brean is buddies with Bobby Harris's mother and she came up with some crap about how it's not fair to report every single time someone does something, and how Mrs. Emerson was just being mean to poor Bobby and Scott and out to get them. Which, I mean, *shouldn't* a teacher be out to get kids like that? You know, like wolves killing the weak and the sick for the good of the species?

Anyway, Emerson wasn't totally stupid, despite all appearances. He knew that alibi was way too good. He knew that the Madmen look out for each other and that Cheryl was a Madman. For that matter he knew Harris and Tierden weren't smart enough to make a story like that up and nobody could be dumb enough to mistake someone else for Squid and Danny.

I mean, trust it, Emerson knew the truth.

But we had set it up so he could *pretend* he believed us. That's why he got that beautiful big weird smile, and he was still smirking up a smirk-storm when he gave Harris and Tierden three-day suspensions for making a false complaint, staggered so they wouldn't have each other to hang out with.

I shrugged and gestured at the now-dry window. "Anyway, like a week after that, Bobby Harris figured out 'water go splash, Karl have to work more.' They're so proud of that. And they do other petty nasty shit, sometimes, too, to Paul, but they sure leave Cheryl alone. The weirdest thing is now they try to make out like they didn't get hurt or it was all their idea or something. Like they think we played a really funny joke on them, you know? *So* weird. Like they'll come over to Paul and me, or Danny and Squid, at Pietro's Pizza and tease us about it like it was something that *we'd* be sensitive about. Danny says if he has to do it again he's going to make them kiss each other and take Polaroids and tape those up around the school."

She laughed. "So that's what the Madmen do? Protect each other like that?"

"No. I wish it was. Usually we can't do a fucking thing for each other, come to admit it. We're a little group of mental-case high school students, not the fuckin' X-Men, you know? But we know each others' stories, and we do try to watch each other's backs, when we can."

"And now I'm in the club."

"Unless you ask Gratz to help you stay out of it, or nobody gives you your ticket. Listen, I have to hang around till time to clock out. That's like another hour. Usually I'd do homework, but I got that done earlier, so I was going to just sit and read; don't let me keep you if you need to get home."

"I need *not* to get home, since our moms are out drinking together. I don't know about yours, but when mine gets home, it's going to get real ugly."

"Hang out as long as you like. The book isn't *that* good. You got a story?"

"Not really. Or just one and it's really long and pointless and I hate it. Will you pretend to listen and sympathize?"

I leaned back and settled in with some cold fries and a little thing of ketchup on my lap. "Pretending to listen and sympathize is my fucking specialty."

Marti had lived a lot of weird places, New Mexico and Washington State and Nevada, usually far away from people, because her dad's work was with "all this wild dangerous atomic shit. And wherever they have a cluster of real smart guys, way out in the desert, they have a genius school, because smart people have smart kids, and I got shipped from one genius school to another, over and over, because Dad has no patience, so as soon as I got nongenius scores, he'd move me again."

Her father had lost some big job with the AEC, and was going to be a physics prof at Plantagenet College.

"He was some kind of a big hero, because there was some report he wouldn't put his name on, and they pressured him, and it turned out he was right and they were wrong. It would have been a big deal except that every single interesting detail is classified. Like every other thing that's any good about my father, I hear rumors about it but I don't get to see it at home."

Marti's mother had been a sixteen-year-old high school dropout waitress with big boobs (resulting in more tips) going out with a twenty-three-year old who had already finished his Ph.D. in physics (resulting in all those weird jobs) when she'd gotten pregnant (resulting in Marti). "Anyway, after I had that nervous breakdown in May—not like a 'nervous breakdown' nervous breakdown, I just cried all the time and couldn't get out of bed for three days—the shrink made Dad agree to let me live somewhere for a while and just be a normal kid."

She'd never been anywhere long enough to have many friends, and her father hadn't really approved of her having the few she sometimes had. She'd gotten locked out a lot but had always spent the night sleeping in her car or at a diner. She couldn't remember a single interesting thing that had ever happened to her.

She looked up at the clock. "Jesus—time for you to clock out. That's a lot of listening to me babble."

"It beats going home," I said.

"Same here. Better than listening to them fight about her drinking and screwing around, him breaking stuff and screwing around, and my grades. Oh, and flying saucers."

"I get the flying saucers, too."

"Yeah, my father is so much of a skeptic and a don't-believe-nonsense guy that Mother takes up flying saucers and quartz crystals and levitation and dowsing and all that just to irritate him."

"I'm afraid our mothers are going to get along just fine." I made a last quick check, and locked the door. We walked across the parking lot to her car. It had still been warm when we had arrived, the air thick with moisture like being wrapped in a blanket, but now it was after midnight and a chill had taken the damp air. We both shivered.

"You can't think of anything that might be making Paul avoid you?" she asked. "Any reason why he wouldn't want to talk to you, or maybe just wouldn't want to be seen with you?"

"That's the weirdest thing of all," I said, "there's one thing I can think of but it makes no sense unless he's telepathic. Can I tell you something I can't tell anyone else?"

"Sure, if you trust me."

We got into her car, and she started it and put the heater on. "Well," I said, "you know the stuff I told you about the Madman Underground. But there's something

I have to do." I took a deep breath and just blurted out everything about Operation Be Fucking Normal. I explained about Dad and AA and "one day at a time," and finally I said, "so that's what I'm trying to do, be normal, one day at a time. So far I've got one day."

"So that's why you said that keeping friends is hard. What a jackass." Marti pushed her glasses up the bridge of her nose. "Maybe I'm just weird but I don't think you should throw away great friends just to sit around all year singing I'm-normal-I'm-normal-I'm-normal to yourself. Your friends are not like a . . . a hairstyle or something."

I felt small, petty, and creepy.

She put the car in gear. "I'm getting mad. But I said I'd give you a ride home. And I like to keep my word." She whipped the car out of the parking lot fast enough to pull me against the door. We said nothing. It seemed like a breath later that we were in front of my house, the brakes screeching loud enough that I figured she'd wake up old Wilson. She said, "I'm sorry. I've only known you a few hours. I really don't have any right to judge you."

"I'd still like to be friends."

"Am I suitable as a friend for a normal guy?" She didn't look at me. "See you in school tomorrow."

"See you in school."

I got out of her car, and the instant that I closed the door she pulled away slow and soft, riding the clutch up into first, not one of her jackrabbit clutch-popping take-offs this time.

Of course Mom wasn't home yet—it was almost an hour till closing time. I tried the back door and it was locked.

I went around front, looked to make sure nobody saw (I didn't want anyone narking me out to Mom), and went in through the window I'd left unlatched. I carefully closed and latched it behind me, in case she came home in one of her paranoid investigative moods.

All the stashes were safe and my door had held.

I undressed into the washer, threw in detergent, made sure it was set for cold, started it.

I treated myself to using up all the hot water, scouring off the smell of burger grease and disinfectant till the shower turned cold.

Tired as I was, I couldn't fall right asleep. I turned on the desk lamp and pointed it at Dad's task list, pinned to my wall. As always, before I got to the third page, I sank into deep sleep.

PART TWO

(Thursday, September 6, 1973)

10

Cussing a Blue Streak Does Not Work on Goddam Ghoul Bastards

MY ALARM WENT off at 5:30—I had work at Thos. Browning Upholster, so I needed to be up. I groaned and pushed myself up off the mattress before sweet sleep could drag me back down, dressed quick, and trotted down the stairs.

Mom was snoring on the living room couch, still wearing her clingy top, baggy hippie-chick long skirt, and Go-Get-Laids—her favorite black leather high-heeled boots. They had huge clunky heels, lots of silver fittings that didn't do anything, and complicated lacing that didn't undo, and they had cost around half a mortgage payment.

She had fallen in love with them in the shoe store window up in Toledo. She'd taken one look and said—

this is how she explained it to me—"They are so perfectly me, Karl. Elegant and sassy, strong and assertive, daring to be all-woman in a man's world." (I noticed later that that was exactly what it said in the magazine ads for the boots.) "I *had* to have them. When you see something that is all you, you've got to have it, it's like a sign that you're meant to have this thing, to be really you." And then she kind of winked and smiled and said, "Especially when it's a perfect pair of Go-Get-Laids." (That part wasn't in the ad.)

She was trying to explain why she'd stolen one of my cash cans to get them. I was pretty upset, though I wasn't going to let her see that—she'd just yell at me, and maybe do something else to spite me. What would be the point? Those boots were about three weeks off my life, but it was gone, you know? No good making it worse by yelling.

Afterwards, she said she was sorry; we agreed it would count as part of what I got her for Christmas (although all by themselves those boots had cost more than I was planning to spend).

I never saw those boots on her without feeling angry and weird. They really were her trademark: all the guys who hung out at Mister Peepers called her "Beth with the boots."

Mom was face down, head turned to the side, snoring with a sound like a just-unclogged toilet drain, but louder. All the authorities say you only snore when you sleep on your back, but Mom was never one to comply with authority. Softandgentle, Prettyangel, Ocean, and Starbeauty lay beside her in a furry row. One booted foot rested on the floor next to the little wad of her underwear. Her long skirt was bunched about halfway up her pasty white thighs.

The front door was unlocked, but the TV and stereo were still there. I'd want to check later to make sure my stashes were still all okay. And she hadn't puked. Really, the morning could've been a lot worse.

She groaned. "Karl?"

"Yeah, Mom."

"Time's it?"

"Quarter till six, Mom, I got a couch pickup this morning."

"That old bastard doesn't pay you enough. And *my* old bastard left. Men. Bastards."

She curled up toward the couch back, erasing the crease where the cats had been sleeping. They flumped to the floor and stalked off, twitching their tails in a parade of indignation.

I went into her bedroom, grabbed the coverlet off the bed, and put it over her. I decided she'd be more comfortable without the boots and pulled those off her as well. She whimpered a little and snuggled into the coverlet. "I'm going to move the clock out here," I said, "and set it for eight thirty."

"'kay." She made a little snork noise, squirming. "Tiger?"

"Yeah, Mom?"

"You're okay. You're really an okay kid." She fell back asleep.

The dim light erased most of the lines on her skin, and smoothed out the dark roots around her part. She was, still, really, kind of pretty. She pouted like a three-year-old who isn't getting her way but isn't sure what her way would be. Except for the hair, she still looked like her class-of-'52 yearbook picture.

Dad always said that when he first saw her after he came back from the service, he knew he'd marry her or nobody. "I'd thought I'd *never* fall in love, but it turned out I was gonna do it *once*," he'd add, and if she was in reach he'd mess her hair a little or run a hand down her back. She'd tell him he was corny and he'd tell her "but you like that."

Last summer, Paul and me had been watching this old Western on TV and that line about "it turned out I was gonna do it once" was in it; John fuck-me-senseless-with-a-flagpole Wayne said it. I wondered whether my dad was so corny he came up with it, too, or he was so corny that when he saw that movie, and heard that line, he slapped it into his favorite story. Anyway it always embarrassed Mom, and it always made her smile. Maybe she never saw that movie.

Looking at the pale tumble of hair around Mom's face,

and the sad little girl expression as she slept, I could sort of see what Dad must've seen.

As I moved the clock to the coffee table, it showed I was only five minutes late. Piece-a-cake. I made back three of the five in a headlong charge through grooming, moving the McDorksuit to the dryer, and catshit patrol. Now if I ran all the way to Courthouse Street, which I enjoyed anyway, I could be right on time.

I slowed as I crossed Courthouse—almost no cars moving yet, just the few people who had to work early. On that block of Shoemaker Avenue, the peeling store-front that read THOS. BROWNING, UPHOLSTER, was the only one not yet boarded up.

Like always, Browning was already out in front of his store, a paper cup of coffee from McDonald's in one gnarled hand, his suit coat draped over his other arm, leaning on the old hearse he used for deliveries. His sludge-gray hair was plastered down with some kind of goop or other, and his hat was on the hood of the hearse beside him. He was wearing his Thursday clip-on tie, the red one of his five flaccid, food-stained clip-ons. His Sunday tie was a real bow tie, blue and red, real ratty and old, and only for church. There was a Saturday clip-on tie but no Monday clip-on tie because he didn't have the shop doors open Mondays, just worked in the back, he said so he could concentrate.

For fifty-some years Browning had been an upholster.

He would threaten to "whack you one upside your empty head with the old mallet" for saying "upholsterer," because "a poet makes poetry but you don't call him a poeter." I thought about asking what about a carpenter but I was afraid he'd have an answer.

"Mister Shoemaker," he said, which was always what he said when he first saw me. After that he would call me Karl like everyone else did. "Just a pickup today, no delivery. 'Fraid it's a long ways out of town—all the way out to Republican Corners—so we'll get you to school on time, but not with much time to spare."

"That's fine, Mister Browning."

"Good, good. I don't want to interfere with your education, Karl. It's important."

Since there was no delivery, there was nothing to carry out of the shop, and we just got into the old hearse. Browning said practically all upholsters did pickups and deliveries in used hearses, because used hearses were cheap, had wide back doors that opened all the way, and came with tackle for handling big, heavy objects.

I could dig that it was practical and cheap. Like me, you know. I still wished he'd just put some cash into fixing up an old bread van or something. Or at least repainted that old hearse some color other than black, and maybe put THOS. BROWN, UPHOLSTER in big letters on it.

We got into the car and he handed me a McDonald's coffee, cream-two-sugars, like I liked it. This was probably my favorite job: good money, in cash so I didn't have to pay Social Security; the hours worked real good for me; and most of all Browning was considerate, like he wanted me to like the job and stick around. "How's it going?" he asked.

"Eahh. Life's busy but I'll live. There's plenty of work, I'm staying up with school, all that."

"Getting out any, got any friends?"

"Oh, I get some time off, Mister Browning, really. I'm friends with a lot of people."

"That's good. You're going to need friends later. Shoemaker is a big name in this town. You remind me a lot of your dad. He carried couches for me back before the war, you know, and did about half an apprenticeship."

"Yeah, well." The tall corn whirred by. Browning reminded me that Dad had worked for him in 1941 every so often; I never knew what to say about it. "Uh, I'm planning to join the army, even though it's got my mom really freaked."

"It would," he said. "Well, hell, when you come back to settle, that time in the service will look good to the voters."

That old hearse didn't have much acceleration but it had quite a top speed and Browning liked to drive at it. I kind of enjoyed the way the old motor would roar and that feeling of barreling along barely in control. Besides, if I got killed I was already in a hearse.

"I'm pretty sure I don't want to live here," I said.

"Your old man was *real* sure of that, himself. Sometimes the Lord has other plans."

Now, *that* was a conversation killer.

"Yeah, well." Might as well put a stake in it.

We shot on down the crumbly pavement ribbon between the fields that stretched right out to the fencerows on the horizon, and the sun climbed up and got brighter and smaller. The heavy-duty shocks on the old hearse could handle all those bumps, lines, and cracks that webbed the asphalt, but they wanted us to know they were working hard, so there was a constant, quick *whuppa-thud whuppa-thud* from the road. In a race between Browning and Marti, she'd have him in a drag, but over distance I wasn't so sure.

I wondered if she and I were still friends, didn't like that thought, and went looking for something to talk about. Lucky I grew up in the Midwest, because I knew just what would restart the conversation.

Blue-brown sky, already starting to silver and it wasn't seven o'clock yet. "Hot one for sure," I said.

"Thank progress for air-conditioning, and God for nothing to do outside after this," Browning agreed.

We kept that one going about five minutes more, and then we got onto the Indians and why they stank this year, and the Oxford reopening, and the fact that neither of us had had a date in a while. Of course my while was the three months since Bonny dumped me, and his was the couple decades since Mrs. Browning had died.

At least I knew if I ever got to his age, I'd still be able to talk to young people.

Republican Corners had been an incorporated town fifty years before. You could still see some foundations in the vacant lots by the road. The old downtown, a block of boarded-up buildings, was still standing. But now there wasn't even a post office, just a little grocery store with gas pumps out front. In one of the dozen or so inhabited houses that huddled around one side street, an old lady named Rose Carson had a sofa that needed re-covered. Browning had gone to high school with her; that was where he got a lot of his business, people he'd known in school. I figured that was probably how he'd gotten his first big break, when he re-covered Moses's living room set.

"Tom," she said as he came in the door, "I can tell you're getting old. You never used to have to bring along a handsome young assistant."

"I used to have a back like steel. Nowadays the doctor says I gotta watch it, so I need help to move a couch."

"Oh, he's to help you with the *couch*. What's he going to do while we're upstairs?" She winked at me. Gross gross gross.

"Don't pick on my help, you shameless old hussy. Not when you got me around and I *like* it."

"Of course you do, you old poop. Or you would if you remembered what it meant."

They were both grinning like this was the funniest shit in the world, and went on into trading jokes about the sex lives of people who were mostly dead now. They'd talk about a time when some guy and girl got caught making out on the hayride, and then they'd suddenly be talking about how nice his funeral was, like fifty years later, or about how her family had had to put her away because she couldn't take care of herself, and like that.

I figured there wouldn't be a quiz so I didn't take notes. I just stood there, smiled nicely, and remembered that at what Browning paid me, so far this conversation had already bought me one more paperback at Philbin's.

They got into more usual old people conversation, too, grandkids and nieces and nephews and stuff. Then she smiled at me and said, "And might I ask, is this the next generation of Browning upholsters?"

"Not a bit," old Browning said, "this is the next Mayor Shoemaker. Doug's boy. Takes after his dad, wants to go into the army. Where his ability to carry large heavy objects around without asking too many questions will come in real handy."

Rose Carson winked. "Well, Tom here's the man to train you. He personally carried General Sherman's sofa all the way from Atlanta to Savannah."

"Why, Rose, you—when you were a senior, I was a sophomore!"

"For the third time!" Then they both got all sentimental and talked about how it was good to see each other again, and he promised that the two of them would have dinner soon.

But they hadn't seen each other in more than a year. I mean, how can you let a friend go for that long, especially when you only live like twenty minutes apart and neither of you has all that much to do in the evening anyway?

What we found when we finally carried that couch out was nothing Browning hadn't seen fifty million times before—figuring one pickup a week and that he'd been in business for a million years—but he overreacted just like it was the first time.

All of Browning's customers were really old because they were the only people with furniture nice enough to be worth fixing. People my mom's age and younger just bought the Sears stuff that, when it starts looking shabby or something breaks, you either sell to a college student or pitch in the Dumpster.

So when Browning and me made pickups and deliveries, it meant there was a hearse in front of some old person's house. In a place like Republican Corners, everybody phoned the neighbors. So now pretty much the whole local population was hanging around on their porches and in the street, waiting to get a look at Mrs. Carson's corpse.

"*Seddidown!*" Browning grunted. I let the couch down and stepped back. I'd seen this show before.

Browning stood up, smacked his palms across each other twice like he had sawdust on them, and stood at the edge of the porch, hollering and flapping his arms around like killer chickens were attacking his legs. "You can all go back inside and take your goddam kids with you, every goddam one of 'em, because you ain't gettin' to see no goddam body this morning! Rose is just fine just like she was yesterday and just like she's gonna be for years to come, except she's got this goddam problem that her goddam neighbors are all goddam ghouls!" He pretty much *howled* "ghouls" at them. Like a goddam dog with its goddam butt on goddam fire, you might say.

"And we ain't burying this couch either so you don't plan to come and sponge off the reception like I'm sure you all goddam do every chance you get! A man ought to be able to conduct his goddam business without having every-goddam-body turn it into a goddam sideshow!"

Same as always. Long pause while they stared, and talked to each other, and then some Einstein among them figured out that this meant no body to look at, and they all just kind of floated back in their front doors, their confused kids trailing after them. We carried that ratty old couch down to the hearse quick.

Usually I didn't bother with the seat belt but I put it on this time, I can tell you that. Browning was still good and mad. The old hearse had a three on the tree;

he slapped it into gear, stood on the gas, and popped the clutch, sending us screaming backwards into the street. He had it floored for full quarter mile, and only upshifted to three when he took his foot off the gas. I think we laid rubber for most of it.

The sun was full up now, the brown ring around the sky was narrow and far away along the horizon, and the cornfields and little strips of woods all around were almost pretty, like a calendar or something, in the deep-yellow light that filtered in through the humidity and dust.

We shot down the narrow channel through the tall corn. "What really gets me, Karl, every single goddam time, is that I'm *trying* to get all those ghoul bastards off the street. I'm trying to make them ashamed of standing around, like goddam ghouls, hoping to get a look at a nice neighbor lady. They only want to look at her when she's cold and stiff and she don't even look like herself anymore. When she would've done anything in the world just to have somebody stop and ask how she was and set with her for half an hour. But nobody wants to do *that*. But for a chance to see her look like a shriveled wax dummy they'll climb the hedge.

"They goddam well *should* be ashamed.

"But I can't seem to *make* them ashamed, so instead I always cuss a blue streak so that the mothers will grab their little brats up and drag 'em off into the house. Only it doesn't work anymore because nobody gives a damn if I cuss in front of their goddam kids!"

It took me a sec to get that by "cussing a blue streak" he meant saying "goddam" a lot. It must be that in his day, *goddam* was kind of like *fuckin'* was to me and my friends. I thought about suggesting that he try saying "fuckin'" instead of "goddam" but I didn't think he'd take the suggestion real well.

When I looked at him again, he was slowly turning his head on his scrawny old neck like a door hanging by one hinge and blowing in the breeze, still trying to work the anger out. "Karl, when you get old, the only thing you got left is your friends. Rose'n'me's the only people that remember some of that stuff we were joking about. Once there's only one of us, which praise the Lord if he's willing won't be for a long time yet, it'll be like all that stuff never happened. That's what happened to my old aunt, she made it to a hundred and four years old with two old friends she'd been in school with, and then both of them died, and she was gone from pure loneliness in just a couple of months. It was like she wasn't there anymore, 'cause there was no one to remind her, or treat her memories like they mattered. So if you don't do anything else, you have to stick up for your friends."

He sped up to pass a tractor, the hearse's old engine thundering as we swung wide. "Hell, I don't even *like* this kind of thing, you know? Now I'll be saying goddam for the rest of the goddam day, too. Probably say it in front of goddam Mrs. Henshaw when she comes in with her son to pick up that big old wrap-around-the-corner couch that she had me get the special leather for. I just know I'm gonna say here's the goddam bill for the goddam couch, Mrs. Henshaw, and be careful your goddam clumsy son don't drop it or drag it, or it will all be for nothing 'cause that goddam leather feels like goddam butter and goddam-well rips about as goddam easy. And them both such big churchies their turds have little halos."

Okay. He was finally funny. I laughed.

"I'm an obnoxious old son of a bitch, ain't I, Karl?"

"I try never to argue with the boss."

He laughed like a goddam idiot. We didn't say anything, either of us, for a few miles of crumbling asphalt and hazy cornfields.

I never understood why grown-ups in general and old farts in particular were always willing to act weird. It was probably the only thing that Mom and Browning would agree about. They both believed in hollering and putting up a fight and standing up for stuff.

It was one big load of crap, I can tell you that. Just because somebody thought something was wrong, everyone else would have to wait around, while Mister Big Ass Defender of Justice went off on his big ego trip. Even if it was embarrassing. Even if it made all your friends want to hide their heads because you were all yelling and mad and weird in public. Most of us don't care and have jobs to do. Why couldn't everyone just shut up and be normal?

11

I Was a Third-Grade Communist

THE YEAR I was in third grade was the first time Dad ever lost an election, when he went for his fourth term as mayor, and it wasn't going real well. By August he knew he didn't have a chance this year, even though he'd always won in a landslide, in '58, '60, and '62.

Trying to stop the whole Oakbrook thing blew up in his face; the real estate bastards beat him down because if Oakbrook didn't happen—or if they had to spend the money to do it as a regular part of Lightsburg—they'd all be broke, and so would a lot of people they'd conned into putting up money for it. So people were *pissed*. Dad had been a big guy that everyone liked, who paved streets, straightened out taxes, and rebuilt the park, but once he tried to say no to Oakbrook, all that stuff was just like it had never been.

Paul's father said it wasn't personal, just that the real estate bastards had to get Dad out of the way. Both Dad and Mr. Knauss always said "real estate bastards" like it was one word.

And then after Dad died, and Mom got busted for possession and couldn't be a substitute teacher anymore, she ended up working at a real estate office. She always said that Cheap Bastard Acres had been a big mistake, too; when she got her license she was going to show people how you *should* do real estate, that there was a right way to do it that built homes and neighborhoods and didn't rip people off. I don't know why, but when she'd say that, I'd kind of believe she meant it, even though I knew you couldn't trust her.

Anyway, getting back to third grade, before I was a Madman and before Paul's mom was killed, and everything, even before Dad got sick, I wanted to be around Dad all the time. I always begged to go to the council meetings with him, where I'd sit in the back and color or do the little bit of homework I had. I just liked hearing his voice; ever since kindergarten it had been a pleasant drone while he ran through all the stuff that needed to get done and asked who was doing it, and people said they had it or there was a committee for it.

But 1964 was real different. Meetings always ran way too late, so by the time we got out the DQ was closed and we couldn't get ice cream on the way home, or sit out on the porch with Mom while I finished my cone and they smoked and talked.

These old guys would stand up and call Dad a dictator, a tyrant, and a Communist, and yell about how stuff wasn't fair or right, or something was or wasn't in the Constitution, and how Dad was trying to control everything and run everything, just to keep them from getting rich.

Last summer, trying to keep Mr. Knauss from getting on Paul and Kimmie's case, I had told Mr. Knauss I'd never really understood what it was all about back then. He shrugged and said, "You were eight, Karl, of course you didn't. What it came down to was they wanted big houses on big lots for the Toledo bedroom market. And to make the costs come out low, so they could promise the investors big profits, they needed to leave out costs like sewer hookups, sidewalk easements, street repairs, all the stuff that makes a place comfortable to live. That was all. It didn't really matter because once the places were built and sold, Gist County went after them anyway, so they get worse services for about the same money, and anyway if you've got to work in Toledo, you might as well live there—the houses aren't any cheaper out here, and there's not much difference between a view of a warehouse and a view of a soybean field. So it was really all for nothing."

The funny thing was, even then, before I had any idea

what it was all about, somehow I knew they were making a mess of Dad's life (and Mr. Knauss's, and mine) for flat nothing. Every Tuesday night the meeting would go way over time and I'd end up going home slung over Dad's shoulder, half-asleep. Sometimes he'd meet some voter on the street, explain he was going home from Council, say that he thought they'd done some good things for the town that night (even if it was just all yelling, he'd say that), and then explain that "this is Karl, my sack of potatoes, and I'd better get him home to bed."

When we got home, he'd just kind of hand me to Mom and she'd more stuff me into bed than tuck me, then go to bed herself. She didn't want to hear about it and he wanted to talk out his fury, so Dad would go to the bar and talk politics with his cronies. That's what Mom called them; I think I was in about sixth grade before I realized that being a crony wasn't a job like being an assistant.

That September, Vietnam was just really getting going. The old farts that were picking on Dad were all for Goldwater and Dad was the city chairman for Johnson. Before then I just knew that good guys rooted for the Indians, voted Democratic, and went to United Methodist. I wasn't sure whether it was Republicans, Tiger fans, or Catholics who were the real source of evil in the world.

But early in third grade I realized it must be Republicans. Everyone was yelling at Dad and writing awful things about him in the paper; what Mom was calling the "Goldwater asshole/cheap bastard axis" was in full swing. I liked the way that when she'd say that, or Dad would, they'd start shushing each other because I wasn't supposed to hear them say bad words, and then they'd get laughing so hard they had to hang on to each other. That was pretty cool.

So sometime in September, Mrs. Baker, the third-grade teacher, who was a Goldwater asshole herself and married to one of the town's leading cheap bastards, tried to tell us about how bad the Russians were and all. My dad said she was putting her politics in her classroom, where it didn't belong, because she was a crazy old lady who wanted to take Grandpa's Social Security away and go to war in Vietnam.

One story hour, Mrs. Baker read us this story about how a bunch of kids were saying the Pledge of Allegiance and their new teacher made them cut up the flag and not pray, and I guess the teacher was Russian. And maybe we were supposed to feel sorry for the old teacher who got taken away at the beginning of the story, because she was a mean old lady like Mrs. Baker.

I thought it was a dumb story with no fighting or danger. Years later when we had U.S. History from Harry we read it again, and I found out what it was about, which was pretty much beyond me when I was eight; it was supposed to warn us that all us kids were all so dumb that we'd fall right into line for the first Communist teacher that walked into the classroom. Like anyone ever believed or did what *any* teacher told us.

Anyway, at the time it was just a dumb story, and after Mrs. Baker read it to us, she started talking about how the way the Communists ran Russia, if people stood up and disagreed and yelled about how something was wrong, the police took them away and they were never seen again.

Now *that* was interesting. (It was also not lost on me that they took mean old teachers like Baker away and shot them.) I thought about that all day. If we had that here in Lightsburg, and put those real estate bastards and Goldwater assholes in jail, meetings could be over in no time. The DQ would still be open, I could walk home with Dad instead of going home slung over his shoulder, and we'd never have to hear from those old hollering booger-faces again.

And it was kind of the perfect day for the idea, because it was Dad's birthday. Also, Dad had lined up a couple contracting jobs for January, after he would stop being mayor, so he'd be able to restart his business and not have to take some clerk job in Toledo. So it was a celebration. They had a bottle of wine before dinner (they let me have some mixed with 7-Up; I'd rather have had plain 7-Up but it was a big deal to them).

Then they had another bottle of wine with dinner, and they were being all loud and silly as they tried to get Dad's Sara Lee birthday cake out of the box and onto a plate so they could put candles on and everything. Big mistake. It went right over the plate, catching the far edge and flipping the plate up into the air, before landing upside down on the floor. The plate shattered next to it.

Mom and Dad started in yelling at each other about it, at the top of their lungs, the usual *You-fucked-it-up/ No*-you-*fucked-it-up* thing they did whenever anything went wrong. It went on for a while. I just sat at the table and thought about poor Dad not getting his cake, and how I had been looking forward to it, too, and it was all very sad.

But at least I had an idea to cheer Dad up—that Russian idea. I was sure it was a good idea because Mrs. Baker didn't approve of it, and Dad didn't approve of Mrs. Baker.

So Mom cleaned up the cake and the smashed plate, and then she made this thing with vanilla ice cream over Oreo cookies, and put candles on it. Dad blew out the candles and they had some more wine, and everything seemed better. Mom was sitting with her arm around him, and he was smiling and holding her hand.

"I learned something in school today that was really good," I told Dad. "In Russia, they just put guys that holler and complain in jail. So they won't bother anybody."

Dad agreed that indeed, they did that, though he wondered why Mrs. Baker was telling little third graders about it and scaring the hell out of them for no good reason.

I explained that if we did that here, we could just take all the people that made the Council meetings take so long, because they were always hollering and objecting, and send them away to jail, the way that they did the mean old lady teacher in that dumb story about kids cutting up the flag.

"You dumb little shit," Dad said. "You dumb, dumb little shit."

"He doesn't know any better!" Mom said.

"He damn well should, he *goes* to Council meetings, we've taught him—"

"How much can you teach a third grader about something like that?" Mom said, her voice tight, holding her breath a little; it was her *please don't* voice, the one she used when he was about to start ranting and yelling, and sometimes it worked, sometimes he'd back off and say she was right.

But not tonight. "Karl, listen. Did you say anything about this to anyone else?"

"I don't know," I said. Actually I'd told Paul and Paul had said he thought we'd get in trouble for that idea. I didn't want to tell on Paul and get him in trouble, too, and I really didn't want to be in trouble for having told him.

Unfortunately Dad knew as well as I did that that

was what I said whenever I was trying to think up a lie. *"Did you talk about this to* anyone *else?"*

"Doug, he's a little boy, you can't expect him—"

"Did. You. Tell. This. To. Anyone. Else?" He stared into my eyes, I think, though I couldn't see through the tears welling up. "Dammit, Betty, if he said anything like that around Baker or her stupid husband or any of the Goldwater assholes or their asshole kids, they're gonna be all over me at the next Council meeting, and I need to know!" He leaned across the table and shouted into my face. *"Now did you say anything about it to anyone?"*

I was blubbering now.

It always made Dad sick to see a boy cry. He said that all the time. He grabbed up the bottle from the table and went out to get drunk by himself on the back porch, like he did when he was really mad, muttering and swearing.

Mom's arms folded around me and I buried my face in her sweater and cried. After a long while, when I'd settled down into sniffles and she'd been holding me and stroking my hair, she got it out of me that I'd talked about it with Paul, and no one else, and that Paul had thought it was a real stupid idea and I'd better keep it secret. "You should listen to Paul more often," Mom said. She sounded really tired, but she kissed me on the forehead and hugged me really hard again. "And when your dad asks you something you should just tell him the truth. I have to talk to him for a few minutes, 'kay, Tiger? Would you like more ice cream treat? Yours got kind of spoiled for you."

It was runny and the Oreos were soggy but getting seconds on dessert was a big deal, so I ate all of it and scraped the bowl pretty much down to the shine. I could hear Mom's voice, soft and pleading, and Dad grouching and grumbling, and then after a while this long sigh from him. "I never could fight you about anything, Betty."

They came in and Dad sat down next to me, put his arm around me, and Dutch rubbed me, not hard, though I was a little scared because sometimes when he was real drunk he was rough. But this time he was gentle, like he was afraid he'd break me.

He said he was sorry he'd yelled at me. He made sure Mom had explained to me that putting people in jail for arguing was wrong and that it was *bad* that the Russians did it. Even if the people arguing were old booger-faces. And he asked if maybe I didn't want to go to Council meetings anymore, since now they were so nasty and taking so long, but I said I still wanted to go.

That settled all the big questions, so Mom got me cleaned up and put to bed. I remember her hugging me extra hard and saying, "Your dad does love you, Tiger, and I know you love him, but try not to be like him, 'kay?"

12

Two Stooges Short of an Act

THINKING ABOUT ALL that now, riding in Browning's hearse, I had about worked myself into hating the whole world. Old people in particular. Why couldn't things just be wrong, and let it go at that? Lots of unfair stuff happened all the time. Lots of things that weren't right happened. You could hear all about them in any therapy meeting.

But that was no excuse for all the hollering. We could all get along a lot better in life if people weren't always standing up and hollering about *this isn't right, that isn't right.* You know what? Maybe it's *not* right. But maybe nobody fucking wants to listen to you holler.

Why did they all think that all that standing-up-for-your-rights bullshit was a good thing? People who said my mom was plain old fucking batshit crazy, and a hippie communist, too, would turn right around and say, "But that Beth sure stands up for what she thinks is right," like that was a good thing. Which makes no fucking sense at all if you think about it. Somebody's not only wrong, but insists on yelling at you about it and not leaving you alone? And that makes it better? Shit.

My hands were squeezing each other in my lap like they did when I wanted to go punch something and make it be afraid of me.

Browning said, quietly, "When I was your age I used to promise myself that I wouldn't ever, ever, ever turn into an old fart that lectures young guys about how to run their lives."

"I was just promising myself the same thing." My fingers were knotting around like spiders at an orgy.

Browning laughed like that was the funniest thing he'd ever heard, and he kept right on laughing as we carried the couch in through the big back door of his workshop, and clapped me on the shoulder and said having me around did him good.

Browning added this trip to my tab—he only paid me once a month, but always the minute it was due, and in cash because he hated all those stupid laws and didn't see any reason why either of us should be paying into Social Security since "I can goddam well work to support myself and you're too young to worry about retiring and we're the only two people that should goddam be involved, and you know they don't save that money, Karl, they're using it to pay off some old poop my age who was too lazy and dumb to save for his own retirement, and thinks he should live off working people now."

I liked the way he put that. He never hollered about it, either. When I staged my Communist coup and took over and put all the people that hollered into concentration camps, maybe I'd put him in the extra-nice one for senior citizens, and give him a private room where he could jump Rose Carson.

Besides, unlike some past employers, Browning had never let my mother sweet-talk him into giving her my wages as an "advance" for an "emergency." I always figured that was the real reason Mom hated him; she was always saying he was a backward, stupid, old small-town bigot who hadn't had a new idea in fifty years. Which he *was*, of course. But there were so many of those around Lightsburg that it was pretty strange that she hated Browning in particular.

Browning dropped me off four blocks from the high school—I had explained to him the year before that it looked pretty weird for me to arrive in a hearse. The streets and sidewalk were already warm in the sun, but in the shadows of the houses the thick lawns were all still soggy with dew, and water ran down the street signs and tree trunks.

I crossed the street to walk in the sun. A car horn honked. When I looked up, it was Marti. She rolled down her window and said, "Hey, little boy. Wanna come for a ride in my car? I have candy!"

There's a rule or something that if a girl can crack you up, you have to do what she says. As soon as I had closed the door, Marti said, "I just wanted to say I'm sorry about blowing up at you last night. I mean, no wonder I've never had any friends, hunh?"

"You're pretty cool," I said.

"Really cool, or just cool for a titless genius?"

"I told you before, those assholes *meant* for you to hear that."

"You know, when someone hurts my feelings, somehow it does not comfort me to know that it was deliberate." She went around a corner with a squeal of tires. "On the other hand, knowing that someone else thinks they are assholes helps a great deal."

"I think that's some kind of rule for the universe."

"Probably. I'm good at figuring out rules for the universe. My dad figures out the rules for manipulating protons, I figure out the rules for manipulating morons."

Okay, come to admit it, if I had to do what Marti said every time she cracked me up, I was pretty much going to be her slave forever. "Listen," I said, "I work at McDonald's Sunday night through Thursday night. Any time you want to avoid going home, knock on the glass, I'll let you in. I like to hear you talk."

"Thank you. I like to hear me talk, too."

"You're on some kind of weird streak this morning," I said, "or I'm just laughing at everything."

"Well, laughing at everything is probably a good idea, considering what everything is like. Want me to be serious for a second?"

"Yeah, I guess."

We slowed down to join the long line of cars that formed a sort of constipated caterpillar hunching into the parking lot. She glanced at me. "I got done being mad at you for not being a perfect friend, and then over being mad at myself for expecting you to be, about fifteen minutes after I got home; I get mad real big and real fast but I come down quick, too, you know? Anyway, I started to think, and, um—your little plan won't work."

"My little plan—"

"To go normal. In the first place, maybe I'm wrong and you're a turd, but you seem like a pretty decent guy. I don't think you have it in you to really cut off all your old friends, and I don't think you're going to *like* being normal. Here's a whole line of cars full of kids; how many of them are normal? Most of them, right, by definition? And if you threw a rock down the line what would be your chance of hitting a happy person?"

"Okay, I see your point."

"Yeah, but I want to explain it some more, till you're pretty much falling asleep. Seriously, your idea won't work. You're trying to do three things that won't go to-gether—be normal, be happy, and keep your friends. I don't even think your odds are that good for two out of three.

"So I'm not worried about your plan to go all normal on us. Even if you manage to avoid therapy. The plan won't work, you can't stay normal for ten minutes on a bet, and you won't fool every single teacher all the way to Thanksgiving.

"Not to mention that your scheme is morally grody.

"But based on knowing you one entire day, I can tell you're *way* too stubborn to be talked out of trying. So go ahead, try, and when it all collapses, you'll find out I'm the horrible kind of person that will drop by McDonald's every night you're there for the rest of the school year, just to say 'nyeah-nyeah-nyeah, told you so!'"

"Yeah, well." I shrugged, afraid she was right and afraid to say it. "I guess I'll enjoy the company. I just wish I knew what's up with Paul."

We were cruising along our third aisle of marked, paved parking, and Marti asked, "Jesus, aren't there any parking spaces in *this* county?"

"The school board doesn't really approve of kids driv-ing. Unless you get here really early, pretty much all the parking is in Crater Field." I pointed the direction.

"And I bet it wasn't named after somebody named Crater." She turned toward the unpaved, pitted, and rutted back lot. "That's going to kill my shocks," she said as the LTD rocked like a boat in a storm.

As we got out of the car, I realized, belatedly, that showing up at school in Marti's car was more embarrassing than arriving in a hearse. But hey, normal guys didn't worry about things like that, right?

As we approached the big main doors, Harris and Tierden were out front, practicing their smoking skills, and they started making hooting noises as we walked into the school.

"Funny, it's fall. Shouldn't the invertebrates be getting ready to hibernate?" I asked Marti, making sure I was loud enough to be heard.

"Only the fit ones. The rest need to perish miserably for the good of the species."

Harris must not have caught it, and ran a couple of steps after us, saying, "What? What?" before Scott stuck out one of his long skinny monkey-arms and dragged his pudgy buddy back.

I held the door for Marti. Holding doors for girls was one of those things Dad taught me by hitting the back of my head. To cover the fact that I was doing it, I kept talking. "You cracked a joke they didn't get. They'll probably forgive you, like, never. Just in case you had your eye on either of them."

"Only for the specimen jar." We were going up the main steps. She held out her hand and we traded fives. "Let me know if you ever need anybody to leave a pound of nails in that puddle."

Without thinking about it, I had followed one of Dad's commandments: *If anyone tries to embarrass you about anything you do, hold your head up and do it more.* He might have been proud of me. Anyway, Marti was still my friend. Maybe today wouldn't completely stink.

Gratz spent half the hour on waste-of-time announcements, reading all of them and taking a minute to comment on each one. Sometimes I thought it would be cool to do extracurriculars, play a sport or something, but once you heard the long catalog of all the stuff at the start of the school year—well, I wouldn't say *not if you paid me* but I'd sure as shit say *only if you paid me.* Science Fair entries were due by November (so get going on that atom smasher now). Show Choir auditions were Friday (don't just be a social, be a singing social). Tryouts for *Barefoot in the Park* were Monday afternoon (you, too, can be in Paul's supporting cast). The debate team needed members (and penises). And like all that, on and on.

Darla kept tweaking Mr. Babbitt's ears and adjusting him and whispering that he was a naughty bunny and this was important, bunnies should listen to the announcements, just quiet enough so that Gratz would have had to ask her what she was saying or doing, and just loud enough to make him a little antsy and nervous; he kept glancing at her like he wanted to ask her to stop but would feel too ridiculous if he did.

It was the thing I liked best about Darla. Well, second best if you counted her big tits. Or was that third best? Anyway, he kept blabbing, she kept talking to the bunny, he got more and more nervous, and I got closer and closer to completely cracking up.

I glanced at Paul, sharing the joke, the way we always did. He jerked his head away like something bit his nose. I looked down at the floor and wished I was dead.

Gratz rambled on through the Future Homewreckers bake sale to buy a new oven, cracking jokes about how if you bought something, you could bring it back and they'd bake it for you. About half the kids in the room laughed, so the percentage of real pathetic loser yummy-yummy-yes-yes-we-love-to-lick-brown-wads-out-of-your-butt-Coach Gratz suck-ups was about average, for a Gratz class.

"All right, now that all of that is out of the way, let's get you started on our first serious project of the term. I'm going to teach you how to read *Huckleberry Finn.* Now, the first thing you have to learn, is how *not* to read *Huckleberry Finn.*" Then he launched into a tirade.

That was how his classes mostly went; he could lay down a half-hour riff on any of his stock subjects, in his sleep—if he didn't yell so much he could have done it in *my* sleep, which I'd have appreciated.

You only needed to take enough notes so that you'd remember to agree with him on the test. And if it looked like he was gonna go into detail and say stuff he'd then want to test us on, we would just ask him about prayer in the schools (for), drugs (against), Vietnam (for), or Nixon (against), and he'd rant away the rest of the time.

He started off by telling us that there were three wrong ways to read *Huckleberry Finn,* and we were going to talk about two of them today. The first way, he said, was the Hollywood way. The movies had made out Huck and Jim to be "just all-American boys on a road trip on a raft, like *Easy Rider* but on the river and without the drugs." (*Easy Rider* was like, years ago, seventh grade or so. I bet it was all cool and groovy when he first used that.)

"But! But! But!" Gratz emphasized, thumping the podium on each *but*. I wished I could smile at Paul and get a smile back. When we were taking "Read Like a Man" from Gratz, we used to count the number of *but!-but!-but!*s in a lecture; there were never fewer than three, and one time there were fourteen. Paul said Gratz was trying to tell us where it hurt, and I said he was telling us what he really wanted out of life.

But, but . . . but. I didn't look at Paul. It was so not the same I wanted to cry.

Meanwhile Gratz got through repeating everything he'd already said, and arrived back at the same place with even more emphasis. "But! But! But! The all-Ameri-can-boys-on-a-road-trip version is *wrong*!"

I managed not to gasp with surprise.

Darla was drawing Mister Babbitt on one side of the page. The other side was filled with neat, careful super-tiny handwriting, no doubt a perfect summary of the lecture.

Since we didn't riot or anything, when we heard that the idea was wrong, Gratz went on to tell us why it was wrong. He had ahold of the podium with both hands now, and he was a-hoppin' and a-boppin', a-reelin' with the fee-lin' as he finished up his point. "So *don't* try to fake your way through class discussion by pretending you got all caught up in the pretty river and how nice it would be to just drift along with a good friend. Even if you do think you'd look cute in overalls and a straw hat, like some breakfast cereal commercial."

Lots of people laughed like they were all surprised that a coach watched television. I thought it was about the least surprising thing I could've thought of.

"Everybody got that?"

"Yes, sir," we all chorused—except Marti.

Gratz glared at her.

"Yes, sir," she said, real meek and stuff. Not like she was challenging him or anything.

He nodded at her, acting all kindly. "You'll get it." He looked down at his notes. "All right, the second way not to read *Huckleberry Finn.* This is really sad. Many, uh, black groups have made an issue of the book, and sometimes even tried to get it banned, because there is a *very* important character in the book called Nigger Jim. And because of that fact we will say the word 'nigger' pretty often in this class. And when you talk about Jim and the way he is treated, sometimes you're going to have to say the word 'nigger.'

"So understand me. First of all and most important, we don't *ever* call anyone a 'nigger.' Not in this class. Not anywhere. When we have to discuss the idea, we always *quote* the word 'nigger.' It is okay to say that Jim is an uh, black person who is mistreated and hated because white people *see him as* a 'nigger.' It is okay to say that thus and so is what those very prejudiced white people meant *when they said the word* 'nigger,' and that they meant it about Jim. It is okay to say that part of how they dominated, controlled, and enslaved uh, black people like Jim was that *they classified them as* 'niggers.' But it is *not* okay to say that—and I am quoting these sentences, from past students who said them and who were made to feel very sorry they said them—'Jim is a nigger,' or that Jim was anybody's 'nigger,' or that 'Jim is running away because he's a nigger.' Is that clearly understood by everyone in the room, or do I need to throw someone out of class right now?"

We all stayed silent.

"Now, tragically, some uh, black people are trying to get *Huckleberry Finn,* of all books, taken off the shelf, because it is a *great* book by a *great American writer* in which he launches a *brilliant* and searching at*tack* on *ra*cism. Far ahead of its time. It showed what was *evil* about slavery and about treating a man, *any* man, as a 'nigger.'

"But to show the evil of racism to anyone, you have to use the words that the racists use. And some *groups* out there insist that *Huckleberry Finn* is a racist book, and that a teacher who teaches it must be racist, and even that the students who read this book will automatically *become* racists, all because"—he whispered dramatically—*"it . . . has . . . that . . . word!"*

Looked to me like Gratz had sure found an excuse for saying "nigger" in class.

Darla had started another sketch of Mister Babbitt. She could really draw.

"So," Gratz said, perching on his desk, "quick review. What do we do with the word 'nigger' in this class? Quote or call?"

"Quote," everyone except Marti said in unison.

"Marti," Gratz said, "I'm sorry, I keep forgetting that you haven't had a class from me before. When I call for a group response like that, I expect everyone to respond, all together."

"I'm sorry, sir."

"Next time." He nodded in a friendly way like he'd scritched her between her fuzzy wittle ears. "Okay, again, in this class, quote the word 'nigger' or call a man a nigger?"

"Quote," we chorused, including Marti.

He made a pencil mark on his notes and said, "Far enough for today. Karl Shoemaker, see me after class."

They all piled out. I approached Gratz's desk slowly, looking down at my friendly shoes.

"Karl." His voice was softer than I'd ever heard it. "I guess by now you must be aware that teachers are always noticing everything you do, how it looks to them, who you seem to be, who it looks like you're trying to become. You know that, right?"

"I guess I do." I wished to God I could forget.

Gratz nodded. "Look, Karl, I knew your dad well, and I could always count on him. Did you know he was my AA sponsor?"

"Uh, yeah, actually, remember, we talked about that last summer." Sometimes Gratz and I were at the same meeting. He'd kind of thought, I think, that I'd have him as my sponsor, like it was hereditary or something, and I think it hurt his feelings when I chose Dick Larren. Or maybe he felt like I'd picked a faggot over him; I guess a lot of men would be mad about that.

Anyway, I think I figured out that Dad was Gratz's AA sponsor even before Dad died. Dad was always doing something for other people—it was just his nature—and while he was still well enough to walk that far, Dad used to hang out at Philbin's, having coffee with Gratz or chatting with Dick Larren.

Both of them had cried like little kids at Dad's funeral.

Sometimes I thought it explained why Mom didn't hate Gratz nearly as much as I'd normally expect her to hate a god-bless-America Vietnam-vet hollering jock churchy asshole, which he still was even if Dad had thought he was the bee's knees.

He sighed and said, "Yeah, of course you're right, I can't believe I forgot that."

I almost asked *forgot what?* until I retraced my thoughts. I wondered if I'd been standing there with my mouth hanging open for a couple of minutes. If I had, was it normal?

Around us, sophomores flowed into the classroom for Read Like a Man. A smooth-faced blond jockish kid walked up to Gratz and started to tell him something about having to have a week off for a family vacation. Gratz held his hand up at the kid and said, "After class. And don't walk into the middle of other people's conversations. Sit down."

"But my mom said that—"

"Sit down."

The kid did. It wouldn't be bad to be Gratz, and have

all the students afraid of you. Of course it would be even better to have them afraid of you and *not* be Gratz.

"What I was gonna say," Gratz said, very low and even, "is this. There's kind of a loophole if you'd like to stay out of therapy this year. If you and a teacher, any teacher, submit a letter that says you are meeting with that teacher, to talk over your problems—and if you do it, regularly—then you can be excused from therapy, unless the school psychologist disagrees. And the school psychologist is so overloaded that unless you're literally foaming at the mouth, she'll probably be glad to let you go.

"So (if you want, it's really up to you, Karl) I'll draw up a letter, and you and I can both sign it tomorrow morning. Then you and I would just meet some time that was convenient for both of us, and, you know, talk about things. Just talk, you know, not too different from what me and your Dad used to do."

It felt like time stopped. Here it was, the Anti-Ticket. My pass to normality. About to be issued by the biggest asshole I knew.

"It's a serious offer," he said.

"I know. I was just really thinking hard for a minute."

"I kind of think you need a year of just being a regular kid."

"I'd love that," I said. Not just not-getting a ticket—being ticket-proof. Shit-Jesus, how could I be hesitating?

"I'll come a little early tomorrow to pick up the letter from you."

"Great." Gratz held out his hand across that big, book-strewn desk, and I took it and shook it. Didn't even count my fingers or wipe it on my pants afterwards.

I followed Gratz's glance at the clock; I had two minutes to get to my next class over in the other wing, and his classroom was almost full already. "Okay, tomorrow morning. I'm glad we're doing this, Karl. Oh—one other thing. Sometimes I get into these beefs with the therapy kids. Like the one you and me had once, you know? Well . . . you seem to be friends with this new girl, Marti—"

"She's not looking for trouble," I said. "She's really not. She's a good kid, Coach. Really. She just doesn't know your system yet."

He made a face. "Believe it or not I'm trying not to get off on the wrong foot any more than she and I already have. So talk to her if you can. Please. See you tomorrow morning."

I had to scramble to get my trig book from my locker, and my butt touched my chair in Hertz's class like a quarter heartbeat before the bell.

I was ticket-proof.

I had a deal.

I had promised to be a stooge for Gratz.

I felt like when he had that letter ready, tomorrow

morning, I'd be signing it in my blood, and he'd be just burning his mark on it with this cloven foot. Well, okay, that's an exaggeration, but I felt like shit, okay?

"Hey, what did Gratz want from you?" Marti said.

"Oh, the usual. Naked pictures of everyone and I'm supposed to plant drugs in your purse," I said. "And I gotta say I saw you at a Communist Party meeting."

Bonny laughed. "Don't do jokes like that on Marti yet, Karl, she's new. She doesn't realize that you're telling the truth."

Today Bon looked like my mom wished she looked, all this shimmery stuff in gauzy layers.

"Yeah, well." I shrugged. "It's complicated."

Hertz came in, smelling like mixed essence of ashtray and old lady, and started pounding through the review. She said she was hurrying because she wanted to "get into the new, fun stuff" on Monday. One good thing about her, she didn't give a shit how we were feeling—she just processed us. Math was fun for her, it was fun for everyone, why would she ask? Load kids into desks, load trig into kids, release kids filled with trig. Like working at the cookie factory and her job was putting on the chocolate sprinkles, she didn't worry too much about any one cookie.

Gratz worried about every cookie, and that's why he broke a lot of them.

See, the thing was, Gratz was sort of right. Usually, if you picked a fight with one Madman, you picked a fight with all of us. Like when Harris and Tierden picked on Cheryl, we were all there, even Darla, who fucking hated everyone.

So two years before, Paul and me had been in Read Like a Man with Gratz. That was right after the assholes on the football team had found out that sometimes Paul went up to hustle in Toledo.

Gratz was trying to get a real stupid football player to admit he could understand a poem. This would happen now and then: Gratz hated the idea that athletes *had* to be stupid, and he tried to fix it by encouraging them to be smarter and shouting their stupid buddies into submission. Which worked great with Danny, who really *was* smart, and pretty good with Squid, who would try; all they needed was a little protection from the Back Row Mandatory Moron Enforcement Squad. But when you're trying to get a big dumb ape to say that he, too, has felt gentle fucking regret just like Emily fucking Dickinson, it fucking doesn't work. At fucking all.

So, anyway, Bongo the Ape Boy was supposed to be getting a major revelation from "Because I could not stop for Death," and Gratz was pushing him real hard, and making Bongo's stupid jock friends shut up so they couldn't take the heat off him. So suddenly the guy says, "Oh, so it's stop like a car stopping for you."

"Yes, yes." Gratz nodded enthusiastically. He was going to *save* this boy for literature, Jesus, and America.

"So like she's like a hooker, she's got cars stopping for her," Bongo explained, "so why don't you ask Paul Knauss about that?"

And, okay, I got up out of my chair and yelled, and next thing I knew, I was headed down to Emerson's office. With Paul because of *course* Paul had caused all the trouble—though actually he'd said nothing because he was just too upset and scared.

This jingly sound beside me . . . I turned and there was Bonny, all those little charms and beads tinkling away, looking like she was going to audition for a job with Jefferson Airplane.

"How did you—?"

"I muttered 'asshole' under my breath," Bonny said.

"Usually you can get away with that."

"I muttered it kind of loud, I think," she said. "Like people started laughing in the next room."

We were twenty minutes on the bench, waiting to see the vice principal, so by the time Mrs. Brean came out and told us to go in and see Emerson, we were goofing and getting silly and having a good old time.

Emerson sighed, shook his head, told us we were better kids than that and he didn't want to see anything more like this. Then he gave us a three-day suspension.

Those are fucking great, because they don't *let* you

make up work, so it's like you get to trade down your grade in a couple of classes in exchange for a vacation. And since it happened on Tuesday, it gave us a five-day break. We weren't even allowed to go to extracurriculars, so on Wednesday and Thursday, Paul just ran through his lines for *Tea and Sympathy* while he watched me turn over some garden beds and rebuild some cold frames. Then we'd go pick up Bonny from her afternoon job where she was getting some extra hours, and get the younger kids from her house, and we'd all go to Pongo's and be silly for an hour, and spend the evenings hanging out at New Life, hassling Rev Dave and shooting pool. It was the funnest week of my sophomore year.

Also, the biggest deal of all, that Thursday night, because Paul had to be at home for something stupid his dad thought up, Bonny and me went to a movie; we smuggled in a big bottle of Rosie O'Grady, and powered by liquid courage, we actually made out. First time I ever got my hand on a boob.

I told Paul we needed to get thrown out of Gratz's classes more often. He said that was fine but next time the jocks could hassle me and he'd do the yelling.

And now I was gonna stooge for Gratz. And Paul wasn't speaking to me. Maybe I could get a non-Madman nickname: instead of Psycho, they could call me Judas. It was hard to concentrate in class; I just kept feeling shittier.

Even gym class wasn't really a relief; I was so distracted that when I tried to serve, the volleyball came down on my head. Coach Stuckey said if I had two more stooges I'd have an act; he said that every time you did something clumsy. I tried not to think about that word *stooge* too much.

About all you can say for the rest of the day was, it went by. Paul ate his lunch outside, again, and I barely ate, and sat in the library so I wouldn't have to goof with Larry because I liked Larry but not when I was bummed, and wondered why I had ever thought *Ice Station Zebra* was a good book. Eventually it sucked so bad I just gave up and did trig homework.

In my notebook, I scrawled:

Notes for review, so far today:
- *Not two hippies on road trip on raft.*
- *Not a racist book, an antiracist book, no matter what anyone uh, black says.*
- *Pythagorean theorem: still good.*
- *I am a stooge, and I can't find two other stooges for an act.*

An Afternoon Down the Toilet

AS I WAS walking home, right where Shoemaker Street crosses Courthouse, there was Browning, carrying his usual late-afternoon doughnut and coffee carefully across the street. "Mister Shoemaker. Today is your lucky day, sir, if you have the time to assist a poor old man . . . and perhaps make twenty dollars yourself?"

"You have my complete attention, Mister Browning."

"See, *anyone* can talk to young people, you just have to know what phrases to use."

I followed him back to his shop.

He'd been busy. "That's a lot more than re-covering," I said.

"Well, Rose herself's a tiny lady, but she has a bunch of ten-ton Tillies as friends. And it probably never occurred to her that her frame would be broken in three places, and anyway I doubt she could afford the actual rebuild it needs. So I'm doing the rebuild, and putting on a nice tough stain-proof fabric, and telling her I used the tag end of a bolt I got on special, and she's getting back a better couch than her old husband ever bought, for half what I'd charge for a repair. Got her fooled completely." He laughed like it was fucking hilarious. "There's near a week of work in this old piece of junk at the usual pace. Rose thinks I'm doing a simple re-cover, so a-course she's planning on getting it back on Monday, and if she finds out how much extra work I did she'll wanna pay me and we'll have to argue. Truth is, this couch was crap to begin with and ten years of ten-ton Tillies have crapped it up a lot more. But I don't want her to know her husband bought a lousy cheap couch, because it was an anniversary present, the last one she ever got from him, and he's been passed on for ten years, and she likes to remember him as the guy who always did everything right."

I looked closer. "Mister Browning, uh, you're building a whole new frame, basically—a lot better one than it had when it came new from the store."

"Right, that's why it's taking a while." He shrugged and spread his hands. "I got no other work that I don't have lots of time for, anyway."

"You're gonna go broke, Mister Browning."

"So I might not have money for when I get old?"

Okay, I laughed too. I like a guy that will do too much for a friend, and try to hide it from them. Makes me feel like I'm just another fool instead of the biggest one in the world.

"Now," he said. "About another problem. I know you take French, Karl. So you will pardon my French. That goddam toilet is jammed up again, because that idiot that worked for me ten years ago poured plaster of Paris down it, which hardened in the goddam trap, and so the drain is only about as big as my constipated old asshole. And I want that bastard out of my bathroom. The toilet, I mean. I already got rid of the idiot, praise the Lord. Then I need a new toilet put in, and I know Doug taught you real well, from what I've heard from people you did some unofficial plumbing for.

"I got all the solder and pipe and slip joints, and the torch, for the hookups, and I just bought me a brand-new toilet. Now, I can pay the plumber, who I have never liked, sixty bucks, which will go into the college fund for his children, and I've never liked them either—hell, I probably don't even like the college he's going to send them to—and the toilet will probably get done in a couple-few days. Or you could do it before dinner today, and I'll give you twenty bucks and take you to dinner."

"Deal."

"Besides, I could use to have a little company around, because I really gotta work late to get this couch finished up and clear the decks for some paying work. So run home, grab your messy-work clothes, and get back here quick as you can."

It beat the hell out of sitting in my room trying to do homework. I covered the half mile to my house in zip flat, and the half mile back in half that because my old painter's pants were easier to run in.

The job wasn't bad at all—Browning was old-fashioned and did regular maintenance, the way my Dad had taught me. So all the valves turned easy enough, and there just wasn't that much trouble getting the old toilet unhooked.

Draining it was gross, of course. But luckily it was up a little above street level, so after I shut off the valves, I just ran a garden hose through the window into the storm drain, siphoned the water out of the tank, the bowl, and the trap, and then cut the toilet free—thirty or forty years of occasionally missing the pot means when it's time to take it out, the bolts are rusted in real good. But that's why they call them bolt cutters.

I hauled it out back to dry out in the sun.

Since Browning had all the tools and stuff in good shape and in the right place, it worked the way stuff does in shop class (well, for me or Squid—I'm not vouching for what happens when Paul takes shop), and the new toilet went in like halfway to magic. It even seemed like the flux and solder behaved extra well; those were some of the neatest joints I ever made. Only banged my head a couple times, got a couple little burns, and left some messy gunk on my painter's pants, but that was why I wore them.

So about the time that I had test flushed it, and was crawling around with the flashlight making sure it was all tight, Browning said his old hands, back, and knees had "about took all they could," looked my work over, and said it was exactly right. He handed me the twenty and told me he'd do the pickup on the bathroom and he had a cleaning lady that would get it shiny again, "so run home and get into something suitable for Pongo's Monkey Burger. Casual tonight—don't go all the way to top hat, white tie, and tails."

Back home, I shot through the door and up the stairs, left my pants on the floor, and pulled on a clean T-shirt and jeans. I was tired. Toilets are heavy and uncooperative and I'd wrestled two of them into submission. But life wasn't sucking too bad, right now. I pretty much flew back; Browning was just locking up.

He had an old Cadillac—another ride in a very big car, but a lot less embarrassing than that hearse.

When Michelsen opened Pongo's, he had dreamed about launching a chain—I knew that the same way everyone did, because Michelsen told us all the time, with this kind of hurt faraway look in his eyes, the same expression (but not as dumb) that Neil had when

he talked about how he'd dreamed about playing football for Ohio State. Pongo's had a fiberglass monkey
squatting on the roof, with his ass right over the kitch-
en. They did make a pretty good hamburger, not as
good as Dick Larren at Philbin's Drug Store, but way
better than McDonald's.

Pongo's had very corny huge menus with photos of all
their food, and cartoons of that same monkey drawn on
and around the photos—hanging from the plates, climb-
ing the straws on milk shakes, sitting on a pile of fries,
whatever Michelson thought was funny. Darla claimed
that "They photographed it the way it comes off the grill.
We have people in the kitchen to shake the monkeys off
the food before the waitresses bring it out. No shit, I'm
not lying. Trust me, that kitchen has a lot more than one
monkey-shaker."

Browning and me took a booth, and he ordered the
salad, soup, and black coffee his doctor made him eat,
and I ordered my usual double bacon cheese half-pound
Pongo Kong burger, large fries, and shake. I held off on
onion rings because I was saving room for apple pie and
ice cream.

Darla scribbled it down. "You guys behave, I don't
want to have to call the cops."

Browning stared at her butt as she walked away.
"Cute."

"Very smart." Mentioning that might make him lose

interest before he started talking about her body.

The food came like lightning, and it went into me about that quick, too. While I wolfed, Browning told stories about Lightsburg back in the twenties and the thirties, and a few about my dad—all ones I'd heard before, but I was never going to point that out to Browning, because, well, shit, it was just nice to listen to them. And Darla kept his coffee cup filled, and every time she came by with the pot, he checked out the side view, getting to know more about how big her breasts were than a bra-fitter would.

He rambled on about how the town used to be very up-and-coming and going somewhere, but it just kind of sagged out of all its ambition thanks to Hoover and Roosevelt, and now it had slid so far down that the C&Es had taken over the churches, and Republicans had taken over the city council, and the goddam high school had goddam hippies and goddam niggers in it.

I swallowed really deep. "I really don't like that word, sir."

He lowered his voice. "I know I say *goddam* a lot but I didn't think I said *fuck*—"

"Uh, 'nigger,'" I said. "I don't like that word. It hurts people, okay? I don't mind—"

"Oh, for Christ's sweet sake. You sure *are* Doug Shoemaker's son. *And* Betty Shoemaker's."

"She likes being called Beth, now."

"Listen, bub, your old man was the best mayor the town ever had, did goddam more for it than any other goddam mayor we ever had, but he sure was a god . . . damn . . . *liberal*. And your mom was always right in there with him, even before he passed, you know, and she got more that way after he died."

I wanted to say *More what way?* or *How do you know what she was like?* or better yet *Well, if you mean not being a racist asshole then I guess I'm glad they were that way and I hope to fuck it's hereditary.* Something like that. I wish I'd said it, but I was full as a tick with food he'd bought, and that made me feel like a cowardly shit. But a well-fed, well-paid cowardly shit. Which is the sort of cowardly shit that keeps his mouth shut.

So he kept going. "I mean, do we have free speech in this country or don't we? I never worried about offending any goddam—" He stared at me like he'd just sat down naked on an electric fence. "Ah, now you've made me goddam self-conscious. Okay, I'll watch how I talk about Neee-groes." (He put about twenty *es* into it). "Just promise me you won't chain yourself to one at the counter here and start singing goddam 'We Shall Overcome.' Christ's sake, the way they brainwash you kids in school nowadays, nobody can talk to you about plain obvious facts anymore."

I still couldn't think of anything to say so I just sat there.

He gave me this big melodramatic sigh, like Harry Weaver did when he said he was "mourning the demise of liberty" six times every day in Honors Gov. "I gotta take a leak."

He stomped off to the men's room. I sat there hoping I hadn't given too much offense; I was sure I still had my job. Still, I didn't want to hurt his feelings any more than I already had, but I was sort-of-okay-friends with both the black kids in the high school and I didn't want him to say that word where they might hear it, since they knew he was my boss. Shit gets complicated a lot.

I mopped up the last melted goop of ice cream, caramel sauce, and pie crust between the tines of my fork, and licked it.

"I can put some papers on the floor, so you can lick the plate like you do at home." Darla scooped up the money from the table, setting her hand gently on my shoulder. "Hey, good job with the old bastard," she whispered. "If he lives to be a thousand or so you might get him civilized."

"For one horrible second I wished I had Gratz there to explain quote-don't-call to him."

"No shit. But thanks for being an influence. He's always better when you're here."

"What's he do when I'm not?"

"He doesn't just stare. He says stuff." She shrugged. "In front of you, it's just his eyes. Oh god, he's coming out of the bathroom and I'm bent over. See you in school tomorrow." She straightened—the uniform skirts Michelson made them wear were short, like 1969 short, and they had to wear heels, too, and you weren't hired at Pongo's if you weren't cute. No doubt Michelson, being a Lightsburg businessman, thought that was a really clever, original idea to improve sales.

Sure enough, when I glanced up at old Browning, he was still tracking Darla's butt. We got into his car without saying anything, and it was a block before he said, "So what were you chatting to the little blonde cutie about?"

"Oh, just school and stuff."

"She likes you, Karl, I can tell. You can probably get her, you know."

"I wasn't really looking to get anyone."

"I didn't mean for a girlfriend, bub. You wouldn't want a girl like that for a *girlfriend*. I mean she's not the type to keep her skirt down."

I thought about asking him if Rose Carson was the type to keep her skirt down, but I was afraid he'd tell me. So instead of being sarcastic, like I wanted to be, I said, "She's a friend . . . I don't know, I'm sorry if it seems like I'm really being touchy tonight."

"Yeah." He drove another block in silence before he said, "Seems to me like people weren't so touchy in the old days, but you know what? I think we were. There were people that would get all bent out of shape over a few hells or goddams, or wouldn't buy anything Jap-made because their brother got killed on Iwo Jima, or wouldn't listen to a radio station if it played nig-Negro music. Even when I was your age a lot of guys were goddam Boy Scouts who would have said 'Would you talk about your sister that way?'"

Browning wasn't the first pushy old fart to tell me that Darla was obviously a slut, and liked me, and I could fuck her if I tried. Hell, Mom had seen Darla and me having a pizza together in Pietro's—it was right after Darla's little brother Logan got taken away for good, after that time she told the cops she was going to blind him with Drano and they had to kick down the bathroom door to get him.

She was going through that hating-herself thing where she'd burn herself with cigarettes and cut bits of skin off, so I hung around till she promised me she wouldn't, which took till like three fucking thirty. (She lied anyway—her arms were all nicked the next time I saw her.)

When I got home, I barely got in the front door before Mom was trying to pump me for details. "How far did you get that little whore to go? You got it dipped yet, Karl?"

She was real drunk, kind of spinning around the living room in her big hippie skirt and singing "Karl got it di-ipped" over and over, that real annoying little kid melody that they use for calling each other sissies and stuff.

Then she knocked over the lamp by the front door, the one Dad and her had bought together one night when they were both pretty drunk. (If you'd seen this lamp, you'd know *how* drunk.) So she knocked it down and smashed glass everywhere, and cried about that and had to be comforted, and finally went back in her bedroom to sleep. I was up till like five cleaning up the broken glass.

This had been a lamp that improved the living room when it left, but I still had to replace it. I didn't want to have to walk across the living room in the dark every night and then have to check my shoes for catshit. So I had to buy a much nicer lamp than the one she broke or I'd never hear the end of it, and that wasn't cheap, I can tell you that.

I still got some fun out of the whole situation though. The next night, before I had time to get her another lamp, she was coming in wearing her Go-Get-Laids, and slipped on a pile of catshit, and landed on it butt first and got it all over the ass of her gypsy skirt. When she turned on the light, the guy she was with saw that big smelly brown smear on her skirt and got all sick and went home, instead of spending the night.

She was mad at the cats, screaming and swinging at them with the broom. I think that might have been when Softandgentle got her limp. The cats all ended up yowling and cowering under the furniture. After some more screaming, and breaking another lamp that I also had to replace, she got all blubbery, and started to beg her precious kitties to come out and comfort her. They, of course, stayed right where they were, especially since she still had that broom.

When I got in from McDonald's, I opened the door to the sight of my mother, sobbing, in front of the couch, on her knees with her face down by the floor, in her Go-Get-Laids and flappy-frilly blouse, cottage-cheesy white and lumpy old butt sticking halfway out of her panties way up in the air. She was still holding that broom, upright in front of her, and pleading with the pileup of cats under the couch; "Mommy's sorry, angels, Mommy's so sorry."

Those cats were not having any of it.

I made her set the broom down, and sit at a kitchen chair, and drink some chamomile tea, to which I added a healthy wallop of gin from my private stash behind the dryer. "They're right, this chamomile really does help someone sleep," I told her.

But nothing was going to stop her from telling me the whole story; it sounded like she wanted to make sure I didn't believe the cats. She put a lot of sobs into it so it took longer. This guy was a really special one, and she loved that skirt, which she had had to throw away. (Later on, I washed it for her—it was just catshit, it came out— and she started wearing it again as soon as she forgot.)

And what if the cats never forgave her?

I let her hang on me and cry a little, then sent her to take a shower. The cats felt safe once the bathroom door closed, and they were all over me, rubbing and begging for attention. So I set out some food to calm them down, and they were pretty much the same as always the next morning.

How good a son am I? I even refrained from laughing till I heard the shower running.

Then I laughed like a crazy bastard, sitting on that filthy floor, cats crawling all over me, bumping me with their heads and kneading with their paws.

"Beth's sorry, preciouses, Bethie is, please come out." *O Mighty Couch, I Bring You the Broom of Righteousness, Yield Up Your Cats.*

I guess if I was serious about my rule that you have to love any girl that cracks you up, I was stuck loving Mom.

Browning went on being creepy about Darla the whole way home. The truth was I was too fucked-up to ever have the confidence to try for her. Drunkenly groping Bonny—when she was drunk enough to pretend she didn't know I was doing it or got carried away—was as far as I'd gotten (and now that I never got drunk, that looked like that was over). Darla probably would know exactly what to do, and would expect me to do it. That scared the shit out of me.

As Browning drove me home, we gossiped a little about whether the minister at First Assembly of God was going to come out against voting for Paul's dad; it might matter because they had more real churchies and fewer C&Es than any other church in town. We worked through all the churches and how they voted, and shit that didn't matter shit, so that by the time he dropped me off, Browning and me were friends again. Somebody liked me, even if it was a dirty old man. At least it was a *straight* dirty old man.

I trotted up the steps. I might have as much as an hour before I'd have to start walking out to McDonald's.

A cat convention in the living room.

Six open cans of tuna, fresh from the store.

The little fuckers were jammed around each can, pounding it down. I yelled "Mom!" several times, just standing there, but she was already gone.

Besides something for the cats to share, she'd have bought herself an expensive blouse or a nice necklace. Very often she left some dumb present that I didn't like—a faggy Qiana shirt, a carved-leather belt, a record album with a guy on the front she thought was good-looking, something that I wouldn't like so she could tell me I ought to like it—on my bed upstairs. In the first hour after she got into one of my cans, she always was just crazy in love with everyone.

But after her little celebration, most of that money can was going into the cash register at Mister Peepers. She'd be buying rounds all night, hanging all over guys, being the center of everything. Then she'd come back here with Neil or some other guy she got off the rack at the Asshole Store, to get high and laid.

Fuck. Twice in two days. I could lose a month's worth every three months or so, like I had been since freshman year, but I couldn't fucking lose it every fucking two fucking days. Fuck fuck fuck. She couldn't keep doing this.

But if I could stop her I'd already have stopped her.

How could she steal that much of my fucking life?

I dragged my feet up the stairs, step by step. There were more money cans hidden in my room than anywhere else, so that was the place to start looking. I thought about just sitting down for a good cry.

Then I saw the great news, through the open door of my room. My dirty painter's pants were in a different corner.

The rest of the room was undisturbed, and there were no little gifts to me like that time she left me a Fleetwood Mac album on my bed because she thought Mick looked like a good lay. She'd just gotten the twenty from my painter's pants, and everything else was safe.

I'd probably never been happier to lose three hours of my life. My spirits rising, I checked in the pockets of the painter's pants and found nothing but lint, then ran around the house like a crazy bastard for like ten minutes, careful not to go too near any of my stashes, as if just looking at one might give it away.

Holy fucking lucky Jesus. It had worked out okay. All she'd taken was that twenty. I went back upstairs almost cheerful.

I realized that she had left my door open, so a fresh pile of catshit lay in the middle of my bed. I cleaned that up and went downstairs.

I still missed that twenty, and I was still mad that I had to live like this. But I took a deep breath, and my back relaxed, and I stopped seeing the world down a blood-red tube. I rubbed my tear-streaked face.

It occurred to me that accidents happened to Mom's cats all the time. She wouldn't take them to the vet because the vet used "chemicals and ucky ucky modern medicine"—and cost money. She wouldn't get them spayed or neutered at the Gist County Humane Society because "kitties need to be free and the world needs lots of kitties and flowers and sunshine"—and because GCHS charged three bucks a cat, the price of a pitcher. She wouldn't do anything to keep them from roaming. So since the cats had come into our lives—the same week, come to admit it, that I'd started drinking and she'd given up on being a mother, which I knew from the date of the first IOU in my book was May 17, 1970—I'd buried thirty-three of them, and maybe another ten had vanished.

Didn't seem like it would be such a bad idea to sort

of select the next one I'd be burying, instead of leaving it to chance.

It felt weird to think about it. The cats actually liked and trusted me more than they did Mom, because I didn't lose it and scream and hit them, and sometimes I fed them. So I knew if I found the bedshitter, I'd have no problem taking him off somewhere to kill him. And Mom never could stand to look at the bodies, so all I'd have to do would be bring the bedshitter back quietly and just plant cat number thirty-four with all the others.

And whatever I did would be quicker and gentler than a coon or a dog. Maybe I could just get Danny, who hunted birds every fall, to shoot the bedshitter out in a field; then it would look completely innocent.

I wasn't sure whether I was thinking about this because I wanted my bed clean, or because I wanted to get even with Mom for taking that twenty. Browning had been proud of me, and you should've seen how nice I soldered those joints.

But come to admit it, it was my fault, too. I'd just left that twenty right there in my pants pockets with my pants out in plain sight, and I knew good and well that Mom went through the pockets of everything, all the time. She had my two little-kid sport coats, from back when we used to go to First United Methodist, hanging in the guest room closet—souvenirs or something—and last year I'd caught her going through *their* pockets, I guess looking for some long-forgotten offering envelope.

So I should have hid that twenty, put it in a stash or changed it to the pocket of my fresh jeans. Losing it was completely my fault; thanks to me getting stupid and being in a hurry, Mom was sitting in Mister Peepers. Some guy in sales (big-lapelled suit, wide blue tie, big teeth yellowed by tobacco and coffee) was nodding and laughing that big *uff uff uff* laugh they do.

She'd be telling him that Watergate was all just part of the plan, the Air Force had to get rid of Nixon because after Cambodia he'd become so infested with evil that his vibrations were keeping the saucer people from being able to land, and once they got him out of the White House, the saucer people could come down and establish universal peace. The sales guy would be nodding and talking about how interesting her ideas were, and what a strong smart independent woman she was, and looking at her breasts and trying to get up the nerve to put his hand on her leg.

Yeah, I guess I did mostly want to find that cat and kill it to get some revenge on Mom, but that wouldn't bring my twenty back. It would make my bed cleaner, of course, but I could do something about that right now.

I went back upstairs, stripped the bed, and took my bedding down to wash. I was still pretty pissed off at Mom. I guess if I'd still been going to Alateen, Danny and Squid would've ridden my ass pretty hard about having enabled her.

By the time I moved the bedclothes from the washer to the dryer, and changed into my McDorksuit, I had the trig and French done, and I had scribbled *freedom* into every blank where it seemed to fit for honors gov, and *free enterprise* into the rest.

Christ, I wished I still had that twenty.

In Their Backseats or at McDonald's,
the Madmen Sleep Tonight

I GUESS IF there was really a low spot in my life it wasn't so much when Dad died as when Mom threw that party. It was the start of booze and cats, and the point where I stopped being able to keep the house all the way nice. Also although by that time, my old Mom was mostly gone, replaced by Flying Saucer Lady, Beth with the Boots, or Neil's Old Lady, somehow that party was like the wake for the mother I'd grown up with.

I don't exactly mean Mom threw a party because Dad was dead. It was more that because Dad was dead, Mom *could* throw the party.

The date on the first IOU pasted into my account book is May 17, 1970. Eighth grade was about over, which was fine with me, since eighth grade stank. Actually that spring was when I'd just gotten comfortable enough with talking dirty to say eighth grade *fucking* stank.

I came home from Sunday afternoon track practice and Mom was running around setting out cereal bowls of potato chips and Fritos, and big bowls of that sloppy red tomato sauce that you got in the El Paso cans. Although I'd just walked two miles home on a warm, sunny day, after running a few miles, there wasn't going to be a shower because the bathtub was full of ice and bottles of beer.

I'd slept over at Paul's on Saturday night, the night before, too, sitting up with Paul and Dennis, watching Houlihan and Big Chuck, two dumb guys that showed stupid old movies and made fun of them. I had stayed to dinner after Mr. Knauss had taken us all into Columbus to see the Jets play—Dad and me were Mud Hen fans, but this was going to be the Jets' last season in Columbus, and Mr. Knauss, a Jets fan forever, had grabbed up a lot of tickets and was always taking his kids' friends along. Between the Jets, Houlihan and Big Chuck, and track, I hadn't actually had a shower since Friday night.

Looked like I was just really going to stink. I'd already learned not to argue about weird shit like a bathtub full of ice and beer.

Mom already looked real different than she had when Dad was alive. Her hair wasn't long yet, but instead of the ash-blonde pageboy, she now had an untidy mop of hooker-blonde yellow hair; she looked sort of like a dandelion smoking a cigarette.

Just now she was in a tie-dyed halter top that she'd bought the week before, and a lot of clunky jewelry, and very low tight jeans. It was like she was going to a costume party as Darla.

She had a cigarette burning in her mouth and she was sticking up posters she's gotten from Judy—Hendrix and some old Beatles and Simon and Garfunkel posters, the kind that came inside the album cover, with these big gross fold lines. They looked shabby as all hell just stuck to the wall with thumbtacks.

I went and got the level so that I could at least get all the posters straight, but she wouldn't let me fix them. She said that worrying about them hanging straight was fascist. "Honestly, Karl, you're more like Doug every day." The way she said it, Dad's name was something like "cocksucker" or "Nixon."

My eyes stung a little, I think because she was standing too close to me with the cigarette and kind of yelling, really, and all of a sudden she was holding me, hanging on to me, and saying, "I'm sorry, sorry, sorry, Tiger Sweetie, that was such a mean thing to say to you. Sorry."

She didn't hug me very often anymore, usually only in front of her new friends from the bar, to show off what a good mother she was. They were always telling me that Mom was a great mother and a fabulous woman and really coming into her own now . . . (after that "now," I could hear them thinking . . . *that your father is dead*). They all thought she was a "super super lady."

This time there was no one around, but she hugged me anyway. "Tiger, I have to tell you about something and give you something."

Poor dumb stupid little eighth-grade me, when she said she was going to "give me something," I still thought she meant something good.

She handed me a piece of typewriter paper, neatly lettered in her precise handwriting. I looked down and read, *May 17, 1970. From Elizabeth (Beth) Shoemaker to Karl Shoemaker. I.O.U. $129.38.*

"It's an IOU," she explained. "I took the money out of your account yesterday, because the bank was open, and I needed to do the shopping on Saturday, while the liquor store was open, to get ready for tonight."

All I could think to ask was, "What's tonight?"

"Well, it's kind of my coming out, my emergence, you know, as a free woman. It's been seven months since your father made the transition, *exactly* seven, and seven is a very powerful number. So I wanted to do something about that and all, anyway. And then, too, it's been two weeks since the terrible thing at Kent State with all those children killed. We just need somewhere to get together and talk and share some feelings, kind of create a safe space where we could talk about Kent State and Cambodia.

And, well, besides, this is sort of my coming-out party, to celebrate really being who I am."

I had no idea what to say.

Then for just a second she was almost her old self. "Tiger, I didn't have the money. I can give you some out of—well, not my next paycheck, but the paycheck after that, and then it shouldn't be long before I've paid it all back. I'm sorry, I know it's your money, sweetie, but I need this party. You know you never spend your money on anything, it's not like you'll miss it before I pay it back."

I just stood there, so confused I wanted to slap myself. My pathetic little savings account had been home to my birthday money; my first paycheck from my paper route, because Dad made a big point about what a great thing it was to save the first money you ever earned; some snow-shoveling money I had left over; some garden-spading and yard-work money, which I'd just started to get about a month ago; and a couple school prizes. I felt like I remembered every deposit there had ever been, and the much less frequent withdrawals.

It was childish of me to feel that it wouldn't be the same when she put the money back, like a little kid worrying about having the exact same dollar bill Grandpa gave him.

The faces weren't new to me. I had met most of Mom's bar crowd before. In Lightsburg, everyone knew everyone, and she'd been bringing some of them around the house a lot. The main thing I noticed was that all of them, men and women, had hair past their shoulders. (Dad had worn a crew cut all his life.)

They spilled a lot of wine and beer on the wall-to-wall shag carpeting, and for a while I tried to get it cleaned up quick with paper towels, but Mom told me not to, that I was embarrassing her, and handed me a beer and told me I could try my first one. I guess I was supposed to feel like a man and stuff. It didn't taste like much of anything. Even later on, when I was drinking all the time, I never liked beer much.

Then Neil showed me how to do boilermakers, and he made me do two to "make sure the little guy gets it right." Whiskey was definitely better than beer, at least by comparison, not much worse than cough syrup.

I didn't have much body weight then, and I'd had a bunch of drinks in less than an hour. So I was real drunk, which at least made the time pass faster; I sat on one end of the couch and watched a lady I didn't know set down her cigarette onto the carpet and grind it out with her boot heel. I wished all these people would go home and that Mom would come back from the bedroom, where she'd gone with Neil.

Judy sat beside me and asked me how I was doing and about school and shit, and she seemed to think everything I said was really funny. She wandered away and I watched people get drunker and smoke pot.

I sort of understood why they drank, though, because with the drinks in me, it all went by faster and didn't hurt as much to watch those people make a mess.

Next morning I woke up on the couch. Everyone was gone except Neil, who was in the bedroom with my mother. I felt like I had been poisoned: head aching, sick to my stomach, sore in every muscle. I puked in the toilet, which helped, except that I realized I might have been the most accurate but I sure hadn't been first. I was the first one to flush, though. I wanted a shower or bath but the tub was full of empties and cigarette butts and mostly-melted ice.

I started picking up empties and putting them in the box to take back to the store, dumping ashtrays in the trash, piling glasses in soapy water in the sink for washing, the usual after-party stuff I realize now, but at the time it was new to me. Red wine splashes and cigarette burns were everywhere in the beige shag carpet. A year ago, when Dad and me had put it in, he'd been so fussy about getting it lined up right—too sick to do it himself but watching me all the time, making me try again when I didn't get it right.

Mom had stood by telling him not to pick on me, I was only a boy and all this didn't matter, while I scuttled around getting the pad underneath just so, and then measuring and cutting and placing. But Dad had told me when it was all over that I'd done a good job, and even

Mom had said that after a while, when she forgot to be mad at him about "making" me do it.

The doorbell rang, and I found Judy on the front porch, a big cardboard box at her feet. "Hey, little guy, how was your first drunk?" she asked.

"I'm kinda sick."

"You just need practice." She lifted the cardboard box and carried it into the house, setting it down in the middle of the living room rug. Mom, wearing just an old T-shirt of Dad's, and Neil, wearing sweatpants, a hair-covered beer gut, and a vacant expression, were staggering out of the bedroom. "Morning, sleepyheads!" Judy said. "Look what I have for everyone!"

She opened the box and turned it gently on its side, and eight kittens came tumbling out. Mom sat down to play with them on the living room floor, and Judy joined her, and the two of them talked baby talk for the next hour or so. With no idea that the kittens would be staying, and turning into cats, and breeding, I thought they were cute, myself.

After he realized Mom and Judy weren't going to give him more dope or have sex with him, Neil left. I washed some dishes to have a clean bowl, but when Mom saw me getting out the box of Cheerios, she said she had some money left over so she took Judy and me out for pizza to celebrate her party, her coming out, and her new kittens. It was my money, but I couldn't see a way to ask her to at least give back what she hadn't spent, so I went along. The pizza tasted like shit and the waiter asked me why I wasn't in school.

Later that day when I was putting laundry together— as long as I'd missed school and track practice I might as well see if I could get the house clean, I thought—I found the IOU in my pants pocket. I pinned the IOU on the bulletin board in my room.

I don't know if Mom ever saw it or took any hint from it. By Christmastime, there was a column of IOUs down one side of the bulletin board, mostly from when she'd borrowed yard-work or paper-route money, and another one from the second time she'd cleaned out my savings account. She hadn't asked that time, either.

That was for her Halloween party. On the first of November I saw the electric bill in the mail, opened it, and saw she hadn't paid for two months, though I'd given her money for it. So I took some money I'd just gotten for turning over a compost pile, put it in a coffee can, and stuck it into the space behind the World Book in the bookcase Dad had built.

About a week before Christmas, I had a couple spare dollars and was getting a paperback in Philbin's when I noticed a little stack of account books. I bought myself one.

That night, stapling the IOUs in next to where I'd recorded them, I decided she owed me for the account book ($0.87 with tax), too, and wrote that in as an entry:

December 17, 1970. For some reason I remember trying to be real quiet with the stapler, so Mom wouldn't hear me.

For some reason tonight while I was cleaning out Mc-Donald's, I kept thinking about that first party, which always got me what Mom called "all full of angry energy," so I burned that energy on work and got done even faster than usual. I was done with everything but the window forty minutes before Harris and Tierden were due to hit the puddle—to my deep disgust, I even rechecked all my homework and reviewed all the reading; it made me feel like a suck-up buttlicker, but I was going to be prepared in class tomorrow.

At least I had *The Three Stigmata* along, so I read that in the back until the pathetic *chungk-splutch*! hit the window—it hadn't rained in days, and the puddle was nearly empty. I went out, hosed the walk and washed the window, and called that good.

They'd been half an hour early. Times must be dull everywhere. Still a long while to clock-out.

With a start, I woke up and sat upright. The clock said twenty minutes till clock-out—

Thumping on the window.

My first thought was that it was Bobby Harris being a jackass and I needed to wake up just a tiny bit more and go outside and kick his pathetic squishy pink pudge-boy frog-face down his throat and out his ass. I sat up and saw Marti. I must've looked like a real duh with my hair all cowlicky and mouth hanging open, but she wasn't laughing.

I opened the door; the parking lot smelled like an open grave, the first breath of cold sludgy Ohio fall.

"I know it's close to time for you to leave but I need a friend real bad." She didn't look at me when she said that.

"Come in, goddammit, of course," I said. "I just woke up, fell asleep over my goddam book." *Goddammit,* I thought, *I am sounding just like goddam Browning.*

"I know, I woke you up."

"I didn't even realize that was what woke me. Food, coffee, anything? I still haven't thrown anything out."

"Yes, please, everything." She sat down at the table where my book was, slumped forward, hands knotting in front of her knees. Her nail polish was all scragged up, and she'd chewed a couple of nails enough to make them bleed. "I'm locked out till Mother gets home, and it was way too damp and cold to sleep in the car, and . . . aw, shit, Karl, I need company." She rubbed her wet face on the back of her hand; I gave her some napkins.

I set the remaining burgers and big pile of room-temperature dried-out fries down in front of her. "Well, I could use some company, too, Marti. It's been kind of an up-and-down day."

"Yeah. Guess there's a lot of it going around. Thanks

for the food. I got home and Dad started right in screaming at me, and Mother was already gone off with your
mother, and . . . well, basically, I just got screamed at
for some hours, and when he was done with that, finally
hoarse I think, he started in crying about it all, and begging me to forgive him. After enough of that I just fuckin'
cruised. I hate the 'I'm a bad Dad' phase even more than
I hate the screaming and yelling . . ." She stopped for
breath and was staring down at her burger.

"Did you get anything to eat?" I asked, feeling like a
mom, though sure as shit not like mine.

She shook her head. "He started the second I walked
in, so nobody made dinner—"

"Eat, Marti. Just eat." As skinny as she was I figured
she probably didn't have any reserves.

"I'll be quick so you can leave on time." She crammed
a third of a burger into her mouth.

"Slow down, and enjoy that stuff if it's possible. Kathy
doesn't care what time I leave, only what time I clock out,
and she knows sometimes I sleep here when I'm locked
out, or have friends over. Everything's cool as long as I
clock out on time."

She swallowed that big bite she'd rammed in, and
said, "Okay. Jeez, I'm so hungry, this stuff is good."

"Ketchup for your fries, miss? I can recommend it—
it's my main source of vitamin C."

She smiled. "Sure. What does Kathy do if you clock
out late?"

"Well, a couple times I've fallen asleep and done it, and gotten off with a warning. Eventually, though, if I made a habit of it, I'd disappear in the middle of the night, and never be seen again, and the only clues the police would have would be a few orange hairs and some enormous shoe prints. But for a few weeks afterward, all over the country, the Quarter Pounders would taste just a little bit more like Lightsburg, Ohio."

She smiled, then looked at me more closely. "Fuck, Karl, you look worse than I do."

"Thanks, I try. Today bounced me all over the place." I mopped my face with a couple of McNapkins and tossed them in the McTrash. "I guess I don't really want to talk about it."

"'Kay." She started into a Quarter Pounder and chewed slowly. "I hate to admit how good this tastes. Sorry to be keeping you up."

"You're not. You did me a favor by waking me up." I looked at the clock; close enough not to lose any pay, so I grabbed my time card from its rack on the wall, and clocked out. "I sometimes sleep here when I get locked out. I just have to get up by three forty-five, when Pancake Pete comes in."

"So we could sleep for like two hours and forty minutes." She reached into her purse and pulled out one of those little fold-down travel alarm clocks, the ones that look like a plastic clam when they're folded down. She saw me glance at that and said, "I always have one of these in my purse because I get locked out a lot."

"It's a good idea. If I had a purse I'd carry one too."

She smiled like we'd traded the secret handshake. "Great. Five more minutes while I swallow more food?"

"Ten if you like. I wasn't going to get much sleep tonight anyway." I grabbed a cheeseburger just to be sociable.

"Karl, are all the Madmen short of sleep?"

"Well, you and me aren't the only ones. Bonny gets to sleep, mostly, because her household is pretty normal, if you don't count that she's the parent and she's blind drunk a lot of nights. Cheryl and her sister, Paul and his sister, Squid and the two younger kids, they have to hide out now and then because it gets dangerous at home. Danny's just a plain old all-American farm boy with a father drinking away the farm. Mostly he just cries because he's exhausted and picked on all the time, but so far he's never been locked out—his dad wouldn't do that because he needs Danny to do the early morning chores, since he's always too hung over himself. So some are better off than us, some worse, I guess."

"Where does a locked-out kid sleep in this town? The last places we lived were warm and dry at night so I'd just sleep in my backseat—I even have toothpaste and toothbrush in the glove compartment."

"Well, you can sleep here if I'm working. Get here before one, Sunday through Thursday nights. Paul can hide you in his basement sometimes, if you sneak in and stay quiet. Bonny or Darla are home alone a lot and they'll let you have a couch, but you have to catch Darla before she leaves Pongo's at nine, because she spends a lot of time over in Vinville with college students. Bonny goes home real early and you do have to put up with little kids who are starved for attention. And I'd stay the hell away from Cheryl's if you're a girl; she's got a real scary grandfather, you'll hear about him in therapy meetings."

"Which you're planning not to be at."

"Well, you know, except for you it's all gonna be reruns, and you already told me your story." I hoped goofing would get her off the subject.

She looked more serious than I wanted her to, but all she said was, "I guess. I still think you're an idiot, even if you're a great idiot to have for a friend. Where do normal kids sleep when they're locked out?"

"I guess I'll find out. Anyway, in a real crisis, especially if you get thrown out real late, the Carrellsen Hotel lobby is okay if it's cold—the clerks will usually let you sleep in an armchair, and sometimes if you have a few bucks and they're not full up they'll give you a break on a room. There's three college guys that are night clerks there—Greg and Don are reasonably cool, Jack's the best one for letting you have a room if he's got one. If you look in the Carrellsen and see a guy with gray hair behind the desk, it's Roy, so *don't* go in. You'll wake up with his hands on you—boy or girl, in the lobby or in a room, Roy doesn't care. On the other hand if you see that the desk clerk is a lady with a dyed-black beehive and Bozo make-up, go right in, because it's Marilyn, and she's the best. She'll almost always give you a room if she's got one, even if you don't have a dime; she's a real churchy but the good generous kind. But she's only at the Carrellsen on Sunday nights.

"If you get locked out early and you don't mind singing and praying a lot before you get your soup and bed, there's the Salvation Army on Wilbur Avenue, but they lock up real early, at eight thirty, and if you're a guy you have to not mind what a room full of winos smells like, and if you're a girl they put you in with the moms with little kids, which is pretty noisy."

"And this place is only good till three forty-five?"

"Kind of. Pancake Pete wouldn't care and he'd never nark anyone out, but he likes to sing while he works, and he tends to get stuck on 'Old McDonald Had a Farm' or 'Polly Wolly Doodle All the Day,' and he goes pretty loud and long. And hell if I'm going to complain and make him be quiet in the best part of his day. Mom always says never fuck with anybody else's bliss, you know?"

We set her little alarm clock for 3:40 and stretched out on the benches, with our heads together and feet pointed in opposite directions. I was just about to nod off when Marti said, "Hey, your friend Paul?"

"Yeah?"

"Is he gay?"

"I don't know if *he* knows what he is. He gets crushes on girls all the time. Why?"

"He asked me to go to the movies with him on Saturday, that rep cinema next to the drugstore where you're going to be working. *Casablanca* and *The Maltese Falcon.* And I said yes, and then I got to worrying—I was afraid my very first date was going to be with a gay guy. Don't tell Paul I asked!"

"I'm not as dumb as I look, Marti. I'm sure six assholes already told you what he does up in Toledo, right?"

"Yeah. Is it true?"

"Sometimes. Not as often as people make out like he does. I wouldn't worry. Him and me might not be getting along right now, but he's still the best guy in the world."

"'Kay." She squirmed a bit to get comfortable. I felt her slip away into sleep, her head lolling over. I watched the little dark bands run around one aging fluorescent tube, overhead, and silently recited Dad's list of household chores until I drifted off.

PART THREE

(Friday, September 7, 1973)

That, Son, Was the Lone Madman

MARTI AND ME woke up with her alarm. We staggered around, throwing away the last couple soggy burgers and dried-out fries, splashed water on our faces in the bathrooms, and looked at each other and sighed. I wiped down where our shoes had been on the benches.

Pancake Pete tapped at the door, so I went over and opened it for him. He came in laughing and gave me a big hug. He always did that.

"Pete," I said, "this is Marti."

"Hi, Marti! Can I hug you?"

"Sure!" So they hugged.

Special Ed had taught him to ask. I understood why, but I thought it was kind of sad that they had to teach him that.

"Now we're friends," Pete said happily. "You have a good day okay?"

"Okay, Pete. Have a good day yourself."

As Marti started her car, I said, "There are times when I think it must be great to enjoy things as much as Pete does."

"I'm always a little nervous around retarded people," Marti said. "My dad says horrible things about them."

"Well, I should probably warn you I've set you up. Now whenever you run into Pete around town, he's going to shout 'Hi, Marti' and wave at you."

"I can deal. I'll wave back and say 'Hi, Pete,' and I bet that'll work. I hope he does it in front of Dad. If he does *I'll* hug *him*." She turned the corner and accelerated into the dark, her headlights reaching just a little way into the shadows under the big old trees. "Do you hate your mom?"

"Sometimes. I try not to. I mean it's not like I can trade her in and get another one." I shrugged. "I guess I can feel sorry for her. She just wants people to like her and think she's cool. I guess I can't really hate her." Then it seemed polite to ask, "Do you hate yours?"

"About as much as I hate my dad."

Neither of us said anything else as we passed through the dark, silent streets just before 4 A.M. When Marti pulled up in front of my house, she said, "See you in school, try not to over-normal it, okay?"

"See you," I said. "No being a genius for you, either."

I felt like we should have shaken hands or something but I just got out of the car in the dark.

Mom must have been mad at me when she came home, and locked the front and back doors, so I got in through the front room window. I peeked and it looked like someone was in the bed with her in her room, so I slipped upstairs, undressed quick, and got into bed; it was 4:02.

My eyes slapped open at 7:15. Something pushed on my chest, and it smelled like Charlie the Tuna was frenching me. Once again, Hairball had managed to work the doorknob—he did that now and then, though he didn't consistently remember how—and now he rested like a hairy Buick on my chest, muzzle against my cheek and paws extending on either side of my face, purring in his sleep.

Gently, I bench-pressed him off my chest. He said something like "qurgle-qurooph," yawned, stretched, and padded away like a surly orange mop.

I trotted down the stairs for a shower, taking a couple extra minutes for a second lather. Lack of sleep crawled around in the back of my head, scraping on the back of my eyeballs, drooling down into puddles of weariness on top of my spine, waiting to knock me unconscious during trig or honors gov. The extremely normal dork in the mirror had Madman-style dark circles under his eyes.

I glanced at my watch. *Damn.* I needed to make it to

school early to get that note from Gratz, but I didn't want to miss any of my Friday ritual. *Butt in gear, right now.*

I finished dressing in a hurry, made sure my door was closed tight, and bounced down the stairs like an amped-up kangaroo.

"Tiger Sweetie?"

"Gotta run, Mom, late."

She lurched into the living room from the bedroom, looking like a housecoat under a haystack. "Are you going to go straight from school to Philbin's?"

"Yeah, I think I'll have to."

"Ucky ucky. You work too much. You should give yourself time to be a kid, it's the best time you're ever going to have. Anyway, will you be around tomorrow?"

"Pretty busy, but Sunday I'll be around most of the day, I think."

"Okay, good." She walked slowly toward me. I wanted to break and run. I could feel the clock ticking away on my Friday morning.

She pressed her soft mouth against my cheek; I'd have to scrub, as soon as I was out of her sight, because that frosted baby pink lipstick she wore stuck like a coat of paint. *Actually it pretty much is a coat of paint,* I thought, so I cheered myself up by thinking, *okay, so I'll say it sticks like napalm to a baby.*

"Listen, Tiger, I just wanted to say . . . I'm really sorry about that twenty. Put it on my tab of IOUs, 'kay? But something—some*body*—wonderful happened while I was out last night. This might be the first man I've brought home that I want you to meet, *really* want you to meet. 'Kay?"

"All right, Mom, Sunday if you want, bring him around and I'll make sure he's okay, and if he's not okay, I'll bop him on the head and put him in the river with the others." She had a new "first man she *really* wanted me to meet" about every two months. They were always more trouble, one way or another, than the ones she just brought home to fuck.

"Oh, you! Have a good day, Tiger Sweetie." She kissed my cheek again. "The glow of the moon bathes your soul because you are a special child of the universe." Her breath wasn't quite as bad as it usually was in the morning.

Old Wilson waved as I shot by his gate. "You keep running like that, Karl, you're gonna give yourself a heart attack," he burbled, through the snot-gorged remains of his lungs.

I ran backwards a few steps and waved back at him. He went off into a coughing fit and I was halfway down the block, probably, before he got enough air to cough up a looger and say, "Goddam doctors."

I spit on my handkerchief and wiped where Mom had planted that kiss on me, checking the pink smear on the cloth and wishing I had a mirror. After the third spit-and-rub nothing more came off. I picked up the pace a little.

By the bank clock at the corner of Church Street, I needed to haul ass, even if I was kind of wasting my morning shower; I wanted to have all my time made up before I got to Philbin's, since breakfast there on Fridays was one of the high points of my week, usually, and this was looking to be a week that would need a high point.

It felt good, before the hot wet air crawled over the town and smothered it, to be running flat out like a crazy bastard with the street to myself. The old trees in the strip between the sidewalk and the street arched over, big deep green leaves not even started to turn yet, and I ran east up Buchanan Street, toward the red ball of the sun coming up between the twin spires of St. Iggy's, staining the street in front of me with the blood-colored glow that seemed to freeze under the deep purples of the thunderheads low overhead. Already the air felt heavy and wet. My legs and lungs warmed to the job, and I flew down the street.

I walked into Philbin's dead on time. Only two booths occupied, no one at the counter—the balled-up blue clouds mashing down over the town must have pinned people into their homes and cars this morning. Dick leaned out of the kitchen and said, "Nobody's ahead of you, Karl, want the usual?"

"Great, sure."

Angie returned from a booth she had been waiting. "I don't know how to break the news to you, but you look awful."

"Eahh. I had a little trouble getting sleep," I said. "I'll get it back Sunday. No biggie."

Dick whomped up my Farmer's Special, a huge skillet full of bacon, potatoes, mixed vegetables, gravy, Amish pepper sausage, Amish baby Swiss, and eggs; Philbin used to claim that he was the major cash income source for six Amishmen. Dick would start it in the skillet with the bacon on the bottom and some of his white pork chop gravy on top, and then when it was sizzling he'd dump it upside down, leaving the skillet over it, onto the hot grill. By the time he lifted the hot skillet off with a pair of channel-locks, and scraped the stuff onto a plate, you had pure ambrosia.

As usual Dick made my Farmer's Special big enough for two farmers, but I managed to find someplace to tuck it in. It came with a big glass of OJ, and coffee, and to make sure you didn't leave hungry they threw in a chocolate frosted cake doughnut. I inhaled all that in about twenty minutes, reading a few pages of *Three Stigmata*. Maybe if I reread it sometime in the next couple weeks, I'd be able to fake understanding it.

"Where's your dad?" I asked Angie. "Resting up for tonight?"

"No, the idiot supplier sent over the wrong stuff, instead of the heart medicine that a third of this town full of geezers is on. Dad *could* just let them send it over by courier car, besides he's got enough to cover twice the usual demand till Monday anyway, but now he doesn't trust 'em, so he's driving to Toledo to do the exchange in person. He was stomping around and yelling that people's lives depended on that stuff. I can never decide whether I'm proud of the old poop or embarrassed to death."

"Can I quote you on that?"

"He'll never believe I said anything as nice as 'old poop.'"

"Actually I'm supposed to tell you that you should give Kathy a call. Some kind of news."

"Cool. Maybe she's finally pregnant. We're hoping that'll make Dad stop being such a shithead." She glanced around; everyone looked okay. "Cover for me, will you? I'd like to call her right away."

I nodded through a mouthful of Farmer's Special.

Caught up with the orders, Dick leaned out of the kitchen. "Hey, you look a little sad, and you've been kind of quiet."

"Just a lot on my mind."

"One day at a time, bro."

"Yeah, well. See you at meeting tomorrow?"

"Never miss."

Angie came back shaking her head; whatever it was, she wasn't about to be an aunt. I washed the last of the doughnut down with the last gulp of coffee, picked up my bag, laid some singles and change on the counter, said good-bye to Angie and Dick, and was off like as much of a shot as you can be when you've swallowed your own weight in breakfast.

Now the early sun had vanished. Growling distant thunder came from the almost-black thunderheads that darkened the deep reds and yellows of the closed, blind brick storefronts to bare tints in the gray. I hurried toward the school bus stop at Pierce.

A blinding *crack-bang!* tore across the sky like God's photo flash, and black lines of rain came racing up the road after me, like the teeth of a mile-high comb. The bus stop was a block away and I sure as hell wasn't running unless I wanted to puke.

A hearse pulled up beside me and a familiar voice said, "Mister Shoemaker, would you rather arrive at school embarrassed, or soaked like a cat in a sack?"

"Embarrassed," I said. "I don't need so many towels to get that off."

I got in just as the first big drops spatted onto my hair and neck, and we hadn't gone ten yards before, instead of a hearse, Browning needed a submarine. "Well," Browning said, "now that was timing. How are you this morning?"

"Oh, exhausted, my life's insane, everybody hates me, and I've decided to renounce Jesus and sell drugs."

We stopped at a light, and two sophomore girls I didn't know ran across the street; their thin shirts were soaked and it was a hell of a good show. "Now tell me that doesn't catch your attention, Karl. You just get hold of those nice big—"

"Uh," I said. "Can we talk about something else?"

"We can, but we can't find a subject that's more interesting. But sure, a-course, suit yourself."

We'd covered another block when we overtook someone running, books held over the head, long hair swinging soggy wet to midback, and low tight jeans seeming to be sprayed on. "Oh, lord God I like driving by the high school in this weather," Browning said.

"You like that butt and hair?" I asked.

"Oh, that sweet little baby—"

"How would you like to have that around the shop all day?" I asked. "I could probably, you know, arrange it."

Browning's breath caught. "You mean—"

"Sure, what the hell, Mister Browning, Larry needs a job."

"That was a *boy*?"

"It's more apparent in the locker room."

We turned again, through a big puddle, and he said, "And people wonder why our country's falling to hell."

I kinda thought I'd teased the old turd enough, lately, so I just said, "Whatever you say, sir."

"No!" he said. "No, no, no, no. *Not* whatever I say.

That's the thing that's wrecking this country. People just going along to be nice. People not standing up for what's right. We used to be a nation that was proud of its dissenters and now we're a whole country of suck-up chickenshits."

I figured if I argued he'd yell at me for being wrong, and if I agreed he'd yell at me for being a suck-up chickenshit, so I just dummied up and enjoyed being out of that cold downpour.

The ride meant I was twenty minutes early, plenty of time to collect my No Ticket This Year letter from Gratz.

Paul was leaning up against my locker, looking at me but not talking. For some weird reason, for just an instant, I thought he might be about to beat me up and take my lunch money, the way old Al used to before I hit him with the bat.

After a long, long second, I said, "Hi."

He looked off to the side. "We ought to talk or something."

"Yeah, we ought to. Are you mad at me?"

"No, not exactly." He paused. "Well, yeah, but it's not exactly your fault. Not exactly. I mean like you couldn't know."

"This isn't making a lot of sense."

He shrugged, meaning it didn't matter whether it

made sense or not, I guess. "Look, you're still my friend but I can't really hang out with you for a while, 'cause it just won't work with what I'm trying to do. Okay?" He was looking at the floor like he was ashamed.

I felt like he'd just punched me in the stomach. "What's wrong with me?" I asked. I thought I might cry.

"Nothing. Nothing wrong with you. Or with me. I just need to kind of get away from the therapy group for a while. You know how we talked about that off and on for years, being tired of it, you know? We talked a lot about that this summer."

Come to admit it, we had. "Yeah, so?"

He raised his chin a little and looked at me like I might hit him. "So I don't want to get the ticket this year."

It clicked. "You don't want to be in the Madman Underground anymore, either!"

I was about to confess that that was the reason I'd been trying to avoid *him*, until *his* avoiding *me* had hurt my feelings, but he grabbed my lapels. "Jesus fucking Christ fuck me up the butt, Karl, you're such a *baby*. Grow up. It's a therapy group, okay? A *therapy* group. Where they put weird loser kids. We don't have some kind of mystical magical Madman mystique. It's not the club where all the geeks get to be special. What it is, is where fucked-up kids go." His twisted, awkward hands pushed hard on my sternum.

Like my body took over on its own, I punched low and

got him in the stomach. "Great," I said. "I'm gonna be fucking normal too. So don't fuck around with me, faggot. I'm tired of you crying on my shoulder and if you're trying to queer me it ain't gonna work."

He was doubled over and breathing hard; I was pretty strong, he was small, and he hadn't expected it. "How normal do you want me to be?" I whispered. "Can't get more normal than beating up a queer, can I?" I couldn't believe what was coming out of my mouth.

He looked up like he'd been poisoned, and I knew he was about to cry and I was about to scream at him.

He made himself stand straight up, which must have hurt. He turned and stalked away in his funny *I'm-mad* stiff-legged strut. *I guess he has a right to be mad,* I thought, and just like that, right as I thought that, I became aware of kids whispering "Psycho," and it was like a red fog just switched off, leaving me standing in an ordinary hallway. At least twenty kids were staring at me. Great. A couple of them were Goody Two-shoes that would nark me out.

I opened my locker and yanked out my books with shaking hands and my eyes full of tears. I still had plenty of time to get to class before anyone else, and to meet with Gratz, and all that, but instead of going to class I went into the boys' restroom, locked myself into a stall, jammed my fist into my mouth so I wouldn't make any noise, and let the tears flow.

I was in there while the hoods came in and out and smoked and made stupid jokes. Nobody even noticed that one stall was locked; those guys only used the toilets for ashtrays anyway.

Class started. They left. All that crying had made me breathe hard, so I couldn't stand any more of the smoke smell. I was about cried out, anyway.

I half-wondered if maybe I'd been there so long that school was over for the day. Jags were like that, and so were rages. My sense of time vanished. By my watch, I was going to be ten minutes late to Coach Gratz's class, and have to take a public reaming. I scoured my face over and over, using the rough paper towels and the harsh hand soap so it wouldn't be so apparent that I'd been crying, and hurried to class.

"Nice you could join us, Karl," Gratz said. "I bet you can explain why you're late."

"I can, sir," I said, "but, it, um, involves the bathroom—"

Everyone, including Gratz, laughed, except Paul, who had his head down on his desk.

Gratz shook his head, smiling. "I think you just explained everything that needs explaining. "

Just like that, I was off the hook.

One problem with fascist dictators is that you never know what's going to happen; *his mercies are as much caprices as his cruelties*, I quoted to myself.

Darla winked at me. I took my seat. Gratz resumed his tirade. "Now, yesterday we talked about two ways not to read *Huckleberry Finn,* and today we're going to talk about the most important way of all *not* to read it, the most absolutely disgusting idea I have ever, ever run into. There's this guy named Leslie Fiedler—a professor at one of those jerkwater cowboy universities out west— who wrote a book called *Love and Death in the American Novel.*"

I wrote down "Leslie Fiedler, Satan," and put a big colon after it. Then I stopped taking notes to wait for The Sentence. Long experience with Gratz's classes had taught me that there would be just one sentence I needed to know about Leslie Fiedler, and I would be hearing that sentence at least six times this morning.

"What Professor Fiedler *says* is that Huck Finn and Nigger Jim go floating down the river together . . . because they're a couple of *fags!*" All the people who thought it was funny to have a teacher say "fag" giggled, but Gratz froze them with his glare; you could tell he was serious as death. "He says their relationship is homosexual. According to *Professor* Fiedler, *Huckleberry Finn* has nothing to do with slavery, nothing to do with the meaning of life—no, sir! *Huckleberry Finn* is the story of two queers on a raft.

"And you know what? If you start to read *any* book, you can find things like that. Sure, Jim calls Huck 'honey'—

because people from his background called all children 'honey.' Sure, when it's cold they huddle up to keep warm. Sure, they'll do anything for each other—they're friends. But the idea—Marti?"

"Uh, at my old school last year, we had to read *Love and Death in the American Novel*, and that's not really what Fiedler says. He's just very into Freud, and Freud thought that boys and girls before puberty, when they get to be like super-intense friends, were in 'homosexual' love, like it was something they'd grow out of later?" She made it sound like a question. "So he's saying that Huck and Jim avoid maturity by being so devoted—"

"*Well.*" Gratz's tone froze *my* blood. "Marti, have you read *all* the books *I've* read?"

"I'm sure I haven't, sir," she said. She spoke slowly and softly, knowing she was right but not how to back out of it. "But I did read *Love and Death in the American Novel*, and I do know that what you were saying was not an accurate version of what Leslie Fiedler was saying."

"Why the hell would I *want* to say what *he* says? If you'd been paying attention in class, instead of getting ready to show off, you'd know that I have been trying to tell you how *not* to read *Huckleberry Finn*."

"What I meant was, sir, I thought you were misrepresenting Leslie Fiedler." I could hear her swallow. "In fact I feel that you still are. Sir." Marti wasn't the type to give up without a fight, especially not if she was very afraid—some people are like that. They lean into the fear. I was starting to wish I had just stayed in the boys' room stall.

"So," Gratz said, "you're going to de*fend* calling one of the *great*est books in American *lit*erature a story about a couple of queers on a raft."

That was the third time I'd heard that phrase. Any time I was asked about Leslie Fiedler, obviously, I was supposed to say that he was the professor who had called *Huckleberry Finn* a story about a couple of queers on a raft. One thing about school, no matter how important or crazy or upsetting things are, there's always something trivial you should be thinking about instead.

"But ... that's ... exactly ... what ... he ... *doesn't* ... say." I could hear the tears in her voice.

With Gratz standing over my desk like that, yelling at the girl behind me, I could have grabbed him by the balls, twisted them up tight, and yanked them down to the floor. It was a very pleasant thought. "See, Pro*fess*or Fiedler is some kind of big name intellectual, very very in the club, so all the big name intellectuals shove his silly ideas down the throat of the next generation at the ex*pen*sive schools. And a kid has *no* ability to resist an idea, no matter how *dumb* it is."

"I'm sorry, sir, I—"

"That's why things are in the mess they are in across this whole country, because the leadership just can't talk to people."

Shit, I'd seen old Gratz lose it before but this was like

ultraGratzical. Maybe I should just suddenly puke on his shoes, as a diversion.

"Like. For. Example. I could talk to my wrestling team about James Joyce. I mean, I have *read* James Joyce, and I can *talk about* James Joyce, so it would be no problem to talk about him to my wrestling team. But! But! But! I know that if I did, they wouldn't wrestle better and they wouldn't get much out of Joyce. It would be for no purpose!"

His face was past red and heading for purple. His diaphragm heaved his little hard round basketball of a belly against his polo shirt. *I could just ram my pencil right up in there, see how deep it would go into him, probably not far, there's still good muscle there, it would probably just scare the piss out of him.*

Of course I didn't, but thinking about it was better than listening to him, or to the little catch-sobs I could hear struggling in Marti's throat. Gratz was going to get what he really enjoyed most—she was going to cry.

Paul tried to jump in. "Sir, I don't think Marti was being disrespectful. I feel as though—"

"What do they do," Gratz snapped at him, "teach you to talk like that in therapy? 'I don't feel this,' 'I don't feel that.' Even if your old man *is* a big deal in this town—"

Cheryl said, "Coach, I think we do understand what—"

"You people really stick together," Gratz said. He sat down on his desk and spread his hands, as if laying out all the cards. "But I'm not running this class based on what students think their psychological needs are. No matter—"

Danny tried. "Coach, uh, Coach Gratz, maybe—"

"Shut up, Danny, this has nothing to do with you!"

Danny started breathing hard, the way he did just before a crying jag. Paul jumped up and started to rub Danny's shoulders, which sometimes kept him from going into it.

In an almost-reasonable tone, Gratz said, "All right, Danny, if you're going to have one of your things, you can go have it in the principal's office, and Paul, you can go with him. And Martinella, don't you even *think* you can get away with stuff like this in my class. You go down to the principal's office, too."

The three of them gathered up their books and papers. I guess Paul must've done some good, getting to Danny's shoulders as quick as he did, because Danny was just making some little spasming sounds in his chest, like fighting down hiccups. They made a strange little trio going through the door—huge Danny, his short hair neatly in place even now, in his eternal FFA jacket, and small skinny Paul and Marti, each topped with a mess of uncontrollable curly hair—like a cathedral with two flanking towers.

As the door closed, Darla stood up. Her books were already stacked against her pink leotard, but she held Mister Babbitt out in front of her, as if he were a microphone, or like she was Hamlet looking at Yorick's skull. "Oh, dear, Mister Babbitt. Oh, dear dear dear. I do believe you are right. Everyone interesting has left the room. There is no one *left* to make the *scene*, and conse*quent*ly, the scene is *not* made.

"What's that you say, Mister Babbitt? You don't want to stay and listen to an asshole shouting at us? Oh, oh, oh dear, Mister Babbitt, you naughty little bunny, don't you know that if people overheard *you* calling that asshole an asshole, they might think that *I* had called that asshole an asshole, and then I could get sent to the principal's office for calling the asshole an asshole? What's that? Don't mumble, you bad little rabbit." She held Mister Babbitt up to her ear like a phone. "Why, Mister Babbitt! Of course you are right. All the cool people are *already* down at the principal's office, so we will *just* be going along there our*self*ies. Say good-bye to the kiddies and the asshole, Mister Babbitt."

She walked to the door in the slinky, hair-flipping way she had perfected for annoying teachers, turned, wiggled Mister Babbitt's arm so that he seemed to wave at us, bowed deeply, and went out, closing the door behind her.

Gratz's mouth could not have hung any more open if she'd kicked him in the balls. I had never been so in love before in my life.

"So," Gratz said. "Now, about Professor Fiedler and—"

Cheryl grabbed her books against her chest, barely keeping them as she ran for the door. Gratz started to say, "I didn't—" and she was gone, leaving the door flapping into the hall behind her. Gratz very slowly walked over, closed it, and began his harangue about Professor Fiedler. He pretty much delivered it all to me, I think watching to see when I was going to stand up and yell, or break for the door, or something. I sat and listened, my face as still as I could keep it. I even took some notes on what he said.

I didn't yet have my ticket-proof letter from him.

So here I was, the Lone Madman. All eyes were on him as the town rode away, and he sat there on his great white chicken. *My work here is done. I'm needed wherever there's another friend to betray, another butt to lick, wherever the people cry out for conformity.* I couldn't draw cartoons because Gratz was standing right over me, and I wouldn't be able to show them to Paul anyway. And since I already had The Sentence about Leslie Fiedler, there wasn't anything left to listen for.

The Value of Anything

WHEN GRATZ FINISHED repeating his variations on The Sentence about Fiedler, he said, "Okay, far enough for today," and made the usual pencil mark on his notes. "Over the weekend, read through to the end of Chapter Six. Karl Shoemaker, don't forget you need to see me for a couple minutes."

Everybody grabbed up their books and piled through the door, taking off to tell all their friends about it, with no crowd in their way because Gratz had let them all go five minutes early. They sprayed out like gas molecules into space, and were gone.

I walked up to Gratz's desk like a lifelong atheist approaching St. Peter. "Sir?"

"Karl, you're a good kid. I know that. So are the ones

that went down to the office. And I'm not happy with how I lost my temper." He was looking down at the desk; his hands were trembling. Poor bastard was really losing it. "Do you still want that letter?"

"Uh, yes, sir, I do."

"Okay. You have to give it directly to the counselor, so you'll need to go to the counseling room a little early, then hurry back here, be on time for class, and that's the deal from then on." He pulled out a sheet of paper, signed it, and pointed to where I was supposed to sign. It said Gratz and I had agreed to meet to talk over my problems and therefore I was requesting to be excused from group therapy.

I signed it. I felt like I was being Paul, in *The Crucible*, last year, when he was talking about signing a death warrant; *I'll not conceal it, my hand shakes yet as with a wound!*

Then Gratz folded it into an envelope and said, "Okay, now we have to sign across the flap, so people can tell if this has been tampered with, since we both sign it. You sign across the flap, too." So we both did that.

I must have looked like I was puzzled (as opposed to sick, which I actually was), because he explained. "They make us take all these precautions to prevent teachers from pressuring kids into leaving therapy; they're afraid a teacher might push a kid who really needs professional help into going to prayer meetings or something instead.

I just can't imagine that any professional educator would do that, but that's what this business is about." He paused for a deep breath. "So, anyway, take that to the counselor on Monday, early, and you're free—except you have to get together and talk with me now and then."

"Thank you, Coach."

He glanced up at me. "I suppose it's not that different from meeting an AA sponsor."

"I'm doing okay with Dick."

"Sorry, didn't mean anything by that. Just thinking out loud. I've never thought the therapists are very good for you kids, and I always thought I could do a better job, but now that I have to do it, it looks bigger and harder than I thought it would." He sighed. "Well, we'll try to figure out whatever it is you need, and do something about that."

I didn't see any way he could give me five extra hours in the day, a mom who wasn't crazy, or a bank account that was safe, but I just said, "Thank you, Coach," again.

"And thank you for not adding to the mess. I behaved inappropriately—funny how the therapy kids can always get to me." He shook his head like he'd just gotten hit with a takedown and pin and lost in ten seconds. "Anyway, please tell your friends that I'm going to apologize publicly on Tuesday when they're back in class. No penalties. I can't believe I acted like that. Oh, and give them the assignment, too—they left before it was given. Jeez, I'm really sorry about everything, Karl."

I couldn't think what to say—I didn't want to say it was all right, because it sure wasn't, but on the other hand, anything that looked faintly like humility in Gratz was something I didn't want to crap on. So I kind of half-waved and shot through the door like my butt was on fire, rushed off to put the letter safely into my locker, and made it to trig still early.

"You okay, Karl?" Bonny asked. She was the only one there so far. Today she was being pretty moderate, just a gauzy blouse over a tie-dye top and some baggy pants I guessed she'd made for herself out of old curtains.

"There was a Madman eruption in Gratz's class. Gratz started it," I said. "Everyone else went to the office, I don't know why I didn't."

She shrugged. "You've been changing. You stopped drinking, you talk to that army recruiter all the time, you stopped going out with me—"

I wasn't up for this, but here it was. "Bonny, you dumped me."

"'Cause you stopped being any fun," she said. "And it wasn't just that you got all holy-roller and stopped drinking. The way you treated me after prom . . ." She shook her head. "Well, I still miss you and we're still friends, but good riddance, asshole."

I thought about pretending I didn't know what she was talking about, but that would never work. Bonny was cute and she cracked me up a lot and I liked being out with her, and talking with her, and the way other guys looked at her. I guess most guys would've said I had a great girlfriend back then.

But Bonny had some weird problems about making out and touching and stuff; actually her rules were pretty simple, just crazy:

1. I was supposed to touch her where and how she liked it.

2. But only when she was drunk enough so it wouldn't be her fault.

3. She wasn't supposed to ever have to say she wanted it.

4. We had to stop and promise never to do it again as soon as she was done.

5. She would never touch me.

6. Except once . . .

After prom, we were in her bedroom, her parents were somewhere in France, the kids were in dreamland, Mom would've been in the cheering section if she could've been, and I was about on the ceiling with nerves, but going ahead bravely. After all, it was good old Bon, and we both had a nice little drunk going from splitting a bottle of champagne she'd liberated while I distracted the caterer at her cousin's wedding.

You'd've thought it'd've been perfect, but, well, it was us. So I was heavy petting her and she seemed pretty close to the point where she usually went "Oh!" and told me to stop.

This time, though, she asked if I wanted to see it—I'd been going by feel all this time. She took off her pants, and I started touching her there again.

Then she said, "Do it."

"Do what?"

"You know. Let's have sex. You brought a rubber, didn't you?"

"Um, I—no."

"Do it anyway. Come on, I'm drunk, and I'm asking you."

Maybe I just never get that drunk. I said, "I don't want to get you pregnant, Bon. We'd have to get married, and it would wreck both our plans."

And she got pissed and threw me out; I didn't even get time to get a good look at her naked. I never quite got if it was because I was supposed to have a rubber, or supposed to want to marry her, or I wasn't drunk enough to get all carried away and just do it, or what. I sure did get that she was pissed, though.

Ten days later, after Mom's stupid thirty-ninth birthday, I gave up drinking, and the next time I saw Bonny at a party, she was mad at me about that too, and went off and made out all night with Chip Neminech, the tackle who demonstrated that not only is there no *I* in *team*, there's no *Q*, either. I suppose, given that my mother was a girl, I shouldn't have been surprised that some of them could get pretty weird.

So I was standing there realizing Bon was still mad about that, and maybe about my quitting drinking, and God knew what else. "So everyone else went down to the office?"

"Yeah, Gratz wanted me to tell them he's sorry, though, and he'll apologize."

"But you didn't go."

"No."

"Remember when you and me and Paul got suspended together, from Gratz's class?"

"Yeah." I was pretty much down to monosyllables.

She glanced at the door to make sure we had no company yet. "I let Chip do it. All summer."

I had no idea what to say to that; she obviously wanted me pissed off or hurt or something, but I had no reaction I could think of. "If you're happy," I said, "Then it's none of my business."

"Exactly." Wow, she was pissed.

"What do you want me to say?" I asked. Sometimes Bonny could confuse me as much as Mom did. "You know I'm your friend, and I want to give you what you need."

"How about a weekend in Detroit with a bunch of geniuses and some horny fat girls from out of town?"

I turned around and of course it was Larry. Much as he wanted to be a weird guy, what was really the weirdest thing about him was that he never noticed anyone else having a conversation. Bonny raised an eyebrow and

I nodded back; if I wanted to talk, I guess she'd talk.

It turned out Larry was talking about one of those sci-fi conventions he was always trying to get me to, sometime next month. He lost his virginity at those about as much as he did at summer camp. (Actually since 0 = 0, *exactly* as much.)

Larry also wasn't real good at noticing when someone was trying to escape from a conversation with him, either, so I kind of had to push past him when Cheryl, Marti, and Danny came in; Gratz must have found a hall monitor to take a note right down to the office right away. "Hey," I said. "Gratz says he was out of line, no punishment, he'll apologize in class on Tuesday, and read through Chapter Six of *Fuckle Hairy Bin* for Monday."

Danny and Cheryl, organized types that they were, pulled out their little assignment books and scribbled. Marti just shrugged. None of them looked the least bit surprised. If you had abusive parents or worshipped a vengeful god, or both, you knew everything about Gratz's sudden reversals.

"Hey," Larry said, "I was talking to you."

"You were," I said, "but now you're just standing there with your mouth open, looking confused."

Nobody laughed or anything. I think I hurt his feelings. I didn't care.

All through math class I kept wanting to run back to my locker and see if my letter was still there. It was what

I'd been dreaming about all summer—the Ticket for No Ticket, my way out of the Madman Underground.

Of course I'd been dreaming about that with Paul . . . who'd've guessed we could *both* be serious? But I guess he was back in the Madman Underground, now, all the way to graduation. And without me. He could be king all by himself.

Along with all my friends. Well, except Squid, who hadn't heard about it yet, and Larry, who was curled over his book, pretending to listen and actually just hugging himself, the way he did when he was really hurt.

Maybe they had a Normal Underground for stooges and sellouts. Come to admit it, my ticket for that was in my locker right now.

"Karl?" Mrs. Hertz asked.

"It's isosceles," I said.

"It is, but the question was the value of theta."

"I guess I don't know."

"Well, if you know it's isosceles," she said, "then you already know everything you need to know about the value of a and b. Doesn't that give you a clue?"

She just kept pushing, and I just kept saying I didn't get it. Finally Larry put his hand up and said, "Pi over four," in this real bored arrogant voice. I know he meant to put me down, but I was glad he let me off the hook. Right now I just couldn't care about the value of anything.

Danny didn't exactly act pissed off in gym class, but then Danny rarely acted pissed off even when he was homicidal. He was always buttoned down tight except when he was crying.

But he didn't say hi, and he didn't look at me, and when we went out to run, he hung in close with his jock buddies. So I might have guessed he was pissed off.

Or I could have just listened to Squid, who ran alongside me for a while. It was being typical Ohio for that time of year—the soaking-cold stormy morning had been replaced by a steaming-damp sunny midmorning. "What'd you do to piss Danny off so bad?"

"Gratz had one of his Gratz-attacks all over Marti, that new girl. Paul backed her up, Gratz let loose at the therapy group, everyone went down to the office except me. So I guess I didn't back the group up. Probably he's pissed about that."

Squid chugged along beside me; I kept my pace down, waiting for the coach to yell at me to pick it up, because just at the moment Squid might be as close to a friend as I had.

After maybe half a lap he said, "That's not actually such a big fuckin' deal, you know?"

"Yeah."

"It'll blow over."

"Yeah."

Then we ran another lap without talking before he said, "I heard something else that was pretty rough, though."

I nodded so he'd know I was listening. By now my heart and lungs had settled into that comfortable groove where I could run the rest of the day, and would have liked to. My shirt was drenched with sweat and my soggy gym shorts were sliding over my wet thighs; it must have been ninety degrees out, and the humidity was like a swimming pool. I paced Squid's heavy-footed trot and waited.

Finally he shrugged and said, "I don't think it's fair."

"What's not?"

"Well, I guess Paul told them all you weren't coming along because you had some deal with Gratz to get out of the therapy group and you didn't want to be friends with them no more."

I felt sick as shit, I can tell you that.

"I can tell you still want to be friends," Squid said, kind of shy, like he was afraid I might snap at him.

"*Yeah!* Yeah, I do."

"Maybe not with Paul right now, hunh?"

"I'll get over it," I said, but I wasn't sure I meant that.

Squid shrugged, and the way he did it said it all: I still had at least one friend. "Paul's a good guy, but sometimes he's a mean little cock-sucking queer-bait, you know? You got to keep a balanced perspective."

I made the mistake of looking sideways at Squid and seeing the twinkle in his eye. It's hard to run well when you're laughing. Then Coach Korviss trotted up beside us and pointed out that Squid was loafing and I was loafing for two, and we put on some speed, which meant Squid didn't have air to talk and I was way out in front of him anyway.

I felt better. For the rest of gym I ran like a crazy bastard, and it made the shower feel like paradise.

I made a point of eating lunch with Larry. He had probably thought I was mad at him, or avoiding him, or something, these last few days. He explained all of *The Three Stigmata of Palmer Eldritch* to me—twice I think. I acted like I was real interested and stuff. He seemed pathetically happy.

Paul was in senior honors gov, and today he was really "on," as he called it, hassling Harry in a friendly way, sucking up and backing off, making old Harry think he was running a real discussion. I tried joining in and Paul acted like I'd pissed in his Cheerios, so I shut up and let Harry and Paul do their show while the rest of the class subsided into a doze.

It wasn't being much of a day but I'd had worse. I figured if I took care of all my other friendships, and just did what I needed to do, I could get it down to aching about Paul maybe once every other breath.

I'd heard the booms of thunder all through French class. We were just doing convo practice and I spent the whole time flirting with Darla, who was being all bitchy and come-here come-here come-here get-away get-away get-away on me. Mr. Babbitt—Monsieur Babbitt, actually, you had to call everything by a French name, which is why I was Claude and Darla was Nathalie—made fun of me, and I tried to rise to the bait, but apparently I was just not doing what Darla wanted.

When we finally got out of class, the temperature had dropped like a brick, there was hail spatting across the parking lot, and the sky was as black as it had been that morning. It wasn't going to last long—these storms never did—but for the moment it was cold, rainy, and nasty, and my house was closer to Philbin's than the high school was. I sprinted to the bus, splashing through the icy puddles on the sidewalk.

"Hey, kiddo." Jolene seemed kind of glum, for her, but glad to see me. "Your mom told you about her new guy?"

"I think so," I said, "if it's the same one it was this morning."

She made a face. "*Nice* way to talk about your mom. She really loves you, you know, she talks about you all the time."

"Yeah, well."

I took a seat toward the back. Just before Jolene pulled out, Paul flopped into a seat way up toward the front, away from me, and stared out the window. I wondered how it felt to be him. He'd been working as hard as I had, apparently, on spending a year not in the Madman Underground. He'd lectured me like I was a bad little kid about it. Then half an hour later he'd kicked the whole idea away. I just didn't get him at all.

His forehead was resting against the bus-window glass, so he must be getting that rattle-buzz in the skull. What I could see of his face—one closed eye and a slack lower lip—looked more dazed and tired than anything else.

Just before his stop, I came up behind him, risking having Jolene yell at me to sit down, and said, "Hey, Gratz is going to apologize Tuesday morning. No penalties for anyone. He wanted you to know the assignment is to read through Chapter Six by Monday, okay? He wanted me to tell you that."

"Good boy," Paul said.

"Fine," I said. "I was supposed to tell you and I did, and fuck you very much. How did you know I'm going to be seeing Gratz instead of going to therapy?"

"I was waiting for you after class, yesterday morning, so I could explain what I told you *this* morning. Fuck, I almost ran in to ask if I could get that deal, too. But I knew it was Gratz, and sure enough, he was real Gratz this morning. Sucking up to him just wasn't worth it no matter what. Not for *me*."

He slung up his books and pushed past me through the bus door into the cold rain at the street corner. As we pulled away I watched him running through the icy silver-gray light, his shirt and pants sticking to him.

I rode the bus to the closest stop to my house, and ran. I don't think I even felt the cold rain.

When I opened the door, Mom hollered, "Hey, Tiger, in here."

In her room, she was packing her suitcase. "You're not gonna believe this one, Tiger," she said. "Not in a million bajillion years."

"Try me."

"That new guy in my life? He's a college prof."

"Somebody has to be."

"That's not what you're not going to believe. So . . . it's after Labor Day and the Erie Islands are cheap. We're going to go check into a cabin up at Put-in-Bay. Tonight *and* tomorrow night."

"Even raining like this?"

"The better excuse to stay in the bedroom all weekend," she said. "Not that Bill needs much of an excuse. He is *so* into me, I can just feel that. You can shift for yourself, right?"

"I'll manage."

"We'll be back Sunday afternoon and then he wants to visit with you and get to know you." She looked at me with a big toothy smile and scared, wary eyes. "Can you . . . is this okay with you, Tiger Sweetie? For your old mom to . . . well, I guess I'm maybe serious about this one?"

"Mom, if he treats you good, I'll be happy for you. Promise. What's he teach?"

"English. Up at Saint Jerome College in Sandusky. He lives right up in Port Clinton, which is how he knew about the cheap cabins at Put-in-Bay. Oh, and they still have the carousel going, and the grapes are getting ripe, and the lake will be all around us and . . . it's just going to be beautiful. Even if it rains we can do that silly romantic thing and walk along the shore in the rain, you know? I need something like this in my life so much."

"Then I'm glad you're getting to do this."

"Really?" She looked so startled.

"No shit, Mom. Really no shit. I'd rather you were happy."

"He's coming by to pick me up in a little bit. And you're sure you can—"

"I can do everything for myself I need to, Mom, you trained me, you should know." That was a lie, but it was one she'd repeated so often she believed it; she was always impressing her friends by telling them that she'd taught me to cook, clean, sew on buttons, and so forth so that I wouldn't be the kind of useless pain in the ass that my father had been.

"Mom," I said, "I have to work tonight and a lot of the

day tomorrow. Do you suppose you could loan me a key so I don't have to leave the house unlocked?"

"Just leave the back door unlocked, sweetie. This is Lightsburg. You don't have to worry about burglars. There's nothing in this house worth stealing."

There was actually just over four thousand dollars, but fuck my ass with a live rabid weasel if I was going to let her know *that*. "Okay."

"You don't need a key. We both live here."

"All right, sorry, just asking."

"But you asked because you worry about property and owning stuff and all that." She sighed, sat down on the bed, and blew out a cloud of smoke; I think she was trying to look thoughtful. "You're so obsessed with the material that you never think about the spiritual or the human, Karl. And I *know* you didn't get that from me." She took another drag on the cigarette, stubbed it out, and exhaled a stream of smoke. Then she really did look thoughtful. "I'm being all preachy, aren't I, Tiger? And I promised Bill I wouldn't be that way. He's *so* different, Karl. So, so very different. He says I talk like I'm translated from a Red Chinese horoscope. Which I don't think is very nice, I mean even Nixon doesn't call them Red Chinese anymore, now that the Cold War is over. Things are getting *so* Aquarian, and what's wrong with sounding like a horoscope? It just means I know what's really going on. But Bill says he wants me to just calm down and hear some poetry and just sit, and just be, and that's why he wants me to go with him to the cabin. Isn't that *so* far-out?" She looked so tired and frantic, and all of a sudden I realized that she might be tired of the way she was living.

I'd seen a lot of "something-betters" come and go, but for her sake I said, "Yeah, Mom, actually, it *is* pretty far-out. A weekend at the lake with a good guy would be really good for you."

She looked at me suspiciously. "You won't mess this up for me?"

"Mom, have I *ever* messed up your dates on purpose?"

"I know, I know, I know. I'm really sorry, Tiger Sweetie, your old mom shouldn't have said that." She set her next cigarette down without lighting it, and came over to have me kiss her cheek. "You forgive Mom?"

"Yeah." I gave her a quick peck on her soft, dry cheek; she had extra powder and foundation on. I didn't smell booze. She was putting jeans and sweaters, not nighties, into the suitcase. I was starting to like this new guy Bill a lot.

By the time I got showered and changed for work, the storm had blown over and there was wet deep yellow sunlight pouring all over the street. I left Mom sitting in a lawn chair under the front porch awning with her suitcase beside her, smoking absentmindedly and trying not to look too nervous and eager. Just before I turned the corner onto Grant Street, she stood up and waved madly, shouting, "The stars shine on you because you are a special light to the universe!" I was glad old Wilson wasn't outside to hear *that*.

Since I'd be working at Philbin's anyway, I figured I might as well have dinner there and be sure I was early. I ate at the counter. Philbin was off getting some last-minute supplies, and Angie and Dick were coping with a bus crowd from the Trailways station.

Eventually Angie brought my burger and fries. While I was eating, something large moved onto the stool beside me. "Karl."

"Squid! Uh, don't you have a game tonight?"

"Don't have to be there for another hour," he said, "and it was getting nasty at home."

"If I buy you dinner, are you gonna get all silly about it, or just let me do it?"

He smiled, which was always something to see, because he had big crooked horsey teeth, and it made his plain features absolutely hideous. "Aw, hell, Karl, I'm starving and was trying to figure out how to eat on what I got. But I wasn't trying to hustle a meal—"

"Hey, Angie, feed this guy. Let me know when I have to rob another bank to keep it coming. And careful not to get between him and his dish."

"Right on it," she said. "Hey, Karl, you're doing better, bud, he's *much* prettier than your last date."

Squid pretty much ordered the menu, and it started to flow out of the kitchen and into him. Even with a maw like that to shove it into, and paws like those to shove it in with, it took Squid a while. Now that Dick had two teenage appetites to feed, he was in heaven.

When Squid finished, he put his head down and muttered for a moment. I glanced his way.

"Oh, Mom always said it was stupid to give thanks before you got the thing, the time to thank was after you had it, so she said grace at the end of the meal. So I— well, you know."

"Yeah. Every time I pick up a tool, I hear my dad's voice."

That pretty much killed the conversation, so I ordered coffee for both of us, and then we decided we needed dessert to give the coffee something to wash down.

After Angie set that up, Squid said, "Hey, so how'd the whole big uproar in Gratz's class turn out, man?"

"I really don't know," I admitted. "I got my magic letter from Gratz, so no therapy for me if I don't want to do it. Just gotta let Gratz be my pal. Paul is acting like this is some big betrayal and I guess I did chicken out—"

Squid rammed in a little more apple pie and chewed like he was thinking. "Naw, *you* didn't chicken out. "

"I don't know, Marti's really gotten to be a friend these past couple days, and of course everybody else was all the old Madmen, and I sat there while Gratz ranted at them like a nut, and I didn't get into it. What do you call that?"

"I don't call it chickening out, because you were the one doin' it. It surprised me when I heard about it, Karl, but you and me know about not running out on nobody. So whatever else it was, I call it a surprise. And that's all."

"I think Gratz was kind of surprised, too. Anyway, he's going to apologize and stuff, and none of them will be in any trouble, and I guess it'll all blow over, like most crap does."

"Yeah, good." He sighed. "Hey, thanks for the dinner—"

"Thanks for the company. Good luck tonight, man."

"Thanks, we gonna need it. Everybody says we gettin' our butts kicked." He squeezed my arm and went out the door in that funny, roll-and-bounce walk that jocks have.

Philbin got back, and I filled out the paperwork for the new job, officially punched in, laid out setups, and waited around for whatever was going to happen. Philbin got lost in an Indians game, and Mrs. P was out in the kitchen whistling and singing to herself and putting the pies together. A couple of junior high hoods came in, but since there was nothing free here, they couldn't smoke, and I was watching too close for them to shoplift, they left.

The first movie let out and I served floats and shakes to a bunch of college couples, most of them trying to explain *Casablanca* to each other. It sounded like it wasn't bad, but when half of the people are trying to explain all the terms they learned from film class and the other half are asking which side France was on, you don't get much of a sense of what happens in the movie. Twenty minutes later, Philbin's was empty again, but that was the biggest crowd it had seen in years.

I had kept up real good with what there was to do, and now I was looking at about an hour of getting paid for sitting. I wanted a story.

I was so lost about what was going on in *The Three Stigmata of Palmer Eldritch* that I might as well try *The Adventures of Huckleberry Finn*. If I found a way to like it, Gratz's class wouldn't be nearly so bad.

Well, I don't know about liking it, but I sure read it. Way past where Gratz told us to stop.

Huck would have been a Madman, for sure, if he'd gone to our school, I can tell you that. His dad was a drunk who was beating him, and kidnapped him, and threatened to kill him, and everybody in that little town knew what was happening—the only people he could trust were other kids.

And not them very much. While Huck had all these problems, Tom Sawyer just wanted to play stupid games about being robbers and things—that was something us

Madmen talked about all the time, the way kids getting raped or beaten were sitting in class next to kids whose biggest concern was what to wear for homecoming.

Anyway, like it or not, *Huckleberry Finn* had my attention. No risk at all that I'd think it was about happy queer hippies on a raft saying "nigger" a lot. I was *pissed* that there wasn't any social services or child welfare to bust Pap Finn, and no therapy group for Huck to hang out with, and the Widow and the Judge were no use, either. Maybe there'd be more slavery or violence, even some sex, or something else cool later, but right now that book was like hearing a new Madman's story at a therapy meeting.

Philbin turned out right: people's noses did the selling. The second movie crowd was much bigger than the first. It was a nice night for early September, the heat of the day gone and the air moist but not really cold. A few girls and old ladies put on light sweaters and left them unbuttoned. The crowd came out of the theater and in that still, cool, wet air, the pies cooking grabbed 'em by the nose and pretty much threw them into the booths and up along the counter. Also Philbin had put a pile of burger and chopped onion on the back of the grill, just to get good smells going.

Despite my predictions, we even got a little postgame crowd. Two tables of band kids, the real nerdy first-in last-out kind that do the instrument check-in and lockup,

wandered in because Pongo's was closed, Pietro's was occupied by the socials and the jocks and their girlfriends,
and they'd heard that Philbin's was going to be open.

I had forty-five crazy minutes waiting tables, then
twenty minutes of hard labor busing and jocking the register. By the time I shoved the third load into the dishwasher, Mrs. P had plenty of pies cooling for tomorrow's
pie-and-cheese breakfast special.

Philbin clapped me on the shoulder, said he figured
we'd do it again tomorrow night, and I slung up my books
and went out the door, turning right to go up Courthouse
Street, looking forward to hauling my butt home to bed.

Tonto Joins the All-Faggot
Midnight Softball League

"KARL." I TURNED and Cheryl was standing there with Marti. "Karl, I—we need you—"

It took me, like, a quarter second to see what this had
to be about. I felt sick and furious and like screaming.
"Oh, *man*. Paul?"

"Yeah. Uh—I grabbed the bat from under my bed, so
we won't have to go by your house. But, um—you don't
have to—"

"Oh, fuckshit shit-eating motherfucking Jesus,
Cheryl, of *course* I have to. Are you parked—"

"Around the corner on Shoemaker," she said. "Marti's
coming, too, she got kind of caught up in this."

"I feel like it's my fault," Marti said. "Paul was talking to his dad, right after the game, and I didn't realize
what kind of a talk it was."

"The usual thing about embarrassing the family by being a drum major?" I said. "'Prancing around in a faggot suit and you never even went out for football'?"

"Yeah." Marti sounded close to crying. "At least I think so. I didn't really hear. I didn't see how upset he was at first. So after his father left, I went up to Paul to ask if he wanted to go to Pietro's after the game, and he threw his baton at me and yelled at me not to pressure him."

"You know that way Paul yells when he loses it," Cheryl said. "I heard that so I ran over to see what was up, and he was halfway across the parking lot, and Marti was just kind of stunned."

"I feel really stupid," Marti said.

"Paul has a way of making people feel stupid," I said, more bitterly than I wanted to. "I wouldn't make a big deal out of it. We'd better get moving."

Cheryl turned and walked fast; I fell into step beside her, with Marti trailing along. Cheryl was ticking things off like she was working out last-minute plans for a formal dance, that super-organized part of her taking over. "Late start, he's probably still in his uniform because some of the men who cruise up there like that. Besides he won't have had any chance to change. We lost real bad, it was forty-two to three, so the guys from the team are going to be worse—"

"We'll manage. Good thinking, having that bat already. So we're ready to go, right?"

"Yeah, but it's going to be *close* this time, Karl. I didn't dare go without you and then you had to work so late—I was *worried*—"

Cheryl leaned over, as we walked, to rest her head on my shoulder. I didn't put an arm around her or anything—she didn't like to feel held. I could smell the clean scent of shampoo, and the sweat because she'd just cheered through a game, and the warm new wool and leather of her cheerleader jacket. The hard, compact weight of her head against my shoulder might as well have been the king touching me with a sword, because it always made me feel like a fucking knight in shining armor.

I said, "You know those guys are going to stop someplace that will take their fake IDs, first. Buying liquor, drinking it, and driving to Toledo will take a while."

She lifted her head off my shoulder, obviously irritated. "I was figuring all that in already. It's gonna be *close*. This is the latest start we've ever had, and we *lost* tonight, Karl, you know it's always worse when we lose."

"Fuck," I said, because that was about all there was to say.

Her car was right at the corner of Shoemaker. She unlocked it and we got in. For this kind of trip I kind of automatically got shotgun; I tossed my books into the back and Marti set them to the side.

"Did you get anything to eat at Philbin's?" Cheryl asked.

"Not recently."

"There's ham sandwiches in a bag by your feet. My step always packs for every game like I'm going to eat enough for five guys while I cheer. What a duh, you know? But I guess she means well and she's trying to do *something* for me. Since she can't keep her creepy dad away from me."

She made another turn, onto Courthouse Street, and headed north.

The sandwich had a lot of mayo and pickle, and the ham was that stringy stuff they sold at delis, not lunch meat. *But*, like the lumberjack said, *good though.* "Bonny couldn't come?"

"She was going out with Chip after the game, so she'd have heard, but maybe couldn't get away. I was so worried that you wouldn't get out of there soon enough that I was thinking of seeing if I could go to Pietro's and get Squid."

"He'd be good," I agreed.

The last streetlights passed behind us, then the golden arches (I was glad not to be working there tonight), then the harsh bars of glare from the sodium lights over the interstate entrance. In a moment we were shooting across the flat land that stretched out to the low rows of trees on both sides, the horizon a range of lumpy glows from little towns, the sky dark fuzzy velvet with the brighter stars peeping through thin clouds.

Marti perched on the edge of the backseat, over the transmission hump, putting her head up between me and Cheryl. "Can you guys explain all this to me? I feel like I came in in the middle of the story."

"Well, it's sort of another tale of the Madman Underground," I said, "maybe one of our most dramatic, or since it's Paul, our most *melo*dramatic. Now and then, when he's been fighting with his dad and is really strung out, Paul goes up on the gay stroll in Toledo. Usually it happens after Paul's dad gets on his ass for not being all manly and stuff. Like whenever Paul gets a lot of attention, say when he has a big part in a play, or a solo in a choir concert, or when it's a home game and he's the drum major for the halftime show, Mr. Knauss catches Paul afterwards and tells him that he's embarrassed the whole family by being Mister Big Public Screaming Faggot, and yells at Paul, and usually tells him to never come home and locks him out that night."

"Now and then," Cheryl said, quietly but perfectly clearly, "one of these blow-ups happens right after Mr. Knauss has gotten caught somewhere, with someone, that he wasn't supposed to be. I always wonder if he's ever seen Paul out on the stroll."

I hadn't planned on clueing Marti in to *that* quite so fast, but what the hell, she had a date with Paul the next night, and maybe she should know; she was bound to know soon, anyway, Paul was such a blabbermouth.

But I still wanted to get off the subject, so I went on as if Cheryl hadn't said anything. "Most of the time when that happens, Paul comes and crashes at McDonald's with me like you did, or one of the other places I told you about.

"But sometimes, he goes up to the interstate entrance, flags down a trucker or a traveling salesman or just some homo, and gives the guy a little action to get a ride up to the stroll in Toledo. Usually by the end of the first night, some older guy takes him home for a few days. It's the main way he gets new clothes. Paul says he's not really queer or anything but you can take his word or not on that, I guess. I think that stuff is pretty gross and when I picture him doing it, I kind of want to puke. But that is what he does."

"And you guys are going up there to make him stop?"

Cheryl sighed. "Well, no. If he was just turning tricks and finding older guys to take care of him, we wouldn't like it but we wouldn't interfere. But two years ago some guys on the team were driving around trying to find the stroll and they found the gay part of it. We were doing *Charley's Aunt* in the Drama Club and Paul did Babbs, which is a guy who wears a dress, and he had a fight with his dad and because of that didn't go to the cast party on closing night. So he was up there in Toledo, hustling men, and those football players saw him and beat him half to death, and bragged it up to the whole school. *And they got away with it.*"

"You sound pretty pissed."

Cheryl sped up. "Shit. Mostly we all feel like such *losers*. Even a guy as brainy as Danny feels that way. But Paul's so talented—sings, draws, acts—everything!—he's just *beautiful*. And those assholes got away with it, beat him so bad his hands were swollen up and he couldn't play the piano or draw, he was too stiff to dance or twirl—it just makes me sick. Because they hate—"

"Cheryl," I said, "we're doing ninety, and we can't afford the time to talk to a statie right now."

"Sorry." The little reflectors on the road-edge markers stopped coming at us quite so fast.

"So what do you guys do?"

"Cheryl hears things," I said, "because, excuse my saying it, she's a social, or at least the other socials think she is. There's always some dumbass trying to impress a popular girl by telling her he's going to beat up that goddam makes-you-sick queer. So Cheryl and me go find Paul—usually it doesn't take long because if he's not right out on the street working, within a few minutes he'll be dropped off again. He listens to Cheryl more than he will to anyone else—uh, because he has had a crush on her forever—"

Cheryl sighed, loudly.

"Well, it's true, and I thought I'd have to explain why he'll get in the car with you—"

"Not the best way to explain it to someone who is turning into his girlfriend, Karl."

"It's okay," Marti said. "Really. Haven't even had the first date yet." I could hear a little puckish smile, and she said, "I'd already figured out Cheryl had kind of a crush on *him.*"

"Yeah," Cheryl said. "It would never work."

I was looking back at Marti, and her eyebrow couldn't have cocked any louder if she'd screamed *Why?*, but instead she asked, "So what happens when Cheryl talks to him?"

"He follows her back to the car—usually after some dramatics—and we bring him back and crash him out somewhere. It works good as long as we get there before the big monkeys do."

"So the bat is in case you get there second?"

Cheryl shrugged. The tires sang on the pavement as we rolled into a patch of deeper darkness, so that Cheryl and I were lit by the dashboard glow, and all that showed of Marti was a vague cloudy glow of hair, and the glint of her glasses frames and braces, like the ghost of Palmer Eldritch in that book.

"Well," Cheryl said, finally, "some years ago when he was really fucked up, Karl did a couple real bad things, which were pretty scary—well, *really* scary—and so a lot of kids that don't know him call him 'Psycho Shoemaker,' which really hurts his feelings and is *so* unfair, but it also means that some kids who don't know him are scared shitless of Karl. And there's a particular reason that football players might be kind of scared of Karl with a bat." She shrugged. "And of course the stroll is in a bad, bad area, and I'm tiny, and Karl's tall and muscular and looks crazy. Sorry, Karl, but you do. I feel a lot better getting out of the car knowing he's in here watching out for me, with that bat across his lap."

"How often do you guys do this?"

"A few times a year," I said. "Not even once a month."

"Eight times in two and a half years," Cheryl said. "Over the summer I got curious and counted them up in my diary."

I nodded. "Seems about right. See, Paul's my best friend from, like, the dawn of time, but he'd never listen to me about this, but he'll listen to Cheryl because she's like his Blanche Fleur, you know? So I have to stay in the car while Cheryl talks him into it, and then when he realizes I've seen him like that again, he'll go way over the top for crying and sobbing and hysteria."

"He doesn't, um, just do it for the attention?"

"He could get just as much attention if he'd just ask us," Cheryl said.

We crossed over the river into Maumee, turned west and then north, and made our way through deserted streets.

"Uh, so—Karl, excuse my being a big chicken, but

what happens when you get out with the bat? Do they just back off?"

"Actually," I admitted, "we've *always* gotten there first. I've never even had to get out—there hasn't even been a bum hassling Cheryl. This time of night, all that's on that street is a few young guys hustling, and we usually get Paul into Cheryl's car in like two minutes. The guys from the team take a long time getting drunk and psyching up for it. That's one reason we're so nervous, is we're cutting it so close this time, and maybe for the first time I'll have to get out of the car."

"So after we get him, what do we do?"

"Traditionally, we go get food at Denny's in Maumee, talk for hours, then head back to Lightsburg, and it's all cool. Of course last year, twice, we didn't hear about it at all till we saw Paul in school, all bruised up. But most of the time we get there in time to save his stupid butt."

For a couple miles of dark silence, I stared out the window and thought. Operation Be Fucking Normal was kind of off track, come to admit it.

Besides saving Paul from ass-thrashings, us Madmen, singly and in combination, also saved Paul from running away, and suicide attempts, and getting into serious drugs. He took a lot of saving, and it wasn't *all* because his dad would slap him around and call him a homo. Hell, Kimmie wasn't half that much a mess for being beat up and called a whore. She was tough and mean and looking for the right guy to run away with and marry, and that's what she'd do as soon as a guy that wasn't a loser hood was interested in her. The thing was, Paul's reaction to all that shit at home was always fucking grand opera, with all the Madman Underground as supporting players.

Actually, maybe more like what my dad called a horse opera, an old western. When I was little one Toledo station showed reruns of *The Lone Ranger* all the time, right after dinner, and I'd sit next to Dad and watch. He'd always be the Ranger and I'd be Tonto. I was thinking that was kind of my life—permanently Tonto. Always the guy who got beat up, never the guy who got the girl; always the one outside making a noise like an owl, or sneaking through the woods to make the plan work, and never the one everybody was thanking.

And being the Tonto I always was, here I was again: Tonto to Paul, who was artistic and beautiful; Tonto to Cheryl, who was off to save the beautiful artist; Tonto to my crazy mom; probably Tonto to old Browning—I was the eternal sidekick.

Once again, Tonto got to get there in time to save Kemo Sabe. Then Kemo Sabe ride off into sunset with both girl. Them share loneliness of masked man.

Meanwhile, back in Lightsburg, Tonto go back to Teepee of Heap Big Heap of Catshit, in case somebody need to save Fucks With Everybody.

Tonto fucking tired. Tonto hardly wait to join pony soldiers. Kill babies and burn villages heap less work than take care of Fucks With Everybody and Kemo Sabe and whole goddam fucking village.

That was one fine set of jokes, to judge by the mood I was getting into. I was kind of hoping the team would show up. Just once maybe I'd get to use the bat; the way that had felt, the shiver in my palm from when I'd whacked Al's elbow, was still something I loved to remember.

Yeah, I did want that. Fuck Jesus if I was gonna let a bunch of big dumb apes pound my best friend.

More of the buildings rolling by were boarded up, smaller and closer together, fewer big plants and more little old shops. We began to see people out walking around, mostly black people, some of them glaring at the car full of white kids.

I couldn't blame them. Assholes from all the little jerkwater towns around thought it was very cool and brave to go "coon calling," which was driving by some black guy who was minding his own business and yelling "coon!" at him. Not just farm boy assholes, either. I'd seen Paul do it, once; I didn't know what to say so I never asked him about it.

When I was a freshman, Gratz had braced up two guys in the parking lot because they'd coon-called Naomi Smith, who was one of our few black students. I didn't see it but from what I heard, Gratz ran in front of the dumbass kids' car and when they slammed on the brakes, he dragged them both out, one in each hand by the collar, hauled them into the school, made them write out confessions and write letters of apology to Naomi. Supposedly he'd stood over Emerson and insisted that that was going to be a week's suspension, too.

It was kind of a legend there in Lightsburg. It was so perfectly Gratzical to go all apeshit about something just because he thought it was important.

To me, he was just one more hollering asshole making more trouble than it was worth. I wondered if somewhere in the tirade he no doubt gave those guys, he told them to quote and not call.

A couple-few more blocks took us into the stroll: lots of cheap featureless brick hotels with red neon VACANCY signs, a couple of yellow-signboard dirty-book stores, mostly just lots of empty storefronts and boarded-up gas stations. Cars started slowing down along the sidewalk. In the left lane one guy with silver hair and a long pointy nose, more or less a big leprechaun or a small elf, pulled up in a Cadillac, looked and saw that Cheryl was in her cheerleader uniform, and leaned over to roll down his window. Before he could say anything to her, Marti shot him the finger and I held up the bat, and he took off.

"I *hate* this part," Cheryl said.

"We need a bumper sticker that says 'We're just here to rescue the fairy,'" I said.

She whooped like a maniac. "Oh, shit, Karl, why am I not in love with you?"

"I always meant to ask. Why *aren't* you in love with me?"

She pretended to think before she answered. "Because neither of us would make enough trouble to keep the other one miserable?"

"Fuck *yeah*," I agreed. "Let's skip the love and just use each other."

"We get too pissed when other people do."

"You guys act like best friends, or a real tight couple," Marti observed.

"We've just been friends a long time," I said.

Cheryl nodded. "Okay, boy zone coming up after the next turn. If we're going to see him we'll usually see him by our third or fourth trip through; he doesn't spend much time with anybody unless someone takes him home."

Cheryl turned the corner into a broad avenue; half the streetlights were out, and the flat bland buildings were peppered with windows as dark and empty as a vice principal's soul. Cars cruised by a few nicely dressed young guys; it wasn't nearly as big and crowded as the regular stroll. No Paul on the first try, and she headed back around.

On our fourth trip through, three cars ahead of us, Paul got out of a big old white Cadillac; probably some guy who'd driven in from Sylvania to get a blow job from a boy, before going home to hear the kids' prayers and read the Bible with his wife. Paul waved good-bye and blew a kiss and then turned and saw us pulling over. He started walking away, obviously angry.

"Shit, he's gonna be a jerk about it," Cheryl said. "What do you think, Karl? We can't stop here."

"Round the corner. You and Marti go together and stick close to each other. I'll get out and stand by the car, with the bat down low so a cop just driving by won't see it. If you yell I'll be right there. Don't get more than half a block away."

"Good." She pulled the car in behind a van and I hopped out, holding the bat down by my leg against the car door. Cheryl handed me her keys and purse, and she and Marti ran around the corner after Paul.

I moved around to lean my ass against the hood of the car, figuring that the way Paul was acting, Cheryl might need some time to get him to come along. I wasn't sure which thing I needed to hide more, my ball bat or her purse. I *really* hoped a cop wouldn't come by. I guess I could try to convince him I was playing midnight softball in the gay league.

I thought how normal kids were spending their Friday nights after a game. Probably having pizza, or road drinking, or making out. Whereas I was standing on Mug Me Street in Toledo, Ohio, with a baseball bat and a purse.

Normal kids would go home and tell their moms nothing much happened, no matter what actually did. My mom wouldn't ask me, I sure as shit wouldn't tell her, and anyway usually *I* was the one waiting up for *her*. Normal kids would be happy because someone they liked had been nice to them, or crying over getting dumped, or lonely and wondering if there was more to life than this. They would know pretty much what they felt, and if they had a story to tell about it later, it would be something like "The Night We Beat the Scumcats" or "The Night I Felt Up Mary Sue."

I didn't have any feelings that I had a name for, and no idea how the story would come out.

Paul came back around the corner with the girls, one on each arm, holding him close as he shuffled along with his head down. I walked toward them.

A girl's voice behind me said, "Don't try it, asshole."

I whipped up the bat, turned around, and found myself face-to-face with Bonny, Danny, and Squid.

There was a very long pause, and then all of a sudden Cheryl whooped—do they teach them to whoop like that at social school, or what? We were all laughing.

I lowered the bat and said, "See here, you savages, stop your violence this moment or I shall strike you with my purse," really hissing all those *s*s, and god we all laughed.

We sorted out the kind of information that you get

from everyone talking at once. Bonny's boyfriend Chip had ditched her to go queer-thumping, which meant he was now her ex-boyfriend, though he didn't know it yet. She'd rushed to Pietro's, because she knew that Danny often took Squid there for postgame pizza. "I knew Karl was working late, and I couldn't find Cheryl, and I was afraid they wouldn't get here in time. And you're new, Marti, I just didn't think of getting you, sorry about that."

Squid had spotted Cheryl's car, and seen a dark figure standing there with an obvious weapon. Danny and Squid decided that the dark figure must be waiting to ambush Paul, Cheryl, and Karl when they got back. So they parked down the street and started stalking me, ready to thwart my evil plan.

Bonny was pretty proud about it, and all. "Okay, we're not the varsity team for Paul-rescues, but I think we're a real strong JV. Strength on the bench and all. I think we did a pretty good job. If Karl had been about to attack Paul with a ball bat, we'd've been right there—"

"That's why I didn't," I said. "Also why I gave back Cheryl's purse. Don't hurt me."

Tales the Madmen Never Tell

SO WE ALL went to Denny's in Maumee, which didn't mind groups of high school students on a weekend night. Not that they were fools about it—the Denny's lady took one look at us and put us at a table away from other people. I ended up perched on the corner of one of those round bench things; Paul was at the center (of course), Marti sitting close beside him on one side, Bonny on the other. Cheryl faced me across the table, and Danny and Squid were in chairs.

We did the usual thing we did when we'd all had a scare and come through it okay; everyone had to tell everyone else the story, all at once, loud. So we did that for a while. When that had about died down, Marti said, "So I guess this is another Madman Underground story."

"I guess so," Paul said. "I'd like to have a few less starring roles, get more character-actor work, in the future, I think." He was still in that drum major uniform, his folded hat like a thick black Frisbee on the table by his plate.

There was an itchy, crawly feeling behind my eyeballs. I wanted to sleep, but I wanted this more. Wedged between Squid and Bonny, I was home.

I dumped my two poached eggs into my bowl of chili and stirred them in; food helped. I thought about coffee, but maybe I would still get some sleep tonight.

The other Madmen were filling Marti in on our history and customs and stuff, I guess you could say, like several different versions of how Squid and Danny beat up the Worthless Brothers and got away with it, and the time Paul decided to take off running instead of coming along, so Cheryl tackled him and had to tell a cop he was her brother, and the night me and Paul and Kimmie and Squid and his two younger sibs ended up all sleeping at Darla's, and it turned into sort of a batshit-weird pajama party. "No shit," Squid said, "and then Darla starts crying because she misses her kid brother—and Marti, I mean this, she'd've *killed* Logan, sooner or later, if he'd stayed there with her. She says so herself when she ain't crying about him being gone. And she took us on like the grand tour upstairs into all the old rooms with sheets over the furniture, like a movie haunted house or something, and she talked about her grandma and she was crying and shit the whole time. I guess she actually lives in about three rooms downstairs. I think she's not real happy."

"Imagine that," Paul said, a little more sarcastic than it needed to be. He pissed me off sometimes because he'd be rude to Squid that way, and though Squid wasn't dumb, it was easy to make him feel dumb. I hairy-eye-balled Paul, and he glared at me, and I knew it wasn't all okay, not yet anyway, we were just having a truce in front of people.

Paul yammered on. Something about getting rescued always made him gabby. When it was just him and me and Cheryl, used to be we'd just sit here or on Cheryl's car hood in some highway rest area or out at the tar pond, and Cheryl and me would listen to him just flow till dawn; he could talk up everything till it was all so much cooler than it really was. I was sorry this wouldn't be one of those nights.

He had finished telling Marti all about half a dozen other stories—well, officially telling Marti, and more like reperforming them for everyone else, but they were good stories and Paul did them well. If I'd had a little more energy and not been so pissed off at the little shit, I'd've been loving the stories, too. Sort of winding down for a breath, he asked, "So anybody got any idea what our new shrink is going to be like?"

"It's a woman," Danny said. "I was in the office this

morning and when Brean turned her back, I read everything on her desk. At least I think it's a woman—Leslie is usually a woman, isn't it? Doctor Leslie Schwinn, like the bicycle. Dibs on the first one to make a joke about sniffing her seat."

Everyone went *yuck!* and started beating on Danny, not hard, just having fun, but I could see the waitress moving our way, so I cued them all she was coming, and we straightened out and Bon and me did the talk-to-grown-ups and got it all cool again.

I could never quite believe how straight-arrow Danny, who wouldn't say "shit" without apologizing, made the grossest jokes of any of us.

Anyway, once we settled back, Danny said, "And she's out of one of those high-speed shrink programs, three years to a doctorate—that place down by Portsmouth, OSU-Hillbilly, whatever they call it. So she'll probably be either one of those that knows the book and nothing else, or one of those old ones that went through those classes ignoring the book, because she had six grandchildren so that was all she needed to know, and now she just wants to help us youths live up to our potentials."

There was some discussion about whether trying to make us fit the book, or trying to help us with all that fucking wisdom and experience, was more obnoxious, before Paul concluded with, "I guess we'll all see on Monday. Except for Karl, of course, who has his magic letter from dear old Gratz, and now carries messages for him."

"I think most of them already know," I said, feeling dead and sick in my stomach.

"Yeah, we all know," Paul said.

"I just don't want to go to therapy anymore," I said.

"But what's your excuse? Because your mommy is crazy and your daddy is dead?"

There was the kind of silence you would get if someone threw a dead cat onto the table.

At least I was wide awake now. I felt like hitting Paul and somehow I thought that was what he wanted me to do, so I knew I wouldn't. And he knew my Psycho act, so it wasn't like I could scare him, either. So I just said, "My mom has a lot of problems. She tries but she fucks up. She's not my excuse for anything. I didn't go to the principal's office with you guys because I didn't. I don't want to be in therapy so I'm not going to be. It doesn't mean anything. I'm still your friend. And leave my mother fucking out of this. Remember what I said to you in the hall."

"I have *not* forgotten."

People looked puzzled. Maybe word hadn't gotten around that we'd had a fight.

I just wanted him to back the fuck off my mom.

We were still staring at each other, and everyone else was dead quiet, when Squid raised his shoulders and let them settle. "If Karl don't want to go to therapy, that's cool with me. I know he's still my friend. Hell, he's up here falling asleep in Denny's because he had to come and take care of a friend."

"Nobody asked you to." Paul looked at me, as if it had been me talking.

Marti was looking at me really strange; Bonny and Danny were looking down at the table like they were playing imaginary chess with each other, and it was a tough spot in the game. I didn't want to look at Cheryl.

"I came out tonight," I said. "That's all. Seemed like the right thing to do. Anytime anyone needs me, you can ask. Probably I'll be there."

"You were real there this morning in Gratz's class, weren't you?" Paul said. "So it looks to me like your get-out-of-therapy magic-bullet letter comes at a price, hunh?"

"Um, look," Cheryl said, "it's pretty late, um, anyone need a ride home?"

"I should get home," I said. "I'm really tired."

I paid for my meal, and Cheryl's and Squid's, and the three of us left together; everyone else would be going home in Danny's huge old Buick Riviera.

We drove for a while, along the river, then out of the lights of the towns and into the dark roads between the cornfields, not taking the interstate because, I guess, Cheryl wasn't in any hurry. Squid was pretty much asleep on my shoulder, muttering now and then. "What?" Cheryl said.

"He just said 'Tony and Junie' a couple times. I think he's asleep," I said, softly. "Considering he played a football game earlier today, and I think he had some kind of fight with his old man, and he probably bagged groceries for a couple hours before I had dinner with him at Philbin's—I guess he's entitled to be tired."

"Yeah, he played both ways, Coach always does that when they're really getting clobbered, puts him on defense too. I don't know why."

I shrugged. "Because Squid plays just as hard when there's no hope. Also because if that big Mexican kid gets hurt in a game that doesn't matter, nobody will care."

"'Cause I *ask* to play a lot, and other guys don't want to, but I do," Squid said, into my shoulder. "It's boring on the bench." A second later he was snoring again.

The car rolled along quietly; at least with the money Cheryl's dad had married, she had a nice car, not like the beaters most of my friends had, or whatever POS I'd have been driving if I'd wanted to afford a car. We slid through the dark tunnel of the willows and cottonwoods along the river road like there was nothing else in the universe but dark, and us, and the headlights; Cheryl had CKLW, "Radio Free Ohio," on, real soft, so I couldn't tell what the song was, but at least it was music and it wasn't country, and that was something.

After a while Cheryl said, "Karl, you're still *my* friend. And you were right there when Paul *really* needed you, and he's being bitchy. I understand how much you just want a year of things being the way they're supposed to be. Shit, when I get home the first thing I do is make sure my grandpa is not in my sister's bed, or she's not curled up someplace crying. And I'm a cheerleader, and popular, and all that crap. I feel like, god, I should only be worrying about cute boys, and what to wear, and college applications."

"You're probably more normal than I'll ever get to be," I admitted.

"Yeah. Right." She turned onto Lightsburg Pike. We blazed through Republican Corners at about eighty, and I wondered about Rose Carson and her couch. Had old Browning, after all his sermons about how important your friends were, gotten around to calling her? Maybe when we took her couch back, I'd help him out, and offer to go outside to holler at the goddam ghouls while he nailed old Rose on the couch to test it out.

"You have the strangest smile, Karl."

"Thinking about horrible things," I said.

We dropped Squid off at his house, and he sort of staggered up to the porch. I think he said something like "See you" but it could have been almost anything.

As Cheryl pulled out, she asked, "Karl, if one of us needs help . . . will you be there?"

"I was here tonight."

"I know. Karl, if Gratz tears into *me* on Tuesday morning . . ."

"I don't know. Fuck, I *could* have stood up to him. He'd still have given me that letter, I think. Because my dad was his AA sponsor, it's like he wants to be my dad or something anyway, and besides I wasn't even sure I wanted that letter by the time it happened. I don't know why I didn't go with you guys." Then I sighed and it just popped out. "I'd just had a big fight with Paul, actually. That's why I was late to class, 'cause I was in the bathroom."

"Crying?"

It was like mentioning it started me off again, my face getting all soggy and runny instantly, like a paper towel settling onto a puddle. "Shit, oh, shit."

She took a turn away from my house.

"Where are we going?"

"Out to the tar pond. You need to talk and it's nicer out there than sitting in my car in your driveway."

The tar pond she was talking about was a couple of miles out of town. See, Lightsburg was rich once and could've joined OPEC, I guess could've *been* OPEC; Gist County produced some huge amount of oil. It's all gone now, because it was all shallow and easy to take out of the ground. And where you have oil close to the surface, you have tar ponds, big puddles of tar that rain and ground seep collects on top of. It poisons the ground for maybe two hundred yards back of the pond, so the farmer usually just throws a low berm around the tar pond to keep it from flooding into his ditches, and grows Christmas trees or firewood there.

The tar pond we all called "*the* tar pond" had a broad dirt beach around it where not much grew, just a few tall, spindly, ill-looking milkweeds. It was a favorite make-out spot, and sometimes a place to smoke a little dope, and all summer long it tended to have a lot of parties at it. You could just drive right up the farm road and over the berm, and park under the big clump of cottonwoods and pine trees, right by the tar pond itself.

It was cold, and damp, and the moonlight shining on the rainbow oil slicks on the black water made it colder still. Even with her cheerleader jacket, Cheryl shivered and pressed against me. We had walked maybe a third of the way around the little quarter-acre pond, kicking beer bottles out of our way, watching the stars jiggle and dance in the drafty wet air around the pond.

Finally she said, "Karl, you and me and Squid . . . we're the ones everyone always counts on, you know?"

"Yeah, I know." The stars really twinkled out here, like tumbling snowflakes sharp as steel between the branches and treetops. "Cheryl, I don't really trust myself, anymore, either."

"So you're saying we *can't* count on you?" She must be tired, too, and worried.

"Remember when Dennis died?"

Paul's big brother had been a big social and stuff in high school, the kid his father had *wanted* to have, a popular-guy athlete that Mr. Knauss was glad to have sitting next to him in the reelection brochure picture, not like his faggot son or his whore-baby daughter, as I'd heard him describe Kimmie more than once. Dennis was the only kid Mr. Knauss didn't consider a "dud."

Dennis had shot himself during his freshman year of college, just three weeks after getting there. No note. No one knew why.

"Yeah," she said. "You and me drove all over hell with Paul while he cried, and then after he fell asleep, you and me sat up all night on the hood of this car, watching waves on Lake Erie. You mean, like, we share that, and we can trust each other?"

"I just happened to think of it," I admitted. "I don't know that I really mean anything. Maybe just thinking about the tales the Madmen never tell, or the way that we only tell the stories about things that worked out okay."

"I'm worried about you," she said, and took my arm, and rested her head with all that soft pretty hair against my shoulder. I could feel a boner stirring and I didn't want to freak her out, I was one of her very few straight guy friends who hadn't actually tried to fuck her. She was freaked about sex after the things her grandfather—and pretty much every boyfriend—had done to her.

So of course she had to turn and hold me. I kind of kept my ass back and didn't quite touch her down below, but it was close enough I could feel her warmth. "You're really the best, Karl, you know that. I'm worried about what's going to become of you. You put so much into taking care of everyone."

She rubbed the back of my neck, and her hair brushed my cheek. I didn't know what to say or think. After a bit she took my hand and we walked back to her car.

Just as we got close, someone loudly said "Shit!" and the lights came on in a car that had pulled up next to ours. I saw a bunch of thrashing around in the front seat and then they pulled out and zoomed away.

Cheryl started to laugh. "Oh, Christ."

"Did you see who it was?"

"Yeah, Stacy Hobbins. Her car, anyway, and that looked like a lot of blonde hair, so that's who I assume it was. She's been getting closer and closer to putting out for Steve for like two months. She has romantic notions, and she's not letting him into the cookie jar till everything is just perfect. I'm afraid we just spoiled it for her, again, like something always does. She's always complaining that it gets to be just the perfect moment and then something goes wrong. So she'll be pissed at me all next week. And she'll probably try to get you into a fight with Bret."

"I'll tell him he can have you."

"Don't you dare. I don't want him to have me. Tell him you're all mine and you'll slam his nuts in a Bible if he ever looks at me again."

"Uh, I guess you don't like him anymore?"

"Two dates with him was three too many. He's such a

good Christian boy. Says grace before he starts trying to feel me up, wants it to be my fault that he's horny. Danny says he's a sneaky bastard too."

"Then why'd you go out with him in the first place?"

"I tend to think it's a compliment when a guy asks me out, and have a hard time saying no unless he's an actual head case. You should keep that in mind in case you ever get desperate for a date."

I was so wiped out I didn't even notice that that might be a hint. I half-fell into her passenger seat, and we didn't say much on the five-minute drive back to my house.

When we got there, all the lights were on. The lawn chair, and Mom's suitcase were still on the porch, but Mom wasn't. "Shit," I said.

"What?"

"Mom was taking off with a guy for the weekend. That's her suitcase. That means she got stood up. There's gonna be a shitstorm waiting inside, one way or another." I reached for the door handle, feeling a thousand years old.

"Hey," Cheryl said.

"What?"

"Turn this way." I did and she hugged me real long and close. It made me feel all warm and supported and like my dick was going to explode, but at least at this angle I didn't have to worry about Cheryl noticing.

She kissed my cheek. "I hope you're my friend,

because I can't help being yours. 'Night, Karl. Get some sleep, as soon as you can."

On the porch, Mom's suitcase sat next to the lawn chair, surrounded by dozens of crushed-out cigarette butts. I was just thinking about what this might mean as Cheryl's car pulled away behind me.

When I went inside, Mom was just lying there, on the couch, hugging herself, still in the nice outfit she'd picked for going up to Put-in-Bay. The coffee table and floor around the couch had maybe ten or so empty beer bottles scattered around, and there was a very full ashtray in the middle of the coffee table as well. There were cats packed all around her like they were trying to keep her warm; they always seem to know when a person feels like crap and is going to hold still long enough to be a good place to nap.

Mom looked up, pushed the thick bright-yellow hair out of her face, and reached for me with both arms. "Got a hug for your mom, Tiger?"

"Sure, always." Seemed to be my night for hugs. I sat down next to her, on the edge of the couch, and she shrugged off all those cats and curled around me like a python, wrapping her arms around my neck and pressing her face into my chest, her body under my arm, her legs pushing against my back. She hung on for a while; every time she'd go to talk, she'd start to sob, and stop and rub her face around on my chest again.

Finally, her voice muffled by my shirt, her lips moving against my chest, she whispered, "Tiger, I sat out on the porch till way, way, way after dark. I smoked all the cigarettes I had. I didn't have a phone number for Bill or anything, couldn't call to see what was going on. After a while it was really cold out there, and it was too dark for anyone to see me, so I just let go and cried, and cried, and cried. Isn't that silly, Tiger?"

"I don't think so, Mom, not at all. You were hurt."

"I mean, isn't it silly for your mom to be crying to you over some boy? It's supposed to be the other way round, isn't it?"

"At least there's someone for you to cry to," I said, feeling practical and tired. "And anyway, you'd be even more upset if *I* was crying over some boy." That made me think of Paul, which I didn't want to do. "So did anything else happen? Have you just been crying here the whole time?"

"Unh-hunh. No Bill. You can hear the phone ring all over the yard, I would have heard him if he'd called." She was crying harder, and I squirmed a little to get more comfortable.

"I'm sorry, Mom. You were hoping—"

"I was *so full* of hope. And besides I *told* all my friends about this and now they're going to ask how it went when I

see them on Monday and I don't know what I'll tell them."
She sobbed again, and clung tighter to me. "I hate myself, Karl. I hate myself. I don't know why I even *thought*
a nice man would want to spend time with me."

"He's not looking like such a nice man to me right
now." I was trying not to fall asleep.

"So finally," she said, "I came inside to wait, and got
into some beer from the fridge, and have been lying here,
crying and drinking ever since, with just the kitties for
company. I tried turning on the TV now and then, but I
was afraid that with it on, I might not hear the phone.
Besides all the programs that were on tonight were sad,
people dying of diseases or getting away with crimes or
things like that, or those mean, mean hateful comedies.
And I can't watch the news, Tiger, you know me, I hate
news, news is bullshit anyway. Thank you for coming
home."

"You're welcome, Mom," I said. The world was kind of
spinning and I really wanted to get to bed.

When she finally eased up her grip, I got up and
brought in her suitcase, and started to steer her toward
the shower. She started to complain that I was "doing all
these Me-Big-Man-Fix-It Things, instead of listening to
me, Tiger, that's what a woman wants, you need to just
listen, I need you to just listen."

"You need a shower and bed. You'll feel better."

"You sound so adult-y. My little man. All grown up

and wants me to get my bath and put my jammies on."

Eventually she disappeared into the bathroom with her robe and towel, and the water started to run, and I could hear her in there singing that "C'mon, People Now Smile on Your Brother" song, in her sharp head voice. She did that when she was starting to feel better, usually, so it was a good sign.

I went upstairs to start getting ready for bed, myself. The door to my room was standing open, but my hiding places weren't disturbed. There was a pile of catshit right in the center of my bed, and one throw rug piss-soaked, which I'd have to wash before I could go to bed.

I wished I knew which cat it was that liked to shit on the bed. Grave Thirty-four in Cat Arlington was waiting.

Hairball was rubbing up against my leg, and I looked down at him and said, "Listen, four cans of tuna, all for you. Just point him out to me, and don't ever mention our conversation, how's the deal sound?"

Unfortunately the purring probably didn't mean "yes."

I lugged my bedding down the stairs. Mom was still in the shower. Groggy as I was, I did one more stupid thing—there's always enough time and energy for that. I forgot to change the settings on the washer to cold.

Mom came out of the shower complaining that the water had started to get cold. Between her long shower and washing my bedclothes, I had used up all the hot water. I took a freezing cold shower—it was better than putting a body cruddy from a day's work into my clean sheets—and then slept in two old sweatshirts on my bare bed, dozing and looking at Dad's notes, until I heard the dryer stop at about three A.M. Between being actually clean and warm, and what the day had been like, I was asleep in an instant.

PART FOUR

(Saturday, September 8, 1973)

19

Love, Waffles, Capitalism, Scooby-Doo,
and a Grave in the Rain

I SAT UPRIGHT in bed like I'd had an electric shock, and sent poor old Hairball tumbling ass over teakettle. The slant of light in the room looked wrong. I grabbed my alarm clock. It wasn't set; I thought I had but I must not have.

Ten thirty. Holy fucking shit. I should already be at my second job of the day.

I was breathing like I'd run six miles, rolling over, yanking on my pants, rehearsing in my mind all the apologies I would have to make to all the nice old ladies because I had missed one, would be late for the next, would have to make it up and that might mean the other two—

As I yanked my pants up, I heard something, realized

I'd been hearing it for a while, and pulled open the curtains of my bedroom window.

It was raining, steady and heavy, a thick curtain of silvery water. MacReady Avenue was flooded three inches deep up at the corner with Grant Street. It must have been doing this for hours.

The sky rumbled low and heavy; brief pale glows of lightning washed everything.

I was saved. I didn't deserve it at all, but I was saved.

I put on a T-shirt and went down to the phone by the front door, and started calling. Even if it cleared up later, the ground would be much too soggy and wet for any of the jobs I had scheduled—turning a compost heap, changing over a bed and replanting it, turning a summer bed under, planting three fruit trees. I called them all up, and even Mrs. Planetari, the job I had missed, seemed surprised, since it was so obvious that I wouldn't be doing any of the work today.

I promised I'd find time to get the fall planting done during the next week, since the flowers and trees were already purchased and needed to get into the ground, and turn the beds and the compost heaps next Saturday. Maybe I could throw Squid and Tony some of the work.

My customers all seemed to think it was noble that I didn't work Sundays. The real reason was because I needed that time to work around the house and get some rest. Dad had kind of made me promise to do that for myself—not for God.

"Karl?" I hung up the phone as I turned; Mom was leaning out of the kitchen. She was wearing her ratty old pink bathrobe and slippers, which she usually only wore in the winter when it got really cold and windy and our poor old furnace couldn't keep up. She grinned through her mop of gold-blonde hair. "Do I look fucking motherly, or what, Tiger?"

"I kind of like it."

"You would, horrible boy. Look, I got up early and had a real attack of maternalism, and I cleaned the kitchen. And then I realized it was raining, so I went in and turned off your alarm, and let you get some sleep."

"That was nice of you."

"It was, wasn't it? Sometimes I'm so motherly I impress myself. Anyway, then I thought I'd like a clean kitchen, and now that I have the pleasure of my son's company, I want to do something so motherly it will make us both puke, and make waffles."

Back when I was a little kid, before all the bad stuff started, waffles had been my favorite. For the last couple of years I'd had them now and then at Philbin's or Pongo's, and at home on my birthday and Christmas Day, maybe.

Next thing I knew she was being all corny and stuff, fixing Belgian waffles. I grabbed an umbrella and pulled on rubbers over my sneakers, and ran up Grant Street to Lawsons to pick up Smucker's Strawberry Syrup and

Reddi-wip, so we had the works; I was soaked and freezing when I got back, but there was time for a fast hot
shower before Mom finished the last of the first batch.

By then the rain had picked up and gotten serious
about soaking the ground. It was one of those nice steady
gully-washers that makes everything grow like crazy; I
figured I'd get some weeding work next weekend, too, and
maybe a couple yards to cut, plenty of work for me, Squid,
and Tony.

We sat in the living room and ate those waffles—
they were great, really, as good as they should be—and
watched *Scooby-Doo*. Now and then a cat would act interested in Reddi-wip but Mom had leaned the broom
up against the back of the couch and most of them were
afraid of it, because it was her weapon of choice whenever
she went batshit-crazy on them. Hairball sat next to my
feet and looked at me mournfully, but knew me too well
to make a move on my food.

Mom cracked me up with some of her work gossip,
and I told her about school and my friends, and we both
skipped everything important: I didn't say a thing about
Paul, and she didn't bring up Wonderful Bill, and we had
a great old time there.

She sighed, carried her plate out to the kitchen, and
said, "Fire it up again? If you have one more waffle, I'm
going to succumb to peer pressure and have another myself."

"Come on, kid, the first one's free, and you don't want to be chicken, and all the kids are doing it," I said.

"Eaah! Can't hold out. Okay, two more waffles starting."

I didn't figure this would be the long-awaited Saturday morning when Velma at last gave in to her obvious lust and jumped Daphne, so I left the TV on to entertain the cats, and went out to keep Mom company.

She was leaning against the counter, looking semi-pensive. I let her have whatever thoughts, and just enjoyed feeling like I had my mom back. I knew it wouldn't last, but a couple hours of total sanity, and a day off from work, was such a blessing I could've shit my pants.

After a while she checked the waffle iron, and apparently didn't see what she wanted to see yet, so she shrugged and leaned back up against the counter, and said, "There seems to be some kind of law about guys. The more regular-guy and John-Wayney straight-shootin' square-dealers they are, the more they turn out to be ucky ucky sons of bitches you can't trust."

"I'm sorry that this one didn't treat you better, Mom," I said, because I wanted her to keep talking, since for once it wasn't about drugs, UFOs, Nixon, or what was wrong with my father. "I know you liked this one."

"No he didn't, and yes I did. He—I don't know, Tiger, do you really want my love life with your waffles?"

"Gotta be more interesting than *Scooby-Doo*, Mom."

"Well, at least my love life is more interesting than *something*." She checked the waffle iron again, but I guess a watched waffle never browns. "Anyway, it's just. It's just. Um." She sighed. "Okay, drop the big one on the boy right now, Beth. All right, I really did love Doug. Really. A lot." She brushed her hair back over her ears. "But you know, if he hadn't gotten sick, we'd probably be divorced by now, and I don't know if I'd be like I am, but I wouldn't be like I was. And I guess you and Doug would be living together as two swinging bachelors, hunh?"

That made me laugh like a crazy bastard. "Right, I'd be bringing home hippie chicks for him to hustle."

She opened the waffle iron up and dumped out two perfect waffles. "How do you know when they're ready?" I asked.

She grinned. "Ancient secret, Tiger Sweetie. You get married very young. You get a waffle iron as a wedding present and you have a husband that you think the sun rises on, and very shortly after a little boy that you think it rises and sets on, and they both love waffles. Then you make about ten thousand burned waffles—and about ten thousand half-raw ones—while your husband gamely eats them, and your little boy doesn't care. Eventually you know what a goopity-gooey uncooked waffle looks like, and what a burned one looks like, and you stand by the waffle iron and when it's been a little bit past raw, but before it's burned, you pop it out. You just don't remember all the crunchy carbon and half-raw batter I put on your plate when you were little. It's like all the assassinations, everything looks fine as soon as none of the witnesses are talking."

"I wish I remembered those times better."

"I wish you did too. They were good times. The waffles got better later, but the times were the best they ever were."

She checked to see if I was smiling, so I did, and she sort of smirked.

We plated up the two round, thick waffles—waffle on an oven-warmed plate, then strawberry syrup, then Reddi-wip, the way Dad always said was right, because that way the syrup didn't defluff the Reddi-wip, and he claimed the Reddi-wip insulated the waffle and syrup and kept it all hot. He also said we had to take that first bite within half a minute of doctoring the waffle, to get the full effect.

The Road Runner theme came from the next room, so by common consent, we grabbed our plates and forks, I popped the Reddi-wip can back into the fridge. The door triggered the usual cat stampede, so that I felt like I was wading to the living room upstream through a river of cats.

Nonetheless, we were on the sofa and digging into the waffles well within the time limit. As Wile E. Coyote was setting up his first trap, something with an Acme

Giant Hammer, Mom said, "See, the world played kind of a dirty trick on me, Tiger. Maybe on every woman my age. When I was ten, the last winter of World War Two, me and all my friends used to say all we really wanted was the five Bs, in the right order—bra, boyfriend, bridal shower, bungalow, baby.

"And then the next spring and summer, all these gorgeous boys—well, they looked like men to me—came home in uniforms, and it just seemed to me like, wow, the best hunting there will ever be, and I barely have boobs yet. So I hurried up, if you see what I mean. By the time I was twelve I was the boy-craziest little flirt you've ever seen, and by the time I graduated, so many boys wanted in my pants so bad that I was a *legend*, an absolute fucking *legend*.

"So there I was hopping the counter for Philbin, slinging burgers for the lunch crowd just like you did all summer, and in came this guy who'd stayed in the service a little longer, still had those hard young muscles even though he was a bit older. And he was the bookkeeper and sold jobs for a contractor here in town, and the day that he bought out the guy he worked for, he took me over to Vinville for dinner, and then back here to see *The Best Years of Our Lives* at the Oxford, and then since I wasn't old enough to get into a bar, he drove us down to that beach along the Little Turtle River, and we drank beer and talked. At first I thought it was so weird, Doug kept going on about how much work he had lined up, and being able to afford a house, and what he had in the bank, until I suddenly realized he was proving he had enough to marry me. I realized that when he pulled out the engagement ring, and got down on his silly knees." She leaned back and looked up at the ceiling. "Funny the things waffles bring to mind. Anyway, a deputy found us sleeping in the car at ten the next morning, and made me prove my age, and we went home hungover and laughing. Next thing I knew, here we all were, and he was running for mayor."

"I never heard that version of it before."

"I think it embarrassed Doug. I always told him it was a shame I was too hungover for practical jokes, or I'd have hidden my I.D. and told the deputy he'd kidnapped me from a convent school." She sighed. "Anyway, that was the good part of the story. After that it was one long dirty trick. I was a real good wife to him, Tiger, you know that."

"He always said so."

"Well, except when he was ranting and screaming at me like a nut, but that came later. But by then I guess I was doing a lot of the screaming too. Was it really scary for you, Tiger?"

On the screen, Wile E. Coyote looked down, saw there was nothing under him, and waved bye-bye. "Sometimes," I said. "When you sounded, I don't know, like you were going to *hurt* each other. Most of the time it just made me really sad."

"You loved us both, didn't you? And now all that seems so weird to me because Doug and I were just so different. He was very Earth, you know, and I'm completely Water, and—"

"I guess that makes me Mud."

"Don't joke about important things, Karl, I don't talk about them very often."

We watched the TV for a while longer, and then I said, "I'm sorry if I sounded like I was making fun of you." I took my last bite of waffle and waited. A bunch of kids on the screen were singing and dancing about chocolate milk. "Those were great waffles."

I got up and carried the plates out to the kitchen. There were so few dirty dishes that it seemed like a good idea just to do a fast wash-rinse-stack.

"Sweetie, you don't have to do that." Mom was posing in the doorway with one hand up on the doorframe and the other arm wrapped over her head, holding a cigarette just above her ear. I was pretty sure I'd seen that pose in an ad someplace.

"You seemed pretty happy with the kitchen being clean, thought I'd give you another few hours of it." I slipped the waffle iron into the soapy water and scoured hard with the net brush. "Besides, this is my sneaky way to make waffles happen again."

She hugged me from behind. "Well, all right, you always did love your waffles. And your friends and your parents . . . you're a good kid, Tiger Sweetie. I know I don't always let you know that, but you are."

She was really in good-mother mode this morning. It never lasted but it was always kind of nice, like getting a short visit from the mother I remembered, although it always ripped out my heart.

Her hug, right now, still felt good.

I moved the waffle iron onto the counter, upside down on top of a dish towel, to drip dry. It was like neither of us knew what to say next, or what the other one was going to say. That was kind of new and weird. "So," she said, "since you can't be a slave of capitalism today, do you have time to catch the second cartoon on Road Runner?"

"I do," I said. I poured us both some fresh coffee from the percolator, and we went back to the living room. It was something with Tweety Bird we'd seen ten thousand times before.

When the commercial started promoting a little plastic guy that threw stuff, Mom said, "My head is full of so much programming from when I was a girl. *Girls* get to be themselves, but as soon as you grow boobs, *bam*, you're not yourself ever again. At least not till you're an old lady. I'm hoping to be one of those really cool old ladies that no one can ever shut up that just tells everyone what she thinks and doesn't let men decide for her whether it makes sense or not." She grinned at me. "Don't say, 'You're pretty far along already,' or you're dead, Tiger. But I have to admit, sometimes I'm just being free and myself and enjoying the day, and sometimes I do like upsetting all the old poops in suits." She sighed. "And sometimes I just wish some big strong guy would ride in on a white horse and rescue me."

"Would the horse get along with all the cats?"

"Good question." She leaned and stretched. "I feel so good and so mellow this morning. If I could just always not care as much as I don't care right now, everything would be okay. But I've spent so much time caring about stuff that doesn't matter. First about getting a man, and then about being a good wife and mommy, and then about being groovy and not missing out on the Revolution. Lately I worry a lot about whether I'm still a fox or turning into an old stove, and whether any nice man will ever like me, and whether Neil is ever going to act like a real boyfriend."

I wouldn't've wasted any of *my* wondering-energy wondering whether Neil would ever act like a real mammal, myself, but it didn't seem like a good time to say that.

"And it's times like that I really miss Doug. He was always so certain and so serious about everything and he was a mean old fascist and he was way too hard on you and made you do all that manly-manly stuff, but at least I knew who I was and where I was."

"I *like* doing all that manly stuff," I said. "I like making things and fixing things and earning money, and if I had time I'd like to play sports. It's just the way I am."

"It's the way you think you are because you've been brainwashed and programmed and stuffed all full of angry energy by all these men in power. This is what so many men do to themselves. You think it's just the way you are but you're really just trying to prove you're male. Why don't you get out a little more, have some fun, maybe go out with somebody like that cheerleader girl again, or Cheryl with the big boobs, or that Darla, she's pretty sexy. Men are always doing all these things to be men, and the only thing that can really make a man a man is a woman. That's what Neil always says."

"And Neil is the authority on being a man?"

"A woman knows, Karl, a woman is the only one who knows. He's a lot more of a man than your father ever was. Being a man is about being what a woman really wants and needs."

The one time I'd tried putting a real lock on my door, to keep out the beautiful free-spirited kitties, who I should be more like instead of always worrying about ucky ucky money, Neil had gone up, while I was at McDonald's, and kicked the whole goddam door down, and then he and Mom had looked hard and found three of my cans. Luckily one of them I had just started and it didn't have much in it. They had rushed off to a dealer and then the bar.

They were planning to go shopping and get a wedding dress and rings and a tux and so forth, too, but they'd drunk and smoked too much of my money before the stores opened the next day, and anyway it wasn't enough, it just looked like a lot to them. It took me a week to put my room back together, and of course I wasn't going to see the money again.

But the thing that pissed me off the most was that if Neil wanted to break into my room, all he had to do was take two little screws out of the hasp; he'd kicked down the door because he was too dumb to figure out how to use a screwdriver. Looked to me like I'd never be dumb enough to be a real man.

I thought about saying a lot of things, but I didn't say them; maybe I wanted to keep the feeling of the waffles, and her talking like her old self, in my head for just a little longer. Maybe I was hoping she'd apologize like she sometimes did, when she said things that really hurt.

What happened instead was that she went to the kitchen for more coffee, and screamed. I ran out to see what was the matter and she was staring out the window over the sink, tears pouring down her face. I looked and saw something that looked like a bit of shredded blue rug out in the yard; then I realized it was blue-gray, and that it was Ocean, one of her prettiest cats.

She was whimpering. "He's all in pieces. Oh, Karl. Oh, Karl. Oh, poor Ocean."

"Oh, crap," I said, and started pulling my rubbers on again.

It would have made sense to leave Ocean out there, of course, and bury him once the rain let up. He wasn't going to be bothered. Or it might have made a certain amount of sense to go out, pick him up in a garbage bag, and bring him in to lie in state before going out to Cat Arlington. But Mom was wailing, and I thought I'd better get him out of sight as soon as possible, so I pulled on an old Boy Scout poncho I had, zipped up the rain hood, and went out there.

Most of the blood had washed away but there was no question, this was another cat pretty much ripped in half by that old coon, or maybe his twin brother. At a guess, he'd probably figured out that this backyard was a reliable source of fresh cat, and acquired a taste for it—raccoons'll do that, they'll eat anything, but if there's something reliable, they'll get to like it. Ocean had been pretty small and didn't stand a chance.

I'd have to tell Wilson to hurry up about letting his buddies in the Coon Hunters' Club know about our local cat-killer. It was one thing when he was getting one or two a year, but this was the second one this week and the fourth since May; he was rapidly overtaking cars as a leading cause of death.

It was messy in the rain and mud, but it didn't take long; Ocean went into the fourth row, fourth grave, right next to Sunflower, and I tamped down the plug, put the sod over him, and figured the headstone could wait till it was dry enough for me to write on it easily.

Ocean had been pretty nice, actually. He'd been the one on Mom's lap when I'd come home and she'd been crying over Wonderful Bill.

I went inside and said, "I'm sorry."

She was still wiping her face, and I guess "I'm sorry" was the wrong thing to say, because she went into her bedroom and turned up *Let It Bleed* real loud on the stereo. Pretty soon the mingled smells of wet rug and litter pan were joined by pot smoke.

It kept raining, and it was pretty cold out, so we had all the windows closed, and that crappy old gravity furnace turned on. The smell was bad enough for me to notice, and there were drafts everywhere because the storm windows weren't up yet. I grabbed a blanket and wrapped up in it in the couch to do the rest of my homework. After a while I was pretty much buried in cats; I wondered if they knew what had happened to Sunflower and Ocean, and were afraid, or maybe they were just cold and wanted company. Hairball got crawling-under-the-blanket privileges and sat in my crossed legs, purring so loud I could feel him through my bones.

After my homework, I read way ahead in *Huckleberry Finn*. I was in some danger of finishing it over the weekend. Now that Huck and Jim were on the river together, though, I could sure as hell see why Gratz kept telling people not to read it as happy hippies on a raft, because the idea of being out there like that, just me and a friend, taking care of ourselves—well, I about cried, come to admit it, when I realized they were bound to get caught.

No way you could do that in Ohio, though, at least not in Gist County. You could walk a lot faster than any of our rivers ran, and most of them were like the Little Turtle—six inches of water on top of four feet of mud. I had kind of a silly daydream about floating away with all the Madmen, it would have had to be a fucker of a big raft of course, and started laughing when I imagined that we'd come down by the gay part of the river, where steamboats stopped to pick up teenage boys turning tricks, and there would be Paul with his shirt open, in hip waders and a lot of gold chains.

"Good book?" Mom asked.

"The best," I said, and held it up for her to see.

"Gratz just makes you read that one so he can intimidate all the black children, you know, because it has 'nigger' on every page. What were you laughing at?"

"I was thinking about whether I would rather own a plantation," I said, "so I could spend my days whipping slaves, or a steamboat, so I could run down rafts full of hippies."

She shot me the finger and went out to the kitchen; in a few minutes she passed back into her bedroom with a pile of sandwiches and a couple of cans of beer. When I

went out to grab my own lunch, later, I saw she'd squirted ketchup all over the wall and the counter, and figured
she was back to being weird and angry. I cleaned it up,
didn't say anything, and warmed up some tomato soup.
After a while she came out and started doing her UFO
and astrology calculations, spreading books and papers
all over the dining room table. She didn't even say hi.

It was down to drizzle, and I had my AA meeting,
so while Mom was engrossed, I put on my work boots,
grabbed up my umbrella, and headed out to my meeting.

I kept my going to meetings semisecret from Mom—
she knew I didn't accept beer and wine from her anymore,
and she knew I had some friends who had been Dad's AA
friends, because they'd say hi to me on the street, but she
didn't officially admit that she knew that I was spending
time with the ucky ucky mean judgmental people who
just want to tell everyone else what to do and never let
anybody have any fun.

Besides, I didn't *really* betray her—I had quit going to
Alateen. Squid and Danny were always on me to go again,
like I had for a while, but they expect you to talk about
your parents' drinking. I was going to be sober and all
that but I wasn't going to get other people involved with
being sober. Kind of like the guys that would smoke but
not deal. That was my ethical position and I was sticking
to it like a coat of paint.

As I stepped off the porch, there, coming up the walk,

was a guy who just had to be Wonderful Bill, holding an umbrella in one hand. In the other he held a bundle of so many roses that I figured maybe Mom had won the Kentucky Derby. He had on a Greek fisherman's cap, which I think the Greek government was exporting as fast as they could, trying to get them out of Greece because they made all their fishermen look stupid. His corduroy jacket (with elbow patches and big lapels) matched his corduroy pants (with big cuffs). He had hair the color of Saturday night bathwater in a big family, all curly and fro'd up to hide its thinness, a big droopy mustache, and huge puppy dog eyes. He looked like an English professor that wanted to be a folksinger, which is to say, a dork who wanted to be a bigger dork.

On the bright side, he had roses, not a bottle. Besides, the last few Wonderfuls before Bill had looked fresh out of jail.

I kind of sauntered, very big and planting my feet firmly, right up the middle of the walk, forcing him to get out of my way and dip his chukka boots in the mud. As I passed him, I said, "Mom's suitcase is still packed," because it was, and he called "Still?" after me, but I was on my way.

"*Still?*" Horseshit. Wonderful Bill was a big fat puregrade lies-just-to-stay-in-practice phony, and if it hadn't been my mother involved, I'd have thought it was pretty funny. He looked like all three of the male teachers at my school that were trying to be the cool teacher, and like the male librarian that was always hitting on the high school girls, except Wonderful Bill was probably older than my mom. Not only a clown—a clown trying to look like a younger clown, and not succeeding.

Strike one, fool.

And somehow he just happened to be carrying like six tons of roses, but he was going to pretend there was some mix-up between what night he was supposed to pick Mom up—like you could get confused about something like that, when you talked to her that morning, *and* somehow just happen to have a bunch of apology-stuff with you?

Strike two, bare-faced liar.

Either he didn't even care enough to make it convincing, or he was too dumb to realize it wasn't.

Sometime real soon I'd be seeing strike three, that magic moment when Mom had had enough of this one— from the looks of Wonderful Bill, it wouldn't take long.

I could have stuck around to hurry the process up a bit, I guess, but I had a meeting to get to.

You Can't Throw Away a Great Deal Like That

NOW THAT THE rain was down to nasty
spitting drizzle, and I had my good boots and umbrella, it was even kind of nice out here, with some summer
warmth still in the air. The gray, flat land stretched to
the horizon, mirrored by low overhead nimbus, like I was
walking between two endless gray planes. In the dim-
ness, the streetlights came on, and most drivers turned
on headlights. On the soft coat of water that blanketed
everything, the bright reflections softened and smeared
poor old workaday Lightsburg into a painting of a quaint
small midwestern town, like what might hang on the
wall of some rich guy who grew up somewhere else.

If you squinted real hard and didn't let yourself look
at the power plant stack to the right, or the freeway ramp

you could just see to the left, then St. Iggy's almost looked like one of those French impressionist pictures, except for the billboard advertising the Men's Fellowship pancake supper.

As I got closer the resemblance to anything artistic faded fast. My AA meeting was in the basement of St. Iggy's. I wasn't going every day like I had been in June, but I made it to at least one a week, and sometimes I'd get to two or three. I secretly felt that everyone else had a cooler story than I did; they'd all done something really wild and gross while drunk, or gotten really sick, or something.

Me, I'd just pitched that bottle in the Dumpster after Mom's unpleasant birthday, and skipped the whole "so I crawled through my own puke in the gutter" story. So I liked other people's stories a lot—it was one of the best parts—but I hardly ever told mine.

St. Iggy's was pretty much the place for AA meetings, that or private homes, because the Catholics didn't have anything against smoking or coffee, and AA meetings were generally held in a blue cloud with everyone drinking a gallon of coffee. Dick always said it just showed that we were all addicts, and all we'd done was change what we were addicted to.

He and I sat together, directly opposite Norm, who was leading this meeting, a local auto sales guy that I didn't know very well. Besides us there were seven other people, nobody I hadn't seen before, and only two with good stories: Kim, a college girl who sometimes told about getting drunk and losing track of who was fucking her; and Don, a real old bum who had stories about being a hobo and his buddy getting killed on the tracks.

I knew it was real wrong and everything for me to enjoy hearing those stories, but I always did anyway.

So we sat there in the cloud of smoke—Dick and me were the only people not smoking—and everyone had a foam cup of hot coffee, and nobody talked.

After we had all refilled, Norm said, "Well, I guess we're in reruns, but we ought to hear some testimony. Dick, would you mind telling us your story again?"

He got up and did the "I'm Dick and I'm an alcoholic" business you start off with, and then laid it out. Fifteen years ago, over in Joffrey, Indiana, he'd drunk himself out of a good job and a family, and now he had a couple kids who were almost grown and hated him and would never speak to him, and he cooked at Philbin's, and he wished he had a do-over on life.

He went over how he had drunk and gambled the rent and the grocery money away, and passed out on a porch three doors from his own, and drove the car through a closed garage door, and so on. That was kind of lively.

He finished up a little teary-eyed because he was realizing next month would be his youngest daughter's eighteenth birthday. She'd refused to see him in his visitation time for the past three years.

Then we heard Dorothy's story about her little boy

getting burned on the iron while she was passed out, and Herb's about having driven his car into pretty much every ditch and tree in Gist County at one time or another, and Norm said he thought that would be enough, and reminded me it was my turn to lead next Saturday, and we prayed. On the way out, Dick asked me if I'd like to go to Pongo's and have one of those general-purpose sponsor conversations.

I said sure, because Dick always bought—that guy was determined to feed me—and it beat the shit out of going home and being introduced to Wonderful Bill officially, since by now Mom had probably found a way to believe every lie he'd told her, and they'd be in the bedroom, where she would be forgiving him. While she was forgiving a guy, she usually moaned and yelled things that made me feel a little sick, loud enough so I think sometimes the neighbors heard.

I knew it was healthy and normal and she was an adult and all. She told me that all the time. But I just really didn't like listening to it, if I could help it.

So I headed off to Pongo's with Dick—walking, neither of us had a car—and on the way we talked about the fall coming on fast now, a good time of year, and that in a couple weeks Philbin's would start opening at five A.M. every morning, for the hunting and the harvesting seasons, because hunters and combine crew wanted to get fed by six. Dick said, "That's why I like to feed teenage boys, to stay in practice for fall. I wish hunting and combining went on for about six months. I get tired, and it's hard to keep up, but it's extra hours, and I think it's what keeps Philbin from going broke every year. I'd hate to think about having some other boss; I may not make much but he treats me pretty good."

"He's one of the best bosses I've ever had." I told Dick about how the postmovie thing had gone the night before, since he hadn't been there. We chewed over that together some, and concluded that if the Ox could stay open, it would sure help Philbin's, which had to be good for us.

Now the sun was out and it was late afternoon. The whole town seemed like it had been washed, all that white paint and red brick gleaming like in a movie, and the air was extra-crisp and clean, like fall was really coming. You're supposed to tell your sponsor everything, but I wouldn't have told Dick about Paul or any of the stuff that had happened last night, and especially not the whole big fucking mess with Gratz. That was Madman-only.

Pongo's was deserted. We sat at the counter where we could goof with Darla, who liked to joke with Dick better than she did most customers.

Mostly I just told him about being tired and not getting enough sleep, and Dick told me I should get more sleep. I told him I knew that.

After making sure there was nothing big, new, or bad,

Dick said, "Well, believe it or not, I have a date. Nice lady from over in Rossford is going to drive all the way down here to look me over and decide whether we ought to get to know each other—I answered her personal ad. I guess we're having dinner at Pietro's because I already ate here today, and if I ever take a date to Philbin's, Karl, I want you to just kill me, right there and right then; make sure you wipe the cleaver for fingerprints and don't forget to forge my handwriting on the suicide note."

"Good luck," I said. "Is she nice?"

"Well, based on three phone calls and five letters, yeah. Now I have to hope *I'm* nice." He turned to Michelson, who was running his own cash register, and said, "How much to buy both these nice kids a dessert and give the attractive one enough time off so they can hang out for a while?"

Michelson laughed and said, "Great idea, Dick, five'll do it—I won't take a dime more," and they set it up. With a friendly swat on my shoulder, Dick was on his way.

Darla and me took a booth way over in the corner, overlooking West Lock Creek. I filled her in about the Gratz assignment and added, "I'd never read it before, but you know, if he was going to Lightsburg High, Huck Finn would be a Madman like us—crazy dangerous father and all. If we weren't reading it with Gratz, it might even be an okay book."

"Yeah, I know, I read it a couple years ago. Trouble

with Gratz is, even when he's right I want to slap him."
She dug into her purse, found a cigarette, and lit up. I
fought off the vision of a wrinkled, gray Darla coughing
up goop-wads and gasping out, "Goddam doctors."

Once she'd blown a couple streams of smoke around
dramatically, I told her about the two rescue missions
last night.

She thought it was pretty funny that we'd all met up
there and claimed she was hurt not to have been invited.
"Maybe if I start walking Dorr Street myself?"

I must've looked pretty startled because she laughed,
blowing a big gust of smoke up toward the ceiling, and
whipped Mister Babbitt out of her purse. "Mister Babbitt, do you think somebody is having naughty thoughts?
Speak up, naughty bunny. Oh, you think this nasty, nasty
young man was getting off on imagining us doing naugh-
ties for money? And you think we should—oh, well, just
whisper it to me." She held Mister Babbitt up to her ear,
then made a shocked face and talked into him like he was
a microphone. "*Mister Babb*itt! I am not going to slap him
there. That would mean having to *touch it!*"

To get off that subject, I said, "Look, you're gonna
hear from everyone else, so I'm just going to tell you,"
and explained about Gratz and my Get Out of Therapy
Free letter and all that.

She shook her head and whacked her forehead. "Oh,
God, Darla. Oh, *God*. Duh-duh, duh-duh-duh. I am the

dumbest fucking bitch that ever fucking walked, and I'm always finding fresh proof." Her eyes met mine. "That would be *such* a great deal. You know you're gonna bullshit Gratz, wall to wall. You know that's not hard at all. He won't have a clue. Whereas some of these therapists are fairly smart people and they catch on to shit and all of a sudden they're not *near* as nonjudgmental as they say they are, and they nark you out to cops and things . . ." She shrugged. "Jesus, what a great deal, Karl, and here I only realize what he was offering us after I went and called him an asshole in class. Now if I want one of those letters, too, I'm gonna have to kiss him where it feels good and he don't wash." She shook her head again. "Oh, Darla."

"He's a fool and a mean bastard of a bully," I pointed out.

"He is, but if he's a big *enough* fool, you can *cope* with the rest." She shook her head. "That letter means you're gonna miss all the reruns. Danny doing his big-strong-gotta-cry number, brave little Cheryl being so courageous about having to blow Grandpa, and Paul playing 'save me I'm having a hissy fit' every time anyone gets more attention than he does."

"I wouldn't let any of them talk that way about you."

"I wouldn't care."

"Yeah, but I would."

She didn't answer right away. Watching Darla, I saw

that one reason why some smart people smoke is all the delays it gives them to rewrite their answers, and the perfect prop for posing when they finally have what they're going to say all composed perfect. It would make them look so classy if it didn't fucking stink.

After a long drag and looking up in the air, Darla said, "Karl, no wonder they all love you, you stupid bastard."

"Darla, they are my friends. I'm sorry if you don't like anybody in the therapy group."

"They're better than the people that aren't in the group." She picked up the ashtray, which was in the shape of the Pongo's monkey's face, with his mouth open. She seemed to make a point of looking into the monkey's eyes as she stubbed out her cigarette hard enough to make a smeary mess, looking exactly like she was grabbing his decapitated head and ramming it down his throat.

While she lit another, I said, "Look, I know they're screwed up, but they're the friends I have. And I'm so pissed that I'd like to kill Paul, but if any shithead lays a finger on him I'd be there with the bat, like Squid says, to explain 'Don't be an asshole' in terms anyone can understand. It might be fucking crazy—in fact I know it is—but those guys are pretty much all the family I want to admit to. Even Paul. Especially even Paul."

She took another drag and shrugged. "I hang out with them too, as much as I hang out with anybody. At least the Madman Underground have a fucking clue what kind of world it is. But the Madman Underground is all about how much everybody needs each other, and hauling my ass out of here is all about *not* needing anybody. And the Madman Underground is all about telling your story to people who already heard it and like you anyway, and I want to live someplace where I have *my* story, not just some things that happened to me.

"Besides, it's not like it's nearly as wonderful as people like Paul make it out to be. You know I'm on probation for possession; who do you think turned me in? Our old pal Vic Marston the Lovable Wonder Shrink. Who smokes the stuff himself. Maybe he wouldn't have turned me in if I'd let him feel me up the time he tried, hunh? Who do you think tipped my parents when I was gonna elope? Shirley Reloso, that shrink we had freshman year, the one who was really nice to me and made me her special friend and all. The one that narked on me that I was beating up that little turd brother of mine in the first place. *Jes*us, it would feel so good to bang his punkin head up against a door one more time and hear him make those whiny crying noises 'cause he was too chickenshit to really cry, he'd get so scared of me."

At least this was familiar territory. Maybe a third of the time Darla was crying about what a bad person she was, and the awful things she'd done to Logan, and how she was a sex kitten for college boys and a dumb bitch and everyone used her and dumped her and like that. Then maybe another third of the time she was basically a grown-up trapped in high school, it was all about her plan to get out and how she was going to get so far away she'd never be bothered again. But then there was that last third of the time, when she was a stone crazy-bastard fucking psycho, bragging up all the shit she'd done and gotten away with. When she was like that she always made me kind of sick to my stomach, but *horny,* too, come to admit it.

Darla glanced to make sure Michelson or some customer wasn't watching her, leaned forward, and spoke very softly. "Now let's talk about some *interesting* issues. You know Carol-Ann, she works in the kitchen here, not real pretty but big boobs, dropped out of school last year because fucking high school was too fucking tough for her?"

"Uh, yeah, I think—"

"She told me about what you do to cats down by Hawthorne Ditch. She's seen them out there twice, and then seen you coming by and getting what was left of the cats. What do you use, Karl, a steak knife? Garden shears, like you did Squid's rabbit? Carol-Ann says sometimes you leave them in fucking *pieces.*"

I felt my whole brain go blank. "I, um—"

"Eddie Cockburn, that kid that stole the money from you one time, out of your shed, he watches your house all the time. He says sometimes you leave the cats out in the yard to get your mom all upset."

"I—It's a fucking *raccoon*, Darla!"

"Oh, no, that's not what they say, those are cats, your mom's cats, and—"

"No, I mean, a raccoon. Kills the cats. An old boar coon that lives right around the Hawthorne Ditch, he kills them and eats them, that's why—"

"Don't treat me like I'm stupid. They eat garbage and corn and things."

"And anything else they can catch, kill, or steal," I said. "A family of them got into the reptile pit at Scout Camp and ate pretty well all the snakes and turtles in one night. They're like giant pretty rats; if it's food and it doesn't eat them, they eat it. This guy's big and old and mean as shit. He's the one that tore up the Schneiders' dog last year—"

"Hey, did you do the dog, too? What happened, did he get away before you got done playing? Do you use that coon to cover everything you do?" Her gaze into my eyes was cold and level. "I know how fucked-up you really are, Karl. Everybody knows what you did to Squid's rabbit. Everyone can see you're running around on like five thousand pounds of anger. You're best buddies with a homo-whore and I just saw you in here letting Lightsburg's favorite old fag buy you dinner. Old boar raccoon. Shit. You probably get a lot of the old people in town to believe that, too, because they believe all kinds of folktales and shit."

Or, I thought desperately, *because they hunted, and ran traplines, and they've come by and found a fox in a trap torn to pieces—*

"Even though you're fucking loaded with all that work you do, and you've got a great body and girls like you and you could, like, bang your way through the school—"

Okay, now I knew she had lost her mind. But I couldn't seem to stop looking into those mad eyes.

"—only girlfriend you've ever had was weird helpless little Bonny. I can guess what kinds of things you do to her because boys talk, you know, and she doesn't keep a boyfriend unless he's pretty physical. Like she's the queen of 'stop that some more,' you know? Old Chip was in here just last week all bragging about pantsing her and not giving her pants back till she put out."

At least that made sense; I knew what to say about that. "And he was out to beat up Paul last night. And Bonny just dumped him. Maybe we need to get together to fucking deal with the son of a bitch."

She rolled her eyes. "Bonny will beg you not to hurt him. He's the only boy she's ever loved besides you." She blew out another cloud of smoke. "Paging Dr. Freud, you know? I've got my bunny, you've got your Bonny. I don't know what you do to enslave her but I'd like to find out." The weird little wickets of her eyebrows bounced up above the tortoiseshell glasses, she performed a big drag and puff on her cigarette; abstractly, I thought Mom's technique of smoking for emphasis was more refined, but Darla's was more dramatic.

Her smile was creepy. "Karl, baby, I know about the cats—half the town has heard stories about what the cats look like before you take them home to bury them."

I wanted to scream or run or something but I just sat there, not knowing what to say, not sure how even to move.

She leaned forward, showing cleavage, and ran a finger around the side of her breast. "We all know about Squid's rabbit."

I was starting to feel a little desperate—well, a lot desperate. "Darla, I have never hurt one of those cats. It's that old coon that tears them up. I just bury them because my mother can't stand to look at them."

"That's not what I hear. Or what the town hears. And we hear it from someone who *knows*," she said. "It's not just seeing cut-up cats and you with your shovel."

I was trying to think what to say, and realizing there must be something that—She had been looking around, and now she just reached into her Pongo's uniform top— they were pretty low cut—and pulled her breast out. Slowly, she ran a finger over the nipple. "Kill me a cat, Karl, and do whatever you want," she said. "Don't pretend you don't want to."

She tucked it back in, sat up, and giggled. "Was that *sexy*, or what?"

"I—it got to me."

"Oh, good, I was afraid you really were queer like Paul." She leaned forward, breathing out smoke, and despite the smell, I leaned in. I faintly remembered that I'd seen a blacksnake get a baby rabbit like this, once, when one of the other Scouts threw it into the pit while the adults weren't watching. I figured I didn't have half the chance that rabbit did.

"And I can tell you're smart about the whole thing. In spite of all the evidence, you're never going to get caught. That's pretty sexy, too, Karl, intelligence is always sexy."

"What am I doing that looks so intelligent?" I wondered if my mouth was hanging open.

She sat back, gave me a wry little smile like she knew she was explaining something I already understood, and said, "Of *course* you wanted to see Gratz instead of a real shrink. Because Gratz would never catch on to you even if you were roasting babies and had a refrigerator full of old lady cutlets. Gratz isn't half as dangerous for you as a smart shrink would be.

"Plus the idea of spending an hour bullshitting Gratz every week, instead of listening to reruns of the Greatest Stories of the Pathetic Losers Club—what a cool deal! I might just go see Gratz after school on Monday, tell him what a bad girl I feel I've been, and see if I can be Gratz's stooge, instead of a Madman, this year.

"You can't throw away a great deal like that, just

because you miss being in the Pathetic Losers Club. They'll still talk with you, bud, they *have* to talk to anyone that'll talk to them, they don't have enough real friends to lose one." She crushed out another cigarette in the monkey's mouth, making a point of looking into his eyes. "To get that letter you've got, I'd do lots of things for it. Maybe I'd even do Gratz."

"Darla," I said, "you scare me."

She turned on a thousand-watt smile, all flirty and cute and come-and-get-me, and said, "Thanks, baby, I try." Then she leaned forward and whispered, "Next time you kill a cat, if you take me along, I'll do anything you want afterward. Whatever you do to Bonny or whatever else you want, and I hope it leaves marks. I don't even want you to wash your hands; I want them on me while they're still warm, damp, and sticky from the cat. This is a guarantee, Karl, take me along when you do a cat, and you're *in*. It would be so cool to do that with a guy who just killed something." She sat back, smiling like she was proud as all shit of herself, and licked her lips at me, half-giggling, like she couldn't believe she was doing this, either.

This was spookier than anything she'd ever done, and I was creeped out, I can tell you that. Also so hard I was afraid to get up from the table. But most of all, I was confused; this looked rehearsed, planned, scripted, like she'd been planning to say these things to me for a long time. What the fuck was she up to?

Michelson called her back to the counter, and she blew a kiss at me and was on her way.

But whatever she was faking, it was clear she wanted me to kill a cat in front of her, and she wanted to have sex with me after I did. Through all my confusion, two thoughts burned like high-beams: a shit-free bed *and* losing my virginity to Darla.

I only hoped nobody saw what a silly sick grin that put on my face, or if they did, they'd think it was because I was checking out Darla's ass in that short tight skirt of her Pongo's uniform.

On my way out, Darla ran around the counter to give me a big hug that involved a certain amount of her chest being up against me and her leg running against mine, the high heel scraping down my calf. Of course I loved it (I mean what guy wouldn't?), but I was kind of wondering what I'd look like walking down the street with a major tent in my pants.

When I turned away from Darla, Stacy Hobbins and some of her other social buddies were just coming in. Her face looked like she'd sat down on a Popsicle naked. Then she looked away. The social platoon, all in their huge platform wedgies and jeans, clip-clopped off to a booth.

Then I realized it looked to Stacy like I was running around on Cheryl. I laughed for most of my way back downtown, kicking an old pop can in front of me, thinking, *Me, Karl Shoemaker, breaker of hearts—the guy that might have to kill a cat to lose his virginity.* Hopefully just one cat to get started having sex, but even if it turned out to be one cat per time, at least I had plenty of cats. I guess when life hands you lemons, chop 'em up and get lemonade; when life hands you cats, chop 'em up and get pussy.

21

How Many Madman Stories Ever Made Any Sense?

THERE WAS A catch to all this. There always is a catch, they say. I was mad at the bedshitter, but I'd been thinking more along the lines of arranging for an encounter with a hunter, something that might be messy but would be over in a second. I felt *sick* about what the coon did to cats. At least I was going to tell Darla that I killed them first, before I cut them up, quick, that there was never any pain.

I had been wanting to fuck Darla since about the time that Paul told me what fucking was and I started noticing those famous boobs growing on her. She was more or less the walking definition of sex.

I was still having some trouble imagining getting in the mood right after cutting up a cat, especially after making the kind of mess the coon had made of Sunflower and Ocean. On the other hand I kept thinking about the way that Pongo's uniform fit Darla. And the way her tight jeans and leotard tops did.

What the fuck *was* her damage, anyway? She might be ten million flavors of pervert, but I was sure that when she was talking to me about killing a cat and having sex with her, there was something—

"Hey, I got a bone to pick with you," a voice said, behind me. I turned. It was Scott Tierden, and sure enough, Bobby Harris was standing just behind him, so that they looked like a skinny guy with a fat shadow.

"'I have a little shadow that goes in and out with me, and what can be the use of him is more than I can see,'" I began, and Tierden, being a dumbass, walked right up and grabbed my lapels, so I slapped him down low. It wasn't the wrack in the sack I was trying for, because he bounced back, glaring.

I gave him my very best Psycho Shoemaker happy-smile, and thought about kicking his head. "Pick your bone, while you still got one."

"I'm fucking tired of you making fun of us and acting all superior, Shoemaker, just cause your drunk dad was the mayor and you think all your mental patient friends are like oh so special hot shit. You make me fucking sick."

"Put your hands on me again and I'll make you so fucking *sore*," I said, "that you'll cry every time Bobby fucks you up the ass."

"Fuck you," Harris said, stretching his vocabulary and displaying more wit than he usually did.

"Your mom's a crazy drunk slut," Tierden said. "She lets Neil Strossman bang her like, all the time."

I could tell he'd been saving that one up. Probably took him like a week to think of it.

I closed the four steps between us real slow; it would bust his balls better if he chickened and ran than if I actually had to slug him. Still, with all the yard work I did I was pretty strong, and come to admit it, I *was* in a mood to hurt something.

"You boys break that up!"

It was Browning, stomping into the middle of things—I hadn't even realized we were right at the alley just behind his shop. Tierden gave me the one-finger salute, and they both ran back to Bobby's car. Bobby popped a u-ey and nearly collided with an old lady driving a Volkswagen.

"He give you any trouble, Karl?"

"Well, I could've been facing a murder rap. I think you saved his life, sir."

Browning laughed and clapped me on the shoulder. "That's the spirit. Jesus, excuse my French, you sure know how to find enemies. Those kids looked like the Grim Reaper out on a date with the Pillsbury Doughboy."

"Sir, I am going to quote that. Often. They're just a couple creepy loser guys that hate everyone, and for some reason my friends are the ones they pick on."

"Glad to be of help, Mister Shoemaker." He dusted his hands as if we'd just won a brawl with those two doofuses. "I'm still planning to have that dining room set done for Tuesday, so make sure you're up early then. And I do have to brag to someone; I think I've honestly made Rose's couch better than new—much better than it was when it was new—and I don't think she'll ever realize that. Want to come in and look?"

Come to admit it, I did, and spent a while looking it over because the old fart was so pleased with himself. Finally I said, "That's a really cool thing to do for a friend. You must be proud."

Browning grinned. "Damn straight. Get to be an old coot like me and all your pleasures come down to a good meal, doing a friend a favor, or seeing an asshole get what's coming to him. Or now and then, if you're real lucky, a real good dump." He brushed the sawdust off his clothes with the little whisk broom he kept on a hook by the vise. "And for once I've got a pretty full shop all next month. I wouldn't want to turn you into an upholster—I think you can do a lot more with your life, even if you go in the army first—but if you'd like to learn a few basics, and have the time, I'll probably be able to use some help here in the shop."

"That would be great."

"Yeah, it would. But there's better places to talk about it than here. Maybe out in the waiting room, where I can fix up a little coffee for us or something?"

"Sure."

The waiting room was this little living-room-like corner he'd fixed up right by the front counter. People didn't bring furniture in through there; couches and chairs and stuff came and went through the big roll-up door on the alley. It was the place where fussy people like the Henshaws sat and had coffee with Browning and looked at the fabric samples, debating endlessly whether they wanted burgundy cowhide or nubbly raw silk on Grandma's Sacred Shield-back Chairs. I guess Browning tried to set it up to be comfortable, but the router, bench sander, and drill press were on all the time, so it was always dusty.

He threw a handful of Maxwell House into the basket, filled the pot, put the percolator on the hot plate, and said, "Now, of course, while we wait for the coffee to make, I have to think of something to say." But then he didn't say anything, and neither did I; there just wasn't much to talk about. Sure, I'd be willing to come in for a couple hours after school most days and do whatever work there was; that was about it.

While we waited, I was watching his hands. You'd think they'd be like old claws, considering all the stuff he did with them, and all the chemicals and calluses, tools and pulling, that would have gone into shaping them, but I realized his habit of using Corn Huskers on them all the time, wearing his rubber gloves, and not whacking himself with the old hammer had stood him in pretty good stead. And his arms, chest, and back were better than half the guys at the school; his face might be able to hold a three-day rain, but he could also probably hold up 120 pounds with one hand if he needed to. I wondered what it would be like to have been alive as long as old Browning, and decided I would be just as happy waiting that long to find out.

The coffee started to perk, and pouring that and getting it doctored right took up some time, too.

We'd each finished about half the cup when Browning said, "Karl, I saw you moving like you were going to kill that boy when he said those things about your mother."

"Well," I said, "she's my mom. And he's an asshole. Mom has a lot of problems, I'm not saying she doesn't, she's a mess, but she's my *mom.*" I kept telling myself to calm down, but I was still so angry, at Harris and Tierden of course, and at Browning for having stopped me, and most of all at Mom, for having put me in this kind of horrible position where this dirty-minded old prejudiced sack of shit was trying to find a nice way to say *Some of us noticed your mom is a crazy drunk slut.*

I pushed my coffee cup away and stood up. Then he really hit me with a hard shot; he said, "Karl, I'm sorry, I wasn't trying to hurt you about your mother, I'd never do that to a man, never, never, never, goddammit. What I was trying to say was things aren't your fault and *they aren't her fault, either.*"

"You mean she can't help that she's crazy? Thanks a lot."

"No—goddammit, Karl, don't goddam walk out on me. Goddammit. What I was trying to say is it don't matter whose fault it is or what went wrong, I see you struggling, trying to take care of your mother—"

"Then leave me alone, and let me do it," I said. Before he could say another word I was out the door and running like a crazy bastard.

I guess I was halfway home by the time the brain cells started firing again and I realized that if I arrived home right now, I'd probably be finding Mom getting drunk or high with Wonderful Bill, in the afterglow, and I really did not want to do that. So I stopped and looked at my watch. Due at Philbin's in an hour; no special reason to be anywhere else. I had *Huckleberry Finn* in my back pocket, so I had a source of amusement. I wasn't hungry yet, but no doubt I would be before my shift started.

I was a little tired of Philbin's but then I was a little tired of a lot of places, such as my house, Lightsburg, Ohio, the United States, and Earth. I turned around and trotted back toward downtown.

As I came in the door, Philbin was arguing with a short, blonde woman who looked like she was trying to be Mom a couple years ago. She wore a crotch-high miniskirt, though the older super super ladies had pretty much given those up in favor of the gypsy-hippie rainbow bag-skirts; those white plastic boots that had gone out a few years before; and a ton of what looked like Christmas ornaments, Ping-Pong balls, and sewing machine parts dangling from each ear.

Philbin waved at me over her shoulder, checking to see if I needed anything; I pointed at the coffeepot, he nodded, and I went around the counter, poured myself a cup, and carried it over to the corner booth, stretching my legs out. The Naugahyde was so shot, and the springs underneath so *more* shot, that I always wondered if maybe some of the dinner crowd had fallen inside the benches and been trapped and mummified; if so, I seemed to have an unusually bony one under me. I'd've moved if I hadn't already known I had the best bench there.

The lady at the counter was trying to talk Philbin into stocking herbal stuff "instead of all these chemicals." He was gently trying to explain that other customers *wanted* chemicals, but he'd be happy to try stocking some herbals if there was anything she especially wanted. Unfortunately she didn't seem to be much more specific than "herbal," probably because she just bought any old thing with "herbal" on the label. After she left I'd point that out to Philbin, he'd order a few herbal remedies, and we'd see if people were gullible enough to buy that crap.

Not that I could put it that way to Philbin. He prided himself on only stocking things that worked. Which might be the other problem she was having with him.

But as I got more into the story, I tuned out the world, and much as I hated to admit it, there I was drifting down the river with Huck and Jim and not having too bad a time at all.

The lady who had been talking to Philbin sat down across from me in the booth and said, "Hi, you're Karl Shoemaker."

"Uh, yeah," I said, displaying the wit that had made me legend.

"I'm Rose Lee Nielsen, Marti's mother. I just thought I'd get a good look at you and introduce myself—Marti talks about you quite a bit."

"She's a really cool girl," I said, because you never say anything less than 100 percent positive to someone's parents, that's a rule.

"You're very kind," Mrs. Nielsen said, in that voice adults have that means *thank you for lying, so nice of you to spare me the truth.* I felt like arguing and saying no, I meant it, Marti was really cool, I liked her, but my past experience with arguing with super super ladies told me to fasten it and hope the subject would change.

Which, of course, it did. "I also wanted to tell you what an amazing lady your mother is. She's just the best thing about having moved to this town."

I let myself look at her just that much more closely, maybe really seeing her for the first time. Mrs. Nielsen was like a lot of the super super ladies—really everyone except Jolene. She looked keyed up, tense, like a tiny dog that is always watching out and ready to yip, afraid someone will step on it. "I'm glad you're friends," I said, not sure what it might be a bad idea to say.

"She just impresses me so much," Mrs. Nielsen said. "She has no fear at all. She doesn't let anything get in her way. No one can tell her what to do, no one can tell her what's true and what's not, she just sees things the way she sees them and acts like she acts. That's so amazing to someone like me, because—I don't know if Marti has told you, but I've been living so much in a man's shadow all my life, really, I got married when I was just a girl, and to see someone who doesn't let anyone put her down or tell her anything, that's just amazing to me."

"I'm always glad when Mom makes another friend," I said, hoping that it would get me out of this.

"Of course you say that," she said, smiling like a real person for the first time, instead of flashing her teeth like a phony. "You don't know me, you have to wonder what I'm up to till you do know me, and of course you're concerned with protecting your mother. That's so lovely." She stood up and stuck out her hand, so I staggered up off that loose and lumpy bench and shook it. "I know we're going to be friends, too," she said. "Marti seems to think the world of you."

She turned, waved, and left. I sat back down wondering what that had been all about, but also knowing that where super super ladies were involved, it wasn't necessarily a good idea to ask.

"Why do I feel like she's trying to sell me a set of encyclopedias?" Philbin said, after a minute.

I laughed and put the book down, and him and me got busy around the place. It was being a very Philip K. Dick kind of night: the world might not make a lot of sense but at least there was work.

It's funny how after you do something, even once, there gets to be a "normal" way for it to be, so anyway, up until the second movie let out, it was a very normal night at Philbin's. For a long while there was nobody and I just laid out setups and read some more of *Huckleberry Finn*.

The first postmovie crowd cleared out, and I bused the last tables and loaded the dishwasher. Philbin was pretty pleased. "We did a little side business, too," he said, "a few idiots that can't go somewhere when stores are open came by and bought aspirin and things. I guess we'll do this as long as the Ox can stay open, and God bless Todd and Mary, I hope that's a long time."

I hurried and mopped the floor up quick, so that the disinfectant smell would be out of the air before the second crowd stuck their heads in and smelled burgers and pie.

The second crowd actually pretty much filled up the tables and the counter. I ran around without a sec to breathe, Philbin seemed to grow three more arms to cook with, and Mrs. P, who was pretty much done with the pies, had to fill in and help both of us. It was at least as crazy as the early shift in combining season.

So I didn't notice Paul and Marti sitting at the very back table till I got there. That wouldn't have been much of a surprise, since I knew they had a date, and there wasn't anyplace else to go in town anyway, but they were there with Bonny, Cheryl, and Squid, all the Madmen except Darla and Danny.

I tried not to let my mouth hang open, and just play it cool. "And what're you kids gonna have? I betcha got them munchies from all that mary-jew-wanna you smoke. Don't try to fool me, I read *Newsweek*, and I know all about you youths. And don't try to get away with no rio-tin' or no protestin', neither."

"Well, I think we can elect him mayor," Paul said, "if he'll stop being such a intellectual egghead."

"A vote wasted on me is a vote you didn't waste on somebody else," I agreed. "Actually I gotta run, so let's get the order."

"Cheeseburger, fries, Coke, and apple pie after," Marti said. "God, I feel so Middle American I could just puke."

"Don't do that, Karl has to mop," Bonny said. "Uh, same for me."

Turned out it was all-round. I couldn't resist saying, "Hey, maybe I can get Philbin to call that the Madman Special."

They all laughed at that, much more than I expected. I shot off to tend three more tables, hung up the orders, and started delivering food.

Note to Philbin, I told myself, *ketchup on every table for the night crowd, that's the third one I've had to go get.*

I wondered about everyone being seen out in public, together, like that. At the Denny's in Maumee, thirty miles away, sure. But we'd always been so careful; now it was going to be obvious that they were a clique. So somebody had decided something. Probably Paul had.

Finally the last plate had landed on the last table, and since Philbin's was pay-at-the-counter, and we were full with nobody waiting, Philbin closed the grill and hung out the CLOSED sign, hollering to everyone to stay as long as they liked, he just didn't want any more coming in.

It looked like it would be calm for a minute or two, so I grabbed a cup of coffee and the stack of remaining tabs to put out on people's tables as I went back to the Madman table. I couldn't sit down, in case anyone needed anything, but at least I could say hi.

"So these two are so hot they need three chaperones?" I asked. Marti stuck her tongue out; from the way Bonny and Cheryl rolled their eyes, I could tell it was an exceptionally dumb joke, even for me. Confirming that, Squid laughed.

"It was just kind of an idea we came up with after you and Cheryl left, at Denny's, last night," Bonny said. "Marti said everyone really knows who the therapy kids are anyway. I mean *we* know who's in the other groups, you know? And we all get teased sometimes, and Gratz practically announces it in class every other day. So Marti said, why not just be friends in public? So here we are."

Squid nodded slowly. "We figured, since you're gonna be stuck working here Saturdays, that we'd be kind of . . . you know, the Saturday movie gang. We know you don't drink no more, and we ain't gonna road drink any time you're out with us, so now and then maybe you'd want to, you know, come along with us after you get off work? Or you'n'me can always go up to Toledo and stand around on a street corner with our purses, even if the rest of the group don't want to come."

"Hey, Mister Social Chairman, there are matters needing your attention," Philbin said. "Mister Social Butterfly, to the cash register please."

I turned and saw three tables waiting in line at the register, and scooted to take care of that. By the time I looked back the Madmen had all gone; they left an okay tip, for high school students.

The Philbins and me cleaned the place as much as it needed—on Sunday evening the regular cleaning people would come in and do the heavy stuff—and Philbin declared it good enough, and we locked up. "Your friends," he observed, "are exactly the kind of business I was hoping to get. And this place really was full. We did two normal breakfast shifts' worth of business in forty minutes. I think you have a job here for a while, Karl, and I sure hope people keep going to see old movies once the novelty wears off. Kind of thing that gives me back a little faith in poor old Lightsburg."

"You get faith easier than I do," I said.

"Yeah, well, it's more fun than getting a cold"—he glanced to see that Mrs. P wasn't standing too close—"but not as much fun as getting laid."

Going out the door I thought, well, if I can catch one stupid cat, and get over being a sissy about what Darla wants me to do, I can find out about getting laid. Who knows, I might even get faith.

I turned the corner and Paul was standing there. "Oh, shit," I said.

"I didn't go out with the rest of them," he said. "I wanted to talk."

"Walk with me," I said, and took a step.

After a block he said, "When we had that fight I was really hurt."

"I'm sorry I called you a faggot. I know you're not."

"But I am." He kicked a pop can, a neat little side shot right into a storm drain. "I mean, I . . . well, like, I love the way Marti's eyes shine when she's with me, and how excited she looks. Whenever I've gone out with Cheryl I like the way she glows and it's like I can picture her getting dressed for a party, her in her evening gown, me in my tux, in our perfect big house up by the marina in Perrysburg, and helping her get her makeup just right . . . and it's great, I love being out with girls. It's just at the end of the evening I want to drop them off with a peck on the cheek, and go find a nice man who's hung like a horse. You know how that is?"

"No, actually."

He sighed. "Yeah, I know you don't. Wanting one, I mean, not being one. You know what I mean."

We walked maybe half a block more, and finally I said, "You're not—um, you don't want me like—"

He sighed. "I do, but it doesn't matter. You're straight as an arrow, Karl, I know that, and I love you and you being a straight guy is part of you. If that makes any sense." I thought he might be crying and I tried not to notice. "That isn't what I stayed to talk about."

Another damp, rain-smelling block, both of us hunching a little against the chill. I was just glad we weren't fighting. I wondered what he had to say.

Finally he just blurted out, "So Gratz let loose with his thing on Marti, and right then I realized I couldn't give the Madmen up. Couldn't. I mean . . . been through too much together, love everybody, all that shit. Couldn't stop being a Madman, you know?"

"Yeah, I know."

"I hope this doesn't sound too weird, but when Gratz yelled at me, I felt *good*, because I knew it was going to be Madman fucking *legend*, the maddest tale of the Madmen ever, all of us walking out on Gratz. Even Darla did, you know?"

"And I didn't."

"And you didn't. And I thought maybe I'd fucked up the friendship so bad you wouldn't ever really be my friend again, and I thought maybe you really had sold out to Gratz and I'd been wrong about you all along, and I thought maybe even you were jealous about Marti—"

"*What?* Why would I be jealous about Marti?"

"Sometimes for the guy I love the most in the whole world you are the stupidest son of a bitch ever born."

Okay, obviously we were friends again, I got that much. So I asked, "If I put an arm around you, you gonna rub wood on me?"

So there we were hanging all over each other, laughing and crying, slapping each other's backs and calling each other assholes.

Car headlights swept over us and stopped. Realizing that we were two guys hugging with tear-stained faces, and this was still Lightsburg, we pretty much flew backwards, each acting like we had no idea where this other guy came from.

I caught a glimpse of the car as it rounded the corner and sped away. I started to laugh, and laughed harder and harder until I was bent over with my hands on my knees, just trying to get air.

"I guess that was a really funny car," Paul said.

"It was Stacy," I said. "Stacy Hobbins."

"Other than holding the unbreakable record for dumbest social, what's so funny about her?"

"She thinks Cheryl is cheating on Bret with me, and I'm cheating on Cheryl with Darla. Or she *thought* that. God *knows* what she thinks now."

"Gotta be a story in there."

"Not much of one," I said. "After Denny's last night Cheryl and I took a walk-and-talk around the tar pond, and we surprised Stacy just when poor old Steve was about to finally get his finger wet. Then this afternoon Stacy saw Darla was humping my leg."

"Why would Darla do *that*?"

"Well, to hump my arm she'd have to jump too high, I guess." This was so old times; I could always make Paul beg for a story, and the longer I made him wait the more fun it was. "Hey, are you still locked out?"

"I don't know if it's cool to go home yet. I slept in Marti's car in her driveway last night, and then hid in her garage. When her folks went out to the liquor store this morning, I got a shower and Marti phoned my house and faked her way past my dad to talk to Kimmie. Kimmie brought over some clothes for me, and took my drum major outfit home. I don't know how I'd survive without her. Hey, I know why you're not in love with me, Karl, but why aren't you in love with my little sister?"

"I'm afraid of who I'd have for a brother-in-law. Well, look, all I was trying to find out was whether you needed crash space. If Mom hasn't locked me out, we can probably crash you in my basement, legit and all. Come on."

Paul and me walked close, like we always had. The wind blew cold wet spray off the streets and lawns into my face, but the storm seemed to have passed over for real this time, and there were some stars peeking through the black boiling clouds. A few leaves on the sidewalk slipped under my boot soles. Looked like they were going to hold fall this year, too.

"Marti sure joined the group in a hurry," Paul said. "Already hiding other Madmen, already been locked out herself, it's like she's always been here."

"She's really changed the group," I agreed. "But I guess it needed changing. I kind of like her knack for upsetting things."

"Well, she can upset the shit out of Gratz," Paul said. "No wonder I'm in love."

"How *does* that work, with being gay and stuff?"

"I don't know, it just does. Probably make my life easier because some football players will decide I can't be gay if I have a girlfriend. Definitely she's cool to go places with." He hesitated as we turned a corner, and then rested his hand lightly on my sleeve. "She talks about you a lot, Karl. It makes me jealous. And I don't even know which one of you I'm jealous *about*."

"Hah," I said, thinking fast because if he stayed on this subject he'd work himself up into an even more major hissy-fit. "If I can just catch a cat shitting on my bed, I can lose my cherry to somebody with *boobs*."

"That's gotta be a story, let's hear it."

I told him.

"Wow," he said. "Little Karl, knocking off a piece of Spooky Darla. All because he's an insane cat killer."

"Well, I *am* insane. I might decide to kill *one* particular cat. But that's not the same thing as being an insane cat killer." We argued about that distinction the rest of the way to my house. Like I said, very old times.

The door was unlocked. When I turned the lights on I saw a folded note taped to the door to the upstairs:

> *Karl-o-Tiger,*
>
> *I've gone up to Put-in-Bay after all! And Bill explained everything, and he's even more wonderful than I thought! See you tomorrow afternoon! I'm so excited!!!!*
>
> *Moms!*

"I guess she's plural when she's that excited," I said to Paul, showing him the letter. "Or she's decided that's a cool pet name and it's her way of telling me to start using it."

"So is Bill really wonderful?"

"Lying sack of shit and a complete bozo," I said, "but a lot classier than Neil and all the other just-outta-jail crowd she's usually with. I guess I'm less worried than I usually am—he's not gonna beat her up or anything."

Paul had a beer and I had some orange juice, and

we washed our glasses neatly; the kitchen had now been clean for almost eighteen hours, a record since Dad had died.

"Thing that worries me," I admitted, "is that when Mom gets to feeling really good, especially about a guy, she always crashes really hard. Every time. So since I know he's a lying bozo—worse yet an *English professor* for fuck's sake—and she's obviously crazy about him, I foresee a major crash about to happen."

We both took quick showers so we could both have it hot; I put Paul's clothes into the wash and loaned him sweats and a T-shirt, which fit him like a tent. We didn't want to stop talking, so we flopped down on my bed side by side, still dressed; after a minute Hairball nosed his way in, jumped up on the bed, and stretched out, purring between us. "I feel so much safer ever since I got my anti-homo cat," I said. "Guard, Hairball."

"Hah. I happen to know this cat is gay. He just wants to protect me from your psychotic queer-bashing ass."

Old times again. I remembered that when one of us got back from camp, back in grade school, Dad would have to clump up the stairs and yell at us to shut up, like, six times before we went to sleep.

Tonight we talked about everybody and everything till one of us fell asleep, and the other went out like a light right after. I don't know that that was even separate events; with Paul and me, there was a lot of stuff you just couldn't separate.

PART FIVE

(Sunday, September 9, 1973)

Paradise Lost, Bedshitter Found,
Paradise Regained

PAUL AND ME got up about eight and goofed
through making fun of the religious programs while we
ate Cap'n Crunch. If I'd felt any happier I'd've wet myself, I can tell you that. In between we told each other
all the stuff we'd been meaning to last night, and got the
rest of the way caught up on our stories. I made a pot of
strong coffee and we drank that while Reverend Billy Bob
Bighair ranted on about the Apocalypse-uh Which-uh
Biblical-uh Prophecy Unquestionably Proved-*duh* Would
Come-uh By 1980. He didn't say you'd get your money
back if it didn't.

None of the Toledo stations showed cartoons or old
movies on Sunday mornings, and the further-away stations were fuzzy this morning.

Paul looked a lot better for having had a safe place to sleep all night.

He had choir at First UM for the second service, and they paid him eighteen dollars a week to do tenor solos, so he really couldn't afford to miss it. He borrowed my razor, stuck in a new blade, shaved and combed his hair, and made himself semipresentable by borrowing one of my shirts and a tie; it was huge on him, but the choir robe would hide everything between his collar and his shoes. Just before he took off he said, "No more bullshit between us, okay? We've been friends all our lives, let's be friends when we're both eighty."

"Well, okay," I said. "But if she's still around, dibs on Rose Carson. Old Browning says she's a piece and a half."

Paul got this smug look and said, "Yeah, well, in that case, dibs on Browning." He could always gross me out *and* crack me up.

After he took off, I did the dishes, wiped the kitchen down, and decided to get going on the storm windows.

While I was in the toolshed, getting out the sawhorses and working my way through the stacked storm windows, I checked around, just casual glances 'cause you never knew which neighbor kids might be watching, and made sure that the four cash stashes I had out there were still in their places.

Only three storms needed reglazing—I'd kept up

pretty regular, and last winter had been mild. Two more needed some dry spots in the glazing broken out and the gaps refilled. All five would need repainting, of course.

If I ate lunch late, I could probably have some real free time this afternoon. And Darla was off work at two on Sundays.

That got me moving a little faster. I pulled out the storms I was going to work on, stacked them by the shed, and set the first one on its sawhorses.

I was about to open the can of glazing compound when the phone rang inside the house. I locked the shed—no matter what, I always did that, after that sneaky little bastard Eddie Cockburn called my house and stole a stash while I was inside getting the phone.

I got to the phone before it stopped ringing. It was Rose Lee Nielsen, Marti's mother, with a super-long super-complicated message for Mom. Apparently this afternoon the super super ladies were getting together to talk about Watergate and "the Bermuda Triangle connection to it," which meant they'd get drunk and agree loudly that elves were good and grays were bad. Rose wanted to show Mom some new documents that would "really reveal something about what's really going on," before they got together with Judy and Jolene to get drunk and smoke pot out back of Judy's place.

After I got all that taken down and read it back twice, she told me a couple more times what a nice young man

I was, and how much Marti liked me. Luckily, a Saab that really wanted tuned rolled up in front of the house. Since it was old and ugly and barely worked, it had to be Wonderful Bill's. "Uh, I think maybe she's coming home now," I said.

A minute later Bill and Mom came in. Her hair had the clean, full look it got when she took time brushing. She wore no makeup, and the sweater and jeans were nothing special, just some stuff I'd gotten her from Sears when she was complaining about being broke and her clothes wearing out (then she'd started complaining about wearing Sears clothing). She was wearing tight jeans tucked into her Go-Get-Laids, the way the college girls were just starting to do, and she had big sunglasses pushed back on her head.

Come to admit it, she looked like she had walked in straight out of a movie, but at least it was a happy movie. Wonderful Bill was in the same corduroy two-piece, but he'd changed his shirt. He was still wearing that Greek fisherman's hat like a smashed pie on top of his head, and it still looked stupid.

He looked like he was trying to be either Peter or Paul, and failing, and Mom looked like she was trying to be Mary and nearly succeeding.

I handed off the phone to Mom and went back out to get those storms glazed and painted.

The thing I like about reglazing windows, it's fussy

and neat but you use your whole arm; you have to put that glazing compound in firm, in one clean stroke, and strike it off neat, or it looks like shit.

I had just broken the old dried-out compound out of the frame and laid down two of the sides of the new compound when I smelled something that was kind of like someone had stuffed old newspapers up an elephant's ass, waited for him to shit them out, dried them, and smoked them. Bill. Puffing on a cigar.

"Your mother's probably gonna be talking for a while," he said.

"Yeah, once she gets rolling, she doesn't stop." I struck off another side, the fresh compound peeling away like dough, and wiped after with my vinegar-wet rag to leave the glass clean right up to the glazing.

"Like some help?"

"You're in a suit."

"It's an old one, and I'm very neat. And I wouldn't've offered if I thought I'd get any on me."

It was less of a faggot-loser answer than I'd been expecting from an English professor. I shrugged. "Suit yourself."

He moved one of the storms that needed a touch-up onto two more sawhorses. He busted out the bad spots in the glazing—didn't need me to tell him which they were, or to tell him that that one just needed a touch-up. And at least now his cigar was downwind of me.

He didn't overpush, letting the tool do the work, quick and clean and controlled. He was at least a step up from that dumbass Neil. Plus Mom had been smiling when she came in. He was still a fool and a liar, but Mom had been with a lot worse.

"So," he said, "your mother says your dad taught you how to do all this home repair stuff."

"Yeah, well."

He borrowed my vinegar rag and wiped. On balance I decided I'd be willing to glaze a window with old Bill.

As he finished striking off, he said, "Um, you probably know that your mother didn't say 'home repairs,' she said 'ucky ucky Mister Fixit Man Things' and complained that you spend too much time on them, especially on Sundays."

"I bet she did."

"She did indeed."

"Indeed."

"Oh, God, did I sound like an English professor?"

"Indeed."

He laughed, which made a big cloud of foul smoke billow up and blow off toward the neighbors' yard. "You know, every single mother I have dated, and there have been quite a few, has told me her kid is funny, and you are the first one who actually is. All right, I did sort of want to talk to you about something sort of serious, which does concern your mother, but you're welcome to avoid that if you prefer."

I shrugged. "There's no ball game on the radio."

"Good point. Well, Beth gave me what I think must be her standard sermon about how you should spend more time being free and that the house gets too much attention and so forth." He finished laying in a side and struck off again; just the right pressure to clean off the excess, not enough to scratch or press the glass. "I said I thought there was something very fine about a man who took care of things, and did them right, and about being a craftsman in a world of bozos." He laid in three gaps at the top.

I still wasn't going to say anything to him that wasn't a direct answer to a question.

After a bit he shrugged and said, "I noticed half a dozen jobs you'd done around here. The painted railings on the back porch. That patch on the roof. The tuck pointing on your chimney. You're good at this stuff, Karl, real good, and what's more, you insist on being good.

"Now, the reason why I'm blowing all this flattering smoke up your kilt here"— he paused to give his full attention to striking off—"is that I am a bit serious about your mother."

"You like my mom?"

"I do. A lot. Unfortunately I have a lifelong habit of falling in love very quickly and then living in an intense state of regret afterward."

"Well, Mom'll get you to *that* pretty quick." Something was making me ask, "What do you like about her?"

"Probably just that she's the sexy J.D. girl that would never speak to a nerd like me in high school."

"J.D.?"

"Juvenile delinquent. I guess I'm revealing my age."

"Naw, I'd already caught on."

He did have a pretty good laugh, for a fool. And at least he appreciated my sense of humor. "All right, then, so we have two things in common: we want your mother to be happy and we like to fix stuff. Thing is, there's a third one you won't like—we both go to AA meetings. Or I did. Anyway, last week I fell off that wagon pretty hard, and ended up at a bar in Lightsburg, and met your mother."

"That would be the place to do it."

He looked over his finished work, and so did I. We both nodded and he moved the window to the completed stack, next to the one I had finished.

"You're good at this," I observed.

"It paid for grad school." He puffed on that horrid cigar again, and said, "Anyway. I'm going to a meeting this evening, and if I stay dry till tomorrow morning, I'm back to one day of sobriety."

"I've got eighty-two days," I said. "The first one's the hard one, and then the rest are hard, too."

"Amen. I had almost three years when I fell off."

"You said you will have one day," I said, calculating, "but you met my mother on Thursday night—"

"And then got so chickenshit-scared that I got drunk after work on Friday and didn't wake up till ten A.M. Saturday. Scared she'd turn me down, scared I'd get there and she would have forgotten, mostly just scared. If there was ever a good reason to stop drinking it's having done something that stupid. But then I already had plenty of good reasons to stop and stay stopped."

"It's staying stopped that matters," I agreed.

We each set up a window on the sawhorses, both of us taking a complete reglaze this time, and worked so much alike we finished at the same time. He said, "Looks like one more to patch the glazing on, and then paint them all?"

"What I had in mind."

Find a good work partner and there's always something to talk about.

We moved the two finished storms to join the others leaning against the wall of the toolshed, and set up the last one on the horses.

Without saying anything, I started knocking out the old dry compound from the top pane, and he started on the bottom.

After a while he said, "You know what they tell you about dating somebody who still drinks. Especially somebody who thinks that your not drinking is criticism of their drinking."

"They say it's pretty stupid, sir."

"Better call me Bill, on the off chance that we have to get used to each other." He sighed. "Yeah, well. I know they say that. And I think . . . look, Karl, your mom told me a lot of stories and I can kind of piece things together. And I'm not exactly the right guy for this job. They say saving people is the biggest addiction of all. Besides, shit, I chickened out on Friday night and went and got drunk instead."

"Should've called her, she'd've come along."

"Yeah, well."

We had that storm mostly done when he spoke again. "Something your mom said—it made me think, uh, for a while you went to Alateen? How is it?"

"A lot like AA. You thinking of Al-Anon?"

"One more meeting a week, in the life of a professor, is another grain of sand on the beach, Karl." He bent to his work. When we finished glazing, he asked, "Think she'll be in there a while longer?"

"Yeah, usually. She's going out drinking with her friend tonight, so first they have to have the predrinking phone call, which takes an hour or two." I was surprised at how blunt I felt like being.

"Yeah. Well, I got a meeting to go to tonight. And I sure shouldn't be out with her when she's that way. Looks like you're planning to prime with oil, paint with latex?"

"Yeah." That had always been what Dad recommended, and it did seem to last longer.

"Might like to help you out. Don't suppose you have an apron?"

I grabbed him mine from the toolshed. We did the little bit of scraping that was needed, just where stuff was crumbly, and then painted. There didn't seem to be much else to say, but he was stranded; he needed to talk to Mom before he went. And he couldn't very well sit there for all the time she'd be on the phone talking about the elves who flew in on spiritual energy to inspire the Beatles and the pyramids, versus the grays who flew in on flying saucers to inspire Nixon and Vietnam, or whatever the mix was today.

We painted for a while. Then he said, "Your mom wanted me to talk to you about going to college, I guess because you're thinking about the army."

"Yeah, I am, it seems like the best way to be sure I'm out of Lightsburg, and I've had enough school for right now."

"Hey, drop those shoulders and relax, man. I'm not doing a sales number on you. College is already full of kids who shouldn't be there and we don't need more. And I *was* in Vietnam—eight years ago—just driving a truck, though. Not as awful as your mom imagines but no fun. So I think you should do what you want, whether it's college or the army." The cigar in his mouth flipped up in a way that I was sure he told himself was "jaunty." "There, now we have talked about your going to college versus your going into the army, which is what I promised I would do. We can have this conversation again as many times as your mom wants us to."

"Thanks." We finished the painting in silence, and I said, "Okay, I should clean up and lock up."

He took off his apron carefully, even though he hadn't gotten paint onto anything, folded it neatly, and handed it to me. "Thank you," he said, "that was definitely better than sitting in there with all the cats."

As he turned to go inside I said, "Good luck," and he said, "Thanks."

His hat still looked stupid. Probably she'd toss him within a week.

Another advantage about having help: even with time to clean the brushes and putty knives, and put the paint away, I was done almost forty minutes before Darla would be getting off work, so I'd have time to shower and change before heading over to Pongo's. I was thinking about that nice body she had, and figuring maybe I'd see if she'd kiss me. *Might even be able to get a feel*, I thought. Definitely the biggest tits I'd ever have felt, too. Like a personal record.

As I hurried through the house, Mom had just opened up a bunch of almanacs and maps to work on her UFO-Nixon thing, a pack of Kents just opened beside a clean ashtray. I waved at her, jogged upstairs, grabbed a change of shirt, and galumphed back down the stairs to the bathroom. The shower felt great, it was nice to have a few hours to do whatever I wanted, and I let myself think about sliding a hand under Darla's bra. It was a little longer shower than I'd intended, but it felt great.

I dried and dressed and sprinted back upstairs to put a couple things away, and make sure the door was locked. I came around the corner from the steps and discovered the door was open a few inches; shit, Hairball must have worked the knob again.

I opened the door, and there was Hairball, squatting right in the middle of my bed, just squeezing out the last of a massive shit.

"Qrph?" he asked. It was almost like he was trying to play innocent.

I almost just whipped the first thing off the dresser at him, but instead I closed the door firmly behind me, sighed, and walked over to him. He mewed again, and I put a hand down and stroked his head.

There's an old saying about being careful what you pray for because you might get it.

I was going to miss him, even if I wouldn't miss his shit on the bed. I picked the pile up carefully with the dustpan and old spatula I kept in my room for these occasions. It was damp but not bad.

I dropped the mess into my wastebasket to be disposed of later, and folded up the bedspread with the damp spot facing out so it wouldn't get gross before I got around to washing it tonight.

Hairball kept bumping his big stupid orange head against my leg and purring. He knew I was mad, and something was up, but I wasn't behaving like I usually did when I was mad at him, and *that* made him nervous.

When I had the mess all under control I took a deep breath, picked up Hairball, and set him on the bed, rubbing his tummy the way he really liked. He blissed out right away, stretching and purring, and hardly fussed at all when I stuffed him into the pillowcase. He squirmed a little, but I petted him and told him he was a good kitty, and he pretty much went to sleep in there. Stupid little fucker trusted me.

I called Pongo's from the upstairs phone, got Darla, and said, "I have a cat in a bag. Would you have some time after work to go down by Makeout Bridge?"

"Romantic bastard, aren't you?" she said, but I could hear the grin in her voice. "You bring the cat, I'll bring the pussy," and kept going with more over-the-top dirty talk till I was about half crazy and Michelson told her to get off the phone.

I gently picked up Hairball—he hardly woke up, snuggled as he was in the warm pillowcase—reached in to stroke him a little, and headed down the stairs and out the door, hollering "Bye, Mom," as I went. From the shed,

I picked up a five-foot length of scrap rope—funny, but I made sure it was nylon, not hemp, I guess I didn't want it to chafe—and a box cutter, and the garden shears. I'd figure out what exactly to do when the time came—it was the same plan I had for Darla.

I wished I had a gun. I didn't care what Darla wanted, this was going to be quick and as near painless as I could make it.

I dropped the rope into the pillowcase with Hairball, who "qrphed" again and rubbed his face on my hand; I tickled under his jaw, I knew he liked that too, and he settled right back in. I picked up the bag and started walking up the alley at the back of our place.

The bridge over West Lock Creek was just a half mile away, and my tunnel into Darla's pants was just as close.

23

*Water Under the Bridge,
Letting the Cat Out of the Bag, Everyone's
Beautiful Naked, and Several Other Clichés*

I'D WALKED ABOUT three blocks when Darla pulled up alongside me in her old Plymouth Spear-a-Chick, as she called it, one of those late-fifties ones that had an ornamental cone right in the middle of the steering wheel, which were pretty cheap used cars if you could find them. She always said she liked the idea of driving with death pointed right at her like that, and besides, with her boobs, probably it wouldn't be able to get anywhere near her sternum.

She opened the passenger-side door and I climbed in; she stayed leaned over, wrapped her arm around my neck, jammed her mouth onto mine, and tongued me deep and hard. The taste of cigarettes on her tongue, and the way she moaned when she kissed, was like everything I'd ever thought about. I told myself to get brave and squeezed her breast, feeling that nip come up against my palm. She kissed me deeper, and I started to slip my hand into her Pongo's uniform, which was so low cut she was halfway out of it anyway. She broke the kiss, gave me a big theatrical sigh, and said, "Well, we should get to our picnic, young man. I take it you've got the cat there."

"Qrph?" Hairball asked.

"Right in the sack."

"Well, you know what I've got," she said, and flicked her skirt way up her thigh. My nuts were throbbing. "I brought you some dinner," she said, "since I figure my insane cat killer needs to keep his strength up, and I think I'll just torment you while we talk, and you eat, and then you can do the kitty, and then . . . do anything you want."

I didn't know what to say so I just looked at her, hoping I was looking cool while trying to figure out, from the angle, whether she was wearing underwear under her uniform. After a minute the silence got so awkward I said, "So work was probably like it always is?"

"Like it always is on Sunday afternoons. It's the Lord's Quarter Shift. This one was thirty-nine dimes, seventeen quarters, and three one-dollar bills. That was *all* my tips, even though all my tables covered at least twice, most three times. Normal for after church. Old Michelson says it's because when it comes time to give a waitress a tip for coping with fifteen people—a lot of them old, fussy, indecisive, and half-fucking-deaf—plus three screaming babies, they suddenly realize they already put their quarter in the offering plate. So he calls it the Lord's Quarter Shift, because you hustle your butt off trying to get the Lord's quarter. But the Lord almost always wins. He gets to try first, and besides, he can send them to hell and all I can do is shoot a nostril inside their sandwich."

She descended the dirt road carefully. There was enough gravel and drainage so there weren't any mud holes, and we drove all the way into the sandy area down below the bridge. We got out and walked over to sit near the creek behind the dredge pile that blocked the view from the bridge.

I set the pillowcase with Hairball down next to me. She handed me a sack that turned out to contain a Pongo's Double Monkey Burger with Three Cheeses and Russian Dressing, the biggest wad of food on the menu, plus a big load of fries. "Weird," I said, "I just realized I'm really hungry."

"Well, that's what the food is for," Darla said. "Eat. You're gonna need your strength, and so am I." It sounded like she wrote it out beforehand, and so did the next thing she said: "I've been thinking about it since eighth grade when you did Squid's little bunny wunny."

The burger smelled good. I started ramming food in,

wanting to make sure I got the meal before everything got weird, and through a full mouth I tried to explain. "I didn't want to hurt it, not really, I wanted to hurt Squid. I almost let it go. I got sick after I killed it. I don't like to kill things."

"And here you are, with a cat, and a knife, and me. I know what you're like whether you'll admit it or not, baby." She stood up and took off her uniform top, and then her skirt. "No hands till I say. Enjoy your dinner with a view." Her bra looked kind of complicated, but she took it off before I had to start figuring out how to.

I made myself not be a chickenshit and not worry about whether someone would see. The hollow behind the low dredge pile, just below Makeout Bridge, had a lot of privacy; hence the name.

She lit a cigarette and sat smoking and watching me eat. Beside me, Hairball stirred and poked his head out. "Qrph?"

"Hey, don't let the cat get away."

"He sticks real close to me whenever he's outside the house," I said. "He's a real fraidy."

Hairball climbed onto my lap, sniffing at the bacon in the burger, so I broke off a piece and gave it to him.

"Ugh, you say *I'm* gross but you let animals touch your food."

I shrugged. "Well, he's kind of the one that's mine."

She licked her lips and said, "This gets better and

better. So this isn't just like any old one of your mom's cats. You picked a special one for me."

He was trying to stand on his hind legs and put his paws around my neck as he sometimes did—he wasn't being affectionate, he was just after the burger. I pushed him down and said, "Hairball, behave." Then I explained to Darla, "I caught him shitting on my bed." Hairball curled up in my lap and batted lazily at the burger; I dripped grease and mayo on his upturned face and he licked at it.

"Hey, you're looking at the wrong pussy." She pulled her panties down and stood in front of me, hands behind her back. Compared to slim, girlish Bonny, Darla really did look like something out of *Playboy*. I felt all stupid and nerdy but I really just wanted to touch and look and find out what her body was like.

Darla pulled that stupid rabbit out of the pile of her clothes and said, "Mr. Babbitt wants to know, isn't this better?"

"It's great," I said, meaning it. I set the last bit of sandwich down and Hairball pounced on it, gobbling at the meat.

"Yuck," she said. "No wonder you want to kill him."

"I don't *want* to," I said.

I was just meaning to correct her, like tell her I really just wanted to lose my virginity with a great-looking friend. That was what I meant when I said that.

But as soon as I said it, I realized it was true.

There was a presentation Don gave once at the AA meeting about life decisions. He said to imagine all the bad parts, and then ask if you'd pay that much, have all the bad parts on purpose, to have the good parts.

How many times would I wash my sheets while dead exhausted, to have this big hairy idiot purring and loving me?

And here was Darla, naked, big tits hanging out for me to look at, posing really, cocking her cigarette to look all slutty and sophisticated, sticking out a shoulder, letting her hair fall half across her face. She put on that pouty sexy face that girls do when they're acting all spoiled and want you to win them a stuffed animal at the carnival, or change a tire for them.

How much would sticking it in Darla compensate me for the look on Hairball's face when he knew I was killing him? And I'd see it; I knew I would.

"Kill it now," she said. "I want to see it thrash around and watch your face while you do that to it."

"Him," I said, because, you know, you correct people about things like that.

Some part of me heard Paul saying there's nothing deader than an overrehearsed show. Right then I knew she wasn't getting to me. So here I was, ten feet from busting my cherry, with the sexiest girl I'd ever seen, and all of a sudden I couldn't even think about reaching into the pillowcase for the rope and the tools. "Tell me what this is about, Darla."

I sat there, rubbing the soft white and orange fur around Hairball's throat, not thinking of anything except that, sexy as Darla was, all I wanted to do was leave.

"Fuck," she said. "You really want to know, don't you, Karl?" I looked up and she was sitting cross-legged, her knees up. I was getting the best view I'd ever had of the whole anatomy thing, but it wasn't sexy at all. She was just sitting. "Fuck," she repeated.

I'd really only gotten as far as deciding not to kill the cat, but obviously she had already slid on over to some other topic.

"Okay," she said, sighing. "So let me explain it to you. I'm smart. I'm rich. I'm young and sexy. I could go anywhere and be anything, be a *legend*, I'm going to be an artist and people are going to know my name and they are going to *die* to be invited to my table and *brag* that they knew me. Except . . . Except when my life really starts a year from now, *what am I going to tell my roommate at Barnard?* 'I'm from this little cornfields town in Ohio and I waited tables a lot and studied hard'? 'My parents left me home from everything and I hung around with losers and read magazines about the cool stuff in the world and now I'm here for it, Miss Dumb Hick With Shit On My Shoes'? 'Hi, I'm nobody from nowhere but I sure am lucky that I had good grades and Daddy had good money, please let me be here'?

"Fuck *that*. I'm not going out into the world as Little Missy Good Grades from Lightsburg, Ohio. I'm going as the wildest most interesting bitch they've ever fucking met. I can already say I gave a guy head while he was driving at ninety on a dirt road, and I've ridden ten miles naked on a motorcycle, and a guy taught me to shoot a gun while I was naked. And I have a year more of stories I'm gonna build up."

She was wiping her eyes and her whine sounded more frustrated than hurt. "I was gonna have this story to tell about fucking the school's crazy killer right after he killed a cat. Fucking stupid, hunh?"

"Everybody wants to have a good story," I said. I'd never quite felt so stupid before in my life.

"Yeah, everybody does, but looks like I'm not going to, hunh? Fuck you, Karl, you like that cat better than you like me."

I thought, *Well, he's not fucking nuts, and he isn't trying to get me to do something awful so he can tell a story about it, and well, shit, yeah, maybe I do.* I asked, "I know this is a dumb question, but . . . uh, why do you want to tell awful stories like that about yourself?"

"So I can be hot shit like my mom, I guess, or be the kind of girl my dad talks about, or maybe . . . fuck. You know how I'm always saying about how places like Manhattan and Acapulco, and Marin County and Jackson Hole, all those places my parents are always flitting around between—you know how I'm always saying they're shitholes? I used to love it when I was little and they'd take me to those places. They always said I was a good little traveler. I had my own suitcase and my own passport and when I was just nine years old, I had to get extra pages in the passport for the visa stamps. Don't laugh at me, it was a big deal."

"How can I laugh? I don't even have a passport." The silly cat settled down to sleeping between my crossed legs; I guess he hadn't ever really been afraid.

She wiped the back of her hand over her face. "Then . . . I don't know. Logan came along. Mom got all this attention for being pregnant with him, but then she didn't really want him. Or me. And I started getting big boobs even when I was eleven, and then it was like those were leprosy, and I had to be a big girl and stay home, and . . . well, and for a while they came back a lot, but then that stopped, and after the big thing with Logan . . . do you know what he did? It's the only thing I'll ever love about the fucking little bastard."

I shook my head.

"About a year after they put him in foster, the county tried to take him back and return him to Mom, and make her promise to spend a lot of time at home. And in the courtroom, Mom was trying to explain to the judge that she needed to spend a lot of time discovering the world, and that was when that dumb little shit figured out they were going to take him away from the Taylors, who are this awful, awful hillbilly family down in Lima with like six other kids in a big dirty house with like cars in the yard and everything—the dad fixes cars, so no kidding, they have like ten of them in the yard all the time—and Logan lets loose with sobbing and crying and screaming he doesn't want to go back to Mom and he doesn't want to go back with Dad and he doesn't want to go back with me. Fucking beautiful. Stupid kid pissed all over Mom and Dad and the money and wants to be a goddam redneck hillbilly. They send pictures almost every month, him in his Little League uniform and the Boy Fucking Scouts and just, you know, out-of-it shit. But that was the best thing he ever did. Yelled it right in everybody's face that he'd rather be with his hillbilly fosters than put up with Mom and Dad's shit." She wiped her eyes again. "He was always useless."

"Anyway," she said, slumping, her rage apparently used up, "there you have it. I'm going to be an *artist*, people are going to know me, I'm gonna be solid cool with all that shit my mother thinks is cool."

"I think you're cool," I protested.

"Well, yeah, *you* think I'm cool. You've never left Lightsfuckingburg and all you want is a job away from your crazy mom, of course *you* think I'm cool. But *my parents are so embarrassed*. Because I'm too old for them to be as young as they pretend they are. Mom throws crying jags over anybody finding out she's over forty, you know." Then she leaned back, putting her hands behind her, which made those big breasts really stand up, and cocked her head like she was pretending to be all whimsical. "How can you stand to have that thing touching you all the time?"

It took me a second to realize she meant Hairball. "Uh, he's my friend?"

"You like him better than you like me."

"It's not like that. I wanted to, Darla—shit, I *still* want to—but Hairball *trusts me*, and I can't kill a friend just to get laid. You know?"

"I never even had goldfish," she said.

"I didn't till after my dad died. He just said having pets meant having animals in your house and he didn't want to live in a damn animal pen. I guess Mom always had pets growing up."

"She sure has them now."

"She's crazy," I said. Hairball rolled over and rubbed the back of his head on my thigh.

"Ewww."

"Come here and pet him," I said.

"No way. All hair and spit and teeth. Be a gentleman while I get dressed, hunh?"

So I turned my back, and kept petting Hairball, and it sounded like she was crying. I asked if she was okay.

She kicked me in the back, hard but not on anything vital, and yelled, "Fuck you, you stupid bastard, fuck you," loud enough they must've heard her in Canada.

Then she ran buck naked out of the hollow, clutching her clothes in a heap to her front, jumped in her car, threw it in gear, and peeled out in reverse, getting like halfway up the road before she made a turnaround. The first stupid thought I had was, well, she's got a garage door opener and an attached garage, I guess as long as the cops don't stop her, she can probably get home without anyone seeing. My second thought was wondering if this was going to be a story for her after all. And my third thought was, *wow, my back really hurts.*

I was just feeling at my back and deciding I didn't have anything worse than a bad bruise and a hole in my T-shirt—when I had an odd sensation of someone watching me. I looked up, and there was Stacy, leaning over the bridge railing.

I didn't know what else to do, so I waved at her, feeling like Pancake Pete, and she half-waved at me, like she was stunned, and then pulled her head back from the bridge railing and was gone.

I was figuring she would probably wear out the dial on her phone tonight.

"Come on, Hairball," I said. "We really should go home." He didn't want to go back in the pillowcase, so I let him climb onto my arm and put his forepaws on my shoulder. All the way home he hung on like that, purring like a crazy bastard. Tears poured down my face, just as if Hairball was dead, and as if I couldn't feel him digging his claws into my T-shirt and scratching my shoulder, or his back paws pushing down on my arm and tiring out my triceps, or his idiot head thumping against mine.

I came in the door, and went to drop him on the couch, but Hairball sank his claws in and meowed—he had discovered he liked riding this way, I guess, and figured he'd just do it for the rest of his life. So I ran up the stairs, still carrying him, to change out of my torn T-shirt and get a look in the mirror at the bruise I was sure I had on my back.

When I found my room door wide open, and Mom in there with her back to me, I nearly screamed. *Not another one of my cans, not so soon after the last one—*

She turned around, stared wildly at me, and said, "Uh." Then her eyes focused on Hairball and she said, "You brought him back. He's alive."

How could she have known what I planned to do?

But she knew.

Then I saw the shredded remains all over my bed, the yellow notebook paper that had already been dry and crumbly, now a pile of loose bits of paper, lint really, if that. Just three corners, from different pages, remained on the wall, clinging to the thumbtacks.

She had torn up Dad's directions for taking care of

the house. Torn them to shreds and beyond, might have torn them all the way down to dust I suppose if she'd had enough time.

Sure as shit, I didn't know what to say, and going by her expression, neither did she. We both just stood there, both knowing all the facts, somehow, without knowing anything that was true. I think if I could have said something about Indians baseball or if she'd said something about flying saucers, we'd both have sighed with relief and babbled for an hour. But we just stood, stared, tried to figure out what we'd be saying if we knew what to say.

After a real long time, she pushed her hair back from around her face and made herself look me in the eye. "I'm sorry. I thought you were going to kill him like you killed the others. It says in a book I was reading that when a teenage boy, um, when he gets to be . . . the way you are, his cycle gets shorter and shorter, and you killed two just in the last two days."

Hairball squirmed, turned, dropped to the floor, and padded out, probably having decided that whatever was going on between the can-opener operators, it would doubtless work out just fine for the cat.

"I didn't kill any of your cats," I said. "I never did. It was a raccoon, like I said."

Her eyes welled with tears and she wiped her face. "First it was Lemondrop, and then Sunblessing, and there was only half of Silvercloud *left*—"

"Mom," I said. "Mom."

She stared at me.

"Mom." I didn't know what to say beyond that. I dropped the bag on the floor, and it made a telltale thud, but I didn't care, I grabbed her and hung on like she was the only tree for a hundred miles and I was surrounded by bears. "Mom, I am telling you the truth. The old raccoon killed them. I just buried them for you."

Her hand rubbed the back of my neck. "I've been having nightmares for years. Officer Williams *told* us what you did to that rabbit, and I have awful dreams about you doing that to Mrs. Fuzzyworth—she was my favorite, of all time, and she just disappeared—"

"Mom, I don't know what happened to Mrs. Fuzzyworth, either."

She went on like she didn't hear me. "—and I can't wake up and I have to watch you and I can't wake up. And the dream just goes on all night. I know you did it to other cats, too, but Mrs. Fuzzyworth was special, I *loved* her, and I see you cutting her up—"

"I never did that to anything but that rabbit, Mom."

She pushed my head back and looked into my eyes, and it was like a tiny, sane bit of my old mother, the one that protected me from Dad, the one I could tell anything to, for just a second. Then she grabbed up the pillowcase and shook it. The garden shears and the box cutter fell out.

It felt like my heart was right there next to them.

And I sat down on my bed, and grabbed my head with both hands like I was going to tear it off, and looked down at the floor, and told her everything—Spooky Darla, that weird idea that Darla had that I slashed up cats, that she was going to have sex with me, the shit on my bed, about getting to see Darla naked and realizing I didn't want to do it, couldn't do it in a million years. I even told her why Darla wanted to do it that way. I finished real stupid, just saying, "I was just real angry."

She didn't speak for so long that I finally looked up, afraid she'd have walked out of the room, afraid she was about to tell me to leave forever, even afraid that she was going to call over a bunch of the super super ladies and they were going to chant to drive the grays out of my room. I mean, it was Mom. Anything was possible.

Instead, very, very softly, she said, "I know where she got the idea that you've been cutting up cats, Karl. I've been worried sick about you. I thought . . . Neil likes to read these books about killers, you know, it's like murderers are his hobby the way mine is UFOs and astrology? Only he's not as serious as I am, but his apartment has all these books. And he said that in all those books, the serial killers start with animals, when they're teenagers, and they're fascinated with weapons and violence, and loners, and they have trouble with girls."

"Shit," I said.

"And I was *afraid*, Karl. Afraid of you. Afraid for you. Afraid that my little son was . . . well, you know what I was afraid you were."

"Didn't you ever ask, you know, a hunter, or a trapper, or just someone who knew—"

"They're all full of male energy and I'll-tell-you-the-truth-little-lady. I felt like I couldn't trust them. Some of them tried to talk to me, I guess because they heard the things Neil was saying—"

"I think I want to kill him."

"He got a lot of it from me, Karl. I didn't know what to do and I was too afraid to do anything. That nice psychiatrist said you were all right, and your father and I thought you were, but then we got the cats after your dad died, and it was only like three months later that I found Lemondrop all torn up in the yard. And you know, I know you don't like Neil, but one thing he did that Doug never did, he *listened*."

He also talked, I thought. "So everyone's been arguing behind my back whether I'm a crazy killer or it's just a raccoon?"

"Not really everyone, just the people at parties. Which is probably where Darla heard it, because, you know, she comes to a lot of parties."

"Yeah." I sat there for a while, trying to see what it felt like to keep breathing. "You must've been scared to death of me."

She shrugged. "Never really scared *of* you. Scared *for* you. Scared you'd do something terrible. Scared you'd be caught." She sighed. "There's something else I guess you'd better see, too. I thought—Karl, that cat should be *special*, he *loves* you, he's *yours*. I couldn't believe it when I saw you taking him down the stairs, you were going to kill *Hairball*, I couldn't believe you had gone so far evil so I—well, I lost my temper and I got all full of angry energy and—you better see this."

She walked past me and I followed her downstairs, like I was a little boy, or maybe like I was a puppy who had messed the rug.

In the backyard, all five of the glazed and primed storm windows were lying in the wet grass, some of their shattered panes knocked all the way out, littering the yard with hundreds of bright glints in the sun.

"You like to be barefoot out here," I said. "This is really stupid."

"I wasn't thinking real clearly." Mom looked it over and said, "I know this was important to you. Will it take much to redo it?"

I shrugged. "I'll need to buy some glass and get a friend with a car to help me move it here. Maybe old Browning would help me out, I kind of like the idea of pulling up a hearse in front of Wilson's place."

Mom made a strangled noise, then coughed way too much like Wilson, then growled, "Goddam undertakers."

I couldn't help it, I started to laugh, and so did she, and we went back inside, almost friends I think, until we got back up to my room.

At first we thought that that sad pile of torn paper could be put back together like a puzzle. But it quickly turned out to be hopeless; the dried-out pieces broke in our hands, that old gravity furnace made it so hot up in my room, and so dry, that four winters had pretty much destroyed it. After a while we both gave up; there was no way to get it all laid out and then tape it together.

"I'm so sorry, Karl," she said. Her eyes were clear and calm, like the Mom I remembered; I almost cried right then.

"It's okay, really," I said. "I pretty much have them all memorized. I'll miss them but I don't *need* them." It was true; even now, just telling Mom about it, I could see all of the four notebook sheets in my mind's eye, and read all sixty-two tasks, spaced two lines apart in case he wanted to add notes (which he sometimes did up till he died), all in Dad's neat bookkeeper's hand lettering. In fact, right now, it would have been so nice to just sit and look at them, or even to stretch out for a nap and read them till I fell asleep.

"Sweetie?" Mom asked.

"Yeah, Mom, I'm just kind of absorbing that it's really gone, right now."

"Tiger, I'm so sorry, this is the kind of thing that happens when we let anger get into our energy."

"I guess it is, Mom."

"This is the kind of thing I wanted to protect you from." She sighed and wiped her eyes. "Actually I don't protect you from much, do I? And your father didn't either, I guess neither of us could." She looked at me, straight and clear and sane as anything, and said, "I'm sorry, Karl. These last few years must have been awful for you."

And something just broke. Not like a dam, crashing slowly down, but like the whole world just ceased to be. I was there in the void with nothing at all, and before I knew it I was running down the stairs, running like a crazy bastard, vaulting over Hairball, out the front door, and on down the street. I didn't hear her call after me or anything. Probably she didn't, come to admit it, but it would have been nice if she had, I can tell you that. It would have been fucking nice.

I ran and ran; like Dad used to say, "the wicked flee when no man pursueth." I ended up in City Park, sitting on a bench, breathing like I'd just come up from five thousand fathoms, hands on my knees, panting like a pervert with a peephole into the girls' locker room. I was two miles from my house, and I'd probably just broken all my previous records—speed, distance, and lunacy. I wanted to cry but I was breathing too hard to do anything but breathe.

I stayed on that bench, by the pool, which had been closed for the season and drained that week. I was a long way from the playground or the basketball courts, just among the picnic tables, but with the cold and rain the day before, no one had planned a picnic I guess, so there was nobody in sight. I sat there because I didn't have anywhere else to be, and stayed until my breathing was slower and I started to come back to myself a little.

It got dark after a while, and I was getting hungry. I looked at my watch, not sure what to do, and saw I had time enough for some basics, and my wallet had enough, so first I walked the mile and a half back to the downtown, taking side streets where I didn't know anybody so I wouldn't have to talk to anyone.

Come to admit it, I was kind of ashamed of how I'd behaved, and really having a hard time figuring out how any guy could be as fucked-up as me and still remember to breathe. Mom acted okay for the first time in years, and I just lost it and ran out on her. Shit-jesus, God only knew what that might have sent her off into. Maybe she was smashing the rest of the windows and looting all my money cans, or more likely she was off with the super super ladies now getting really drunk, even more weird ideas, seriously horny, and a lot of sympathy. I'd have to go home eventually, but I admitted to myself I was just too chickenshit to think about that now, too afraid of what I could find.

Plenty of cash in my wallet. Kathy had let me do my shift without my McDorksuit before, when I'd been locked out or not able to go home; I should find a pay phone and call her.

I could get a single room at the Carrellsen tonight; probably Paul wouldn't be able to smuggle me into his basement, and there was nobody else I felt comfortable asking, and besides, this was Marilyn's night on the front desk, and she was a real bud. Getting a room would set me back a couple days' work but it beat trying to get by on four hours of McSleep.

I took a deep breath and kind of put it in perspective; by dawn Mom would be passed out drunk for sure. I had reset the window sash lock earlier that day. I could sneak in and get what I needed for school, neat and easy, at around eight in the morning or so. Then when she got home from work tomorrow I could try to have it together enough to tell her . . .

Well, I'd figure out what to tell her later.

I'd left home without any books, and I was done with everything but the windows, but I didn't want Harris and Tierden to see me just catching a nap in here. It was always possible they'd figure out the way I'd been avoiding having to double-clean the windows. Since it had rained all day Saturday, the McPuddle by the window was all filled up. They'd make their big splash, I'd wash the windows that I had to wash anyway, and we'd be all even and done.

So I wanted them to think I'd already gone home for the night, and therefore I was hiding from their view, since they never got out of that car. I was sitting reading on the bathroom floor, with the bathroom door propped open. I'd fished out a Sunday *Toledo Blade* that wasn't all grody from having been in the trash, and was trying to keep all the Watergate crap straight because Harry would be telling us what to think about it tomorrow.

Instead of the big splash, I heard a knock on the window. I came out of the bathroom. Marti was looking in the window like a puppy in a pet store. I went outside, but she didn't come right in the door, so I walked up to her. She stood like she didn't want to be touched.

"Locked out?"

"My parents were fighting. Mother was yelling at Dad because he created an ugly geek daughter, and I will never get a date because I'm too brainy and too weird and I'll never learn to do anything like a normal person, and my boyfriend is the biggest fag in the high school. Dad was blaming Mom for having contaminated his genius bloodline with crazy drunken whore blood. I don't think they noticed when I left, which was six hours ago, and they might not have noticed yet. I drove halfway to Cleveland, and then realized I only had enough money for gas to make it back here. So I turned around and now I'm here. Are you going to let me in?"

"Of course. I only came out because you didn't move."

Once I had her seated at the counter, and put a couple of the remaining hamburgers in front of her, she just kind of sat there, head down, like the kind of rescued baby animal situation when you know you're going to be up all night but the poor little thing isn't going to make it.

"I'm locked out, too," I said, lying or maybe not. "I have a room at the Carrellsen. There's room on the bed for two, or there's a couch in the room; either way I'm pretty much a gentleman. Might take some smuggling to get you up there, but we'll manage." I picked up one of the burgers. "If you're not going to eat that, I've always got room."

"Help yourself." She sat there while I finished. "Are you just waiting for the assholes to splash water on the windows?"

"Pretty much. Then I have to hang out here till I can clock out. Get a nap if you need one, and I'll wake you up when it's time to go to the Carrellsen."

"My first time checking into a hotel room with a guy. My mom will be so proud."

She slept, and I read the paper. It got close to closing, and Harris and Tierden didn't show up, so I finally just washed the windows, woke Marti, and clocked out. Marti parked her car on the side of the Carrellsen that you can't see from the front desk.

I went in the front entrance, chatted with Marilyn for a minute, went up the steps towards my room, descended the stairs to the side entrance, looked all around the parking lot to be on the safe side, and gestured for Marti. She slipped out from between two parked trucks and hurried into the doorway beside me. I pulled the door closed, careful to keep it quiet, and we went up the stairs together.

"How close is the front desk?" she breathed in my ear. "Where do I hide if she comes up the hall?"

"About a mile and a half beyond some closed doors," I said in my normal voice, "and Marilyn won't leave that front desk to walk the halls. She's the only staff here, and she's so conscientious about staying at the desk that I don't think she ever takes a pee break for her whole shift."

Marti made that snorting, fizzy laugh, pinned her back against the wall, and moved sideways like she was in a commando raid in a movie, quietly singing the *Mission Impossible* theme—"Bump-bump-bump bump-BAH-dump, Bump-bump-bump bump-BAH-dump." I about bust a gut. "Come on," I said, "We should get into the room anyway."

As I closed the door, Marti said, "Well, yeah, okay, I *am* a hopeless romantic, but this is the cheapest-looking hotel room I've ever been in, exactly like the kind of place I always figured I'd be staying in when I started having real adventures out in the real world, and I think this is cool."

I'd lost track of how many times I'd crashed out in one of these rooms, so "cool" was not a word that would have occurred to me. The Carrellsen was old; it had been a railway hotel, then a bum bin, and though for the moment it was back to being sort of a hotel, it made most of its money off the bar on the ground floor, and you could tell it would be a bum bin again in a few years.

The room had hairy gold wallpaper with a red rope pattern on it, and a tall ceiling. There was an ancient radiator that had been painted so many times it looked like it was made out of dirty yellow snow and the spring thaw was on. The gray-beige carpets were the color of the local mud. The furniture was a lumpy old double bed, a desk taken up entirely by a TV, a hard-back chair that looked stolen from somebody's dinette set, and an old couch, one of those thirties designs that was all curves, sagging so much it looked like Dr. Seuss had drawn it. The bathroom contained a greasy mirror, two big towels, two little towels, and one really ancient pink toilet that didn't match either the tiny sink on a stand or the old claw-foot tub with an aluminum-tube circle above it, from which hung a plastic shower curtain dirtier than Mom's bathroom floor.

"Well," she said, "embarrassment time if you want to be embarrassed. What do we do about showers and jammies and all that?"

"Humph," I said. "Well, we each get a bath or shower,

then get dressed in our dirty clothes, and come out and sleep in them. That's what I'd say."

"Or," she said, "how much of a gentleman are you? We move the coverlet to the couch, where I'm going to sleep. You won't need it, this place is too warm anyway. We each take a shower and come out wearing a towel, with our dirty clothes on hangers. We hang up the dirty clothes on the rack so they at least get some air. The second one out turns off the lights and then you get into the bed, because you paid for the room, and I get under the coverlet on the couch, in our nice clean skin. That way we just wear our stinky clothes for a few minutes tomorrow morning. Unless, of course, knowing there are naked ta-tas in the same room is going to keep you awake all night."

Hunh, no naked ladies in my life for seventeen years, and now twice in a day. By the time I was thirty I might get to touch one.

I wanted to flip a coin to see who got first shower, but Marti insisted that paying for the room trumped on that, so I got my shower, tied on the towel, and went out and got between the sheets. I figured if I was already asleep I could trust myself to be a gentleman.

I drifted off but woke when she sat on the edge of the bed. "Um, Karl, this is embarrassing. I need your help for something."

"It can't be any more embarrassing than anything else today has been," I said. "What do you need?"

"There's this cream," she said, "for my acne. When I get a real bad flare-up, like I'm having now, it itches and gets sore. And I've got a patch on my back I can't reach. Could you, um—"

"Just get me the stuff and I won't open my eyes till you tell me you're stretched out on your stomach," I said. "Then you close your eyes, unless you want to be struck with awe at my manly equipment. I rub it in where you say, and get back under the covers, and we reverse the process. Duck soup."

In a minute she had it all together and was lying on the bed, with the sheet down to her waist, on her stomach. In the light of the crappy little lamp, all I was looking at was a frizzy mop of blonde hair and a bare back with one big angry red patch on it, but Jesus fucking God she was beautiful, and if you don't understand that, I'm sorry for you.

When I went to rub it in, I could see the skin was badly broken and erupted down in the lower part between her shoulder blades. "That looks awful," I said.

"It doesn't feel good, either. But the cream kills the itch and dries it out. You have to kind of work it in."

"Let me know if this hurts." I rubbed a little of the cream in, and she said, "You can rub harder." So I did, and reflected that here I'd been wishing to touch a naked girl and I was getting to. Obviously God or somebody had one hell of a sense of humor.

Once she wasn't itching and hurting, it kind of turned into an overall back rub; she just seemed so small and her skin was so soft, and, well, we had the time. "That couch looks like it's uncomfortable," I said. "Not to mention like it's probably rough on your skin. There's room in the bed for two of us to sleep without touching."

She breathed in and out before saying, "If you turn out the lights, and we both get under the sheet, are you gonna turn into a crazy rapist?"

"I don't think so."

I don't know if she peeked but I didn't; it wouldn't have felt right.

I was tired, and so was Marti, and we were almost asleep when a big old thunderstorm came booming in, filling the room with flashes of bright light. "I'm a little scared of storms," she said. "If I take your hand, you won't break out in hair and go for my throat or anything, will you?"

"When there's a thunderstorm on," I said, "I can't see the moon anyway."

So we fell asleep holding hands. If married couples got to do this all the time, shit if I could understand how there were ever divorces, or even fights.

PART SIX

(Monday, September 10, 1973)

24

The Long End of the Stick Isn't So Hot Either

THE DOOR BOOMED.

I opened my eyes to see it was five fifteen just after I jumped out of bed with a yell, because I thought it was one of Mom's crazy boyfriends coming upstairs to beat me up because Mom was mad at me.

I remembered where I was in about half a second. We had set the alarm for five forty-five, so we could slip out before anyone saw us—the bedroom lamp came on, and I looked back to see Marti sitting up, clutching a sheet around herself. I turned back to the door and shouted, "What!"

"Police. Open up."

"We have to get some clothes on," I said, not thinking very clearly.

Behind me, Marti was scrambling to get into hers. I dove for my T-shirt and jeans.

But I hadn't put the chain on, so Marilyn just used her key to unlock the door, and a whole parade came through—first Marilyn in her dyed-black beehive, dumpy brown dress, and sensible shoes, hand to her mouth, looking perfectly like a cartoon of a middle-aged lady being shocked. Then Officer Williams, Lightsburg's family court officer, a big man with a heavy black mustache, his level gaze appraising everything in an instant—two kids frantically putting clothes on, one bed with covers flung all over.

Behind them came Mom, and Mrs. Nielsen, both of whom had that hard-set mother-jaw that means: "You have embarrassed me."

And behind all of that, looking like the most embarrassed guy in the world, which he couldn't possibly be, since I was right there, was Mom's Wonderful Bill.

Mrs. Nielsen shrieked first. "Oh my god, oh honey, what did that boy *do* to you?"

Marti blinked. "Mom, we—"

Mrs. Nielsen and Marilyn had rushed to her like she was bleeding to death and they were trying to win the International Special Tourniquet Award. "Did he hurt you? Did he leave marks? Oh honey—"

"Now *just* a minute," Mom said. "Just a damn *minute*. Karl would *never*—"

"How fast can we get a pregnancy test?" Mrs. Nielsen demanded.

Officer Williams opened his mouth but didn't seem to have anything to say, maybe trying to decide which craziness to deal with first. Just as he seemed to settle on Mrs. Nielsen, Marilyn asked, "Can the Carrellsen Hotel get into legal trouble about this? I don't think it's fair if we can get in trouble for people doing things like this."

Williams froze again. I don't know how they let a guy like that be a cop; what would he do in the middle of a bank robbery?

I looked away—really looking for anything besides two raging moms, one beehived old church lady, a bewildered old cop, and a bum-bin hotel room. Bill was standing halfway in the door—the room was a little big for the crowd and he couldn't quite get in past Williams's broad, lardy back. Bill was wearing big old tire-tread sandals, chinos that looked like they'd been fished out of the laundry basket, an untucked Mud Hens T-shirt with holes in the belly, and one of those silly patch-on-the-elbows corduroy jackets. He looked so disheveled and out of it that the pathetic stupid fisherman's cap, perched on the back of his head like a lost pancake, sort of helped by at least hiding some of the mess of his hair.

Out of nowhere he gave me this funny little sideways smile and a wink.

I didn't know what the fuck he meant, but it did make me feel better, come to admit it.

Meanwhile, everyone else except Marti had gotten into yelling at each other, trying to settle whether I was a rapist psycho, or Marti was an out-of-control little slut who lured me here to give me VD and trap me into a loveless marriage with a baby that probably wasn't even mine. At least I think that's what the two mothers were saying, trying to shout over each other, and over Marilyn, and over Williams asking them to calm down.

At first I thought they were drunk. Then I realized Mrs. Nielsen had what Mom called a "slamover," a sleepless hangover that you get by sobering up while staying up all night. And Mom—I didn't know. She just looked sick for some reason.

It was kind of hard to keep it all straight with both of them going at the same time, and Marilyn asking if the hotel was in trouble and helpfully suggesting that all of us ought to be tested for drugs. All three of them were pretty much drowning out Officer Williams, who seemed to be trying to get them to just come at him one at a time.

Finally Williams's patience wore out just as Mom and Mrs. Nielsen paused for breath, which left Marilyn pointing out that all this was probably because of *drugs*, if you just *look*ed at the *people* in*volv*ed, and Williams lost it and barked *"Shut up!"* at her, kind of loud.

She got an expression like he'd just given her ten million volts across the nipples, and her face started folding and crumpling like a soggy paper towel in a campfire, and it was like you could see poor old Williams brace himself for half a second before Marilyn let loose with a wail like she just saw her kitten go under a tire. She flumped down on the bed and just sobbed, because it all wasn't fair, the Carrellsen was going to be *closed* because of this, she *knew* it, and she'd *lose her job* and it was all because some people couldn't keep their kids away from *drugs*. Her beehive was kind of working its way loose, shaking more and more as she talked and sobbed, and it looked like in no time it would be all down around her face.

Williams sat down next to her, and patted her arm, and told her everything would be fine, the Carrellsen and her job would survive, really, and she should just go on down to the desk, he'd handle everything and it would all work out.

She sniffled once, then fled like her butt was on fire; her cheeks were streaked with makeup and eye shadow avalanches and the beehive was more like a squirrel nest.

Williams looked a little at loss for words.

Bill said, "Look, I'm just the chauffeur here, but I think somebody ought to ask and give them a chance to just tell us. Did you kids have sex?"

"No!" Marti and I both said, pretty loud.

At least that seemed to surprise Mom and Mrs. Nielsen. Williams opened his mouth again, but Bill rolled on. "And did you come here to have sex?"

"No," I said.

"We were locked out and we needed somewhere to sleep, sir," Marti said, in that stubborn-sincere way that seemed to drive Gratz apeshit (but I could tell Bill believed her).

"*You* weren't locked out, Karl," Mom said. She didn't sound happy. She was on probation for marijuana possession, and locking your kid out, unless they were violent, was a crime.

"I *thought* I was locked out, Mom, I was *sure* I would be."

She stared at me, and I realized her confusion was real. "Karl, I've been out looking for you for most of the night. And Rose has been looking for Marti. Bill was driving us around. I was *worried*."

That was so weird—Mom worrying about what was happening when I was out—that she and I just kind of stared at each other for a second while the weirdness washed over us.

"I want to go to the hospital," Mrs. Nielsen announced.

I swear I was still so freaked-out that for one crazy second I wondered if she was sick.

Unfortunately she wasn't. I mean, not that it would have been fortunate if she'd been sick or anything like that. I mean, she didn't want to go to the hospital for herself. "We've got to find out what this creepy little boy did to Martinella right now," she said, arms folded across her chest. "That's all there is to it. You're not going to railroad me with any small-town bullshit, Officer, we are going to make sure the truth comes out. Martinella is going straight to the hospital for a pregnancy test and a VD test and whatever kind of whatever else they can do for her."

"Uh, ma'am," Officer Williams said, "neither one of those tests would show anything right now, if she just now got pregnant or infected. I guess if we test them both we can find out whether either one could have infected the other—"

"He could not have gotten it from Martinella! He could not! We are just going to test to see whether she got it from this—this—"

"If you are going to be that way about it, Rose," Mom said, with a voice that would freeze vodka solid, "then I think Karl had *better* be tested for VD. You never know what he might have gotten off a girl like that."

"*Fine!*" Mrs. Nielsen was pretty loud; I felt sorry for anyone trying to sleep. For a second there I thought we might get to see our moms brawling on the floor. But instead they seemed to agree on something while communicating entirely by glare. All of a sudden we had grabbed up our few things, and Mrs. Nielsen took Marti's car, Bill took Mom in his car, and Williams took me and Marti in the oinkmobile. "Probably it will be better if you two don't communicate, officially," he said. "But was what you said true, you didn't have sex, you were just sleeping, and didn't want to put dirty clothes back on?"

"We didn't have sex, we didn't plan to have sex, we just needed a place to sleep," I said.

"Martinella?"

"Same thing," she said. "Christ, my mother is embarrassing."

Williams sighed. "She's upset and terrified and you're gonna have to take care of her. She thinks she's a complete failure because of this, you know."

That kind of killed the conversation for the next three miles as we rumbled onto the interstate and out through the cornfields. It was the same time of day I was used to being out with Browning, gray-white sky that would be blue as soon as it got more light, sun crawling up over the distant tree line, but I wasn't getting paid for this one.

After a while Williams said, "So, Karl, no drugs?"

"No."

"Drinking?"

"No, really, we just needed to sleep some—"

"Who killed Squid's rabbit?"

"I did," I said. "Everybody knows that." Then I realized

what a cheap trick that was, and didn't care, because obviously I'd passed the test. I'm sure old Williams thought he was the cleverest son of a bitch of a pig old Lightsburg had ever produced, but if he was willing to believe us because of it, I guess he was welcome to think he was Sherlock Fucking Holmes.

He was nodding. "You're acting like a kid who isn't lying. Keep that up and we can probably get you through all this bullshit okay. You do the same, Martinella, and this can just be a mildly unpleasant day or two."

"All right," she said.

It was grayish dawn with the sun just coming up when we turned into the driveway for the emergency room at Gist County Hospital in Vinville. There was no one waiting this morning.

Marti's mom was already there, having captured a very embarrassed young doctor. "All right, now I want both of them tested," she barked, in a tone I wouldn't use on a bad waiter.

"Ma'am," he said, "now that everyone is here, let me just repeat, a pregnancy test is useless right now. The tests we do here don't even *start* to mean anything until about a week after a missed period, and for the new tests we still need to wait at least two weeks and then send a urine sample to the lab in North Carolina. This is just going to be money down the—"

"Money!" Mrs. Nielsen got madder, which I wouldn't

have thought was possible. "This is the care of my daughter we are talking about! I want a pregnancy test and right now. My husband has good insurance, he's an important scientist and a professor. This is the kind of thing we *have* insurance for. Give her whatever the best test is—give her the expensive one. And I want her tested and treated for VD. *That* is what she was with," she said, pointing at me.

Bill had had Mom by the elbow and been talking to her quietly, but now she shook him off and said, "You go right ahead and do that, Rose Lee Nielsen."

I had a feeling old Rose was no longer a super super lady.

Williams stepped between them. We all watched Marti, her mother, and the doctor disappear down the white, fluorescent-lit corridor. When he could see they were all out of earshot, Williams said, "Look, Mrs. Shoemaker, I think we can trust your son and the girl, they really didn't have sex, and there's really no reason for him to have that test or—"

"I don't care," Mom said. "If that bitch is going to talk about my son like that, and call him a liar and say he raped that ugly little zit-face girl—"

"Mom, Marti is my friend—"

"Karl, don't argue, I mean it. If that bitch, who just got to this town a month ago, is going to say that kind of crap about my son—I mean, a *Shoemaker*—well, then *we're* going to act just like he was with a whore."

"Uh," Bill said, "I think what Officer Williams is trying to tell you is that the test is pretty uncomfortable
and if we—" He stopped because she was glaring at him.
"Karl," he said, "I am sure Officer Williams will say it's
up to you, and I have to tell you—"

"You don't have to tell him anything. He's taking the
test." It was so weird to see Mom so angry and not yelling, just hissing everything through a clenched jaw. I
hadn't seen that since Dad died.

"Mom," I said, "I really wasn't with anyone, but if it'll
keep the peace, I'll have the test."

Williams and Bill both seemed to shrug, like they'd
tried, and then Mom and me filled out the forms and they
led me back to a little room. They told me this was something Mom wouldn't want to see.

The nurse was Mrs. Freeberg. She went to First
United Methodist and was super-active there, so I figured she wouldn't be too happy with me. Her husband,
Hal, bought a ton of radio ads from me every month for
his car dealership. I really hoped this wasn't going to cost
me an account that good.

Mrs. Freeberg had big curls of gray hair, soft and
loose. Her thick red cheeks looked like they'd been slabbed
on with a tuck-pointing trowel, and her little blue eyes behind her horn-rimmed glasses were hard and business-
like, so I guess she knew what I was in for. The set of her

jaw made her look ready to bite somebody. But her voice
was soft and sympathetic when she told me to get into
that little green gown.

After I'd sat scratching, and trying to find a way
to get it to close around my butt, and squirming to try
to find a comfortable position on that silly Naugahyde-
covered table, and gotten bored enough to wonder if it
would be okay to lay down to go to sleep, this million-
year-old white-haired guy that stank of cigarettes came
in and said he was Doctor Adler. He asked me a bunch
of questions, all the stuff everyone had already asked,
and finally said, "Well, you say you didn't have sex, and
I believe you, but your mother is insisting that you be
treated, and that guy with her—is he your stepdad?"

"Her boyfriend. He's okay."

"Well, he's definitely on your side, trying to talk her
out of this, but she's pretty determined that you be tested. I was trying to give him a little more time to work on
her, but it looks like she won't change her mind."

"Nobody ever gets her to do that. It's nice that you
tried, and Bill tried. I suppose we'd better get it over
with." I guess I was thinking, how bad can it be?

"You're a good sport," the doctor said. "Mrs. Freeberg
will come in to take the samples for the tests, and give
you the shot and the pro."

"The pro?"

"Prophylaxis. Prevents gonorrhea. Technically it's re-
dundant with the big shot of antibiotics we're giving you,

but we're supposed to play it safe." Then he was out that door like a greased coward.

Mrs. Freeberg came back in and said, "Okay, Karl, this is not going to be fun. And Dr. Adler says it's unnecessary, so I'm *really* sorry you have to go through with this. There's a blood test, a shot, a swab test, and the pro, and we'll do them in that order because that's the order that doesn't mess up the test results. I guess your mother is having some kind of fight with the girl's mother, and this is some kind of proving a point, and I have to say it's really nice of you to go along with it. Okay, blood sample first."

That was almost interesting; she put a needle in to connect the vein in my arm to a test tube and filled the tube up with my fresh dark blood. "We check this for syphilis," she said. "It won't tell us if you just caught it but it will tell us if you might have given it to the girl. If you both come up blanks, then neither of you had a developed-enough case to give it to the other one. Next is your ampicillin. It's like more-modern penicillin, and it should kill everything—for sure it will kill any syphilis you have. It should also kill gonorrhea, but we still do the swab and pro for that."

"Okay," I said.

She prepped the shot and gave it to me in the butt, because there was a lot of it; it stung a little and I could tell I might be sore there for a day.

"Most men tell me the swab is the worst," she said.

"Stand up and lift your gown and hold very still. For the swab test most guys are more comfortable if they don't look."

She got out a container of individually wrapped, sealed sticks that ended in little cotton tips, and a sample bottle, and I suddenly knew what she was going to do. "We need to get a sample swabbed from the site of the infection," she said, pulling on her rubber gloves. "For gonorrhea, that's the interior of the urethra. It has to go a long way in, and stay there for a bit, and I'm supposed to rotate it a little to make sure I pick up whatever's in there. It won't get any easier if we wait or talk it over, so raise your gown, hold still, and look away."

I did.

She pulled my dick out straight, gently enough but firmly, and then that little stick went in and kept going. The swab was dry, I guess to catch more goop, and it hurt going in, staying in, turning around, and coming out. It felt like it was in me for like three thousand years.

She dropped it into the sample bottle, closed it, and wrote something on the label.

"All right," she said. "The pro goes to the same place, but not as deep. Thanks for being a big boy about this."

I sighed and lifted my gown. I was still hurting, but I wasn't going to be a pussy.

The gadget was sort of a plunger syringe without a needle; it hurt a little as she fit it into me, and it felt weird to have that goo squirting up there inside, but compared to the swab, it wasn't much. When she'd squirted it and pulled out the syringe, she said, "There will be some yellow glop in the toilet, next time you pee, with perhaps a few drops of blood, and it might sting a little bit. That's just the pro coming back out, and you might have gotten a little scraped up inside from the swab. County Health will call you if it comes out positive." She shook her head. "It makes *no* sense to give you a swab *and* a pro. If you had it, you don't now." She scribbled a few notes on my chart, and put it on the outside of the door. "Stacy, chart up." She closed the door. "Okay, get dressed and go out to the waiting area. Your mom is out there." She went out into the hallway, closing the door after her.

As I dressed, I thought, *Stacy?* and figured there had to be a lot of girls with that name, and besides, the one I knew didn't seem like the brainy type that becomes a candy striper, or the ambitious type that takes the early-morning shift.

I continued to reassure myself on that subject until I came around the corner on my way back to the waiting room. Headed my way, carrying a bunch of file folders, was *that* Stacy, the same one who had seen me by the tar pond with Cheryl, and a couple of times with Darla, and hugging Paul on the street. She wore a dorky uniform that looked very 1962, thin red stripes on a white, knee-length dress, and silly white cap and shoes, kind of like a cover on a Harlequin novel, but not so classy.

For a second she looked like she was trying not to see

me. I don't know what my facial expression was, but it must've been something, because all of a sudden she gave me this big goofy grin and said, "See you in school."

Something about that grin made me want to laugh. "Believe it or not, I can explain everything."

Damn if she didn't smile like she thought I was cute or something, and over her shoulder, as she walked away, she even gave me the cutesy-wave social girls do. Okay, it wasn't just my mom and all my female friends, *all* girls made no sense.

It also occurred to me that aside from being with two different naked girls in twenty-four hours, I'd also just been touched on the dick by someone female for the first time since I'd been toilet trained. I decided if that was how it was going to be, I'd just look from now on, thanks.

At the waiting room, Mom had sort of settled into exhaustion, and was about half asleep on Bill's shoulder. "Williams already left," Bill said, "and he said that officially you're free to go. They have one of those new answer-machine things at your mother's office, so she's already called in sick. My plan is, I'm taking you both to the Elias Brothers here in Vinville for the breakfast bar, ramming food into all of us, and then taking you and this young lady home"—he squeezed Mom's shoulder and she looked sort of happy through her tired—"where you will change clothes. Then I'll drop you at the high school. Good chance you'll actually be on time."

It seemed strange, but it'd only been about an hour

and a half since Marti and me had been awakened at the Carrellsen, and there was actually plenty of time.

Mom was rubbing her face. "God, food," she said. "I don't know if I can face it."

Bill shrugged. "It's plain old breakfast. Easy on the stomach." He glanced sideways and then asked sharply, "How long have you been sweating like that?"

Her clothes were drenched; she looked like she'd been in a rainstorm, and her face shone from the sweat.

"I don't know," she said. "I feel really upset."

"Okay," Bill said. "Let me check something. You didn't drink while we were up at Put-in-Bay. And I know you didn't have any while we were out looking for Karl. Did you have any in between?"

"No. Things got kind of . . . you know, fraught," she said.

"Welcome to alcohol withdrawal."

"You mean DTs?"

"Alcohol withdrawal," I said. I'd been through the Ala-teen classes enough, before she got so nasty about them, to know this stuff, too. "DTs is seeing snakes and bugs on your skin and seizures. This is just withdrawal. I had it a little when I quit."

"I had it a lot when I did," Bill said.

"Don't you have to be an alcoholic to get it?" Her whine was pretty desperate, and she was rubbing her head like it ached.

"Yep," Bill said, and he was smart enough not to give

her any more time to argue. "We're going to pour water and coffee into you, and food if your tummy will take it, and then take you home and put you to bed. Best way through is to sleep it off and sweat it out."

Neither Bill nor me was gonna mention the hair of the dog.

She thought about that for a while and said, "Shit."

"Just have water and coffee if it's all you can handle, but food will do you good if you can keep it down," Bill said. "Then home to bed. And stay there. You weren't lying about phoning in sick, Beth, not anymore. You've got a day or two of something that's going to feel a lot like the worst flu you've ever had. But I'll take care of you, and Karl will."

She groaned, but she didn't argue.

At Elias Brothers, Bill had the waitress set up a pitcher of ice water for her and kept filling her glass, too. Mom actually had about half a pot of coffee, plus some scrambled eggs and a couple waffles from the buffet. We made a few lame jokes about the waffles not being up to our standards, and told Bill he'd have to come by some morning for those. He looked almost as happy as his hat looked stupid.

Aside from having to squirm a bit to find a comfortable position to sit in, I enjoyed the breakfast. Once Mom settled down and fell half asleep on his shoulder, Bill was smart enough not to talk. I concentrated on exploring the wonderful concept of "all you can eat."

On the way back to Lightsburg, Mom suddenly asked, "Karl?"

"Yeah?"

"Are you not kidding, you really didn't have sex with her?"

"I really didn't, Mom."

"But you were naked."

"We didn't have any pajamas. We held hands and stuff. We just didn't do anything else, that's all, Mom. Honest."

"I bet she was nice and tight."

"Mom!" I said, just as Bill said, "Oh, for Christ's sake, Beth!"

"Just testing. As long as you don't get them pregnant, Tiger, have all the fun you want. The way girls are today you might as well."

"Mom, I didn't—"

"And remember, even if you are a dreadful perverted boy with a taste for ugly girls—"

"Mom, Marti is my friend!"

"—the starlight shines on you just as much as it does on anything else in the universe. Even that stupid cat. By the way, before Rose called to say Marti was missing, and I went out to look for you, and Bill talked Rose into not driving drunk—it was a complex kind of evening, you know?—I did make sure your door was closed tight, and if Hairball did get in there, this one'll be on me—I'll wash your sheets this time."

As we came in off the interstate, I saw Pancake Pete in the McDonald's window, sitting at that counter that faced outward, finishing his shift with a big pile of breakfast and having a good old time. I waved and he waved back, though I doubt he knew who it was. I just figured, *somebody* might as well be happy and having a normal day.

25

A Completely Normal Monday,
If You Happen to Be a Madman

BILL'S LITTLE SAAB would have been embarrassing to drive, but it was okay to be dropped off in.
Not nearly as embarrassing as arriving with Marti, let
alone in a hearse.

A couple of blocks from the school, Bill said, "I'm planning to go to every meeting I can get to today, here, Vinville, all around. You go have a completely normal school
day."

"Aren't you teaching?"

"Phoned in sick. First time I've done that since
I stopped drinking. I figure if I could take time off to
drink—like it added up to a couple weeks out of every
term, it was getting like that—I can take one day to get
better."

"You know everyone will tell you you're crazy to get involved with Mom. And chances are once she's slept for a while, she'll get up and head right for the booze in the house."

"Yeah, well." He made the last turn, and the high school loomed before us. "Sometime soon we should all go out for Chinese—there's a place in Port Clinton I love—and we can have a four-hour conversation in which nothing serious comes up. What do you think?"

"Is that Jade Lotus Blossom?" I asked. "My friends and I have gone there a couple times, it's awful."

"Yeah, but it's awful *exactly* the way a Chinese restaurant on a Lake Erie beach ought to be awful. That's why I love it. It's just so fucking au*then*tic."

I liked the way he said "fucking" around me. Like grown-up to grown-up, and all that shit. Like I figured I'd say it after I'd been in the army. "Sounds fucking great," I said.

I looked at my watch; I was going to be on time, even early. Driving took a lot less time than the school bus or walking. I guess if more people were to realize that, these automobile-thingies might really catch on.

At the curb, Bill asked, "Are you going to be okay?"

I wasn't sure if he meant emotionally, financially, socially, or what. He might even have been asking if my dick was still hurting from having a giant Q-tip poked up it and twirled around. Anyway, not knowing what he meant, I said, "Yeah," and knowing he meant it kindly I said, "Thank you" as I got out of the car.

I closed his car door behind me and semiwaved. He flipped his hand up and popped into gear, a crazy little gnome dressed in sandals, jacket, and a rumpled pile of laundry, with gray Bozo flyers sticking out around his stupid fisherman cap. As he thundered away—had to be some major holes in that muffler—I thought, *damn, she'll get rid of him in a week, and I'll* miss *him.*

At the top of the front steps to the main entrance, there was one of those excited, bunched little crowds you see sometimes in a high school, that mean something is happening that everyone wants to see and nobody wants adults to notice (at least not yet). Sometimes it would be something good for a laugh, like maybe Paul doing an imitation of some teacher, or some goofy piece of weird porno. Sometimes it would be shitheads on a rampage, like one time two years ago it was a couple jocks playing keepaway with Pancake Pete's glasses, until I told them to stop (I had Squid standing beside me, which helped concentrate their attention). Most usually it would be some dumbass thing that just didn't interest me, but you know how it goes—you can't *not* look.

So I climbed the front steps with only mild curiosity, figuring at best there might be a cheap laugh in it. But it got real quiet, and everyone turned around to stare at me.

My first thought was that Stacy had gotten to school before I had.

Then Paul stepped out of the crowd, with Danny and Squid right behind him. Squid's arms were folded like a cop who doesn't believe you, and Danny had his hand in the pockets of his FFA jacket and his shoulders hunched forward, so that I thought *like he's expecting a fight*, and then I realized.

Paul stepped forward. "So about you and Marti."

"Yeah," I said. Something made me glance at Squid. There was something tight, almost too tight, about his expression, wound up and straining forward, like he was psyched for something.

Of course.

I stepped forward to Paul and said, "Yeah, yeah, I'll do what I want, I've told you to get out of my way before. You gonna cry about it, pussy boy?"

I had to kind of skip forward and turn my head to make sure I met his fist with my jaw, and even then I wasn't sure I could block that slow, but then just in the last hair of a second, he figured out how to get his back and shoulder into it for real. He actually socked me a pretty good one, and I didn't have to fake falling over at all, I can tell you that. I tumbled back about three steps on my ass and had to save myself with my hands, skinning them up a little.

Paul glared down at me. He must not have thought of

a good curtain line, because he just turned and walked away like Dirty Harry after a gunfight. Danny slouched off after him, being the solid sidekick. Squid chanced a wink to me, then did the same.

I climbed to my feet, a little unsteady because that punch really had landed. I was the center of attention for just an instant, then the kids who had been the crowd started to fade away, going to find someone they could tell the story to: Psycho Shoemaker, decked by the school fairy.

Operation Be Fucking Normal did not appear to be working out.

In my locker, on top of everything, I found Gratz's get-out-of-therapy letter, still in its signed and sealed envelope. I held it in my hand for a long time, like it was a feather from an angel wing. Then all the people crashing around the hall behind me pulled me back to reality, and I grabbed up what I needed.

I walked into Gratz's class like two minutes before class time, with almost everyone except the Madmen already there. I walked up to his desk, where he was pretending to review notes, and set my letter down firmly but gently in front of him, like it was covered with adhesive and I needed to stick it to the desk.

He looked up. I said, loud enough for everyone to hear,

"Sir, I've thought about it ever since Friday, and, um. Um. What I mean to say is—" Then it just popped out of my mouth, like when you try to sneak a fart in church, planning to just barely raise up the old butt cheek and let it escape quietly, but instead, uncontrollably, massively, and with a noise like an elephant being raped by a tuba, you shit your pants. "Coach," I said, "I can't help myself. It's the peer pressure. Or maybe it's all the drugs I take. But I read those chapters of *Huckleberry Finn* and I just kept thinking, *two queers on a raft.*"

"Are you making fun of me?!"

"Well, I'm trying, but I'm not sure you're getting it."

He turned purple, and looked about ready to belt me, and finally he said, "Hunh." Then he heaved a big sigh, dropped the sealed letter into the trash can beside him, and said, "You better hurry, you'll be late."

Dip me in shit and paint me blue if I'll ever understand Coach Gratz.

From the way it got quiet, I could guess what the subject of conversation had been just before I walked into the therapy room. I sat down. "Sorry, guys, I know you weren't expecting me, but I just did some major disrupting in Gratz's class and, well, here I am."

Paul, who had been sounding real excited just as I came in, and then gone dead quiet, didn't look at me. "Are you okay?"

"Yeah, you got a real solid punch on me and I think I'll have a lump on my jaw, so it's lucky I never *have* used my head for much. But I really didn't know you had a punch like that in you, Paul, and considering what it did to my jaw—is your hand okay? Can you still play your instruments and draw?"

"I'm fine," Paul said—always generous when people gave him attention and praise, and who knew that better than me? "And *I* didn't know that I had that in me, either. I wanted to hit you but I didn't mean to hit you that hard. It looks like you're getting a bruise, too."

I touched my jaw; it was tender and I could feel stuff gooshing around a little. "Think you're right."

"Boys," Marti said, in about the tone she'd use to say "dogshit," if there'd been some on the floor.

"Yeah," Darla said, agreeing hard enough to freeze the rest of us. She and Marti were glaring, and Bonny and Cheryl didn't exactly look extra happy, either.

"Uh," I said. "We needed to talk cause we had a fight."

"Oh, boy, did you have a fight," Bonny said, "like the biggest fight since maybe World War Two. Now if you *boys* are done congratulating each other over that manly sock in the jaw, can we talk about the fact that Marti is going to be hassled by every dumb ass loser in the school now, because they're going to figure she's easy?"

"Plus they've realized her standards are low," Darla said, looking right at me to make sure I got it, because she clearly doubted I was smart enough. "Karl gets to be all cool and dangerous and the bad boy. Marti just got stuck being a slut. And you guys can't stop talking about what big balls Paul has."

"Now, wait a sec," Danny said, in that reasonable-guy commentator voice that he used to impress teachers with how mature he was. "In the first place, punching out another guy for messing with your girlfriend is like *primo* antihomo for Paul's image. No more dumbasses from the team hassling him. That's why Squid and I were cheering for you, Paul, and made sure no one interfered."

"And we kept you from getting carried away and really hurting Karl," Squid added.

I was about to say, *like shit, I took one punch and I knew what for, but in a real fight I'd've pounded Paul into the pavement*, when I realized what Squid was doing for Paul. Not for the first time, I thought, *okay, I understand why adults think Squid is stupid, because he's big and talks slow and his parents were tomato pickers, and that's how adults think, the stupid bastards. But why the hell did I ever think that?*

"Well, this is all great and wonderful and shit," Darla said, "and just so groovy. For the guys. So Paul doesn't get beat up. But Marti still gets labeled, and she's gonna have Scott Tierden-type creeps trying to get into her pants, and if you guys'd just stop banging your damn antlers a minute you'd see what a fucked-up mess Karl just made out of Marti's life, hanging all this shit around her neck."

I was stunned. "But you tell everyone that you—"

"Karl, don't be a bigger social retard-o than you have to be, okay? Just this once try to see how things really work? Okay, so like it's the seventies and all, I am woman hear me roar, a girl can do whatever she wants and brag about it. Except one thing: she can't get caught. Getting caught makes her look stupid and slutty, at least to every half-brained slimeball in the fucking world, and she—"

"*Good* morning, *ev*eryone!" The lady who floated through the door in a cloud of books, papers, briefcase, and clipboard, like she'd just shoplifted a whole stationery store but didn't have a bag for anything, was kind of tall and thin, with a pixie face and blonde hair down to the middle of her back with bangs all down her forehead. She wore a short brown leather dress with a big brass zipper that went from the neck to the hem, over a white fuzzy sweater. She had big honking Ping-Pong ball earrings like my mom wore, and textured panty hose, and black plastic clunky-wedgy shoes. You could just tell she'd been the cutest chick in her sorority three years ago, or maybe the lead singer in a Jesus-rock antidrug band, but she hadn't been able to afford new clothes during her three years of shrink school.

"I'm Doctor Leslie Schwinn," she said, dropping that whole huge heap of books and papers on one end of the table. Looked like Theory One was right; she would try to make us fit all that stuff from the book. "And I'm going to start off by sharing my biggest fear. This is the first real therapy group of my professional career, and my biggest fear is that I'm just not ready for this yet."

"My name is Darla Pilsudski, and I'm going to share with you that your biggest fear is probably right."

Schwinn drew a breath, but before she could speak, Darla had sat straight up, brightly exclaimed, "What's that, Mr. Babbitt?" and pulled her stuffed bunny out of her purse, listening to him like a phone. "Mr. Babbitt wants to know what kind of shrink you are? We've had TA a lot lately but we're also experienced with Freudians and there was a sort of half-ass Maslow-man we all liked."

"Your file mentioned Mr. Babbitt, and—"

"Did it mention that Mr. Babbitt is usually the smartest person in the room?" Squid asked.

Schwinn was hanging on to that poise for all it was worth, and she brightened and smiled at him. "You must be Esquibel."

"Well, if you say I must be. I was gonna be Cheryl this year, for a change."

Schwinn laughed, not making it convincing at all. "I can tell we'll all enjoy your sense of humor. I thought we should start out kind of light today, just sort of build the group—"

"The thing is," Danny said, leaning forward, and

looking pretty much like your shrewd old farmer type if you could look like that at seventeen, "it's built. Most of us have been here through ten or twenty therapists. We kind of lose count."

"Oh, that's not a problem," Cheryl said. "I keep a diary and I just counted last summer."

"That's interesting, but—" Schwinn was still trying to hang in there, but now we had something to run with.

Cheryl rolled right on. "If you count from seventh grade, when Karl, Paul, and Bonny came in from Lincoln Elementary and me, Danny, and Hank came in from McKinley—Hank moved in tenth grade, Doctor Schwinn, we don't have a lot of stories about him—then counting Doctor Schwinn here, it's been eighteen therapists from seventh grade to date. My grade school group at McKinley had four before we got here."

"Paul and me just had two, and Bonny joined halfway through sixth grade," I said, filling in some more, "along with Amy, who left the group in eighth and then got killed in a car wreck last year. What happened to Peter?"

"Moved to Tiffin in the middle of the school year, but he was so quiet no one noticed," Darla said. "One of those rock and drool types. So just keeping track, then, Mr. Babbitt says that eighteen plus four plus two is twenty-four in Ohio, although some of the churchies will tell you that's just a theory. But I also had private therapists all along—"

"I had private ones besides my group ones too," Marti

said. I'd been noticing that she almost busted out in a metal-mouth grin once she saw what we were all doing, but she had her game face on now and was ready to play with us. "It's what weird girls with rich parents *do*."

"Then you're a weird girl with rich parents and a private shrink *too*!" Darla exclaimed, like she'd just realized it. "*And* we both know that Gratz is an evil bully and Karl and Paul are complete shits. We are *so* bonded." She threw her arms around Marti.

"Cool! Do I get a rabbit?"

"You can use mine till you get your own."

"This is all very funny," Schwinn said, meaning it wasn't. "Now if you're all done—"

"*Done?*" I don't know why but she'd just pissed me off completely, or maybe I was mad at Darla and taking it out on Schwinn, which was a good place to take it out. "Lady, some of us have been here eight or ten years and we're *never* getting 'done.' We're just graduating. I mean, that's our point, if you haven't got that yet. We need the group to get by, but we ain't getting better."

"Nonetheless," Schwinn said, putting on a toothy smile so fake it should've gone to church, "I need to get acquainted with all of you, and we need to discuss our goals in therapy for this year—"

"*You* need to do all that," Bonny said. She seemed to have leaped right over gypsy and gone for fairy princess when she dressed this morning, with a billowy rainbow skirt, about ten iridescent blouses that stuck out through each other, stripey socks I think she stole from the Wicked Witch of the West, and huge wedge heels. "*You* are the one who has to do paperwork and report on how we're doing and all that shit. *You* have to do that because that is your job. *We* have other stuff to do. You happened to turn up when we've got some urgent things to do, and we have to do them today, so we don't have time to do the usual shrink thing of pretending we're all going to be great friends. Now *if* you are nice to us, *and* we get to trust you in a few weeks or so, we'll *let* you hang around and take the credit. So just write down on your little pad that you met the group, many of us have serious problems, and you are especially worried about Paul, Marti, and Karl, because that will make you look real smart if any bad shit happens, which it is likely to do if we don't get going on fixing things—which is a *hint*, guys, let's stop clowning and figure out what we need to do."

Schwinn looked shocked and confused. I think that happens because the shrink schoolteachers all did their therapy work, if they ever did it, back in the 1950s when no one outside of shrink school had ever even heard of the whole shrinkamatology routine, so they never had kids who knew what the game was. So the teachers at shrink school didn't *tell* little bookaholic positive-attitude moron-girls like Leslie Schwinn, who probably got into psych because it was just such a *super* thing to be able to *help* people, that the clowns might already know what the ringmaster had in mind, and have other plans for the circus.

"I'm not going to forge my *records*," Schwinn said, sounding really shocked for the first time. You could tell some prof she'd liked had told her the records were the most important thing.

This was a perfect moment. I'd recognized Bon's tactics; good thing the Madmen had two sales people in the group, because Bon's "are you gonna buy or should I walk" needed the walk-out close to complete it, and I knew how to do that one. "No one is asking you to forge the records," I said, turning up the charm. "Look, you seem nice and all. We don't want you to be in trouble. But we have a big mess to cope with, and we know how to handle it, and you're coming in too late for this one. Just the way it goes. We need this time.

"So grab your pen. We've been through this with so many shrinks that we know all about first meetings, which is why Darla asked what kind of therapy you do. Now, if *you* let *us* get you through this first-day thing in like five minutes, so we can use the rest of the time to sort out the group emergency, *we* will *let you* just watch and listen while we solve our problems, and you will know a fuckload more than the average shrink knows about us at the end of the first month, I can tell you that. *And* have all your paperwork right." Continuing to be a sales guy, I assumed the close and proceeded like she'd already signed. "Okay, then. Pencil ready, Doctor Schwinn? Now, everybody just spit it out, you know the basics she needs to get down on paper today, and *no bullshit*." I made a point of glaring at Darla. "Doctor Schwinn needs us to keep our side of the deal."

"Um, actually, um. I prefer that you call me Leslie—"

"Oh, you're one of the nice informal ones!" Cheryl turned on a smile as fake as Schwinn's. "Okay, Leslie, I'm Cheryl Taliaferro, I lose my temper and have crying fits and have trouble saying no to sex, and I'm an incest victim." Schwinn's pencil was moving; whether she wanted to or not, she was writing it down.

Squid said, "Ready? Okay, you got my name right, except everyone calls me Squid and I like that. I have depression and anger and I've done some binge drinking and I got some stuff on my rap sheet for fighting. My mom committed suicide, and my dad is remarried to a real bitch and he drinks and hits me."

Bonny and Darla explained about being abandoned while their parents went off to do their silly things, and about having to keep their houses running, and Darla even mentioned that Logan had been taken away because she'd kept hurting him, which she usually saved to spring on a shrink when she thought it would upset them; it was in the files, but most of them were too lazy to read those. (Maybe Darla was just guessing that Schwinn, bright-eyed and fresh from grad school, would be the thorough type.)

Then Danny shocked us all by just opening right up: "My father's a drunk who hates me." He explained how his dad hit him, belittled him, made him do a lot of the work, and was letting the farm go all to shit, so that it was an even bet which would happen first, whether Danny would inherit it in horrible shape, or his father would lose it. "The plumbing hasn't worked in the house for two years, which is why I play sports and take gym—showers every day—and I want to go to ag school but I figure without me working, Dad'll just lose it while I'm away learning how to run it." He finished in better shape than he usually did when he talked about this stuff, just wiping his face with his hands. This was way early for Danny; every year before he'd pretended that nothing was wrong until at least Christmastime, when the Holiday Hammer would fall on his house and his crying jags would become constant.

That left me, Paul, and Marti, and we all stared at each other for a long breath before I swallowed hard. "I'm Karl Shoemaker. Last night I was locked out, and so was Marti. I usually have plenty of cash, so I got us a room at a hotel, and we slept naked in the same bed because there was only one bed, and we didn't want to put our dirty clothes back on. We didn't touch each other except for like back rubs and hugs and friend stuff like that.

We got caught, and our crazy mothers threw huge shit fits, and brought the cops into it, and now it's all over the school. Now, Paul is Marti's boyfriend, so he punched me out this morning, but he's also my best friend so I'm cool about that, I understand that he had to do it."

Schwinn, scribbling fast, asked, very reasonably, "Why did Paul have to do *that*?"

"Because I'm the biggest homo in the school," Paul said, angrily. "At least everyone says I am. And my best friend Karl is a crazy dangerous son of a bitch that people are afraid of. So kids in this school are so stupid that they think that just because I had a fistfight with a scary guy, about a girl, that means I can't be a queer, and that will probably help keep me from getting beaten up."

"This *is* complicated," Schwinn said, her face down in her notes and pencil flying. "And you're Paul Knauss, of course. So then—"

"Well," Marti said, "it's even more complicated than that. Because, see, it's a big deal to my mother whether or not I have a boyfriend, because as far as she's concerned that is what high school is about, and I never did have one because I'm not exactly pretty. So now I have a boyfriend, which is a big deal, except everyone knows he's gay, so now Mom is mad at me for having my first boyfriend be a homo. Plus as Karl says I've just been labeled a slut. And besides all that I have some problems."

"Did, um, er." Schwinn looked down at her pad and

squirmed. "Did you *want* something to happen, Marti?"

Damn, you can't trust anything. A shrink straight out of school and she asks the most embarrassing possible question.

Marti blushed purple and said, "Yeah, but Karl here is Sir Galahad. But the way he looked at me, it made me feel, I don't know, like, beautiful." She was studying her sneaker really hard.

Bonny chuckled. "This is so *typical*, Karl."

I could see the headline in *Stars and Stripes* already: MASTER SERGEANT RETIRES AFTER 30 YEARS, STILL A VIRGIN.

Paul was wrapped up in a tight little ball, arms around himself, and I knew he was furious. "So you'd rather be with Karl," Paul said. "But you'll go out with the fag so he doesn't get beat up?"

The room got real cold and quiet.

"Aw, shit," Squid said, which was about the smartest thing I'd heard all day.

Then Schwinn said, "Right *on*, Squid. I was just thinking that."

We all laughed, even Paul, though I could sure tell he was still sore. Then we started figuring out what to do, which basically came down to three things:

1. The other girls would look out for Marti and straighten out the gossip;
2. Paul and me would make a big point of stressing that we were friends again because

now he knew nothing had happened;

3. Marti and Paul would talk things over soon because she liked him and didn't want to lose him.

"And," Danny said, "Squid and I can probably sit on some of the jock humor about the subject. Like two percent of it. But it'll blow over as soon as something else happens, and, guys, it's high school. There'll be somebody new to pick on by tomorrow morning."

Schwinn took her notes while we worked all that out, and when we'd finished, she scanned over the three pages on her pad, and shook her head. "This is *so* like the group I was in, in high school, and then another therapy group I was in, in college." She let us go a little early.

"I kind of hope she sticks for the whole year," I admitted to Danny, Cheryl, and Marti.

"Yeah," Danny said as we all walked to trig together. "An ex-Madman herself. Hunh."

"I have a horrible feeling that when we did the runaround on her, at the start, she was trying not to laugh," Cheryl said.

Darla ran up and stopped in front of me and said, "Mister Babbitt needs to talk to Mister Shoemaker."

"Later," Cheryl said, and she, Marti, and Danny shot out of sight, not quite fast enough for me to miss all the smirking.

Darla grabbed my shirt, held up Mister Babbitt, and

said, "Mister Babbitt would like to know if what Marti said about you was the truth?"

I held up my hand in the Cub Scout sign. "Wall to wall and ten feet tall. Cross my heart and hope to die. Stick a needle in my eye. And I'd rather talk to you than to a stuffed rabbit."

She held Mister Babbitt up to her ear, then in front of herself. "Because, Mister Babbitt, you silly little bunny, I have to be sure that what we have here is a goddam prince of a guy like I think we do. A guy who would give a girl a place to sleep, just because she was a friend, and not try to get anything from her, and never ever brag, or even suggest, to other guys, that she did something that she didn't, might be a real cool guy. He might be so cool that even though he is not up to our usual standards, Mister Babbitt, by which I mean he does not have a motorcycle, a portfolio of disturbing art, or a prison record, I might want to see more of him." She dropped her voice so only I heard. "Even if he won't kill cats. Especially if he won't because he won't hurt a friend." She stepped back, planted her hands on her hips, pulled her elbows back a bit to improve my view, and said, "So I was just explaining to Mister Babbitt that I might want to see what it's like to go out with a goddam prince of a guy, even if he is still in high school and grounded until the year two thousand.

"But. But. But. As Gratz might say.

"Suppose it turned out the goddam prince of a guy actually *lied* about what happened, and either messed with a girl when she had nowhere else to go, or is just waiting to start hinting to the other guys that she put out for him. Now, Mister Babbitt, *that* would be a different matter. A guy like that has probably touched his last boob, because I would take his hands off at the neck, along with a trophy for my first apartment's mantel, which will look very much like a mushroom floating in an olive jar full of rubbing alcohol.

"So last chance for complete truth here, Karl. The thingie you save may be your own, unless I decide to take it." She took a slow step toward me with a hair flip that put blonde hair down around her face in a way that was so sexy I figured she'd probably spent weeks practicing it. Softly, she said, "Did you and Marti tell the truth in therapy group?"

"Yes, Darla, I—*mrmph.*"

Kissing in the halls was a one-full-demerit offense which was really unfair, because if an ordinary kiss was one, what Darla did should have been like eight. Right in front of Mrs. Greimiladi, the Latin teacher, who had probably been Poster Bitch of 1925 for the National Pickle Up The Butt Association.

She shouted "Stop that this instant!" and "That's a demerit for each of you!" and finally pushed us apart, huffing out "Well, I never!"

"Well, you should try," Darla said, "it's great," and went slinking away.

"I know who you are, Darla Pilsudski! I'm writing you up!"

"Just so she spells our name right, Mister Babbitt," Darla said, turning, flipping her hair, and rolling her hips as she strutted away. She blew me a kiss before she vanished around the corner. Greimiladi stared at me like I was a newly arrived Martian.

Something touched my elbow. I turned and saw Cheryl grinning like a fucking moron; Marti was pretty much limp with giggles, hanging on Danny. "Hey," Cheryl said. "For some reason I was just thinking about something in bio class. Before she mates with him, the female praying mantis eats the male's head. What do you think?"

It was one of those moments when, "Yeah, well," comes in handy.

How Uncle Al Became My Favorite Hollering Asshole, and Vice Versa

BY NOON EVERYONE had heard that I had spent a night with Marti in a hotel room and when the cops came by, with our mothers, I had asked for time to get dressed. It was also all over the school that I had deliberately provoked Gratz and lived to tell of it, and that Paul had knocked me flat. And on top of that, that Spooky Darla had given me a thermonuclear kiss in public.

No getting away from it: I was now Public Madman Number One.

At least nobody had said anything about Cheryl by the tar ponds, naked Darla down by the creek, or hugging Paul on a street corner. Maybe Stacy had laryngitis.

Paul ate outside again, but Larry seemed to be very pleased to sit with me; he explained *The Three Stigmata of Palmer Eldritch* to me twice and I still had no idea what he was talking about, but it was clear we were in-tight friends again, even though I didn't want to go to Detroit and lose my virginity to a fat girl.

Just after lunch, Harris and Tierden stopped me in the hall to tell me I wasn't so tough and I wasn't so spe-cial and that they were gonna have to teach me a les-son and I wouldn't be protected by old man Browning forever, and I better watch my ass and they'd get me even if I did, and stuff, but that was a pretty one-sided con-versation, and it got broken up when Mrs. Hertz noticed them hassling me and walked over to see what was go-ing on. I told her "nothing" as those two stood behind her giving me the finger, and while I was talking to her, I gave Harris such a big smile, and focused my eyes on his crotch so much, that he moved over to hide behind Tierden. There was going to be a lot of bragging about which one of them had really scared me most, I figured, in that big heap of a car tonight.

And after all that, the strange thing was that despite all the strange stories, and people coming up to ask me about them, all I had to do was keep saying, "We were locked out, we just shared a room, and we didn't have pa-jamas," "He knows I didn't do anything with his girl now, but he didn't then and I don't blame him for hitting me," and "Well, I was kind of pissed off at Gratz about some-thing else, and I guess he just decided to cut me some slack," over and over, and mostly it was all still okay. I guess everyone loves a good story and they're willing to let you be normal if you'll tell one.

After French, I went to my locker to stash the textbooks and get a couple things to take home with me, and while I was fiddling around in there, I felt a hand on my shoulder. I turned and discovered Stacy; she had a shy little smile and she looked like she'd just freshened her makeup and fluffed her blonde mane. "Hey," she said, "can you still explain everything?"

"Well, there's a *lot* of everything."

She stood a little closer. "Sometime soon, I want to hear the whole story."

"Will you promise to believe it?"

"If it's true."

"Then I'd love to have an excuse to talk about myself." I figured I was totally misunderstanding something somewhere—I mean, I'd always been invisible to popular socials—so I was just kind of playing, being a little cool and cracking jokes, while I figured out what was up with her.

But she grinned and said, "Don't be too slow about calling," and walked away, giving me the little social-wave over the shoulder for the second time that day. Maybe Cheryl could interpret this for me, if that wouldn't violate the Secret Protocols of the Socials or something. Anyway, the view of Stacy walking away was pretty nice.

"Karl."

I turned around and it was Gratz and for one crazy second I felt like blurting out *Okay, you saw me looking at her ass, but I can explain.*

Not seeing any way to escape, I said, "Coach Gratz," and waited to see what would happen next.

Strangely, nothing did happen for a couple seconds. Like he had some other script in mind entirely and was baffled by what I'd said. Finally he seemed to shake himself and make himself say, "I've been thinking," he said. "Which is not an easy thing for a teacher to admit to. If you don't mind, I've got a couple important things to discuss with you—I promise, I'm not still angry about this morning—and what I'd like to do is give you a ride home."

Getting into Gratz's car was weird enough to begin with; he kept it so pristine that I was really hoping my feet were clean enough for it. It was a big Continental, white, black landau roof, with those silly wire spoke wheels that were so hot in 1960, and you could tell it was absolutely his baby. I felt like I was sitting on an old lady's antique chair.

He drove a couple blocks before he said, "In my planning period, I was noticing that I was wanting to kill you, and *that* was making me want to drink. So I decided that I wouldn't kill you and I wouldn't drink, and instead, I went and caught a midday meeting at Saint Iggy's. I'm sure you know how that goes."

"Oh, yeah."

"Well, there was a new guy at the meeting, name of Bill, an English professor, but not one of those jerks I try to warn you all about, the good kind that loves books and wants people to love them and could do something besides teach English. And he was trying to figure out what to do about a big problem."

I almost told him to turn at MacReady, but then he put his blinker on. Of course he knew the way.

Gratz seemed to be thinking hard. "So I'm violating a lot of the traditional rules, but, sheesh, Karl, you know the way that is, it's a small town. Like it or not, most of the stuff that comes up in meetings, you know *what* it's about and you know *who* it's about. So, all right, it seems that Bill has been having some trouble with this new girlfriend who he is crazy about for all the wrong reasons, and who is absolutely everything that a guy in Bill's situation should be running away from, and I'm sorry to say that about your mom but—"

"But it's true," I said. "That's why I don't go to Alateen meetings, to avoid hearing true stuff about my mom. But I sure know it anyway. Did Mom do something new, since I saw her this morning?"

"I guess so, from what Bill says. He went back to your house to check on her after an eleven A.M. meeting and she was drunk, setting up a night at the bars with Rose Lee Nielsen on the phone, doing a lot of things that aren't good for her. Bill didn't stop her—you never can—but he was dumb enough or infatuated enough to try, and he had a quarrel with her, and felt awful. So he did the right thing—finally—and went to another meeting, and that's where Dick Larren and I ran into him." He made a strange little face, and the deep tan crinkled around the blue eyes. "Dick got most of the story out of him, and he's kind of taking care of Bill and they're kind of taking care of things together, and so now I'm Dick's relief, because he'll need to get down to Philbin's and cook pretty soon. We've got kind of a plan we want to present to you, and if you say it's okay, we'll do it right away."

We pulled up at my house, the Continental floating up to the curb like riding a cloud, and I got out, wondering what I was about to find.

Dick and Bill were in the backyard, just finishing painting the now-reglazed storm windows. I could tell at a glance that they'd picked up the glass from the lawn, too.

Bill was puffing away on a vile cigar and still wearing that damned cap, but I couldn't seem to come up with any disgust at all. "Karl," Bill said, "you should know that Dick here can be trusted to do perfectly acceptable work, in case you ever want to hire him."

"I did this stuff for *years*," Dick said. "I'm just *rusty*, is all."

I realized I was wiping my eyes, and the two of them were improvising because they were embarrassed that I was crying. I also realized I didn't give a shit, wiped my face one more time, and said, "So what's going on? Coach says you have a plan."

"We do," Dick said. "And we're going to try to make it work. You know how trying can go, Karl, no one knows it better than you do, but we want to try this."

Bill puffed out a big foul cloud, set a piece of cut milk carton against one of the stiles, and painted that side in one neat stroke, no drips, no hurry. He turned the cardboard around and did the other side, backhanded, and then one clean stroke long the top of the stile.

I looked around. The reglazed window so far was perfect; I suppose I knew it would be, but I liked to see for myself.

Coach Gratz must have seen me look. He shook his head, grinning sadly. "You're lucky I had to teach this afternoon, Karl, or I'd've insisted on helping and it wouldn't have looked half as nice."

Bill stepped back and looked at the finished storm; it was really good as new now. "Well," he said, "we're delaying because we're scared to death you'll say no. But we have to tell you sooner or later. So here it is: when I got here after the eleven o'clock meeting, your mother had already had most of a six-pack from the fridge and was working the phone pretty hard to line up her evening. She's definitely back to being buddies with Rose Nielsen, which is not necessarily a good thing, as you know. It bothered me to find this going on, and it bothered me a lot more that she kept demanding that I come along on the binge she was planning with her buddies, but what really upset me was that she wanted me to help look for one of your stashes of money, which she told me all about." He took the cigar out of his mouth, tapped ash onto the grass, smeared it around with his foot, and kept his gaze on his foot. "So as I found out more and more about her taking that money, she said a lot of things that made me angry, or I got angry about things she said, anyway. She pounded down another couple of beers to show me I couldn't stop her, and shouted at me, and I felt like shit but I stuck to what I was saying and kept it cool. So she stormed out and that was the last I saw of her. Didn't know what else to do so I ended up going to the meeting, where I found these guys."

He made himself look me in the eye and said, "After she left I snooped in your room. I knew a meticulous, systematic guy like you would be keeping some kind of record. I didn't have to snoop much because it was right on the desk."

"My IOU book? You read that?" I asked. It was like I was so stunned that I was getting things down to the smallest idea I could.

"Yeah. I'm a snoop, a spy, a rat, and a dick. But I did."

"I left it out in plain sight 'cause I was always hoping

Mom would read it," I said. "It never worked."

"Anyway, I didn't understand why you didn't have your money safe in a bank account, till Al Gratz explained to me about the adult cosigner rule here in Ohio. And Dick pointed out that either he or Gratz could cosign, just say they were your uncle, any bank outside Lightsburg. Nobody would ever check. Dick was pretty upset—"

"Shoot, Karl, I'm your sponsor. If you'd only told me—"

"You don't have a car, Dick." I still couldn't quite get used to the idea that someone else knew, I mean besides my mother, and Neil, and her drunk asshole friends, I mean. Someone that wasn't throwing it in my face, or telling me to stop thinking I was better than they were.

Someone that said they were going to try to do something.

That was the really hard idea to latch on to.

Dick shrugged. "I'd've found us both a ride, or gotten Philbin to take us over there, or something. It wouldn't have been *anything* for me to take care of that for you, Karl."

I could tell he was still hurt, and I didn't know how to apologize for not asking for help.

Gratz cleared his throat; it was sort of his teacher-noise, same sound he used in class, or at school board meetings when he was going to straighten everyone out about the Youths of Today, or pretty much whenever he was about to lay down the law. "Dick, don't take it personally, it isn't that Karl didn't trust you. Kids are that way, if they're getting hurt bad. They think it's their fault, they think it's something wrong with them, they won't tell anyone. It's just how kids are." His hands were dug into his hips and he was standing like a phys ed teacher about to lead calisthenics, and then suddenly he said, "Shit."

Coach Gratz swearing. Okay, the world was ending.

"Shit," he repeated. "Dick, I'm lecturing you like my hollering asshole self. All I should've said was you have to figure Karl's a kid. Even if he's a great one and even if he's Doug's kid."

Dick smiled a little. "We need to get Karl moving if you're going to get to the bank before it closes."

"The bank?" I asked.

"Yep. You're opening a bank account in Vinville. With 'Uncle Al'—i.e., me—as your cosigner," Gratz explained. "Get those cans of money down into my car and we'll go right now, we just have time before they close."

I stared at all three of them, just managed to squeak out a "thank you," and ran to get the money cans. There were nineteen in all, from most rooms of the house, plus two outside behind removable stones in the exposed basement wall, plus the ones from the toolshed. I think they were a little surprised there were so many, but it took me almost no time to get them all into Gratz's trunk. I could have grabbed them all twice as fast except I kept stopping to wipe my eyes.

It's funny how Vinville is only eight miles from Lightsburg, along the cleverly named Vinville Road, but it might as well be another world. Vinville has the college, built on the slope of Gravel Ridge down toward the town, with old maples, oaks, ginkgos, and buckeyes on it, tended for a hundred years, and the red brick of the college buildings peeks out from between all those trees, making the whole thing look like a tiny slice of a movie college stuck in the middle of all those flat Ohio fields.

Lightsburg has more going for it if you think about money—the interstate ramp, more stores, the high school, and a couple little factories; in the old days it had Prentiss Petroleum. But Vinville can look like a little chunk of somewhere nice, picket fences and red bricks and all that, when the right light hits it.

Which the right light was doing right now. We were coming into Vinville from the west, with the sun at our backs, and maybe I was seeing it like the cavalry making it back to Fort Apache or some knight catching his first glimpse of Camelot, but it was also just great photographer's light—this would have been a calendar shot, I can tell you that. The steeples and the Augelsmann Brothers department store glowed above the just-changing trees, fall colors swarming over the green, and behind them, the red brick college did a real good job of faking being like someplace out of *A Separate Peace* or every college movie ever made.

Gratz said, "We don't want you to keep more than a

couple of days of your cash earnings in the house, from now on. So try to make a deposit three times a week or so. If you can't get a ride with a friend, ask me, or ask Dick and he'll find you one. I kind of think he'd appreciate it if you asked him for some help, too. Tom Browning would do it for you, too, you know."

"Yeah, I know. I didn't know how to ask." How do you say *My mom is crazy and her friends are dangerous and they're robbing me*, when you figure the next thing it leads to is cops and family court and maybe not having a mom anymore? At least Gratz had understood that much, though he blamed it on being a kid, and I figured it just kind of went with moms and love and stuff.

"Anyway," he said, never moving his eyes from the road, he was that kind of obsessive careful driver, "no matter what, keep your money here in your account. Not just so it doesn't get stolen. We want to make sure your mom can't get it to go on a bender, and we think if she doesn't have those windfalls to rip through, a lot of her friends will drift away."

"Like Neil?"

"Like Neil. Some of us would like to help him drift a little faster but I think Bill's opposed to that, says it would alienate Beth if we talked to him directly."

Something about the way he said *directly* made me feel just a little good down inside. I would have loved to see Dick and Coach "talk" to Neil *directly*. If I couldn't do the job myself. I owed him a few for convincing my mother that I was Young Charlie Manson. But I'd like to see Neil after a couple men got *direct* on his worthless ass.

While I'd been thinking about that pleasant thought, Gratz had still been making sure I knew that I had to keep the money away from my mother. "It's important for *both* of you, Karl."

We were coming into the town now, and I said, "I'll do like you say. Why are you making such a big deal about it?"

He ran a tanned hand through the perfect hair; it had too much Brylcreem in it to move, of course, but I guess it showed off the big biceps. Probably Mrs. Gratz had unconsciously trained him to do that. "Well," he said, and then I realized he wasn't sure he wanted to tell me. "When I get back, after Dick gets off at Philbin's, Dick and me and Bill are going to go find your mother and have a long talk with her, one she probably won't like. But it's way overdue."

"She'll say it's because you're ucky ucky men who want to stop her being a free woman."

"Well, maybe we are. Nonetheless we thought maybe we'd see if we could get her to dry out and take some control of her life. And she won't do that unless she's cut off from the benders with her asshole friends."

Wow. First *shit*, now *asshole*. Coach Gratz was getting a real vocabulary.

"I guess she can run around and pretend she's twenty, and give the finger to all us bad old men, all she wants, after you leave. She's a grown-up, at least officially. We just don't want her to screw up your life before you get out the door, and we don't want to be the friends that stood around and did nothing while you got worked over like that. That was part of why I . . . well, shit."

I looked down at the perfectly new-car clean carpet, wondering how many times he vacuumed and shampooed the inside of this big old boat. "Coach, if I could have all my years back to fourth grade as a do-over, I'd take it in a minute."

"Yeah," he said. "I know. Let me tell you something stupid and ugly about myself. Every single teacher in the school knew how tight the Madman Underground was, and how much you all pretended not to be a group. We'd talk about it in the lounge. And for years it just ate at me that you were in there—"

"Coach, they're the friends I've got. And that's who I am."

"I *know. That's* the thought that made me want to go buy a bottle: I looked at that letter I'd thrown away, lying in the wastebasket, and I just couldn't stop thinking, *Karl can't let a friend down, and they can't let him down, and that's really the way Karl is most Doug Shoemaker's son.* The only people who were really helping my old friend's son were all those crazy kids I despised. They were a lot better friends than I was. Maybe better people.

"So just as I walked into the meeting, stewing about all that, I found myself thinking, 'I wish I had friends as good as Karl's,' and there was Dick, who I hadn't talked to in years because of all that stuff they teach in my church about giving up the bad influences in your life . . . well. Here we are. About to commit financial fraud." He turned into the parking lot for First Gist County Bank and Trust.

"Someday I wanna be a felon just like you, Uncle Al," I said, and we both laughed like two stupid kids trying to get up their nerve to buy booze underage.

Counting all the money took more time than anything else. The forms were real simple to fill out. It finally came to $4,364.91, which was three dollars and twenty-four cents more than I thought it was but I didn't figure I'd fight them about it. We set it up as a passbook savings account because it didn't seem like a good idea to have checks around that Mom or one of her buds might try to forge. And the bank had early hours on Monday and Friday, late Friday hours, and Saturday morning hours, so one way and another I figured I'd be able to make it work. They even had a night depository so whenever a Madman with a car turned up at McDonald's, I had a way to get money in there in the middle of the night.

We finished up at like five minutes to five, and Gratz told me he was buying and we were going to get sandwiches from the sub shop that catered to the college students, eat in the park, and talk things over some more.

"Okay, as long as Mrs. Gratz won't be on your case about missing dinner," I said.

"It's a Monday night. She works late, so we both grab something early, and then later we watch *Monday Night Football* together and cook up hot dogs and popcorn, because we used to love to go to games together in college, and I suppose it will seem corny and silly to you, but *we* think it's romantic."

The guy at the counter handed us our sandwiches and we walked out into the late afternoon sun. "Actually you're scaring me, Coach, because that *sounds* romantic."

The park was one of those old-style Ohio town squares, the kind they plowed up and turned into streets in bigger cities years ago, where the four main roads converge but then they inset a four-block area with trees and sidewalks and no streets running through it. There were a fair number of old guys on benches sitting around trying to remember a story the other old guys hadn't already heard, and college students trying to pretend they were studying instead of checking each other out, and little kids running around like nuts on the playground. It occurred to me that if I could get Paul and Marti to hang out with me, we ought to drag Marti over here because it was the kind of thing she'd describe as being so American she could just shit.

The sandwiches were good and I wolfed mine down. I

noticed Gratz was actually a pretty fastidious type, and I suppose that went with keeping himself in perfect shape and so forth. It was very annoying to realize that I might be getting to like this particular rude hollering asshole, but I consoled myself that there would always be plenty more of them to hate.

When we'd finished and splashed some water on our faces from the old-style pump drinking fountain (sulfur water, so I was sort of damp and eggy-smelling around the face), Gratz said, "Well, we should get back, but there was one more thing I wanted to ask you about, and you don't have to answer if you don't want to."

"Uh, if it's about Marti, I'd rather not."

He laughed. "Oh, no, it's not. I can see why you might be worried, but it's not. No, I just figure I'll try to be nice to Marti, and more important be fair around her, and she'll probably never like me but we can both get through the year."

Then a thought kind of hit me, and I said, "Coach, if there's a way you could help her—as much as you're help-ing me—do you suppose you and some of the other people in town could, you know, help?"

That one seemed to rock him back, but he thought for a bit and said, "I guess if we knew someone was in the kind of bad spot you're in—and there was anything anybody could do—I guess we'd have to. Is Marti in some kind of trouble like that? Or one of the other Madmen?"

Now it was my turn to think. "I don't know what to say just yet. I'd've been mad at any of the Madman Underground"—it still felt so weird to speak those words to Gratz—"if they'd narked on me and my situation. I would bet they'd feel the same. And anyway I think there probably are adults who know some of what's happening to some of us, and aren't doing anything, for one reason or another, good or bad. I don't know."

"Nobody can do anything if nobody talks."

"Yeah, I know, Coach." I looked at the people playing, walking, loafing, hurrying, or sauntering across the little park in front of us. How many terrible stories were there, just there in front of me, never to be spoken? "Uh, I guess I'm going to think for a little while. You know, when you gave me that letter, I thought you wanted me to stooge for you."

"Maybe I did, though I wouldn't have put it that bluntly."

"Well, maybe I ought to be your informant. Or maybe I should keep people's trust. Or maybe it's kind of case by case."

"Karl, how about . . ." He thought for a moment, and finally said, "Okay, how's this? I promise that if you come to me with anyone's story—no matter whose and no matter how tough it is—I will at least tell someone who would be able to do something about it. But I won't push you, and you'll have to tell me."

"Deal, Coach."

We sat there and, shit, like it or not, I was kind of comfortable with him. I turned over the Madmen in my mind; it was the old, old problem, would Squid be better off without the kids who depended on him? If people knew the truth about what Mr. Knauss did in his rages, and Paul and Kimmie were fostered out somewhere, taken away from the town where they at least had some friends and support . . . did I want to have that kind of power over my friends' lives? Hadn't I always had it anyway?

Finally, to stop my thoughts from circling on forever, I asked, "Was *that* the 'last thing' you said you wanted to talk about?"

"No," he said. "I—well, look, Karl, this is just something I've kind of noticed and wasn't sure how to ask you about. You hear a lot about your dad, even now. He was a big guy in Lightsburg."

"Yeah," I said.

"So how come you seem angry about him? I mean, is it one of those shrink things where you're mad at him for deserting you and leaving you with your mother?"

"Maybe," I admitted. "And for leaving my mother to get lost among all the hippie shitheads, there's so much crap floating around in the world and he never let her think for herself enough to learn to sort it out. He told her to be a Democrat and a Methodist, so she was; now Neil tells her to be a pothead and Judy tells her to be a paranoid lunatic, so she is. And right now her best hope is that Bill will tell her to be a responsible grown-up; she won't do it for herself. So I sure as shit know that Dad could've left her better able to take care of herself."

"He could," Gratz said, noncommittally.

I knew right then I had to either say "I won't talk about it" or just lay it right out there in front of Gratz, so I could see it myself, and see if it changed anything.

It had been a long day. I was tired. This was easier than anything else: "Coach," I said, "my parents were screwed-up people who drank together a lot. You probably know that the cops spiked the police report that time Dad got busted for drunk driving and pissed into the police car to make his point. Mom and Dad had drunk fights and drunk make-ups and drunk sex, and I was scared to death a lot of the time. They tucked me in when they were drunk, and I got myself cereal while they sat at the breakfast table holding their heads and groaning about their hangovers. They loved me and they fought each other and they did stupid things and, well, it was a lot like some of my friends' houses, too, you know?

"And then Dad found out he was dying, and he finally put his act together, and those were the best years of my life—while he dried out, getting ready to die. So it kind of feels like . . ." I didn't know what to say next, so I watched a young couple throwing a Frisbee back and forth, her trying to look ditzy and silly, him trying to look cool and athletic. She was succeeding.

Finally, still with no idea of the right way to say it, I said, "Well, while he was dying, I was around Dad all the time. He showed me how to fix everything around the house, how to rebuild a chimney and spade a garden and rehang a door and all that stuff he'd been good at once, and was good at again now that he wasn't drinking. We'd do stuff all day and he'd add it to that list that—the list that used to be on my wall, and then we'd sit and watch old stupid movies together. He used to do that when he was drunk with Mom, but now he did it with me.

"He was dying, but life was better than it had ever been. I loved that. But after a while I knew it wasn't for me; a lot of ways, I realized, it didn't have much to do with me except I was his son and he needed to prove to himself he could be a good father. He wasn't doing it for anyone but himself, Coach. He had just decided to die sober. He was a proud old bastard, under all the aw-shucks routine he did when he was running for office, he was proud as all shit. So he didn't get sober to spend the time with me. He could have done that anytime. But he didn't do it for me. I wasn't worth it."

"He loved you," Gratz said. "He liked being around you. I *know* that."

"Yeah, I do too, but that wasn't why he got sober."

Gratz sighed. "Karl, I ought to get on your case right

now." He made a sour little smile and I could tell he was trying to lighten the mood but didn't feel like it. "This is a lot worse than thinking Huck Finn and Jim are two queers on a raft."

I made myself smile, knowing he meant well.

Then he shrugged and said, "No one can get sober except for themselves. That's what we'll be trying to tell your mother tonight. She has to do it because *she's* worth it. Not for you, though God knows she owes you the moon and the stars after all you've been through. Not for Bill, though I think the crazy guy really is in love with her and she's what he's wanted all his life, and I don't understand that, either. If she's going to get it together, she has to be the one to do it, just because she'd rather have it together than not. Nothing else will work, Karl, you know that. And it doesn't mean she doesn't love you and want the best for you. And it doesn't mean your dad didn't."

"That's what my friends try to tell me all the time in therapy group," I admitted. "Cheryl is always saying to remember Dad liked my company and *did* spend all that time with me. Squid tells me how lucky I was to have a great dad for that long. One night for like four hours Darla kept telling me that it didn't matter whether he got sober and then realized he loved me, or he realized he loved me and then got sober, she said either way my dad loved me and I ought to hang on to that with both hands."

"I can tell I've misjudged therapy."

"You've misjudged the group. Therapy is crap, it's the friends that are great."

"Friends *are* great, aren't they?" Gratz said. "I guess I should get back to mine. Wish us luck, and if she does get better, forgive your mother for it, okay?"

"Okay," I said. "Promise."

Damn if we didn't laugh and joke, just gossip about every old thing, the whole way back to Lightsburg. He dropped me off at my house. I waved as he drove off.

I headed right for the kitchen. I had no idea how Mom would be coming back, or with who, but I wanted it clean when she did. She'd gotten such a kick out of her clean kitchen on Saturday.

I Love the McDonald's Crowd,
I Always Feel Like I'm Coming Home Here

THAT NIGHT, I had just finished *Huckleberry Finn* and was thinking maybe I should do some math homework, it was looking that dull. There was a tap at the McDonald's window, which I kind of expected, but I was surprised at the size of the crowd: it was everyone— Marti, Darla, Paul, Danny, Bonny, Cheryl, and Squid.

I opened the door, not sure what to say.

Marti looked from Paul to me and back, and said, "I don't know what guy friends do about something like this in the real world. In the movies I think you'd go out and have a fistfight or something. But you already did and it didn't work. If you want to have a fistfight about me, well, hell, fellas, you go right ahead, but it didn't turn out to be nearly as romantic as I would have thought. Maybe you can have a fistfight over who gets to be the biggest queer on the raft.

"Now, the reason for our visit: I was just lamenting, over Cokes at Pongo's with Cheryl, that you two idiots still hadn't made up, really, which is a hell of a way to treat a friendship that practically goes back to the womb. So we figured you wouldn't act badly if the whole crowd was watching you, and then we recruited Darla because she was getting off work and we thought she might be a good influence, which gives you an idea what a mess you are if she can be a good influence."

"Think we can get them to fight?" Darla asked. "That *would* be cool. Actually I just came along because I had a car, and Marti's keys have been confiscated, and Cheryl doesn't have a car because her dad is grounded."

"Uh, what?" I asked, trying to follow this.

"I have no idea either," Danny said, "but it sounds like another good story."

Cheryl shrugged with a funny smile. "Cops came by the house at dinnertime tonight to talk to Dad. Seems a car registered to him—that one I always drive—was spotted cruising on the gay stroll in Toledo on Saturday night. My stepmom doesn't believe his alibi, so I couldn't have it tonight because she's out there with a flashlight searching the car for whatever it is you find if your husband is going to gay prostitutes."

"Fairy dust," Paul said, and we all groaned and made

faces at him. "Thank you, thank you," he said, putting on his Vegas-show voice, though of course he was getting it from television, not from having been to a Vegas show. "I love the McDonald's crowd, I always feel like I'm coming home here."

There was a brief, awkward silence as we all contemplated how little that sounded like a joke.

"Anyway," Darla said, "from the pay phone at Pongo's, we called Danny and he picked up Bonny, and the two of them went over to grab Paul from auditions for *Barefoot in the Park*."

Paul said, "Those ran late because I had to read with everybody," but for once we didn't all stop to tell him how talented he was.

"Meanwhile," Marti explained, "at first we thought we'd have to not include Squid because he wasn't at his house when we called, but then the three of us spotted Squid just walking down Courthouse Street, minding his own business. Naturally all us little ladies realized at once that, if we had guessed wrong, and you guys had no shame at all and would quarrel and refuse to make up in front of us terrific women, then we could go to plan B, and Squid would pound you both into a single greasy smear on the floor."

"Just for your own good," Squid assured us. "Nothing personal, you know?"

"So we met up at the high school parking lot, four people in Darla's car and three in Danny's," Cheryl finished. "This leaves us an empty seat, which you *will* be getting into pretty soon, because you *will not* duck out on the group."

"But first," Marti announced, arms widespread, "now and for the first time in any McDonald's parking lot, gather round because—" She gestured at the other girls, who all sang "Doot doo doo doo!" in a really bad imitation of a trumpet, which told me they'd rehearsed. "Yes, right now, before our very eyes, Paul and Karl are both going to shake hands and come out admitting you are idiots."

"Or be pounded into a single greasy smear on the floor," Squid said hopefully.

"Well, I know I am an idiot," I said, and stuck out my hand. Paul shook it, and we looked each other right in the eye. I nearly blurted out that I loved him or some fucking stupid thing like that.

"Now here's the rest of the plan," Bonny said. "Back when we were going out, Karl, being Karl, told me he has some way to fake out the time clock, but doesn't usually do it, because if he does it too often he's afraid of getting caught. So you are going to leave a note saying that it was very late and somebody just vandalized the windows and you can't possibly get them clean because you have a test tomorrow. And we are all going to go to the tar pond—"

"Hold on," I said, "What if Harris and Tierden don't come tonight? I could get caught."

Bonny shook her head. "I saw the trouble they got into

at lunchtime for picking on you. They were *mad*. I think we can depend on the asshole wagon to hit the windows tonight. Now write that note, Karl—late, windows vandalized, gotta go, very sorry. Ready-set-go, done yet?"

I grabbed the memo pad and started writing.

"Now, once that is done," Marti added, "Karl will fuck over the clock the way he knows how to do, and punch out with his full hours. And we will grab all this food—jeepers there's a lot tonight—"

"The crew left a lot and I wasn't very hungry—"

She rolled right over me. "And go sit by the tar pond, look up at the infinite universe, and eat McFood and talk about absolutely everything, and you will all tell me sad and funny tales of the Madman Underground, like old friends, which we are all going to be. After which we will all be so bonded that we'll just shit. How's that sound?"

"Fucking great," I said.

Paul said, "Double fucking great."

Squid said, "Duh, what comes after double."

"Fucking," Danny said. "Weren't you listening?"

It was going to be a night to goof, if the girls didn't kill us, anyway.

Cheryl nodded emphatically. "At the end of all this, we will be friends, and if I ever hear the word *normal* out of either of you again, I'll tie your scrotums around your necks. Clear?"

"Clear," I said.

"Scrota," Paul corrected, "it's a neuter third-declension noun." So while I finished writing the note he tried to explain how a scrotum was neuter rather than masculine, which Squid got right away, because he said it kind of worked like Spanish, but Danny had a little trouble with.

So I finished the note, and worked my little trick with a paper clip and a plastic fork on that time clock, and packed all the food into triple bags for insulation. I locked up, and we were just walking along the sidewalk beside the building when tires screamed.

With a mighty *wa-chow!* of its expiring shocks, Harris's car tore around the corner and hit that puddle. Tonight, though, not quite so much went on the window, because eight people were standing in the way.

We all got covered. The car shrieked to a halt, fine-stone gravel howling out from under the locked rear tires as it slewed halfway round to face us. Scott Tierden emerged from the passenger side, looking like the Ghost of World Hunger Day Past, laughing like it was the funniest, cleverest thing in the world, and staring at Cheryl and Darla, who were pretty impressive in thin wet tops, come to admit it, though at the time I didn't exactly appreciate it, being drenched with muddy water myself.

Tierden, on the other hand, was hypnotized and paying no attention to anything else. I suppose, to be fair, I should mention that Cheryl and Darla in soaking wet shirts could have distracted most average males from Godzilla, a bagpipe band, and the Second Coming, all at once.

But when Squid covered the twenty feet between him and Tierden in two big leaps, with ten times the enthusiasm he ever put into going after a quarterback, he got Tierden's undivided attention. Scotty-poo ran right into the puddle behind him, Squid splashing after. Before Tierden got to the car, Squid had picked him up by the collar and belt. He threw him into the puddle, getting about as much on himself as he got onto Tierden. Tierden scrambled out like an underfed king crab with terrible hair, and ran to the car yelling, "They're crazy! They're crazy! *Bobby, start the fucking car!*"

As Tierden slammed the door, the car lurched into motion and spun around, heading across the lot; Marti ran past me to the puddle, scooped a handful of mud, and did a high, arcing throw that would have been a first-rate Hail Mary pass. The mudblob came down almost vertically, making a real pretty *whap-splat* on the hood of Harris's car, and must have scared him, or maybe splashed enough on the windshield to blind him, so he swerved and his right wheels ran over the ends of two parking bumpers, his prehistoric shocks creaking and smashing and the whole car bucking like a cat in a pillowcase.

Harris got it straightened out, went over the curb into

the street, peeled out, and roared away up the freeway ramp. Of course an old rust bucket like that roars when it's doing forty.

"Somebody say something positive," Marti said, after a second.

"*This* sack of food seems to be okay," Paul said.

We went back inside, cleaned ourselves and the bathrooms, and then ate the food. We never did get out to the tar ponds. We just sat around talking, one of those nothing conversations that go on for, like, forever, not getting anyplace except closer to each other.

By the time Darla dropped me off at my house, giving me another kiss that made the whole world spin, I was pretty tired, I can tell you that, and it was almost two. The front door was unlocked, and the lights were on.

Bill was sitting on the couch with Mom, and she was just leaning on his shoulder. She looked up and said, "Oh, it must be late," and I was about to ask something inane, like if she'd had a nice evening or something, when she said, "Tiger, your sheets are in the dryer, if you don't mind putting them on the bed yourself, and could you shake us awake when you get up? We both should at least try to make it to work tomorrow."

"Sure," I said, and then remembered I'd be getting up extra early 'cause Browning and me were going out to deliver Rose Carson's couch. "Uh, that's going to be about five thirty in the morning."

"We'll manage," Bill said, and Mom nodded; he stood up and offered his hand to her like she was a duchess, and after looking a little startled, she took it. He brought her up from the couch and they went into the bedroom.

"Hey," I said, "you guys didn't just wait up for me, did you?"

"Not intentionally," Mom said. "But if it makes you feel like a special child of the universe, pretend we did."

I put the sheets on my bed, grabbed a quick wonderful hot shower, and made it back upstairs. In less than ten minutes, I was setting down the alarm clock and turning out the light.

As I dragged my clean sheets up over me, I felt Hairball walking up the mattress to lie down in the small of my back. He settled in with a little *Qrph?* and the tension flowed out of me like it had been flushed. My eyes came to rest on the alarm; the hour hand was already close to the alarm hand. I would get exactly three hours and eleven minutes of sleep tonight.

I guess I should have regretted the extra time I'd spent with the other Madmen at McDonald's, but fuck it, I'd really lost only one lousy hour of sleep. So I was going to be tired tomorrow. So what? Once I got going, with so much to do and so much in front of me, I'd be up on my feet again, running like a crazy bastard.

ACKNOWLEDGMENTS

This book would be a great deal more confusing, and far less a reflection of what I was trying to say, without the diligence, intelligence, and perception of Sharyn November, the editor, and Shelly Perron, the copy editor. Any remaining errors are deliberate, or my own damned fault, or both.

Join the conversation...

Point of View books are riveting novels that capture the hard truths about **life as a teen**.

These novels **start a conversation**, and you won't be able to ~~put~~ down.

WITHDRAWN

poin view

Check out **www.pointofviewbooks.com** for author interviews, trailers, discussion materials, and more!

Penguin Group (USA) • penguin.com/teen